BARED TO YOU

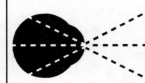

This Large Print Book carries the
Seal of Approval of N.A.V.H.

CROSSFIRE, BOOK 1

BARED TO YOU

SYLVIA DAY

THORNDIKE PRESS
A part of Gale, Cengage Learning

Detroit • New York • San Francisco • New Haven, Conn • Waterville, Maine • London

GALE
CENGAGE Learning®

LIBRARY OF CONGRESS CATALOGING-IN-PUBLICATION DATA

Day, Sylvia.
    Bared to you / by Sylvia Day.
       pages ; cm. — (Thorndike Press large print romance) (Crossfire series ; #1)
    ISBN-13: 978-1-4104-5560-4 (hardcover)
    ISBN-10: 1-4104-5560-2 (hardcover)
    1. Large type books. I. Title.
PS3604.A9875B37 2013
813'.6—dc23   2012045026

Published in 2013 by arrangement with The Berkley Publishing Group, a member of Penguin Group (USA), Inc.

Printed in the United States of America
1 2 3 4 5 6 7 17 16 15 14 13

This one is for Dr. David Allen Goodwin.
My love and gratitude are boundless.
Thank you, Dave. You saved my life.

ACKNOWLEDGMENTS

I have great appreciation and respect for my editor, Cindy Hwang, for so many things involved in the process of turning over this series from my loving hands to hers. She wanted this story and fought hard to get it, and I'm grateful for her enthusiasm. Thank you, Cindy!

I can't say enough about my agent, Kimberly Whalen, who brings so much energy and drive to the table. She exceeded my expectations over and over again, leaving me in the lovely and much-longed-for position of saying, "Run with it." Thank you, Kim, for being just what I needed!

Behind Cindy and Kim are dynamic teams at Berkley and Trident Media Group. In every department, on every level, the support and excitement for the Crossfire series has been amazing. I'm so thankful, and I feel very blessed.

My deepest gratitude to editor Hilary

Sares, who really dug into this story and made me work for it. Basically, she kicked my ass. By not pulling her punches or letting me shortchange the details, she made me work harder, and because of that, this story is a much, *much* better book. *Bared to You* wouldn't be what it is without you, Hilary. Thank you so much!

My thanks to Martha Trachtenberg, copy editor extraordinaire, and Victoria Colotta, interior text designer, for all their hard work on the self-published version of this book.

To Tera Kleinfelter, who read the first half of *Bared to You* and told me she loved it. Thank you, Tera!

To E. L. James, who wrote a story that captivated readers and created a hunger for more. You rocked it!

To Kati Brown, Jane Litte, Angela James, Maryse Black, Elizabeth Murach, Karla Parks, Gitte Doherty, Jenny Aspinall . . . oh, there are so many of you I need to thank for sharing *Bared to You* with others and saying such wonderful things about it! If I missed your name here, please believe I didn't miss you in my heart. I'm so grateful!

To all the girls who were at Cross Creek at some point in your adolescence: May all your dreams come true. You deserve it.

And to Alistair and Jessica, from *Seven Years to Sin,* who inspired me to write Gideon and Eva's story. I'm so glad the inspiration struck twice!

1

"We should head to a bar and celebrate."

I wasn't surprised by my roommate's emphatic pronouncement. Cary Taylor found excuses to celebrate, no matter how small and inconsequential. I'd always considered it part of his charm. "I'm sure drinking the night before starting a new job is a bad idea."

"Come on, Eva." Cary sat on our new living room floor amid half a dozen moving boxes and flashed his winning smile. We'd been unpacking for days, yet he still looked amazing. Leanly built, dark-haired, and green-eyed, Cary was a man who rarely looked anything less than absolutely gorgeous on any day of his life. I might have resented that if he hadn't been the dearest person on earth to me.

"I'm not talking about a bender," he insisted. "Just a glass of wine or two. We can hit a happy hour and be in by eight."

"I don't know if I'll make it back in time." I gestured at my yoga pants and fitted workout tank. "After I time the walk to work, I'm going to hit the gym."

"Walk fast, work out faster." Cary's perfectly executed arched brow made me laugh. I fully expected his million-dollar face to appear on billboards and fashion magazines all over the world one day. No matter his expression, he was a knockout.

"How about tomorrow after work?" I offered as a substitute. "If I make it through the day, that'll be worth celebrating."

"Deal. I'm breaking in the new kitchen for dinner."

"Uh . . ." Cooking was one of Cary's joys, but it wasn't one of his talents. "Great."

Blowing a wayward strand of hair off his face, he grinned at me. "We've got a kitchen most restaurants would kill for. There's no way to screw up a meal in there."

Dubious, I headed out with a wave, choosing to avoid a conversation about cooking. Taking the elevator down to the first floor, I smiled at the doorman when he let me out to the street with a flourish.

The moment I stepped outside, the smells and sounds of Manhattan embraced me and invited me to explore. I was not merely across the country from my former home in

San Diego, but seemingly worlds away. Two major metropolises — one endlessly temperate and sensually lazy, the other teeming with life and frenetic energy. In my dreams, I'd imagined living in a walkup in Brooklyn, but being a dutiful daughter, I found myself on the Upper West Side instead. If not for Cary living with me, I would've been miserably lonely in the sprawling apartment that cost more per month than most people made in a year.

The doorman tipped his hat to me. "Good evening, Miss Tramell. Will you need a cab this evening?"

"No thanks, Paul." I rocked onto the rounded heels of my fitness shoes. "I'll be walking."

He smiled. "It's cooled down from this afternoon. Should be nice."

"I've been told I should enjoy the June weather before it gets wicked hot."

"Very good advice, Miss Tramell."

Stepping out from under the modern glass entrance overhang that somehow meshed with the age of the building and its neighbors, I enjoyed the relative quiet of my tree-lined street before I reached the bustle and flow of traffic on Broadway. One day soon, I hoped to blend right in, but for now I still felt like a fraudulent New Yorker. I had the address and the job, but I was still wary of the subway and had trouble hailing cabs. I tried not to walk around wide-eyed and distracted, but it was hard. There was just *so much* to see and experience.

The sensory input was astonishing — the smell of vehicle exhaust mixed with food from vendor carts, the shouts of hawkers blended with music from street entertainers, the awe-inspiring range of faces and styles and accents, the gorgeous architectural wonders . . . And the cars. *Jesus Christ.* The frenetic flow of tightly packed cars was unlike anything I'd ever seen anywhere.

There was always an ambulance, patrol car, or fire engine trying to part the flood of yellow taxis with the electronic wail of earsplitting sirens. I was in awe of the lumbering garbage trucks that navigated tiny one-way streets and the package delivery drivers who braved the bumper-to-bumper traffic while facing rigid deadlines.

Real New Yorkers cruised right through it all, their love for the city as comfortable and familiar as a favorite pair of shoes. They didn't view the steam billowing from potholes and vents in the sidewalks with romantic delight, and they didn't blink an eye when the ground vibrated beneath their feet as the subway roared by below, while I

14

grinned like an idiot and flexed my toes. New York was a brand-new love affair for me. I was starry-eyed and it showed.

So I had to really work at playing it cool as I made my way over to the building where I would be working. As far as my job went, at least, I'd gotten my way. I wanted to make a living based on my own merits, and that meant an entry-level position. Starting the next morning, I would be the assistant to Mark Garrity at Waters Field & Leaman, one of the preeminent advertising agencies in the United States. My step-father, megafinancier Richard Stanton, had been annoyed when I took the job, pointing out that if I'd been less prideful I could've worked for a friend of his instead and reaped the benefits of that connection.

"You're as stubborn as your father," he'd said. "It'll take him forever to pay off your student loans on a cop's salary."

That had been a major fight, with my dad unwilling to back down. "Hell if another man's gonna pay for my daughter's educa-tion," Victor Reyes had said when Stanton made the offer. I respected that. I suspected Stanton did, too, although he would never admit it. I understood both men's sides, because I'd fought to pay off the loans myself . . . and lost. It was a point of pride for my father. My mother had refused to marry him, but he'd never wavered from his determination to be my dad in every way possible.

Knowing it was pointless to get riled up over old frustrations, I focused on getting to work as quickly as possible. I'd deliberately chosen to clock the short trip during a busy time on a Monday, so I was pleased when I reached the Crossfire Building, which housed Waters Field & Leaman, in less than thirty minutes.

I tipped my head back and followed the line of the building all the way up to the slender ribbon of sky. The Crossfire was seriously impressive, a sleek spire of gleaming sapphire that pierced the clouds. I knew from my previous interviews that the interior on the other side of the ornate copper-framed revolving doors was just as awe-inspiring, with golden-veined marble floors and walls and brushed-aluminum security desk and turnstiles.

I pulled my new ID card out of the inner pocket of my pants and held it up for the two guards in black business suits at the desk. They stopped me anyway, no doubt because I was majorly underdressed, but then they cleared me through. After I completed an elevator ride up to the twentieth floor, I'd have a general time frame for the whole route from door to door. Score.

I was walking toward the bank of elevators when a svelte, beautifully groomed brunette caught her purse on a turnstile and upended it, spilling a deluge of change. Coins rained onto the marble and rolled merrily away, and I watched people dodge the chaos and keep going as if they didn't see it. I winced in sympathy and crouched to help the woman collect her money, as did one of the guards.

"Thank you," she said, shooting me a quick, harried smile.

I smiled back. "No problem. I've been there."

I'd just squatted to reach a nickel lying near the entrance when I ran into a pair of luxurious black oxfords draped in tailored black slacks. I waited a beat for the man to move out of my way and when he didn't, I arched my neck back to allow my line of sight to rise. The custom three-piece suit hit more than a few of my hot buttons, but it was the tall, powerfully lean body inside it that made it sensational. Still, as impressive as all that magnificent maleness was, it wasn't until I reached the man's face that I went down for the count.

Wow. Just . . . *wow.*

He sank into an elegant crouch directly in front of me. Hit with all that exquisite masculinity at eye level, I could only stare. Stunned.

Then something shifted in the air between us.

As he stared back, he altered . . . as if a shield slid away from his eyes, revealing a scorching force of will that sucked the air from my lungs. The intense magnetism he exuded grew in strength, becoming a near-tangible impression of vibrant and unrelenting power.

Reacting purely on instinct, I shifted backward. And sprawled flat on my ass.

My elbows throbbed from the violent contact with the marble floor, but I scarcely registered the pain. I was too preoccupied with staring, riveted by the man in front of me. Inky black hair framed a breathtaking face. His bone structure would make a sculptor weep with joy, while a firmly etched mouth, a blade of a nose, and intensely blue eyes made him savagely gorgeous. Those eyes narrowed slightly, his features otherwise schooled into impassivity.

His dress shirt and suit were both black, but his tie perfectly matched those brilliant irises. His eyes were shrewd and assessing, and they bored into me. My heartbeat quickened; my lips parted to accommodate faster breaths. He smelled sinfully good. Not cologne. Body wash, maybe. Or shampoo. Whatever it was, it was mouthwatering, as was he.

He held out a hand to me, exposing gold and onyx cuff links and a very expensive-looking watch.

With a shaky inhalation, I placed my hand in his. My pulse leaped when his grip tightened. His touch was electric, sending a shock up my arm that raised the hairs on my nape. He didn't move for a moment, a frown line marring the space between arrogantly slashed brows.

"Are you all right?"

His voice was cultured and smooth, with a rasp that made my stomach flutter. It brought sex to mind. Extraordinary sex. I thought for a moment that he might be able to make me orgasm just by talking long enough.

My lips were dry, so I licked them before answering. "I'm fine."

He stood with economical grace, pulling me up with him. We maintained eye contact because I was unable to look away. He was younger than I'd assumed at first. Younger than thirty would be my guess, but his eyes were much worldlier. Hard and sharply intelligent.

I felt drawn to him, as if a rope bound my waist and he were slowly, inexorably pulling it.

Blinking out of my semidaze, I released him. He wasn't just beautiful; he was . . . enthralling. He was the kind of guy who made a woman want to rip his shirt open and watch the buttons scatter along with her inhibitions. I looked at him in his civilized, urbane, outrageously expensive suit and thought of raw, primal, sheet-clawing fucking.

He bent down and retrieved the ID card I hadn't realized I'd dropped, freeing me from that provocative gaze. My brain stuttered back into gear.

I was irritated with myself for feeling so awkward while he was so completely self-possessed. And why? Because I was dazzled, damn it.

He glanced up at me, and the pose — him nearly kneeling before me — skewed my equilibrium again. He held my gaze as he rose. "Are you sure you're all right? You should sit down for a minute."

My face heated. How lovely to appear awkward and clumsy in front of the most self-assured and graceful man I'd ever met. "I just lost my balance. I'm okay."

Looking away, I caught sight of the woman who'd dumped the contents of her purse. She thanked the guard who'd helped her; then she turned to approach me, apologizing profusely. I faced her and held out the handful of coins I'd collected, but her gaze snagged on the god in the suit and she promptly forgot me altogether. After a beat, I just reached over and dumped the change into the woman's bag. Then I risked a glance at the man again, finding him watching me even as the brunette gushed thank-yous. *To him.* Not to me, of course, the one who'd actually helped.

I talked over her. "May I have my badge, please?"

He offered it back to me. Although I made an effort to retrieve it without touching him, his fingers brushed mine, sending that charge of awareness into me all over again.

"Thank you," I muttered before skirting him and pushing out to the street through the revolving door. I paused on the sidewalk, gulping in a breath of New York air redolent with a million different things, some good and some toxic.

There was a sleek black Bentley SUV in front of the building, and I saw my reflection in the spotless tinted windows of the limo. I was flushed and my gray eyes were overly bright. I'd seen that look on my face before — in the bathroom mirror just before I went to bed with a man. It was my I'm-ready-to-fuck look and it had absolutely no business being on my face now.

Christ. Get a grip.

Five minutes with Mr. Dark and Dangerous, and I was filled with an edgy, restless energy. I could still feel the pull of him, the inexplicable urge to go back inside where he was. I could make the argument that I hadn't finished what I'd come to the Crossfire to do, but I knew I'd kick myself for it later. How many times was I going to make an ass of myself in one day?

"Enough," I scolded myself under my breath. "Moving on."

Horns blared as one cab darted in front of another with only inches to spare and then slammed on the brakes as daring pedestrians stepped into the intersection seconds before the light changed. Shouting ensued, a barrage of expletives and hand gestures that didn't carry real anger behind them. In seconds all the parties would forget the exchange, which was just one beat in the natural tempo of the city.

As I melded into the flow of foot traffic and set off toward the gym, a smile teased my mouth. *Ah, New York,* I thought, feeling settled again. *You rock.*

I'd planned on warming up on a treadmill, then capping off the hour with a few of the machines, but when I saw that a beginners' kickboxing class was about to start, I followed the mass of waiting students into that instead. By the time it was over, I felt more like myself. My muscles quivered with the perfect amount of fatigue, and I knew I'd sleep hard when I crashed later.

"You did really well."

I wiped the sweat off my face with a towel and looked at the young man who spoke to me. Lanky and sleekly muscular, he had keen brown eyes and flawless café au lait skin. His lashes were enviably thick and long, while his head was shaved bald.

"Thank you." My mouth twisted ruefully. "Pretty obvious it was my first time, huh?"

He grinned and held out his hand. "Parker Smith."

"Eva Tramell."

"You have a natural grace, Eva. With a little training you could be a literal knockout. In a city like New York, knowing self-defense is imperative." He gestured over to a corkboard hung on the wall. It was covered in thumbtacked business cards and flyers. Tearing off a flag from the bottom of a

23

fluorescent sheet of paper, he held it out to me. "Ever heard of Krav Maga?"

"In a Jennifer Lopez movie."

"I teach it, and I'd love to teach you. That's my website and the number to the studio."

I admired his approach. It was direct, like his gaze, and his smile was genuine. I'd wondered if he was angling toward a pickup, but he was cool enough about it that I couldn't be sure.

Parker crossed his arms, which showed off cut biceps. He wore a black sleeveless shirt and long shorts. His Converse sneakers looked comfortably beat up, and tribal tattoos peeked out from his collar. "My website has the hours. You should come by and watch, see if it's for you."

"I'll definitely think about it."

"Do that." He extended his hand again, and his grip was solid and confident. "I hope to see you."

The apartment smelled fabulous when I got back home, and Adele was crooning soulfully through the surround sound speakers about chasing pavements. I looked across the open floor plan into the kitchen and saw Cary swaying to the music while stirring something on the range. There was an open bottle of wine on the counter and two goblets, one of which was half-filled with red wine.

"Hey," I called out as I got closer. "Whatcha cooking? And do I have time for a shower first?"

He poured wine into the other goblet and slid it across the breakfast bar to me, his movements practiced and elegant. No one would know from looking at him that he'd spent his childhood bouncing between his drug-addicted mother and foster homes, followed by adolescence in juvenile detention facilities and state-run rehabs. "Pasta with meat sauce. And hold the shower, dinner's ready. Have fun?"

"Once I got to the gym, yeah." I pulled out one of the teakwood bar stools and sat. I told him about the kickboxing class and Parker Smith. "Wanna go with me?"

"Krav Maga?" Cary shook his head. "That's hard-core. I'd get all bruised up and that would cost me jobs. But I'll go with you to check it out, just in case this guy's a wack."

I watched him dump the pasta into a waiting colander. "A wack, huh?"

My dad had taught me to read guys pretty well, which was how I'd known the god in the suit was trouble. Regular people offered token smiles when they helped someone, just to make a momentary connection that smoothed the way.

Then again, I hadn't smiled at him either.

"Baby girl," Cary said, pulling bowls out of the cupboard, "you're a sexy, stunning woman. I question any man who doesn't have the balls to ask you outright for a date."

I wrinkled my nose at him.

He set a bowl in front of me. It contained tiny tubes of salad noodles covered in a skimpy tomato sauce with lumps of ground beef and peas. "You've got something on your mind. What is it?"

Hmm . . . I caught the handle of the spoon sticking out of the bowl and decided not to comment on the food. "I think I ran into the hottest man on the planet today. Maybe the hottest man in the history of the world."

"Oh? I thought that was me. Do tell me more." Cary stayed on the other side of the counter, preferring to stand and eat.

I watched him take a couple bites of his own concoction before I felt brave enough to try it myself. "Not much to tell, really. I ended up sprawled on my ass in the lobby of the Crossfire and he gave me a hand up."

"Tall or short? Blond or dark? Built or lean? Eye color?"

I washed down my second bite with some

wine. "Tall. Dark. Lean *and* built. Blue eyes. Filthy rich, judging by his clothes and accessories. And he was insanely sexy. You know how it is — some good-looking guys don't make your hormones go crazy, while some unattractive guys have massive sex appeal. This guy had it all."

My belly fluttered as it had when Dark and Dangerous touched me. In my mind, I remembered his breathtaking face with crystal clarity. It should be illegal for a man to be that mind-blowing. I was *still* recovering from the frying of my brain cells.

Cary set his elbow on the counter and leaned in, his long bangs covering one vibrant green eye. "So what happened after he helped you up?"

I shrugged. "Nothing."

"Nothing?"

"I left."

"What? You didn't flirt with him?"

I took another bite. Really, the meal wasn't bad. Or else I was just starving. "He wasn't the kind of guy you flirt with, Cary."

"There is no such thing as a guy you can't flirt with. Even the happily married ones enjoy a little harmless flirtation now and then."

"There was nothing harmless about this guy," I said dryly.

"Ah, one of those." Cary nodded sagely. "Bad boys can be fun, if you don't get too close."

Of course he would know; men and women of all ages fell at his feet. Still, he somehow managed to pick the wrong partner every time. He'd dated stalkers, and cheaters, and lovers who threatened to kill themselves over him, and lovers with significant others they didn't tell him about . . . Name it, he'd been through it.

"I can't see this guy ever being fun," I said. "He was way too intense. Still, I bet he'd be awesome in the sack with all that intensity."

"Now you're talking. Forget the real guy. Just use his face in your fantasies and make him perfect there."

Preferring to get the guy out of my head altogether, I changed the subject. "You have any go-sees tomorrow?"

"Of course." Cary launched into the details of his schedule, mentioning a jeans advertisement, self-tanner, underwear, and cologne.

I shoved everything else out of my mind and focused on him and his growing success. The demand for Cary Taylor was increasing by the day, and he was building a reputation with photographers and accounts for being both professional and prompt. I was thrilled for him and so proud. He'd come a long way and been through so much.

It wasn't until after dinner that I noticed the two large gift boxes propped against the side of the sectional sofa.

"What are those?"

"Those," Cary said, joining me in the living room, "are the ultimate."

I knew immediately they were from Stanton and my mom. Money was something my mother needed to be happy, and I was glad Stanton, husband number three, was able to fill that need for her and all her many others as well. I often wished that could be the end of it, but my mom had a difficult time accepting that I didn't view money the same way she did. "What now?"

He threw his arm around my shoulders, easy enough for him to do because he was taller by five inches. "Don't be ungrateful. He loves your mom. He loves spoiling your mom, and your mom loves spoiling you. As much as you don't like it, he doesn't do it for you. He does it for her."

Sighing, I conceded his point. "What are they?"

"Glam threads for the advocacy center's fund-raiser dinner on Saturday. A bombshell dress for you and a Brioni tux for me, because buying gifts for me is what he does for you. You're more tolerant if you have me around to listen to you bitch."

"Damn straight. Thank God he knows that."

"Of course he knows. Stanton wouldn't be a bazillionaire if he didn't know everything." Cary caught my hand and tugged me over. "Come on. Take a look."

I pushed through the revolving door of the Crossfire into the lobby ten minutes before nine the next morning. Wanting to make the best impression on my first day, I'd gone with a simple sheath dress paired with black pumps that I slid on in replacement of my walking shoes during the elevator ride up. My blond hair was twisted up in an artful chignon that resembled a figure eight, courtesy of Cary. I was hair-inept, but he could create styles that were glamorous masterpieces. I wore the small pearl studs my dad had given me as a graduation gift and the Rolex from Stanton and my mother.

I had begun to think I'd put too much care into my appearance, but as I stepped into the lobby I remembered being sprawled across the floor in my workout clothes and I was grateful I didn't look anything like *that* graceless girl. The two security guards

30

didn't seem to put two and two together when I flashed them my ID card on the way to the turnstiles.

Twenty floors later, I was exiting into the vestibule of Waters Field & Leaman. Before me was a wall of bulletproof glass that framed the double-door entrance to the reception area. The receptionist at the crescent-shaped desk saw the badge I held up to the glass. She hit the button that unlocked the doors as I put my ID away.

"Hi, Megumi," I greeted her when I stepped inside, admiring her cranberry-colored blouse. She was mixed race, a little bit Asian for sure, and very pretty. Her hair was dark and thick and cut into a sleek bob that was shorter in the back and razor sharp in the front. Her sloe eyes were brown and warm, and her lips were full and naturally pink.

"Eva, hi. Mark's not in yet, but you know where you're going, right?"

"Absolutely." With a wave, I took the hallway to the left of the reception desk all the way to the end, where I made another left turn and ended up in a formerly open space now partitioned into cubicles. One was mine and I went straight to it.

I dropped my purse and the bag holding my walking flats into the bottom drawer of my utilitarian metal desk, then booted up my computer. I'd brought a couple of things to personalize my space, and I pulled them out. One was a framed collage of three photos — me and Cary on Coronado Beach, my mom and Stanton on his yacht in the French Riviera, and my dad on duty in his City of Oceanside, California, police cruiser. The other item was a colorful arrangement of glass flowers that Cary had given me just that morning as a "first day" gift. I tucked it beside the small grouping of photos and sat back to take in the effect.

"Good morning, Eva."

I pushed to my feet to face my boss. "Good morning, Mr. Garrity."

"Call me Mark, please. Come on over to my office."

I followed him across the strip of hallway, once again thinking that my new boss was very easy to look at with his gleaming dark skin, trim goatee, and laughing brown eyes. Mark had a square jaw and a charmingly crooked smile. He was trim and fit, and he carried himself with a confident poise that inspired trust and respect.

He gestured at one of the two seats in front of his glass-and-chrome desk and waited until I sat to settle into his Aeron chair. Against the backdrop of sky and

32

skyscrapers, Mark looked accomplished and powerful. He was, in fact, just a junior account manager, and his office was a closet compared to the ones occupied by the directors and executives, but no one could fault the view.

He leaned back and smiled. "Did you get settled into your new apartment?"

I was surprised he remembered, but I appreciated it, too. I'd met him during my second interview and liked him right away.

"For the most part," I answered. "Still a few stray boxes here and there."

"You moved from San Diego, right? Nice city, but very different from New York. Do you miss the palm trees?"

"I miss the dry air. The humidity here is taking some getting used to."

"Wait 'til summer hits." He smiled. "So . . . it's your first day and you're my first assistant, so we'll have to figure this out as we go. I'm not used to delegating, but I'm sure I'll pick it up quick."

I was instantly at ease. "I'm eager to be delegated to."

"Having you around is a big step up for me, Eva. I'd like you to be happy working here. Do you drink coffee?"

"Coffee is one of my major food groups."

"Ah, an assistant after my own heart." His

smile widened. "I'm not going to ask you to fetch coffee for me, but I wouldn't mind if you helped me figure out how to use the new one-cup coffee brewers they just put in the break rooms."

I grinned. "No problem."

"How sad is it that I don't have anything else for you?" He rubbed the back of his neck sheepishly. "Why don't I show you the accounts I'm working on and we'll go from there?"

The rest of the day passed in a blur. Mark touched bases with two clients and had a long meeting with the creative team working on concept ideas for a trade school. It was a fascinating process seeing firsthand how the various departments picked up the baton from one another to carry a campaign from proposition to fruition. I might've stayed late just to get a better feel of the layout of the offices, but my phone rang at ten minutes to five.

"Mark Garrity's office. Eva Tramell speaking."

"Get your ass home so we can go out for the drink you rain-checked on yesterday."

Cary's mock sternness made me smile. "All right, all right. I'm coming."

Shutting down my computer, I cleared

out. When I reached the bank of elevators, I pulled out my cell to text a quick On my way note to Cary. A ding alerted me to which car was stopping on my floor and I moved over to stand in front of it, briefly returning my attention to hitting the send button. When the doors opened, I took a step forward. I glanced up to watch where I was going and blue eyes met mine. My breath caught.

The sex god was the lone occupant.

2

His tie was silver and his shirt brilliantly white, the stark absence of color emphasizing those amazing blue irises. As he stood there with his jacket open and his hands shoved casually into his pants pockets, the sight of him was like running smack into a wall I hadn't known was there.

I jerked to a halt, my gaze riveted to the man who was even more striking than I'd remembered. I had never seen hair that purely black. It was glossy and slightly long, the ends drifting over his collar. That sexy length was the crowning touch of bad-boy allure over the successful businessman, like whipped cream topping on a hot-fudge brownie sundae. As my mother would say, only rogues and raiders had hair like that.

My hands clenched against the urge to touch it, to see if it felt like the rich silk it resembled.

The doors began to close. He took an easy

step forward and pressed a button on the panel to hold them open. "There's plenty of room for both of us, Eva."

The sound of that smoky, implacable voice broke me out of my momentary daze. *How did he know my name?*

Then I remembered that he'd picked up my ID card when I'd dropped it in the lobby. For a second, I debated telling him I was waiting for someone so I could take another car down, but my brain lurched back into action.

What the hell was wrong with me? Clearly he worked in the Crossfire. I couldn't avoid him every time I saw him, and why should I? If I wanted to get to the point where I could look at him and take his hotness for granted, I needed to see him often enough that he became like furniture.

Ha! If only.

I stepped into the car. "Thank you."

He released the button and stepped back again. The doors closed and the elevator began its descent.

I immediately regretted my decision to share the car with him.

Awareness of him prickled across my skin. He was a potent force in such a small enclosure, radiating a palpable energy and sexual magnetism that had me shifting restlessly on my feet. My breathing became as ragged as my heartbeat. I felt that inexplicable pull to him again, as if he exuded a silent demand that I was instinctively attuned to answering.

"Enjoy your first day?" he asked, startling me.

His voice resonated, flowing over me in a seductive rhythm. *How the hell did he know it was my first day?*

"Yes, actually," I answered evenly. "How was yours?"

I felt his gaze slide over my profile, but I kept my attention trained on the brushed-aluminum elevator doors. My heart was racing in my chest, my stomach quivering madly. I felt jumbled and off my game.

"Well, it wasn't my first," he replied with a hint of amusement. "But it was. successful. And getting better as it progresses."

I nodded and managed a smile, having no idea what that was supposed to mean. The car slowed on the twelfth floor and a friendly group of three got on, talking excitedly among themselves. I stepped back to make room for them, retreating into the opposite corner of the elevator from Dark and Dangerous. Except he sidestepped along with me. We were suddenly closer than we'd been before.

He adjusted his perfectly knotted tie, his arm brushing against mine as he did so. I sucked in a deep breath, trying to ignore my acute awareness of him by concentrating on the conversation taking place in front of us. It was impossible. He was just so *there.* Right there. All perfect and gorgeous and smelling divine. My thoughts ran away from me, fantasizing about how hard his body might be beneath the suit, how it might feel against me, how well endowed — or not — he might be . . .

When the car reached the lobby, I almost moaned in relief. I waited impatiently as the elevator emptied, and the first chance I got, I took a step forward. His hand settled firmly at the small of my back and he walked out beside me, steering me. The sensation of his touch on such a vulnerable place rippled through me.

We reached the turnstiles and his hand fell away, leaving me feeling oddly bereft. I glanced at him, trying to read him, but although he was looking at me, his face gave nothing away.

"Eva!"

The sight of Cary lounging casually against a marble column in the lobby shifted everything. He was wearing jeans that showcased his mile-long legs and an oversized sweater in soft green that emphasized his eyes. He easily drew the attention of everyone in the lobby. I slowed as I approached him and the sex god passed us, moving through the revolving door and sliding fluidly into the back of the chauffeured black Bentley SUV I'd seen at the curb the evening before.

Cary whistled as the car pulled away. "Well, well. From the way you were looking at him, that was the guy you told me about, right?"

"Oh, yeah. That was definitely him."

"You work together?" Linking arms with me, Cary tugged me out to the street through the stationary door.

"No." I stopped on the sidewalk to change into my walking flats, leaning into him as pedestrians flowed around us. "I don't know who he is, but he asked me if I'd had a good first day, so I better figure it out."

"Well . . ." He grinned and supported my elbow as I hopped awkwardly from one foot to the other. "No idea how anyone could get any work done around him. My brain sort of fried for a minute."

"I'm sure that's a universal effect." I straightened. "Let's go. I need a drink."

The next morning arrived with a slight

throbbing at the back of my skull that mocked me for having one too many glasses of wine. Still, as I rode the elevator up to the twentieth floor, I didn't regret the hangover as much as I should have. My choices were either too much alcohol or a whirl with my vibrator, and I was damned if I'd have a battery-provided orgasm starring Dark and Dangerous. Not that he'd know or even care that he made me so horny I couldn't see straight, but *I'd* know, and I didn't want to give the fantasy of him the satisfaction.

I dropped my stuff in the bottom drawer of my desk, and when I saw that Mark wasn't in yet, I grabbed a cup of coffee and returned to my cubicle to catch up on my favorite ad-biz blogs.

"Eva!"

I jumped when he appeared beside me, his grin a flash of white against his smooth dark skin. "Good morning, Mark."

"Is it ever. You're my lucky charm, I think. Come into my office. Bring your tablet. Can you work late tonight?"

I followed him over, catching on to his excitement. "Sure."

"I'd hoped you'd say that." He sank into his chair.

I took the one I'd sat in the day before

and quickly opened a notepad program.

"So," he began, "we've received an RFP for Kingsman Vodka and they mentioned me by name. First time that's ever happened."

"Congratulations!"

"I appreciate that, but let's save them for when we've actually landed the account. We'll still have to bid, if we get past the request-for-proposal stage, and they want to meet with me tomorrow evening."

"Wow. Is that timeline usual?"

"No. Usually they'd wait until we had the RFP finished before meeting with us, but Cross Industries recently acquired Kingsman and C.I. has dozens of subsidiaries. That's good business if we can get it. They know it and they're making us jump through hoops, the first of which is meeting with me."

"Usually there would be a team, right?"

"Yes, we'd present as a group. But they're familiar with the drill — they know they'll get the pitch from a senior executive, then end up working with a junior like me — so they picked me out and now they want to vet me. But to be fair, the RFP provides a lot more information than it asks for in return. It's as good as a brief, so I really can't accuse them of being unreasonably demanding, just meticulous. Par for the course when dealing with Cross Industries."

He ran a hand over his tight curls, betraying the pressure he felt. "What do you think of Kingsman Vodka?"

"Uh . . . well . . . Honestly, I've never heard of it."

Mark fell back in his chair and laughed. "Thank God. I thought I was the only one. Well, the plus side is there's no bad press to get over. No news can be good news."

"What can I do to help? Besides research vodka and stay late."

His lips pursed a moment as he thought about it. "Jot this down . . ."

We worked straight through lunch and long after the office had emptied, going over some initial data from the strategists. It was a little after seven when Mark's smartphone rang, startling me with its abrupt intrusion into the quiet.

Mark activated the speaker and kept working. "Hey, baby."

"Have you fed that poor girl yet?" demanded a warm masculine voice over the line.

Glancing at me through his glass office wall, Mark said, "Ah . . . I forgot."

I looked away quickly, biting my lower lip to hide my smile.

A snort came clearly across the line. "Only two days on the job, and you're already overworking her and starving her to death. She's going to quit."

"Shit. You're right. Steve honey —"

"Don't 'Steve honey' me. Does she like Chinese?"

I gave Mark the thumbs-up.

He grinned. "Yes, she does."

"All right. I'll be there in twenty. Let security know I'm coming."

Almost exactly twenty minutes later, I buzzed Steven Ellison through the waiting area doors. He was a juggernaut of a fellow, dressed in dark jeans, scuffed work boots, and a neatly pressed button-down shirt. Red-haired with laughing blue eyes, he was as good looking as his partner was, just in a very different way. The three of us sat around Mark's desk and dumped kung pao chicken and broccoli beef onto paper plates, then added helpings of sticky white rice before digging in with chopsticks.

I discovered that Steven was a contractor, and that he and Mark had been a couple since college. I watched them interact and felt awe and a dash of envy. Their relationship was so beautifully functional that it was a joy to spend time with them.

"Damn, girl," Steven said with a whistle,

as I went for a third helping. "You can put it away. Where does it go?"

I shrugged. "To the gym with me. Maybe that helps . . . ?"

"Don't mind him," Mark said, grinning. "Steven's just jealous. He has to watch his girlish figure."

"Hell." Steven shot his partner a wry look. "I might have to take her out to lunch with the crew. I could win money betting on how much she can eat."

I smiled. "That could be fun."

"Ha. I knew you had a bit of a wild streak. It's in your smile."

Looking down at my food, I refused to let my mind wander into memories of just how wild I'd been in my rebellious, self-destructive phase.

Mark saved me. "Don't harass my assistant. And what do you know about wild women anyway?"

"I know some of them like hanging out with gay men. They like our perspective." His grin flashed. "I know a few other things, too. Hey . . . don't look so shocked, you two. I wanted to see if hetero sex lived up to the hype."

Clearly this was news to Mark, but from the twitching of his lips, he was secure enough in their relationship to find the whole exchange amusing. "Oh?"

"How'd that work out for you?" I asked bravely.

Steven shrugged. "I don't want to say it's overrated, 'cause clearly I'm the wrong demographic and I had a very limited sampling, but I can do without."

I thought it was very telling that Steven could relate his story in terms Mark worked with. They shared their careers with each other and listened, even though their chosen fields were miles apart.

"Considering your present living arrangement," Mark said to him, catching up a stem of broccoli with his chopsticks, "I'd say that's a very good thing."

By the time we finished eating, it was eight and the cleaning crew had arrived. Mark insisted on calling me a cab.

"Should I come in early tomorrow?" I asked.

Steven bumped shoulders with Mark. "You must've done something good in a past life to score this one."

"I think putting up with you in this life qualifies," Mark said dryly.

"Hey," Steven protested, "I'm housebroken. I put the toilet seat down."

Mark shot me an exasperated look that was warm with affection for his partner.

"And that's helpful how?"

Mark and I scrambled all day Thursday to get ready for his four o'clock with the team from Kingsman. We grabbed an information-packed lunch with the two creatives who would be participating in the pitch when it got to that point in the process; then we went over the notes on Kingsman's Web presence and existing social media outreach.

I got a little nervous when three thirty rolled around because I knew traffic would be a bitch, but Mark kept working after I pointed out the time. It was quarter to four before he bounded out of his office with a broad smile, still shrugging into his jacket. "Join me, Eva."

I blinked up at him from my desk. "Really?"

"Hey, you worked hard on helping me prep. Don't you want to see how it goes?"

"Yes, absolutely." I pushed to my feet. Knowing my appearance would be a reflection on my boss, I smoothed my black pencil skirt and straightened the cuffs of my long-sleeved silk blouse. By a random twist of fate, my crimson shirt perfectly matched Mark's tie. "Thank you."

We headed out to the elevators and I was

briefly startled when the car went up instead of down. When we reached the top floor, the waiting area we stepped into was considerably larger and more ornate than the one on the twentieth. Hanging baskets of ferns and lilies fragranced the air and a smoky glass security entrance was sandblasted with CROSS INDUSTRIES in a bold, masculine font.

We were buzzed in, and then asked to wait a moment. Both of us declined an offer of water or coffee, and less than five minutes after we arrived, we were directed to a closed conference room.

Mark looked at me with twinkling eyes as the receptionist reached for the door handle. "Ready?"

I smiled. "Ready."

The door opened and I was gestured in first. I made sure to smile brightly as I stepped inside . . . a smile that froze on my face at the sight of the man rising to his feet at my entrance.

My abrupt stop bottlenecked the threshold and Mark ran into my back, sending me stumbling forward. Dark and Dangerous caught me by the waist, hauling me off my feet and directly into his chest. The air left my lungs in a rush, followed immediately by every bit of common sense I possessed.

Even through the layers of clothing between us, his biceps were like stone beneath my palms, his stomach a hard slab of muscle against my own. When he sucked in a sharp breath, my nipples tightened, stimulated by the expansion of his chest.

Oh no. I was cursed. A rapid-fire series of images flashed through my mind, showcasing a thousand ways I could stumble, fall, trip, skid, or crash in front of the sex god over the days, weeks, and months ahead.

"Hello again," he murmured, the vibration of his voice making me ache all over. "Always a pleasure running into you, Eva."

I flushed with embarrassment and desire, unable to find the will to push away despite the two other people in the room with him. It didn't help that his attention was solely on me, his hard body radiating that arresting impression of powerful demand.

"Mr. Cross," Mark said behind me. "Sorry about the entrance."

"Don't be. It was a memorable one."

I wobbled on my stilettos when Cross set me down, my knees weakened from the full-body contact. He was dressed in black again, with both his shirt and tie in a soft gray. As always, he looked too good.

What would it be like to be that amazing looking? There was no way he could go anywhere without causing a disturbance.

Reaching out, Mark steadied me and eased me back gently.

Cross's gaze stayed focused on Mark's hand at my elbow until I was released.

"Right. Okay then." Mark pulled himself together. "This is my assistant, Eva Tramell."

"We've met." Cross pulled out the chair next to his. "Eva."

I looked to Mark for guidance, still recovering from the moments I'd spent plastered against the sexual superconductor in Fioravanti.

Cross leaned closer and ordered quietly, "Sit, Eva."

Mark gave a brief nod, but I was already lowering into the chair at Cross's command, my body obeying instinctively before my mind caught up and objected.

I tried not to fidget for the next hour as Mark was grilled by Cross and the two Kingsman directors, both of whom were attractive brunettes in elegant pantsuits. The one in raspberry was especially enthusiastic about garnering Cross's attention, while the one in cream focused intently on my boss. All three seemed impressed by Mark's ability to articulate how the agency's work — and his facilitation of it with the client —

created provable value for the client's brand.

I admired how cool Mark remained under pressure — pressure exerted by Cross, who easily dominated the meeting.

"Well done, Mr. Garrity," Cross praised lightly as they wrapped things up. "I look forward to going over the RFP when the time comes. What would entice you to try Kingsman, Eva?"

Startled, I blinked. "Excuse me?"

The intensity of his gaze was searing. It felt as if his entire focus were on me, which only reinforced my respect for Mark, who'd had to work under the weight of that stare for an hour.

Cross's chair was set parallel to the length of the table, facing me head on. His right arm rested on the smooth wooden surface, his long, elegant fingers stroking rhythmically along the top. I caught a glimpse of his wrist at the end of his cuff and for some crazy reason the sight of that small expanse of golden skin with its light dusting of dark hair arrested my attention. He was just so . . . *male.*

"Which of Mark's suggested concepts do you prefer?" he asked again.

"I think they're all brilliant."

His beautiful face was impassive when he said, "I'll clear the room to get your honest

51

opinion, if that's what it takes."

My fingers curled around the ends of my chair's armrests. "I just gave you my honest opinion, Mr. Cross, but if you must know, I think sexy luxury on a budget will appeal to the largest demographic. But I lack —"

"I agree." Cross stood and buttoned his jacket. "You have a direction, Mr. Garrity. We'll revisit next week."

I sat for a moment, stunned by the break-neck pace of events. Then I looked at Mark, who seemed to be wavering between astonished joy and bewilderment.

Rising to my feet, I led the way to the door. I was hyperaware of Cross walking beside me. The way he moved, with animal grace and arrogant economy, was a major turn-on. I couldn't imagine him not fucking well and being aggressive about it, taking what he wanted in a way that made a woman wild to give it to him.

Cross stayed with me all the way to the bank of elevators. He said a few things to Mark about sports, I think, but I was too focused on the way I was reacting to him to care about the small talk. When the car arrived, I breathed a sigh of relief and hastily stepped forward with Mark.

"A moment, Eva," Cross said smoothly, holding me back with a hand at my elbow.

"She'll be right down," he told Mark, as the elevator doors closed on my boss's astonished face.

Cross said nothing until the car was on its way down; then he pushed the call button again and asked, "Are you sleeping with anyone?"

The question was asked so casually, it took a second to process what he'd said.

I inhaled sharply. "Why is that any business of yours?"

He looked at me and I saw what I'd seen the first time we'd met — tremendous power and steely control. Both of which had me taking an involuntary step back. Again. At least I didn't fall this time; I was making progress.

"Because I want to fuck you, Eva. I need to know what's standing in my way, if anything."

The sudden ache between my thighs had me reaching for the wall to maintain my balance. He reached out to steady me, but I held him at bay with an uplifted hand. "Maybe I'm just not interested, Mr. Cross."

A ghost of a smile touched his lips and made him impossibly more handsome. *Dear God . . .*

The ding that signaled the approaching elevator made me jump, I was strung so tight. I'd never been so aroused. Never been so scorchingly attracted to another human being. Never been so offended by a person I lusted after.

I stepped into the elevator and faced him.

He smiled. "Until next time, Eva."

The doors closed and I sagged into the brass handrail, trying to regain my bearings. I'd barely pulled myself together when the doors opened and revealed Mark pacing in the waiting area on our floor.

"Jesus, Eva," Mark muttered, coming to an abrupt halt. "What the hell was that?"

"I have no freakin' clue." I exhaled in a rush, wishing I could share the confusing, irritating exchange I'd had with Cross, but well aware that my boss wasn't the appropriate outlet. "Who cares? You know he's going to give you the account."

A grin chased away his frown. "I'm thinking he might."

"As my roommate always says, you should celebrate. Should I make dinner reservations for you and Steven?"

"Why not? Pure Food and Wine at seven, if they can squeeze us in. If not, surprise us."

We'd barely returned to Mark's office when he was pounced on by the executives — Michael Waters, the CEO and president, and Christine Field and Walter Leaman, the executive chairman and vice chairman.

I skirted the four of them as quietly as possible and slid into my cubicle.

I called Pure Food and Wine and begged for a table for two. After some serious groveling and pleading, the hostess finally caved.

I left a message on Mark's voice mail: "It's definitely your lucky day. You're booked for dinner at seven. Have fun!"

Then I clocked out, eager to get home.

"He said *what*?" Cary sat on the opposite end of our white sectional sofa and shook his head.

"I know, right?" I enjoyed another sip of my wine. It was a crisp and nicely chilled sauvignon blanc I'd picked up on the walk home. "That was my reaction, too. I'm still not sure I didn't hallucinate the conversation while overdosing on his pheromones."

"So?"

I tucked my legs beneath me on the couch and leaned into the corner. "So what?"

"You know what, Eva." Grabbing his netbook off the coffee table, Cary propped it on his crossed legs. "Are you going to tap that or what?"

"I don't even *know* him. I don't even

know his first name and he threw that curveball at me."

"He knew yours." He started typing on his keyboard. "And what about the thing with the vodka? Asking for your boss in particular?"

The hand I was running through my loose hair stilled. "Mark is very talented. If Cross has any sort of business sense at all, he'd pick up on that and exploit it."

"I'd say he knows business." Cary spun his netbook around and showed me the home page of Cross Industries, which boasted an awesome photo of the Crossfire. "That's his building, Eva. Gideon Cross owns it."

Damn it. My eyes closed. *Gideon Cross.* I thought the name suited him. It was as sexy and elegantly masculine as the man himself.

"He has people to handle marketing for his subsidiaries. Probably dozens of people to handle it."

"Stop talking, Cary."

"He's hot, rich, and wants to jump your bones. What's the problem?"

I looked at him. "It's going to be awkward running into him all the time. I'm hoping to hang on to my job for a long while. I really like it. I really like Mark. He's totally involved me in the process and I've learned so much from him already."

"Remember what Dr. Travis says about calculated risks? When your shrink tells you to take some, you should take some. You can deal with it. You and Cross are both adults." He turned his attention back to his Internet search. "Wow. Did you know he doesn't turn thirty for another two years? Think of the stamina."

"Think of the rudeness. I'm offended by how he just threw it out there. I hate feeling like a vagina with legs."

Cary paused and looked up at me, his eyes softening with sympathy. "I'm sorry, baby girl. You're so strong, so much stronger than I am. I just don't see you carrying around the baggage I do."

"I don't think I am, most of the time." I looked away because I didn't want to talk about what we'd been through in our pasts. "It's not like I wanted him to ask me out on a date. But there has to be a better way to tell a woman you want to take her to bed."

"You're right. He's an arrogant douche. Let him lust after you until he has blue balls. Serves him right."

That made me smile. Cary could always do that. "I doubt that man has ever had blue balls in his life, but it's a fun fantasy."

He shut his netbook with a decisive snap.

"What should we do tonight?"

"I was thinking I'd like to go check out that Krav Maga studio in Brooklyn." I'd done a little research after meeting Parker Smith during my workout at Equinox, and as the week passed, the thought of having that kind of raw, physical outlet for stress seemed more and more ideal.

I knew it wouldn't be anything close to banging the hell out of Gideon Cross, but I suspected it would be a lot less dangerous to my health.

3

"There's no way your mom and Stanton are going to let you come out here at night multiple times a week," Cary said, hugging his stylish denim jacket around him even though it wasn't more than slightly chilly.

The converted warehouse Parker Smith used as his studio was a brick-faced building in a formerly industrial area of Brooklyn presently struggling to revitalize. The space was vast, and the massive metal delivery-bay doors offered no exterior clue as to what was taking place inside. Cary and I sat in aluminum bleachers, watching a half dozen combatants on the mats below.

"Ouch." I winced in sympathy as a guy took a kick to the groin. Even with padding, that had to sting. "How's Stanton going to find out, Cary?"

"Because you'll be in the hospital?" He glanced at me. "Seriously. Krav Maga is brutal. They're just sparring and it's full contact. And even if the bruises don't give you away, your stepdad will find out somehow. He always does."

"Because of my mom; she tells him everything. But I'm not telling her about this."

"Why not?"

"She won't understand. She'll think I want to protect myself because of what happened, and she'll feel guilty and give me grief about it. She won't believe my main interest is exercise and stress relief."

I propped my chin on my palm and watched Parker take the floor with a woman. He was a good instructor. Patient and thorough, and he explained things in an easy-to-understand way. His studio was in a rough neighborhood, but I thought it suited what he was teaching. It didn't get more reality based than a big, empty warehouse.

"That Parker guy is really hot," Cary murmured.

"He's also wearing a wedding band."

"I noticed. The good ones always get snatched up quick."

Parker joined us after the class was over, his dark eyes bright and his smile brighter. "What'd ya think, Eva?"

"Where do I sign up?"

His sexy smile made Cary reach over and squeeze the blood out of my hand.

"Step this way."

Friday started out awesome. Mark walked me through the process of collecting information for an RFP, and he told me a little more about Cross Industries and Gideon Cross, pointing out that he and Cross were the same age.

"I have to remind myself of that," Mark said. "It's easy to forget he's so young when he's right in front of you."

"Yes," I agreed, secretly disappointed that I wouldn't see Cross for the next two days. As much as I told myself it didn't matter, I was bummed. I hadn't realized I'd been excited by the possibility that we might run into each other until that possibility was gone. It was just such a rush being near him. Plus he was a hell of a lot of fun to look at. I had nothing nearly as exciting planned for the weekend.

I was taking notes in Mark's office when I heard my desk phone ringing. Excusing myself, I rushed over to catch it. "Mark Garrity's office —"

"Eva, love. How are you?"

I sank into my chair at the sound of my stepfather's voice. Stanton always sounded like old money to me — cultured, entitled, and arrogant. "Richard. Is everything okay?

Is Mom all right?"

"Yes. Everything's fine. Your mother is wonderful, as always."

His tone softened when he spoke of his wife, and I was grateful for that. I was grateful to him for a lot of things, actually, but it was sometimes hard to balance that against my feelings of disloyalty. I knew my dad was self-conscious about the massive differences in their income brackets.

"Good," I said, relieved. "I'm glad. Did you and Mom receive my thank-you note for the dress and Cary's tuxedo?"

"Yes, and it was thoughtful of you, but you know we don't expect you to thank us for such things. Excuse me a moment." He spoke to someone, most likely his secretary. "Eva, love, I'd like us to get together for lunch today. I'll send Clancy around to collect you."

"Today? But we'll be seeing each other tomorrow night. Can't it wait until then?"

"No, it should be today."

"But I only get an hour for lunch."

A tap on my shoulder turned me around to find Mark standing by my cubicle. "Take two," he whispered. "You earned it."

I sighed and mouthed a thank-you. "Will twelve o'clock work, Richard?"

"Perfectly. I look forward to seeing you."

I had no reason to look forward to private meetings with Stanton, but I dutifully left just before noon and found a town car waiting for me, idling at the curb. Clancy, Stanton's driver and bodyguard, opened the door for me as I greeted him. Then he slid behind the wheel and drove me downtown. By twenty after the hour, I was sitting at a conference table in Stanton's offices, eyeing a beautifully catered lunch for two.

Stanton came in shortly after my arrival, looking dapper and distinguished. His hair was pure white, his face lined but still very handsome. His eyes were the color of worn blue denim, and they were sharp with intelligence. He was trim and athletic, taking the time out of his busy days to stay fit even before he'd married his trophy wife — my mom.

I stood as he approached, and he bent to kiss my cheek. "You look lovely, Eva."

"Thank you." I looked like my mom, who was also a natural blonde. But my gray eyes came from my dad.

Taking a chair at the head of the table, Stanton was aware that the requisite backdrop of the New York skyline was behind him, and he took advantage of its impressiveness.

"Eat," he said, with the command so easily wielded by all men of power. Men like Gideon Cross.

Had Stanton been as driven at Cross's age?

I picked up my fork and started in on a chicken, cranberry, walnut, and feta salad. It was delicious, and I was hungry. I was glad Stanton didn't start talking right away so I could enjoy the meal, but the reprieve didn't last long.

"Eva love, I wanted to discuss your interest in Krav Maga."

I froze. "Excuse me?"

Stanton took a sip of iced water and leaned back, his jaw taking on the rigidity that warned me I wouldn't like what he was about to say. "Your mother was quite distraught last night when you went to that studio in Brooklyn. It took some time to calm her down and to assure her that I could make arrangements for you to pursue your interests in a safe manner. She doesn't want —"

"Wait." I set my fork down carefully, my appetite gone. "How did she know where I was?"

"She tracked your cell phone."

"No way," I breathed, deflating into my seat. The casualness of his reply, as if it were the most natural thing in the world, made

64

me feel ill. My stomach churned, suddenly more interested in rejecting my lunch than digesting it. "That's why she insisted I use one of your company phones. It had nothing to do with saving me money."

"Of course that was part of it. But it also gives her peace of mind."

"Peace of mind? To spy on her grown daughter? It's not healthy, Richard. You've got to see that. Is she still seeing Dr. Petersen?"

He had the grace to look uncomfortable. "Yes, of course."

"Is she telling him what she's doing?"

"I don't know," he said stiffly. "That's Monica's private business. I don't interfere."

No, he didn't. He coddled her. Indulged her. Spoiled her. And allowed her obsession with my safety to run wild. "She has to let it go. *I've* let it go."

"You were an innocent, Eva. She feels guilty for not protecting you. We need to give her a little latitude."

"Latitude? She's a stalker!" My mind spun. How could my mom invade my privacy like that? *Why* would she? She was driving herself crazy, and me along with her. "This has to stop."

"It's an easy fix. I've already spoken with Clancy. He'll drive you when you need to venture into Brooklyn. Everything's been arranged. This will be much more convenient for you."

"Don't try to twist this around to being for my benefit." My eyes stung and my throat burned with unshed tears of frustration. I hated the way he talked about Brooklyn like it was a third-world country. "I'm a grown woman. I make my own decisions. It's the goddamn law!"

"Don't take that tone with me, Eva. I'm simply looking after your mother. And you."

I pushed back from the table. "You're enabling her. You're keeping her sick, and you're making me sick, too."

"Sit down. You need to eat. Monica worries that you're not eating healthy enough."

"She worries about *everything,* Richard. That's the problem." I dropped my napkin on the table. "I have to get back to work."

I turned away, striding toward the door to get out as quickly as possible. I retrieved my purse from Stanton's secretary and left my cell phone on her desk. Clancy, who had been waiting for me in the reception area, followed me, and I knew better than to try to blow him off. He didn't take orders from anyone but Stanton.

Clancy drove me back up to midtown, while I stewed in the backseat. I could bitch all I wanted, but in the end I wasn't any better than Stanton because I was going to give in. I was going to cave and let my mom have her way, because it hurt my heart to think of her suffering any more than she already did. She was so emotional and fragile, and she loved me to the point of being crazy about it.

My mood was still dark when I got back to the Crossfire. As Clancy pulled away from the curb, I stood on the crowded sidewalk and looked up and down the busy street for either a drugstore where I could get some chocolate or a cellular store where I could pick up a new phone.

I ended up walking around the block and buying a half dozen candy bars at a Duane Reade on the corner before heading back to the Crossfire. I'd been gone just about an hour, but I wasn't going to use the extra time Mark had given me. I needed work to distract me from my crazy-ass family.

As I caught an empty elevator car, I ripped open a bar and bit viciously into it. I was making strides toward filling my self-imposed chocolate quota before I hit the twentieth floor when the car stopped on the fourth. I appreciated the added time the stop gave me to enjoy the comfort of dark

chocolate and caramel melting over my
tongue.

The doors slid apart and revealed Gideon
Cross talking with two other gentlemen.

As usual, I lost my breath at the sight of
him, which reignited my fading irritation.
Why did he have that effect on me? When
was I going to become immune?

He glanced over and his lips curved into a
slow, heart-stopping smile when he saw me.

Great. Just my crappy luck. I'd become
some kind of challenge.

Cross's smile faded into a frown. "We'll
finish this later," he murmured to his companions without looking away from me.

Stepping into the car, he lifted a hand to
discourage them from following him. They
blinked in surprise, glancing at me, then
Cross, and then back again.

I stepped out, deciding it would be safer
for my sanity to take a different car up.

"Not so fast, Eva." Cross caught me by
the elbow and tugged me back. The doors
shut and the elevator glided smoothly into
motion.

"What are you doing?" I snapped. After
dealing with Stanton, the last thing I needed
was another domineering male trying to
push me around.

Cross caught me by the upper arms and

searched my face with that vivid blue gaze. "Something's wrong. What is it?"

The now-familiar electricity crackled to life between us, the pull made fiercer by my temper. "You."

"Me?" His thumbs stroked over my shoulders. Releasing me, he withdrew a lone key from his pocket and plugged it into the panel. All the lights cleared except for the one for the top floor.

He wore black again, with fine gray pinstripes. Seeing him from behind was a revelation. His shoulders were nicely broad without being bulky, emphasizing his lean waist and long legs. The silky strands of hair falling over his collar tempted me to clench them and pull. Hard. I wanted him to be as pissy as I was. I wanted a fight.

"I'm not in the mood for you now, Mr. Cross."

He watched the antique-style needle above the doors mark the passing floors. "I can get you in the mood."

"I'm not interested."

Cross glanced over his shoulder at me. His shirt and tie were both the same rich cerulean as his irises. The effect was striking. "No lies, Eva. Ever."

"That's not a lie. So what if I'm attracted to you? I expect most women are." Wrap-

69

ping up what was left of my candy bar, I shoved it back into the shopping bag I'd tucked into my purse. I didn't need chocolate when I was sharing air with Gideon Cross. "But I'm not interested in doing anything about it."

He faced me then, turning in a leisurely pivot, that ghost of a smile softening his sinful mouth. His ease and unconcern aggravated me further. "*Attraction* is too tame a word for" — he gestured at the space between us — "this."

"Call me crazy, but I have to actually *like* someone before I get naked and sweaty with him."

"Not crazy," he said. "But I don't have the time or the inclination to date."

"That makes two of us. Glad we got that cleared up."

He stepped closer, his hand lifting to my face. I forced myself not to move away or give him the satisfaction of seeing me intimidated. His thumb brushed over the corner of my mouth, then lifted to his own. He sucked on the pad and purred, "Chocolate and you. Delicious."

A shiver moved through me, followed by a heated ache between my legs as I imagined licking chocolate off his lethally sexy body.

His gaze darkened and his voice lowered

70

intimately. "Romance isn't in my repertoire, Eva. But a thousand ways to make you come are. Let me show you."

The car slowed to a halt. He withdrew the key from the panel and the doors opened.

I backed into the corner and shooed him out with a flick of my wrist. "I'm really not interested."

"We'll discuss." Cross caught me by the elbow and gently, but insistently, urged me out.

I went along because I liked the charge I got from being around him and because I was curious to see what he had to say when afforded more than five minutes of my time.

He was buzzed through the security door so quickly there was no need for him to break stride. The pretty redhead at the reception desk pushed hastily to her feet, about to impart some information until he shook his head impatiently. Her mouth snapped shut and she stared at me, her eyes wide, as we passed at a brisk pace.

The walk to Cross's office was mercifully short. His secretary stood when he saw his boss's approach but remained silent when he noted that Cross wasn't alone.

"Hold my calls, Scott," Cross said, steering me into his office through the open glass double doors.

Despite my irritation, I couldn't help but be impressed with Gideon Cross's spacious command center. Floor-to-ceiling windows overlooked the city on two sides, while a wall of glass faced the rest of the office space. The one opaque wall opposite the massive desk was covered in flatscreens streaming news channels from around the world. There were three distinct seating areas, each one larger than Mark's entire office, and a bar that showcased jeweled crystal decanters, which provided the only spots of color in a palette that was otherwise black, gray, and white.

Cross hit a button on his desk that closed the doors, then another that instantly frosted the clear glass wall, effectively shielding us from the view of his employees. With the beautiful sapphire-hued reflective film on the exterior windows, privacy was assured. He shrugged out of his jacket and hung it on a chrome coatrack. Then he returned to where I'd remained standing just inside the doors. "Something to drink, Eva?"

"No, thank you." Damn it. He was even yummier in just the vest. I could better see how fit he was. How strong his shoulders were. How beautifully his biceps and ass flexed as he moved.

He gestured toward a black leather sofa. "Have a seat."

"I have to go back to work."

"And I have a meeting at two. The sooner we work this out, the sooner we can both get back to business. Now, sit down."

"What do you think we're going to work out?"

Sighing, he scooped me up like a bride and carried me over to the sofa. He dropped me on my butt, then sat next to me. "Your objections. It's time to discuss what it's going to take to get you beneath me."

"A miracle." I pushed back from him, widening the space between us. I tugged at the hem of my emerald green skirt, wishing I'd worn pants instead. "I find your approach crude and offensive."

And a major turn-on, but I was never going to admit it.

He contemplated me with narrowed eyes. "It may be blunt, but it's honest. You don't strike me as the kind of woman who wants bullshit and flattery instead of the truth."

"What I want is to be seen as having more to offer than an inflatable sex doll."

Cross's brows shot up. "Well, then."

"Are we done?" I stood.

Wrapping my wrist with his fingers, he pulled me back down. "Hardly. We've established some talking points: We have an intense sexual attraction and neither of us wants to date. So what do you want — exactly? Seduction, Eva? Do you want to be seduced?"

I was equally fascinated and appalled by the conversation. And, yes, tempted. It was hard not to be while faced with such a gorgeous, virile male so determined to get hot and sweaty with me. Still, the dismay won out. "Sex that's planned like a business transaction is a turnoff for me."

"Establishing parameters in the beginning makes it less likely that there'll be exaggerated expectations and disappointment at the conclusion."

"Are you kidding?" I scowled. "Listen to yourself. Why even call it a fuck? Why not be clear and call it a seminal emission in a pre-approved orifice?"

He pissed me off by throwing his head back and laughing. The full, throaty sound flowed over me like a rush of warm water. My awareness of him heightened to a physically painful degree. His earthy amusement made him less sex god and more human. Flesh and blood. Real.

I pushed to my feet and backed out of reach. "Casual sex doesn't have to include wine and roses, but for God's sake, whatever else it is, sex should be personal. Friendly even. With mutual respect at the very least."

His humor fled as he stood, his eyes darkening. "There are no mixed signals in my private affairs. You want me to blur that line. I can't think of a good reason to."

"I don't want you to do jack shit, besides let me get back to work." I strode to the door and yanked on the handle, cursing softly when it didn't budge. "Let me out, Cross."

I felt him come up behind me. His palms pressed flat to the glass on either side of my shoulders, caging me in. I couldn't think of my own self-preservation when he was so close.

The strength and demand of his will exuded an almost tangible force field. When he stepped close enough, it surrounded me, closing me in with him. Everything outside that bubble ceased to exist, while inside it my entire body strained toward his. That he had such a profound, visceral effect on me while being so damn irritating had my mind spinning. How could I be so turned on by a man whose words should've turned me completely off?

"Turn around, Eva."

My eyes closed against the surge of arousal I felt at his authoritative tone. God, he smelled good. His powerful frame radiated heat and hunger, spurring my own wild desire for him. The uncontrollable response was intensified by my lingering frustration with Stanton and my more recent aggravation with Cross himself.

I wanted him. Bad. But he was no good for me. Honestly, I could screw up my life on my own. I didn't need any help.

My flushed forehead touched the air-conditioned glass. "Let it go, Cross."

"I am. You're too much trouble." His lips brushed behind my ear. One of his hands pressed flat to my stomach, the fingers splaying to urge me back against him. He was as aroused as I was, his cock hard and thick against my lower back. "Turn around and say good-bye."

Disappointed and regretful, I turned in his grip, sagging against the door to cool my heated back. He was curved over me, his luxurious hair framing his beautiful face, his forearm propped against the door to bring him closer. I had almost no room to breathe. The hand he'd had at my waist was now resting on the curve of my hip, tightening reflexively and driving me mad. He stared, his gaze searingly intense.

"Kiss me," he said hoarsely. "Give me that much."

Panting softly, I licked my dry lips. He groaned, tilted his head, and sealed his mouth over mine. I was shocked by how soft his firm lips were and the gentleness of the pressure he exerted. I sighed and his tongue dipped inside, tasting me in long, leisurely licks. His kiss was confident, skilled, and just the right side of aggressive to turn me on wildly.

I distantly registered my purse hitting the floor; then my hands were in his hair. I pulled on the silky strands, using them to direct his mouth over mine. He growled, deepening the kiss, stroking my tongue with lush slides of his own. I felt the raging beat of his heart against my chest, proof that he wasn't just a hopeless ideal conjured by my fevered imagination.

He pushed away from the door. Cupping the back of my head and the curve of my buttocks, he lifted me off my feet. "I want you, Eva. Trouble or not, I can't stop."

I was pressed full-body against him, achingly aware of every hot, hard inch of him. I kissed him back as if I could eat him alive. My skin was damp and too sensitive, my breasts heavy and tender. My clit throbbed for attention, pounding along with my raging heartbeat.

I was vaguely aware of movement, and

then the couch was against my back. Cross was levered over me with one knee on the cushion and the other foot on the floor. His left arm supported his torso while his right hand gripped the back of my knee, sliding upward along my thigh in a firmly possessive glide.

His breath hissed out when he reached the point where my garter clipped to the top of my silk stocking. He tore his gaze away from mine and looked down, pushing my skirt higher to bare me from the waist down.

"Jesus, Eva." A low rumble vibrated in his chest, the primitive sound sending goose bumps racing across my skin. "Your boss is damned lucky he's gay."

In a daze, I watched Cross's body lower to mine, my legs sliding apart to accommodate the width of his hips. My muscles strained with the urge to lift toward him, to hasten the contact between us that I'd been craving since I first laid eyes on him. Lowering his head, he took my mouth again, bruising my lips with a fine edge of violence.

Abruptly, he yanked himself away, stumbling to his feet.

I lay there gasping and wet, so willing and

ready. Then I realized why he'd reacted so fiercely.

Someone was behind him.

4

Mortified by the sudden intrusion into our privacy, I scrambled up and back into the armrest, yanking down my skirt.

". . . two o'clock appointment is here."

It took an endless moment to realize Cross and I were still alone in the room, that the voice I'd heard had come through a speaker. Cross stood at the far end of the sofa, flushed and scowling, his chest heaving. His tie was loosened and the fly of his slacks strained against a very impressive erection.

I had a nightmare vision in my head of what I must look like. And I was late getting back to work.

"Christ." He shoved both hands through his hair. "It's the middle of the fucking day. In my goddamn fucking office!"

I got to my feet and tried to straighten my appearance.

"Here." He came to me, yanking my skirt up again.

Furious at what I'd almost let happen when I should be at work, I smacked at his hands. "Stop it. Leave me alone."

"Shut up, Eva," he said grimly, catching the hem of my black silk blouse and tugging it into place, adjusting it so that the buttons once again formed a straight row between my breasts. Then he pulled down my skirt, smoothing it with calm, expert hands. "Fix your ponytail."

Cross retrieved his coat, shrugging into it before adjusting his tie. We reached the door at the same time, and when I crouched to fetch my purse, he lowered with me.

He caught my chin, forcing me to look at him. "Hey," he said softly. "You okay?"

My throat burned. I was aroused and mad and thoroughly embarrassed. I'd never in my life lost my mind like that. And I hated that I'd done so with *him,* a man whose approach to sexual intimacy was so clinical it depressed me just thinking about it.

I jerked my chin away. "Do I *look* okay?"

"You look beautiful and fuckable. I want you so badly it hurts. I'm dangerously close to taking you back to the couch and making you come 'til you beg me to stop."

"Can't accuse you of being silver-tongued," I muttered, aware that I wasn't offended. In fact, the rawness of his hunger

81

for me was a serious aphrodisiac. Clutching the strap of my purse, I stood on shaky legs. I needed to get away from him. And, when my workday was done, I needed to be alone with a big glass of wine.

Cross stood with me. "I'll juggle what I have to and be done by five. I'll come get you then."

"No, you won't. This doesn't change anything."

"The hell it doesn't."

"Don't be arrogant, Cross. I lost my head for a second, but I still don't want what you want."

His fingers curled around the door handle. "Yes, you do. You just don't want it the way I want to give it to you. So, we'll revisit and revise."

More business. Cut-and-dried. My spine stiffened.

I set my hand over his and yanked on the handle, ducking under his arm to squeeze out the door. His secretary shoved quickly to his feet, gaping, as did the woman and two men who were waiting for Cross. I heard him speak behind me.

"Scott will show you into my office. I'll be just a moment."

He caught me by reception, his arm crossing my lower back to grip my hip. Not wanting to make a scene, I waited until we were by the elevators to pull away.

He stood calmly and hit the call button. "Five o'clock, Eva."

I stared at the lighted button. "I'm busy."

"Tomorrow, then."

"I'm busy all weekend."

Stepping in front of me, he asked tightly, "With whom?"

"That's none of your —"

His hand covered my mouth. "Don't. Tell me when, then. And before you say never, take a good look at me and tell me if you see a man who's easily deterred."

His face was hard, his gaze narrowed and determined. I shivered. I wasn't sure I'd win a battle of wills with Gideon Cross.

Swallowing, I waited until he lowered his hand and said, "I think we both need to cool off. Take a couple days to think."

He persisted. "Monday after work."

The elevator arrived and I stepped into it. Facing him, I countered, "Monday lunch."

We'd have only an hour, a guaranteed escape.

Just before the doors closed, he said, "We're going to happen, Eva."

It sounded as much like a threat as a promise.

■ ■ ■ ■

"Don't sweat it, Eva," Mark said, when I arrived at my desk nearly a quarter after two. "You didn't miss anything. I had a late lunch with Mr. Leaman. I just barely got back myself."

"Thank you." No matter what he said, I still felt terrible. My kickass Friday morning seemed to have happened days ago.

We worked steadily until five, discussing a fast-food client and contemplating some possible tweaks to ad copy for a chain of organic grocery stores.

"Talk about strange bedfellows," Mark had teased, not knowing how apt that was in regard to my personal life.

I'd just shut down my computer and was pulling my purse out of the drawer when my phone rang. I glanced at the clock, saw it was exactly five, and considered ignoring the call because I was technically done for the day.

But since I was still feeling shitty about my overly long lunch, I considered it penance and answered. "Mark Garrity's —"

"Eva, honey. Richard says you forgot your cell phone at his office."

I exhaled in a rush and sagged back into

84

my chair. I could picture the handkerchief wringing that usually accompanied that particular anxious tone of my mother's. It drove me nuts and it also broke my heart. "Hi, Mom. How are you?"

"Oh, I'm lovely. Thank you." My mom had a voice that was both girlish and breathy, like Marilyn Monroe crossed with Scarlett Johansson. "Clancy dropped your phone off with the concierge at your place. You really shouldn't go anywhere without it. You never know when you might need to call for someone —"

I'd been debating the logistics of just keeping the phone and forwarding calls to a new number I didn't share with my mom, but that wasn't my biggest concern. "What does Dr. Petersen say about you tracing my phone?"

The silence on the other end of the line was telling. "Dr. Petersen knows I worry about you."

Pinching the bridge of my nose, I said, "I think it's time for us to have another joint appointment, Mom."

"Oh . . . of course. He did mention that he'd like to see you again."

Probably because he suspects you're not being forthcoming. I changed the subject. "I really like my new job."

"That's wonderful, Eva! Is your boss treating you well?"

"Yes, he's great. I couldn't ask for anyone better."

"Is he handsome?"

I smiled. "Yes, very. And he's taken."

"Damn it. The good ones always are." She laughed and my smile widened.

I loved it when she was happy. I wished she were happy more often. "I can't wait to see you tomorrow at the advocacy dinner."

Monica Tramell Barker Mitchell Stanton was in her element at society functions, a gilded, shining beauty who'd never lacked male attention in her life.

"Let's make a day of it," my mom said breathlessly. "You, me, and Cary. We'll go to the spa, get pretty and polished. I'm sure you could use a massage after working so hard."

"I won't turn one down, that's for sure. And I know Cary will love it."

"Oh, I'm excited! I'll send a car by your place around eleven?"

"We'll be ready."

After I hung up, I leaned back in my chair and exhaled, needing a hot bath and an orgasm. If Gideon Cross somehow found out I masturbated while thinking about him, I didn't care. Being sexually frustrated was weakening my position, a weakness I knew he wouldn't be sharing. No doubt he'd have a preapproved orifice lined up before day's end.

As I swapped out my heels for my walking shoes, my phone rang again. My mother was rarely distracted for long. The five minutes since we'd ended our call was just about the right length of time for her to realize the cell phone issue hadn't been resolved. Once again, I debated ignoring the phone, but I didn't want to take any of the day's crap home with me.

I answered with my usual greeting, but it lacked its usual punch.

"I'm still thinking about you."

The velvet rasp of Cross's voice flooded me with such relief that I realized I'd been hoping to hear it again. Today.

God. The craving was so acute I knew he'd become a drug to my body, the prime source of some very intense highs.

"I can still feel you, Eva. Still taste you. I've been hard since you left, through two meetings and one teleconference. You've got the advantage; state your demands."

"Ah," I murmured. "Lemme think."

I let him wait, smiling as I remembered Cary's comment about blue balls. "Hmm . . . Nothing is coming to mind. But

I do have some friendly advice. Go spend time with a woman who salivates at your feet and makes you feel like a god. Fuck her until neither of you can walk. When you see me on Monday you'll be totally over it and your life will return to its usual obsessive-compulsive order."

The creak of leather sounded over the phone and I imagined him leaning back in his desk chair. "That was your one free pass, Eva. The next time you insult my intelligence, I'll take you over my knee."

"I don't like that sort of thing." And yet the warning, given in that voice, aroused me. Dark and Dangerous for sure.

"We'll discuss. In the interim, tell me what you *do* like."

I stood. "You definitely have the voice for phone sex, but I've got to go. I have a date with my vibrator."

I should've hung up then, to gain the full effect of the brush-off, but I couldn't resist learning if he'd gloat like I had imagined he would. Plus, I was having fun with him.

"Oh, Eva." Cross spoke my name in a decadent purr. "You're determined to drive me to my knees, aren't you? What will it take to talk you into a threesome with B.O.B.?"

I ignored both questions as I slung my

bag and purse over my shoulder, grateful he couldn't see how my hand shook. I was *not* discussing Battery-Operated Boyfriends with Gideon Cross. I'd never discussed masturbation openly with a man, let alone a man who was for all intents and purposes a stranger to me. "B.O.B. and I have a long-time understanding — when we're done with each other, we know exactly which one of us has been used, and it isn't me. Good night, Gideon."

I hung up and took the stairs, deciding the twenty-floor descent would serve double duty as both an avoidance technique and a replacement for a visit to the gym.

I was so grateful to be home after the day I'd had that I practically danced through my apartment's front door. My heartfelt "God, it's good to be home!" and accompanying spin was vehement enough to startle the couple on the couch.

"Oh," I said, wincing at my own silliness. Cary wasn't in a compromising position with his guest when I barged in, but they'd been sitting close enough to suggest intimacy.

Grudgingly, I thought of Gideon Cross, who preferred to strip all intimacy out of the most intimate act I could imagine. I'd had one-night stands and friends with benefits, and no one knew better than I that sex and making love were two very different things, but I didn't think I'd ever be able to view sex like a handshake. I thought it was sad that Cross did, even though he wasn't a man who inspired pity or sympathy.

"Hey, baby girl," Cary called out, pushing to his feet. "I was hoping you'd make it back before Trey had to leave."

"I have class in an hour," Trey explained, rounding the coffee table as I dropped my bag on the floor and put my purse on a bar stool at the breakfast bar. "But I'm glad I got to meet you before I left."

"Me, too." I shook the hand he extended to me, taking him in with a quick glance. He was about my age, I guessed. Average height and nicely muscular. He had unruly blond hair, soft hazel eyes, and a nose that had clearly been broken at some point.

"Mind if I grab a glass of wine?" I asked. "It's been a long day."

"Go for it," Trey replied.

"I'll take one, too." Cary joined us by the breakfast bar. He was wearing loose-fitting black jeans and an off-the-shoulder black sweater. The look was casual and elegant and did a phenomenal job of offsetting his dark brown hair and emerald eyes.

I went to the wine fridge and pulled out a random bottle.

Trey shoved his hands in the pockets of his jeans and rocked back on his heels, talking quietly with Cary as I uncorked and poured.

The phone rang and I grabbed the handset off the wall. "Hello?"

"Hey, Eva? It's Parker Smith."

"Parker, hi." I leaned my hip into the counter. "How are you?"

"I hope you don't mind my calling. Your stepdad gave me your home number when I couldn't reach you on your cell."

Gah. I'd had enough of Stanton for one day. "Not at all. What's up?"

"Honestly? Everything's looking up right now. Your stepdad is like my fairy godfather. He's funding a few safety improvements to the studio and some much-needed upgrades. That's why I'm calling. The studio's going to be out of commission next week. Classes will resume a week from Monday."

I closed my eyes, struggling to tamp down a flare of exasperation. It wasn't Parker's fault that Stanton and my mom were overprotective control freaks. Clearly they didn't see the irony of defending me while I was surrounded by people trained to do that very thing. "Sounds good. I can't wait. I'm really excited to be training with you."

"I'm excited, too. I'm going to work you hard, Eva. Your parents are going to get their money's worth."

I set a filled glass in front of Cary and took a big gulp out of my own. It never ceased to amaze me how much cooperation money could buy. But again, that wasn't Parker's fault. "No complaints here."

"We'll get started first thing the next week. Your driver has the schedule."

"Great. See you then." I hung up and caught the glance Trey shot Cary when he thought neither of us was looking. It was soft and filled with a sweet yearning, and it reminded me that my problems could wait. "I'm sorry I caught you on the way out, Trey. Do you have time for pizza Wednesday night? I'd love to do more than say hi and bye."

"I have class." He gave me a regretful smile and shot another side glance at Cary. "But I could come by on Tuesday."

"That'd be great." I smiled. "We could order in and have a movie night."

"I'd like that."

I was rewarded with the kiss Cary blew me as he headed to the door to show Trey out. When he returned to the kitchen he grabbed his wine and said, "All right. Spill it, Eva. You looked stressed."

"I am," I agreed, grabbing the bottle and moving into the living room.

"It's Gideon Cross, isn't it?"

"Oh, yeah. But I don't want to talk about him." Although Gideon's pursuit was exhilarating, his goal sucked. "Let's talk about you and Trey instead. How did you two meet?"

"I ran across him on a job. He's working part time as a photographer's assistant. Sexy, isn't he?" His eyes were bright and happy. "And a real gentleman. In an old-school way."

"Who knew there were any of those left?" I muttered before polishing off my first glass.

"What's that supposed to mean?"

"Nothing. I'm sorry, Cary. He seemed great, and he obviously digs you. Is he studying photography?"

"Veterinary medicine."

"Wow. That's awesome."

"I think so, too. But forget about Trey for a minute. Talk about what's bugging you. Get it out."

I sighed. "My mom. She found out about my interest in Parker's studio and now she's freaking out."

"What? How'd she find out? I swear I

haven't told anyone."

"I know you didn't. Never even crossed my mind." Grabbing the bottle off the table, I refilled my glass. "Get this. She's been tracking my cell phone."

Cary's brows rose. "Seriously? That's . . . creepy."

"I know, right? That's what I told Stanton, but he doesn't want to hear it."

"Well, hell." He ran a hand through his long bangs. "So what do you do?"

"Get a new phone. And meet with Dr. Petersen to see if he can't talk some sense into her."

"Good move. Turn it over to her shrink. So . . . is everything okay with your job? Do you still love it?"

"Totally." My head fell back into the sofa cushions and my eyes closed. "My work and you are my lifesavers right now."

"What about the young hottie bazillion-aire who wants to nail you? Come on, Eva. You know I'm dying here. What happened?"

I told him, of course. I wanted his take on it all. But when I finished, he was quiet. I lifted my head to look at him, and found him bright-eyed and biting his lip.

"Cary? What are you thinking?"

"I'm feeling kind of hot from that story." He laughed, and the warm, richly masculine sound swept a lot of my irritation away. "He's got to be so confused right now. I would've paid money to see his face when you hit him with that bit he wanted to spank you over."

"I can't believe he said that." Just remembering Cross's voice when he made that threat had my palms damp enough to leave steam on my glass. "What the hell is he into?"

"Spanking's not deviant. Besides, he was going for missionary on the couch, so he's not averse to the basics." Cary fell into the sofa, a brilliant smile lighting up his handsome face. "You're a huge challenge to a guy who obviously thrives on them. And he's willing to make concessions to have you, which I'd bet he's not used to. Just tell him what you want."

I split the last of the wine between us, feeling marginally better with a bit of alcohol in my veins. What *did* I want? Aside from the obvious? "We're totally incompatible."

"Is that what you call what happened on his couch?"

"Cary, come on. Boil it down. He picked me up off the lobby floor and then asked me to fuck. That's really it. Even a guy I take home from a bar has more going for him than that. 'Hey, what's your name?

Come here often? Who's your friend? What are you drinking? Like to dance? Do you work around here?' "

"All right, all right. I get it." He set his glass down on the table. "Let's go out. Hit a bar. Dance 'til we drop. Maybe meet some guys who'll talk you up some."

"Or at least buy me a drink."

"Hey, Cross offered you one of those in his office."

I shook my head and stood. "Whatever. Let me take a shower and we'll go."

I threw myself into clubbing like it was going out of style. Cary and I bounced all over downtown clubs from Tribeca to the East Village, wasting stupid money on cover charges and having a fabulous time. I danced until my feet felt like they were going to fall off, but I toughed it out until Cary complained about his heeled boots first.

We'd just stumbled out of a techno-pop club with a plan to buy me flip-flops at a nearby Walgreens when we ran across a hawker promoting a lounge a few blocks away.

"Great place to get off your feet for a while," he said, without the usual flashy smile or exaggerated hype most of the hawk-

96

ers employed. His clothes — black jeans and turtleneck — were more upscale, which intrigued me. And he didn't have flyers or postcards. What he handed me was a business card made from papyrus paper and printed with a gilded font that caught the light of the electric signage around us. I made a mental note to hang on to it as a great piece of print advertising.

A stream of quickly moving pedestrians flowed around us. Cary squinted down at the lettering, having a few more drinks in him than I did. "Looks swank."

"Show them that card," the hawker urged. "You'll skip the cover."

"Sweet." Cary linked arms with me and dragged me along. "Let's go. You might find a quality guy in a swanky joint."

My feet were seriously killing me by the time we found the place, but I quit bitching when I saw the charming entrance. The line to get in was long, extending down the street and around the corner. Amy Winehouse's soulful voice drifted out of the open door, as did well-dressed customers who exited with big smiles.

True to the hawker's word, the business card was a magic key that granted us immediate and free entrance. A gorgeous hostess led us upstairs to a quieter VIP bar that overlooked the stage and dance floor below. We were shown to a small seating area by the balcony and settled at a table hugged by two half-moon velvet sofas. She propped a beverage menu in the center and said, "Your drinks are on the house. Enjoy your evening."

"Wow." Cary whistled. "We scored."

"I think that hawker recognized you from an ad."

"Wouldn't that rock?" He grinned. "God, it's a great night. Hanging out with my best girl and crushing on a new hunk in my life."

"Oh?"

"I think I've decided to see where things go with Trey."

That made me happy. It felt like I'd been waiting forever for him to find someone who'd treat him right. "Has he asked you out yet?"

"No, but I don't think it's because he doesn't want to." He shrugged and smoothed his artfully ripped T-shirt. Paired with black leather pants and spiked wristlets, it made him look sexy and wild. "I just think he's trying to figure out the situation with you first. He wigged when I told him I lived with a woman and that I'd moved across the country to be with you. He's worried I might be bi-curious and secretly hung up on you. That's why I wanted you two to meet today, so he could see how you and I are together."

"I'm sorry, Cary. I'll try to put him at ease about it."

"It's *not* your fault. Don't worry about it. It'll work out if it's supposed to."

His assurances didn't make me feel better. I tried to think of a way I could help.

Two guys stopped by our table. "Okay if we join you?" the taller one asked.

I glanced at Cary, and then back at the guys. They looked like brothers and they were very attractive. Both were smiling and confident, their stances loose and easy.

I was about to say, *Sure,* when a warm hand settled on my bare shoulder and squeezed firmly. "This one's taken."

Across from me, Cary gaped as Gideon Cross rounded the sofa and extended his hand to him. "Taylor. Gideon Cross."

"Cary Taylor." He shook Gideon's hand with a wide smile. "But you knew that. Nice to meet you. I've heard a lot about you."

I could've killed him. I seriously thought about it.

"Good to know." Gideon settled on the seat beside me, his arm draped behind me so that his fingertips could brush casually and possessively up and down my arm.

99

"Maybe there's hope for me yet."

Twisting at the waist, I faced him and whispered fiercely, "What are you doing?"

He shot me a hard glance. "Whatever it takes."

"I'm going to dance." Cary stood with a mischievous grin. "Be back in a bit."

Ignoring my pleading glance, my best friend blew me a kiss and the guys followed him. I watched them all go, my heart racing. After another minute, ignoring Gideon became ridiculous, as well as impossible.

My gaze slid over him. He wore dress slacks in graphite gray and a black V-neck sweater, the overall effect being one of careless sophistication. I loved the look on him and was attracted to the softness it gave him, even though I knew it was only an illusion. He was a hard man in a lot of ways.

I took a deep breath, feeling like I needed to make an effort to socialize with him. After all, wasn't that my big complaint? That he wanted to skip past the getting-to-know-you stage and jump straight into bed?

"You look . . ." I paused. *Fantastic. Wonderful. Amazing. So damn sexy . . .* In the end, I went with the lame, "I like the way you look."

His brow arched. "Ah, something you like about me. Is that a general like of the overall package? Or just the clothes? Only the sweater? Or maybe it's the pants?"

The edge to his tone rubbed me the wrong way. "And if I say it's just the sweater?"

"I'll buy a dozen and wear them every damn day."

"That would be a shame."

"You don't like the sweater?" He was pissy, his words coming clipped and fast.

My hands flexed restlessly in my lap. "I love the sweater, but I also like the suits."

He stared at me a minute, and then nodded. "How was your date with B.O.B.?"

Oh hell. I looked away. It was a lot easier talking about masturbation over the phone. Doing it while squirming under that piercing blue stare was mortifying. "I don't kiss and tell."

He brushed the backs of his fingers over my cheek and murmured, "You're blushing."

I heard the amusement in his voice and swiftly changed topics. "Do you come here often?"

Shit. Where did that clichéd line come from?

His hand dropped to my lap and caught one of mine, his fingers curling into my palm. "When necessary."

A quick stab of jealousy made me stiffen. I glared at him, even though I was mad at myself for caring either way. "What does that mean? When you're on the prowl?"

Gideon's mouth curved into a genuine smile that hit me hard. "When expensive decisions need to be made. I own this club, Eva."

Of course he did. Jeez.

A pretty waitress set two pinkish-colored iced drinks in square tumblers on the table. She looked at Gideon and gave him a flirtatious smile. "Here you go, Mr. Cross. Two Stoli Elit and cranberries. Can I get you anything else?"

"That'll be all for now. Thanks."

I could totally see that she wanted to get on the preapproved list and I bristled at that; then I was distracted by what we'd been served. It was my beverage of choice when clubbing and what I'd been drinking all night. My nerves tingled. I watched him take a drink, swirl it around in his mouth like a fine wine, and then swallow it. The working of his throat made me hot, but that was nothing compared to what the intensity of his stare did to me.

"Not bad," he murmured. "Tell me if we made it right."

He kissed me. He moved in fast, but I saw

it coming and didn't turn away. His mouth was cold and flavored with alcohol-laced cranberry. Delicious. All the chaotic emotion and energy that had been writhing around inside me abruptly became too much to contain. I shoved a hand in his glorious hair and clenched it tight, holding him still as I sucked on his tongue. His groan was the most erotic sound I'd ever heard, making the flesh between my legs tighten viciously.

Shocked by the fury of my reaction, I wrenched away, gasping.

Gideon followed, nuzzling the side of my face, his lips brushing over my ear. He was breathing hard, too, and the sound of the ice in his tumbler clinking against the glass skittered across my inflamed senses.

"I need to be inside you, Eva," he whispered roughly. "I'm aching for you."

My gaze fell to my drink on the table, my thoughts swirling around in my head, a clusterfuck of impressions and recollections and confusion. "How did you know?"

His tongue traced the shell of my ear and I shivered. It felt like every cell in my body was straining toward his. Resisting him took an impossible amount of energy, draining me and making me feel tired.

"Know what?" he asked.

"What I like to drink? What Cary's name is?"

He inhaled deeply and then pulled away. Setting his drink down, he shifted on the sofa and drew a knee up onto the cushion between us so that he faced me directly. His arm once again draped over the sofa back, his fingertips drawing circles on the curve of my shoulder. "You visited another of my clubs earlier. Your credit card popped and your drinks were recorded. And Cary Taylor is listed on the rental agreement for your apartment."

The room spun. *No way* . . . My cell phone. My credit card. My fucking apartment. I couldn't breathe. Between my mother and Gideon, I felt claustrophobic.

"Eva. Jesus. You're white as a ghost." He shoved a glass into my hand. "Drink."

It was the Stoli and cranberry. I pounded it, draining the tumbler. My stomach churned for a moment, then settled. "You own the building I live in?" I gasped.

"Oddly enough, yes." He moved to sit on the table, facing me, his legs on either side of mine. He took my glass and set it aside, then warmed my chilled hands with his.

"Are you crazy, Gideon?"

His mouth thinned. "Is that a serious question?"

"Yes. Yes, it is. My mom stalks me, too, and she sees a shrink. Do you have a shrink?"

"Not presently, but you're driving me crazy enough to make that a possibility."

"So this behavior isn't normal for you?" My heart was pounding. I could hear the blood rushing past my eardrums. "Or is it?"

He shoved a hand through his hair, restoring order to the strands I'd mussed when we'd kissed. "I accessed information you voluntarily made available to me."

"Not to you! Not for what you used it for! That has to violate some kind of privacy law." I stared at him, more confused than ever. "Why would you do that?"

He had the grace to look disgruntled, at least. "So I can figure you out, damn it."

"Why don't you just *ask* me, Gideon? Is that so fucking hard for people to do nowadays?"

"It is with you." He grabbed his drink off the table and tossed back most of it. "I can't get you alone for more than a few minutes at a time."

"Because the only thing you want to talk about is what you have to do to get laid!"

"Christ, Eva," he hissed, squeezing my hand. "Keep your voice down!"

I studied him, taking in every line and

105

plane of his face. Unfortunately, cataloging the details didn't lessen my awe even a tiny bit. I was beginning to suspect I'd never get over being dazzled by his looks.

And I wasn't alone; I'd seen how other women reacted around him. And he was crazy rich, which made even old, bald, and paunchy guys attractive. It was no wonder he was used to snapping his fingers and scoring an orgasm.

His gaze darted over my face. "Why are you looking at me like that?"

"I'm thinking."

"About what?" His jaw tightened. "And I'm warning you, if you say anything about orifices, preapprovals, or seminal emissions, I won't be held accountable for my actions."

That almost made me smile. "I want to understand a few things, because I think it's possible I'm not giving you enough credit."

"I'd like to understand a few things myself," he muttered.

"I'm guessing the 'I want to fuck you' approach has a high success rate for you."

Gideon's face smoothed into unreadable impassivity. "I'm not touching that one, Eva."

"Okay. You want to figure out what it's going to take to get me into bed. Is that why you're here in this club right now?

Because of me? And don't say what you think I want to hear."

His gaze was clear and steady. "I'm here for you, yes. I arranged it."

Suddenly the threads the street hawker had been wearing made sense. We'd been hustled by someone on Cross Industries' payroll. "Did you figure that getting me here would get you laid?"

His mouth twitched with suppressed amusement. "There's always the hope, but I expected it would take more work than a chance meeting over drinks."

"You're right. So why do it? Why not wait until Monday lunch?"

"Because you're out trolling. I can't do anything about B.O.B., but I can stop you from picking up some asshole in a bar. You want to score, Eva, I'm right here."

"I'm not trolling. I'm burning off tension after a stressful day."

"You're not the only one." He fingered one of my silver chandelier earrings. "So you drink and dance when you're tense. I work on the problem that's making me tense in the first place."

His voice had softened, and it stirred an alarming yearning. "Is that what I am? A problem?"

"Absolutely." But there was a hint of a

smile around his lips.

I knew that was a lot of the appeal for him. Gideon Cross wouldn't be where he was, at such a young age, if he took "no" gracefully. "What's your definition of dating?"

A frown marred the space between his brows. "Lengthy social time spent with a woman during which we're not actively fucking."

"Don't you enjoy the company of women?"

The frown turned into a scowl. "Sure, as long as there aren't any exaggerated expectations or excessive demands on my time. I've found the best way to steer clear of those is to have mutually exclusive sexual relationships and friendships."

There were those pesky "exaggerated expectations" again. Clearly, those were a sticking point with him. "So, you do have female friends?"

"Of course." His legs tightened around mine, capturing me. "Where are you going with this?"

"You segregate sex from the rest of your life. You separate it from friendship, work . . . everything."

"I've got good reasons for doing that."

"I'm sure you do. Okay, here are my thoughts." It was difficult concentrating when I was so close to Gideon. "I told you I don't want to date and I don't. My job is priority number one and my personal life — as a single woman — is a close second. I don't want to sacrifice any of that time on a relationship, and there's really not enough left over to squeeze in anything steady."

"I'm right there with you."

"But I like sex."

"Good. Have it with me." His smile was an erotic invitation.

I shoved his shoulder. "I need a personal connection with the men I sleep with. It doesn't have to be intense or deep, but sex needs to be more than an emotionless transaction for me."

"Why?"

I could tell he wasn't being flippant. As bizarre as this conversation must be for him, Gideon was taking it seriously. "Call it one of my quirks, and I'm not saying that lightly. It pisses me off to feel used for sex. I feel devalued."

"Can't you look at it as *you* using *me* for sex?"

"Not with you." He was too forceful, too demanding.

A sizzling, predatory glimmer sparked in his eyes as I bared my weakness for him.

"Besides," I went on quickly, "that's

semantics. I need an equal exchange in my sexual relationships. Or to have the upper hand."

"Okay."

"Okay? You said that really quickly, considering I'm telling you I need to combine two things you work so hard to avoid putting together."

"I'm not comfortable with it and I don't claim to understand, but I'm hearing you — it's an issue. Tell me how to get around it."

My breath left me in a rush. I hadn't expected that. He was a man who wanted no complications with his sex and I was a woman who found sex complicated, but he wasn't giving up. Yet.

"We need to be friendly, Gideon. Not best buds or confidants, but two people who know more about each other than their anatomy. To me, that means we have to spend time together when we're not actively fucking. And I'm afraid we'll have to spend time not actively fucking in places where we're forced to restrain ourselves."

"Isn't that what we're doing now?"

"Yes. And see, that's what I mean. I wasn't giving you credit for that. You should've done it in a less creepy manner" — I covered his lips with my fingers when he tried to cut me off — "but I admit you did try to set up a time to talk and I wasn't helpful."

He nipped my fingers with his teeth, making me yelp and yank my hand away.

"Hey. What was that for?"

He lifted my abused hand to his mouth and kissed the hurt, his tongue darting out to soothe. And incite.

In self-defense, I tugged my hand back to my lap. I still wasn't completely confident that we'd worked things out. "Just so you know there are no exaggerated expectations — when you and I spend time together not actively fucking, I won't think it's a date. All right?"

"That covers it." Gideon smiled, and my decision to be with him solidified for me. His smile was like lightning in the darkness, blinding and beautiful and mysterious, and I wanted him so badly it was physically painful.

His hands slid down to cup the backs of my thighs. Squeezing gently, he tugged me just a little bit closer. The hem of my short black halter dress slipped almost indecently high, and his gaze was riveted to the flesh he'd exposed. His tongue wet his lips in an action so carnal and suggestive I could almost feel the caress on my skin.

Duffy began begging for mercy, her voice

drifting up from the dance floor below. An unwelcome ache developed in my chest and I rubbed at it.

I'd already had enough, but I heard myself saying, "I need another drink."

5

I had a vicious hangover on Saturday morning and figured it was no less than I deserved. As much as I'd resented Gideon's insistence on negotiating sex with as much passion as he would a merger, in the end I'd negotiated in kind. Because I wanted him enough to take a calculated risk and break my own rules.

I took comfort in knowing he was breaking some of his own, too.

After a long, hot shower, I made my way into the living room and found Cary on the couch with his netbook, looking fresh and alert. Smelling coffee in the kitchen, I headed there and filled the biggest mug I could find.

"Morning, sunshine," Cary called out.

With my much-needed dose of caffeine wrapped between both palms, I joined him on the couch.

He pointed at a box on the end table.

"That came for you while you were in the shower."

I set my mug on the coffee table and picked up the box. It was wrapped with brown paper and twine and had my name handwritten diagonally across the top with a decorative calligraphic flourish. Inside was an amber glass bottle with HANGOVER CURE painted on it in a white old-fashioned font and a note tied with raffia to the bottle's neck that said, *Drink me.* Gideon's business card was nestled in the cushioning tissue paper.

As I studied the gift, I found it very apt. Since meeting Gideon I'd felt like I'd fallen down the rabbit hole into a fascinating and seductive world where few of the known rules applied. I was in uncharted territory that was both exciting and scary.

I glanced at Cary, who eyed the bottle dubiously.

"Cheers." I pried the cork out and drank the contents without thinking twice about it. It tasted like sickly sweet cough syrup. My stomach quivered in distaste for a moment and then heated. I wiped my mouth with the back of my hand and shoved the cork back into the empty bottle.

"What was that?" Cary asked.

"From the burn, it's hair of the dog."

His nose wrinkled. "Effective but unpleasant."

And it was working. I already felt a little steadier.

Cary picked up the box and dug out Gideon's card. He flipped it over, then held it out to me. On the back Gideon had written *Call me* in bold slashing penmanship and jotted down a number.

I took the card, curling my hand around it. His gift was proof that he was thinking about me. His tenacity and focus were seductive. And flattering.

There was no denying I was in trouble where Gideon was concerned. I craved the way I felt when he touched me, and I loved the way he responded when I touched him back. When I tried to think of what I *wouldn't* agree to do to have his hands on me again, I couldn't come up with much.

When Cary tried to hand me the phone, I shook my head. "Not yet. I need a clear head when dealing with him, and I'm still fuzzy."

"You two seemed cozy last night. He's definitely into you."

"I'm definitely into him." Curling into the corner of the couch, I pressed my cheek into the cushion and hugged my legs to my chest. "We're going to hang out, get to know

115

each other, have casual-but-physically-intense sex, and be otherwise completely independent. No strings, no expectations, no responsibilities."

Cary hit a button on his netbook and the printer on the other side of the room started spitting out pages. Then he snapped the computer closed, set it on the coffee table, and gave me all his attention. "Maybe it'll turn into something serious."

"Maybe not," I scoffed.

"Cynic."

"I'm not looking for happily-ever-after, Cary, especially not with a mega-mogul like Cross. I've seen what it's like for my mom being connected to powerful men. It's a full-time job with a part-time companion. Money keeps Mom happy, but it wouldn't be enough for me."

My dad had loved my mom. He'd asked her to marry him and share his life. She'd turned him down because he didn't have the hefty portfolio and sizable bank account she required in a husband. Love wasn't a requisite for marriage in Monica Stanton's opinion, and since her sultry-eyed, breathy-voiced beauty was irresistible to most men, she'd never had to settle for less than whatever she wanted. Unfortunately she hadn't wanted my dad for the long haul.

116

Glancing at the clock, I saw it was ten thirty. "I guess I should get ready."

"I love spa day with your mom." Cary smiled, and it chased the lingering shadows on my mood away. "I feel like a god when we're done."

"Me, too. Of the goddess persuasion."

We were so eager to be off that we went downstairs to meet the car rather than wait for the front desk to call up.

The doorman smiled as we stepped outside — me in heeled sandals and a maxi dress, and Cary in hip-hugging jeans and a long-sleeved T-shirt.

"Good morning, Miss Tramell. Mr. Taylor. Will you need a cab today?"

"No thanks, Paul. We're expecting a car." Cary grinned. "It's spa day at Perrini's!"

"Ah, Perrini's Day Spa." Paul gave a sage nod. "I bought my wife a gift certificate for our anniversary. She enjoyed it so much I plan to make it a tradition."

"You did good, Paul," I said. "Pampering a woman never goes out of style."

A black town car pulled up with Clancy at the wheel. Paul opened the rear door for us and we climbed in, squealing when we found a box of Knipschildt's Chocopologie on the seat. Waving at Paul, we settled back and dug in, taking tiny nibbles of the truffles that were worth savoring slowly.

Clancy drove us straight to Perrini's, where the relaxation began from the moment one walked in the door. Crossing the entrance threshold was like taking a vacation on the far side of the world. Every arched doorway was framed by lushly vibrant striped silks, while jeweled pillows decorated elegant chaises and oversized armchairs.

Birds chirped from suspended gilded cages, and potted plants filled every corner with lush fronds. Small decorative fountains added the sounds of running water, while stringed instrumental music was piped into the room via cleverly hidden speakers. The air was redolent with a mix of exotic spices and fragrances, making me feel like I'd stepped into *Arabian Nights.*

It was *this close* to being too much, but it didn't cross the line. Instead, Perrini's was exotic and luxurious, an indulgent treat for those who could afford it. Like my mother, who'd just finished a milk-and-honey bath when we arrived.

I studied the menu of treatments available, deciding to skip my usual "warrior woman" in favor of the "passionate pampering." I'd been waxed the week before, but the rest of the treatment — "designed to make you sexually irresistible" — sounded like exactly what I needed.

I'd finally managed to get my mind back into the safe zone of work when Cary spoke up from the pedicure chair beside mine.

"Mrs. Stanton, have you met Gideon Cross?"

I gaped at him. He knew damn well my mom went nuts over any news about my romantic — and not-so-romantic, as the case may be — relationships.

My mother, who sat in the chair on the other side of me, leaned forward with her usual girlish excitement over a rich, handsome man. "Of course. He's one of the wealthiest men in the world. Number twenty-five or so on *Forbes*'s list, if I'm remembering correctly. A very driven young man, obviously, and a generous benefactor to many of the children's charities I champion. Extremely eligible, of course, but I don't believe he's gay, Cary. He's got a reputation as a ladies' man."

"My loss." Cary grinned and ignored my violent headshaking. "But it'd be a hopeless crush anyway, since he's digging on Eva."

"Eva! I can't believe you didn't say anything. How could you not tell me something like that?"

I looked at my mom, whose scrubbed face

appeared young, unlined, and very much like mine. I was very clearly my mother's daughter, right down to my surname. The one concession she'd made to my father had been to name me after his mother.

"There's nothing to tell," I insisted. "We're just . . . friends."

"We can do better than that," Monica said, with a look of calculation that struck fear in my heart. "I don't know how it escaped me that you work in the same building he does. I'm certain he was smitten the moment he saw you. Although he's known to prefer brunettes . . . Hmm . . . Anyway. He's also known for his excellent taste. Clearly the latter won out with you."

"It's not like that. Please don't start meddling. You'll embarrass me."

"Nonsense. If anyone knows what to do with men, it's me."

I cringed, my shoulders creeping up to my ears. By the time my massage appointment came around, I was in desperate need of one. I stretched out on the table and closed my eyes, preparing to take a cat-nap to get through the long night ahead.

I loved dressing up and looking pretty as much as the next girl, but charity functions were a lot of work. Making small talk was exhausting, smiling nonstop was a pain, and conversations about businesses and people I didn't know were boring. If it weren't for Cary benefiting from the exposure, I'd put up a bigger fight about going.

I sighed. Who was I fooling? I'd end up going anyway. My mom and Stanton supported abused children's charities because they were significant to me. Going to the occasional stuffy event was a small price to pay for the return.

Taking a deep breath, I consciously relaxed. I made a mental note to call my dad when I got home and thought about how to send a thank-you note to Gideon for the hangover cure. I supposed I could e-mail him using the contact info on his business card, but that lacked class. Besides, I didn't know who read his inbox.

I'd just call him when I got home. Why not? He'd asked — no, *told* — me to; he'd written the demand on his business card. And I'd get to hear his luscious voice again.

The door opened and the masseuse came in. "Hello, Eva. You ready?"

Not quite. But I was getting there.

After many lovely hours at the spa, my mom and Cary dropped me off at the apartment; then they headed out to hunt for new cuff links for Stanton. I used the time alone to call Gideon. Even with the much-needed privacy, I punched most of his phone number into the keypad a half dozen times before I finally put the call through.

He answered on the first ring. "Eva."

Startled that he'd known who was calling, my mind scrambled for a moment. *How did he have my name and number in his contact list?* "Uh . . . hi, Gideon."

"I'm a block away. Let the front desk know I'm coming."

"What?" I felt like I'd missed part of the conversation. "Coming where?"

"To your place. I'm rounding the corner now. Call the desk, Eva."

He hung up and I stared at the phone, trying to absorb the fact that Gideon was moments away from being with me again. Somewhat dazed, I went to the intercom and talked to the front desk, letting them know I was expecting him, and while I was talking, he walked into the lobby. A few moments after that, he was at my door.

It was then that I remembered I was dressed in only a thigh-length silk robe, and my face and hair were styled for the dinner. What kind of impression would he get from my appearance?

I tightened the belt of my robe before I let him in. It wasn't like I'd invited him over for a seduction or anything.

Gideon stood in the hallway for a long moment, his gaze raking me from my head down to my French-manicured toes. I was equally stunned by his appearance. The way he looked in worn jeans and a T-shirt made me want to undress him with my teeth.

"Worth the trip to find you like this, Eva." He stepped inside and locked the door behind him. "How are you feeling?"

"Good. Thanks to you. Thank you." My stomach quivered because he was here, with me, which made me feel almost . . . giddy. "That can't be why you came over."

"I'm here because it took you too long to call me."

"I didn't realize I had a deadline."

"I have to ask you something time-sensitive, but more than that, I wanted to know if you were feeling all right after last night." His eyes were dark as they swept over me, his breathtaking face framed by that luxurious curtain of inky hair. "God. You look beautiful, Eva. I can't remember ever wanting anything this much."

With just those few simple words I became hot and needy. Way too vulnerable. "What's so urgent?"

"Go with me to the advocacy center dinner tonight."

I pulled back, surprised and excited by the request. "You're going?"

"So are you. I checked, knowing your mother would be there. Let's go together."

My hand went to my throat, my mind torn between the weirdness of how much he knew about me and concern over what he was asking me to do. "That's not what I meant when I said we should spend time together."

"Why not?" The simple question was laced with challenge. "What's the problem with going together to an event we'd already planned on attending separately?"

"It's not very discreet. It's a high-profile event."

"So?" Gideon stepped closer and fingered a curl of my hair.

There was a dangerous purr to his voice that sent a shiver through me. I could feel the warmth of his big, hard body and smell the richly masculine scent of his skin. I was falling under his spell, deeper with every minute that passed.

"People will make assumptions, my mother in particular. She's already scenting your bachelor blood in the water."

Lowering his head, Gideon pressed his lips into the crook of my neck. "I don't care what people think. We know what we're doing. And I'll deal with your mother."

"If you think you can," I said breathlessly, "you don't know her very well."

"I'll pick you up at seven." His tongue traced the wildly throbbing vein in my throat and I melted into him, my body going lax as he pulled me close.

Still, I managed to say, "I haven't said yes."

"But you won't say no." He caught my earlobe between his teeth. "I won't let you."

I opened my mouth to protest and he sealed his lips over mine, shutting me up with a lush wet kiss. His tongue did that slow, savoring licking that made me long to feel him doing the same between my legs. My hands went to his hair, sliding through it, tugging. When he wrapped his arms around me, I arched, curving into his hands.

Just as he had in his office, he had me on my back on the couch before I realized he was moving me, his mouth swallowing my surprised gasp. The robe gave way to his dexterous fingers; then he was cupping my breasts, kneading them with soft, rhythmic squeezes.

"Gideon —"

"Shh." He sucked on my lower lip, his fingers rolling and tugging my tender nipples. "It was driving me crazy knowing you were naked beneath your robe."

"You came over without — Oh! Oh, God . . ."

His mouth surrounded the tip of my breast, the wash of heat bringing a mist of perspiration to my skin.

My gaze darted frantically to the clock on the cable box. "Gideon, no."

His head lifted and he looked at me with stormy blue eyes. "It's insane, I know. I don't — I can't explain it, Eva, but I have to make you come. I've been thinking about it constantly for days now."

One of his hands pushed between my legs. They fell open shamelessly, my body so aroused I was flushed and almost feverish. His other hand continued to plump my breasts, making them heavy and unbearably sensitive.

"You're wet for me," he murmured, his gaze sliding down my body to where he was parting me with his fingers. "You're beautiful here, too. Plush and pink. So soft. You didn't wax today, did you?"

I shook my head.

"Thank God. I don't think I would've made it ten minutes without touching you, let alone ten hours." He slid one finger carefully into me.

My eyes closed against the unbearable vulnerability of being spread out naked and fingered by a man whose familiarity with the rules of Brazilian waxing betrayed an intimate knowledge of women. A man who was still fully clothed and kneeling on the floor beside me.

"You're so snug." Gideon pulled out and thrust gently back into me. My back bowed as I clenched eagerly around him. "And so greedy. How long has it been since the last time you were fucked?"

I swallowed hard. "I've been busy. I had my thesis, then job hunting and moving . . ."

"A while, then." He pulled out and pushed back into me with two fingers. I couldn't hold back a moan of delight. The man had talented hands, confident and skilled, and he took what he wanted with them.

"Are you on birth control, Eva?"

"Yes." My hands gripped the edges of the cushions. "Of course."

"I'll prove I'm clean and you'll do the same, and then you're going to let me come in you."

"Jesus, Gideon." I was panting for him, my hips circling shamelessly onto his thrusting fingers. I felt like I'd spontaneously combust if he didn't get me off.

I'd never been so turned on in my life. I was near mindless with the need for an orgasm. If Cary walked in right then and found me writhing in our living room while Gideon finger-fucked me, I didn't think I'd care.

Gideon was breathing hard, too. His face was flushed with lust. For me. When I'd done nothing more than respond helplessly to him.

His hand at my breast moved to my cheek and brushed over it. "You're blushing. I've scandalized you."

"Yes."

His smile was both wicked and delighted, and it made my chest tight. "I want to feel my cum in you when I fuck you with my fingers. I want *you* to feel my cum in you, so you think about how I looked and the sounds I made when I pumped it into you. And while you're thinking about that, you're going to look forward to me doing it again and again."

My sex rippled around his stroking fingers, the rawness of his words pushing me to the brink of orgasm.

"I'm going to tell you all the ways I want you to please me, Eva, and you're going to do it all . . . take it all, and we're going to have explosive, primal, no-holds-barred sex. You know that, don't you? You can feel how it'll be between us."

"Yes," I breathed, clutching my breasts to

ease the deep ache of my hardened nipples. "Please, Gideon."

"Shh . . . I've got you." The pad of his thumb rubbed my clitoris in gentle circles. "Look into my eyes when you come for me."

Everything tightened in my core, the tension building as he massaged my clit and pushed his fingers in and out in a steady, unhurried rhythm.

"Give it up to me, Eva," he ordered. "Now."

I climaxed with a thready cry, my grip white-knuckled on the sides of the cushions as my hips pumped onto his hand, my mind far beyond shame or shyness. My gaze was locked to his, unable to look away, riveted by the fierce masculine triumph that flared in his eyes. In that moment he owned me. I'd do anything he wanted. And he knew it.

Searing pleasure pulsed through me. Through the roaring of blood in my ears, I thought I heard him speak hoarsely, but I lost the words when he hooked one of my legs over the back of the couch and covered my cleft with his mouth.

"No —" I pushed at his head with my hands. "I can't."

I was too swollen, too sensitive. But when his tongue touched my clit, fluttering over it, the hunger built again. More intense than the first time. He rimmed my trembling slit, teasing me, taunting me with the promise of another orgasm when I knew I couldn't have one again so quickly.

Then his tongue speared into me and I bit my lip to bite back a scream. I came a second time, my body quaking violently, tender muscles tightening desperately around his decadent licking. His growl vibrated through me. I didn't have the strength to push him away when he returned to my clit and sucked softly . . . tirelessly . . . until I climaxed again, gasping his name.

I was boneless as he straightened my leg and still breathless when he pressed kisses up my belly to my breasts. He licked each of my nipples, then hauled me up with his arms banded around my back. I hung lax and pliable in his grip while he took my mouth with suppressed violence, bruising my lips and betraying how close to the edge he was.

He closed my robe, then stood, staring down at me.

"Gideon . . . ?"

"Seven o'clock, Eva." He reached down and touched my ankle, his fingertips caressing the diamond anklet I'd put on in preparation for the evening. "And keep this on. I

want to fuck you while you're wearing nothing else."

6

"Hey, Dad. I caught you." I adjusted my grip on the phone receiver and pulled up a stool at the breakfast bar. I missed my father. For the last four years we'd lived close enough to see each other at least once a week. Now his home in Oceanside was the entire country away. "How are you?"

He lowered the volume on the television. "Better, now that you've called. How was your first week at work?"

I went over my days from Monday through Friday, skipping over all the Gideon parts. "I really like my boss, Mark," I finished. "And the vibe of the agency is very energetic and kind of quirky. I'm happy going to work every day, and I'm bummed when it's time to go home."

"I hope it stays that way. But you need to make sure you have some downtime, too. Go out, be young, have fun. But not too much fun."

"Yeah, I had a little too much last night. Cary and I went clubbing, and I woke up with a mean hangover."

"Shit, don't tell me that." He groaned. "Some nights I wake up in a cold sweat thinking about you in New York. I get through it by telling myself you're too smart to take chances, thanks to two parents who've drilled safety rules into your DNA."

"Which is true," I said, laughing. "That reminds me . . . I'm going to start Krav Maga training."

"Really?" There was a thoughtful pause. "One of the guys on the force is big on it. Maybe I'll check it out and we can compare notes when I come out to visit you."

"You're coming to New York?" I couldn't hide my excitement. "Oh, Dad, I'd love it if you would. As much as I miss SoCal, Manhattan is really awesome. I think you'll like it."

"I'd like anyplace in the world as long as you're there." He waited a beat, then asked, "How's your mom?"

"Well . . . she's Mom. Beautiful, charming, and obsessive-compulsive."

My chest hurt and I rubbed at it. I thought my dad might still love my mom. He'd never married. That was one of the reasons I never told him about what happened to me. As a cop, he would've insisted on pressing charges and the scandal would have destroyed my mother. I also worried that he'd lose respect for her or even blame her, and it hadn't been her fault. As soon as she'd found out what her stepson was doing to me, she'd left a husband she was happy with and filed for divorce.

I kept talking, waving at Cary as he came rushing in with a little blue Tiffany & Co. bag. "We had a spa day today. It was a fun way to cap off the week."

I could hear the smile in his voice when he said, "I'm glad you two are managing to spend time together. What are your plans for the rest of the weekend?"

I hedged on the subject of the charity event, knowing the whole red-carpet business and astronomically priced dinner seats would just highlight the gap between my parents' lives. "Cary and I are going out to eat, and then I plan on staying in tomorrow. Sleeping in late, hanging out in my pajamas all day, maybe some movies and food delivery of some sort. A little vegetating before a new workweek kicks off."

"Sounds like heaven to me. I may copy you when my next day off rolls around."

Glancing at the clock, I saw it was creeping past six. "I have to get ready now. Be careful at work, okay? I worry about you, too."

"Will do. Bye, baby."

The familiar sign-off had me missing him so much my throat hurt. "Oh, wait! I'm getting a new cell phone. I'll text you the number as soon as I have it."

"Again? You just got a new one when you moved."

"Long, boring story."

"Hmm . . . Don't put it off. They're good for safety as well as for playing Angry Birds."

"I'm over that game!" I laughed, and warmth spread through me to hear him laughing, too. "I'll call you in a few days. Be good."

"That's *my* line."

We hung up. I sat for a few moments in the ensuing silence, feeling like everything was right in my world, which never lasted long. I brooded on that for minute; then Cary cranked up Hinder on his bedroom stereo and that kicked my butt into gear.

I hurried to my room to get ready for a night with Gideon.

"Necklace or no necklace?" I asked Cary, when he came into my bedroom looking seriously amazing. Dressed in his new Brioni tux, he was both debonair and dashing, and certain to attract attention.

"Hmm." His head tilted to the side as he studied me. "Hold it up again."

I lifted the choker of gold coins to my throat. The dress my mom had sent was fire engine red and styled for a Grecian goddess. It hung on one shoulder, cut diagonally across my cleavage, had ruching to the hip, and then split at my right upper thigh all the way down my leg. There was no back to speak of, aside from a slender strip of rhinestones that connected one side to the other to keep the front from falling off. Otherwise, the back was bared to just above the crack of my butt in a racy V-cut.

"Forget the necklace," he said. "I was leaning toward gold chandeliers, but now I'm thinking diamond hoops. The biggest ones you've got."

"What? Really?" I frowned at our reflections in my cheval mirror, watching as he moved to my jewelry box and dug through it.

"These." He brought them to me and I eyed the two-inch hoops my mother had given me for my eighteenth birthday. "Trust me, Eva. Try 'em on."

I did and found he was right. It was a very different look from the gold choker, less glam and more edgy sensuality. And the earrings went well with the diamond anklet on my right leg that I'd never think of the same way again after Gideon's comment. With my hair swept off my face into a cascade of thick, deliberately messy curls, I had a just-screwed look that was complemented by smoky eye shadow and glossy nude lips.

"What would I do without you, Cary Taylor?"

"Baby girl" — he set his hands on my shoulders and pressed his cheek to mine — "you'll never find out."

"You look awesome, by the way."

"Don't I?" He winked and stepped back, showing off.

In his own way, Cary could give Gideon a run for his money . . . er, looks. Cary was more finely featured, almost pretty compared to Gideon's savage beauty, but both were striking men who made you look twice, and then stare in greedy delight.

Cary hadn't been quite so perfect when I met him. He'd been strung out and gaunt, his emerald eyes cloudy and lost. But I'd been drawn to him, going out of my way to sit next to him in group therapy. He'd finally propositioned me crudely, having come to believe the only reason people associated with him was because they wanted to fuck him. It was when I declined, firmly and irrevocably, that we finally connected and became best friends. He was the brother I'd never had.

The intercom buzzed and I jumped, making me realize how nervous I was. I looked at Cary. "I forgot to tell the front desk he was coming back."

"I'll get him."

"Are you going to be okay riding over with Stanton and my mom?"

"Are you kidding? They love me." His smile dimmed. "Having second thoughts about going with Cross?"

I took a deep breath, remembering where I'd been earlier — on my back in a multiorgasmic daze. "Not really, no. It's just that everything's happening so fast and going better than I expected or realized I wanted . . ."

"You're wondering what the catch is." Reaching out, he tapped my nose with his fingertip. "He's the catch, Eva. And you landed him. Enjoy yourself."

"I'm trying." I was grateful that Cary understood me and the way my mind worked. It was just so easy being with him, knowing he could fill in the blanks when I couldn't explain something.

"I researched the hell out of him this morning and printed out the interesting recent stuff. It's on your desk, if you decide you want to check it out." ⸸

I remembered him printing something before we got ready for the spa. Pushing onto my tiptoes, I kissed his cheek. "You're the best. I love you."

"Back atcha, baby girl." He headed out. "I'll head down to the front desk and bring him up. Take your time. He's ten minutes early."

Smiling, I watched him saunter into the hallway. The door had closed behind him when I moved into the small sitting room attached to my bedroom. On the very impractical escritoire my mother had picked out, I found a folder filled with articles and printed images. I settled into the chair and got lost in Gideon Cross's history.

It was like watching a train wreck to read that he was the son of Geoffrey Cross, former chairman of an investment securities firm later found to be a front for a massive Ponzi scheme. Gideon was just five years old when his dad committed suicide with a gunshot to the head rather than face prison time.

Oh, Gideon. I tried to picture him that young and imagined a handsome dark-haired boy with beautiful blue eyes filled with terrible confusion and sadness. The image broke my heart. How devastating his father's suicide — and the circumstances around it — must have been, for both him and his mother. The stress and strain at such a difficult time would've been enormous, especially for a child of that age.

His mother went on to marry Christopher Vidal, a music executive, and had two more children, Christopher Vidal Jr. and Ireland Vidal, but it seemed that a larger family and financial security had come too late to help Gideon stabilize after such a huge shakeup. He was too closed off not to bear some painful emotional scars.

With a critical and curious eye, I studied the women who'd been photographed with Gideon and thought about his approach to dating, socializing, and sex. I saw that my mom had been right — they were all brunettes. The woman who appeared with him most often bore the hallmarks of a Hispanic heritage. She was taller than me, willowy rather than curvy.

"Magdalene Perez," I murmured, grudgingly admitting that she was a stunner. Her posture had the kind of flamboyant confidence that I admired.

"Okay, it's been long enough," Cary interrupted with a soft note of amusement. He filled the doorway to my sitting room, leaning insolently into the doorjamb.

"Really?" I'd been so absorbed; I hadn't realized how much time had passed.

"I would guess you're about a minute away from him coming to find you. He's barely restraining himself."

I shut the folder and stood.

"Interesting reading, isn't it?"

"Very." How had Gideon's father — or more specifically, his father's suicide — influenced his life?

I knew that all the answers I wanted were waiting for me in the next room.

Leaving my bedroom, I took the hallway to the living room. I paused on the threshold, my gaze riveted to Gideon's back as he stood in front of the windows and looked out at the city. My heart rate kicked up. His reflection revealed a contemplative mood. His gaze was unfocused and his mouth grim. His crossed arms betrayed an inherent unease, as if he were out of his element. He looked remote and removed, a man who was inherently alone.

He sensed my presence, or maybe he felt my yearning. He pivoted, then went very still. I took the opportunity to drink him in, my gaze sliding all over him. He looked every inch the powerful magnate. So sensually handsome my eyes burned just from looking at him. The rakish fall of black hair around his face made my fingers flex with the urge to touch it. And the way he looked at me . . . my pulse leaped.

"Eva." He came toward me, his stride graceful and strong. He caught up my hand and lifted it to his mouth. His gaze was intense — intensely hot, intensely focused.

The feel of his lips against my skin sent goose bumps racing up my arm and stirred memories of that sinful mouth on other parts of my body. I was instantly aroused. "Hi."

Amusement warmed his eyes. "Hi, yourself. You look amazing. I can't wait to show you off."

I breathed through the delight I felt at the compliment. "Let's hope I can do you justice."

A slight frown knit the space between his brows. "Do you have everything you need?"

Cary appeared beside me, carrying my black velvet shawl and opera-length gloves. "Here you go. I tucked your gloss into your clutch."

"You're the best, Cary."

He winked at me — which told me he'd seen the condoms I had tucked into the small interior pocket. "I'll head down with you two."

Gideon took the shawl from Cary and draped it over my shoulders. He pulled my hair out from underneath it and the feel of his hands at my neck so distracted me, I barely paid attention when Cary pushed my gloves into my hands.

The elevator ride to the lobby was an exercise in surviving acute sexual tension. Not that Cary seemed to notice. He was on my left with both hands in his pockets, whistling. Gideon, on the other hand, was a tremendous force on the other side of me. Although he didn't move or make a sound, I could feel the edgy energy radiating from him. My skin tingled from the magnetic pull between us, and my breath came short and fast. I was relieved when the doors opened and freed us from the enclosed space.

Two women stood waiting to get on. Their jaws dropped when they saw Gideon and Cary, and that lightened my mood and made me smile.

"Ladies," Cary greeted them, with a smile that really wasn't fair. I could almost see their brain cells misfiring.

In contrast, Gideon gave a curt nod and led me out with a hand at the small of my back, skin to skin. The contact was electric, sending heat pouring through me.

I squeezed Cary's hand. "Save a dance for me."

"Always. See you in a bit."

A limousine was waiting at the curb, and the driver opened the door when Gideon and I stepped outside. I slid across the bench seat to the opposite side and adjusted my gown. When Gideon settled beside me and the door shut, I became highly conscious of how good he smelled. I breathed him in, telling myself to relax and enjoy his company. He took my hand and ran his fingertips over the palm, the simple touch sparking a fierce lust. I shrugged off my shawl, feeling too hot to wear it.

"Eva." He hit a button and the privacy glass behind the driver began to slide up. The next moment I was tugged across his lap and his mouth was on mine, kissing me fiercely.

I did what I'd wanted to do since I saw him in my living room: I shoved my hands in his hair and kissed him back. I loved the way he kissed me, as if he *had* to, as if he'd go crazy if he didn't and had nearly waited too long. I sucked on his tongue, having learned how much he liked it, having learned how much *I* liked it, how much it made me want to suck him elsewhere with the same eagerness.

His hands were sliding over my bare back and I moaned, feeling the prod of his erection against my hip. I shifted, moving to straddle him, shoving the skirt of my gown out of the way and making a mental note to thank my mom for the dress — which had such a convenient slit. With my knees on either side of his hips, I wrapped my arms around his shoulders and deepened the kiss. I licked into his mouth, nibbled on his lower lip, stroked my tongue along his . . .

Gideon gripped my waist and pushed me away. He leaned into the seat back, his neck arched to look up at my face, his chest heaving. "What are you doing to me?"

I ran my hands down his chest through his dress shirt, feeling the unforgiving hardness of his muscles. My fingers traced the ridges of his abdomen, my mind forming a picture of how he might look naked. "I'm touching you. Enjoying the hell out of you. I want you, Gideon."

He caught my wrists, stilling my movements. "Later. We're in the middle of Manhattan."

"No one can see us."

"That's not the point. It's not the time or place to start something we can't finish for hours. I'm losing my mind already from this afternoon."

"So let's make sure we finish it now."

His grip tightened painfully. "We can't do that here."

"Why not?" Then a surprising thought struck me. "Haven't you ever had sex in a limo?"

"No." His jaw hardened. "Have you?"

Looking away without answering, I saw the traffic and pedestrians surging around us. We were only inches away from hundreds of people, but the dark glass concealed us and made me feel reckless. I wanted to please him. I wanted to know I was capable of reaching into Gideon Cross, and there was nothing to stop me but him.

I rocked my hips against him, stroking myself with the hard length of his cock. His breath hissed out between clenched teeth.

"I need you, Gideon," I said breathlessly, inhaling his scent, which was richer now that he was aroused. I thought I might be slightly intoxicated, just from the enticing smell of his skin. "You drive me crazy."

He released my wrists and cupped my face, his lips pressing hard against mine. I reached for the fly of his slacks, freeing the two buttons to access the concealed zipper. He tensed.

"I need this," I whispered against his lips. "Give me this."

He didn't relax, but he made no further attempts to stop me either. When he fell heavily into my palms, he groaned, the sound both pained and erotic. I squeezed him gently, my touch deliberately tender as I sized him with my hands. He was so hard, like stone, and hot. I slid both of my fists up his length from root to tip, my breath catching when he quivered beneath me.

Gideon gripped my thighs, his hands sliding upward beneath the edges of my dress until his thumbs found the red lace of my thong. "Your cunt is so sweet," he murmured into my mouth. "I want to spread you out and lick you 'til you beg for my cock."

"I'll beg now, if you want." I stroked him with one hand and reached for my clutch with the other, snapping it open to grab a condom.

One of his thumbs slid beneath the edge of my panties, the pad sliding through the slickness of my desire. "I've barely touched you," he whispered, his eyes glittering up at me in the shadows of the backseat, "and you're ready for me."

"I can't help it."

"I don't want you to help it." He pushed his thumb inside me, biting his lower lip when I clenched helplessly around him. "It wouldn't be fair when I can't stop what you do to me."

I ripped the foil packet open with my teeth and held it out to him with the ring of the condom protruding from the tear. "I'm not good with these."

His hand curled around mine. "I'm breaking all my rules with you."

The seriousness of his low tone sent a burst of warmth and confidence through me. "Rules are made to be broken."

I saw his teeth flash white; then he hit a button on the panel beside him and said, "Drive until I say otherwise."

My cheeks heated. Another car's headlights pierced the dark tinted glass and slid over my face, betraying my embarrassment.

"Why, Eva," he purred, rolling the condom on deftly. "You've seduced me into having sex in my limousine, but blush when I tell my driver I don't want to be interrupted while you do it to me?"

His sudden playfulness made me desperate to have him. Setting my hands on his shoulders for balance, I lifted onto my knees, rising to gain the height I needed to hover over the crown of Gideon's thick cock. His hands fisted at my hips and I heard a snap as he tore my panties away. The abrupt sound and the violent action behind it spurred my desire to a fever pitch.

"Go slow," he ordered hoarsely, lifting his hips to push his pants down farther.

His erection brushed between my legs as he moved and I whimpered, so aching and empty, as if the orgasms he'd given me earlier had only deepened my craving rather than appeased it.

He tensed when I wrapped my fingers around him and positioned him, tucking the wide crest against the saturated folds of my cleft. The scent of our lust was heavy and humid in the air, a seductive mix of need and pheromones that awakened every cell in my body. My skin was flushed and tingling, my breasts heavy and tender.

This was what I'd wanted from the moment I first saw him — to possess him, to climb up his magnificent body and take him deep inside me.

"God. Eva," he gasped as I lowered onto him, his hands flexing restlessly on my thighs.

I closed my eyes, feeling too exposed. I'd wanted intimacy with him, and yet this seemed too intimate. We were eye-to-eye, only inches apart, cocooned in a small space with the rest of the world streaming by around us. I could sense his agitation, knew he was feeling as off-center as I was.

"You're so tight." His gasped words were threaded with a hint of delicious agony.

I took more of him, letting him slide deeper. I sucked in a deep breath, feeling exquisitely stretched.

Pressing his palm flat to my lower belly, he touched my throbbing clit with the pad of his thumb and began to massage it in slow, expertly soft circles. Everything in my core tightened and clenched, sucking him deeper. Opening my eyes, I looked at him from under heavy eyelids. He was so beautiful sprawled beneath me in his elegant tuxedo, his powerful body straining with the primal need to mate.

His neck arched, his head pressing hard into the seat back as if he were struggling against invisible bonds. "Ah, Christ," he bit out, his teeth grinding. "I'm going to come so hard."

The dark promise excited me. Sweat misted my skin. I became so wet and hot that I slid smoothly down the length of his cock until I'd nearly sheathed him. A breathless cry escaped me before I'd taken him to the root. He was so deep I could hardly stand it, forcing me to shift from side to side, trying to ease the unexpected bite of discomfort. But my body didn't seem to care that he was too big. It was rippling around him, squeezing, trembling on the verge of orgasm.

Gideon cursed and gripped my hip with his free hand, urging me to lean backward as his chest heaved with frantic breaths. The position altered my descent and I opened, accepting all of him. Immediately his body temperature rose, his torso radiating sultry heat through his clothes. Sweat dotted his upper lip.

Leaning forward, I slid my tongue along the sculpted curve, collecting the saltiness with a low murmur of delight. His hips churned impatiently. I lifted carefully, sliding up a few inches before he stopped me with that ferocious grasp on my hip.

"Slow," he warned again, with an authoritative bite that sent lust pulsing through me.

I lowered, taking him into me again, feeling an oddly luscious soreness as he pushed *just* past my limits. Our eyes locked on each other as the pleasure spread from the place where we connected. It struck me then that we were both fully clothed except for the most private and intimate parts of our bodies. I found that excruciatingly carnal, as were the sounds he made, as if the pleasure were as extreme for him as it was for me.

Wild for him, I pressed my mouth to his,

my fingers gripping the sweat-damp roots of his hair. I kissed him as I rocked my hips, riding the maddening circling of his thumb, feeling the orgasm building with every slide of his long, thick penis into my melting core.

I lost my mind somewhere along the way, primitive instinct taking over until my body was completely in charge. I could focus on nothing but the driving urge to fuck, the ferocious need to ride his cock until the tension burst and set me free of this grinding hunger.

"It's so good," I sobbed, lost to him. "You feel . . . Ah, God, it's too good."

Using both hands, Gideon commanded my rhythm, tilting me into an angle that had the big crown of his cock rubbing a tender, aching spot inside me. As I tightened and shook, I realized I was going to come from that, just from the expert thrust of him inside me. *"Gideon."*

He captured me by the nape as the orgasm exploded through me, starting with the ecstatic spasms of my core and radiating outward until I was trembling all over. He watched me fall apart, holding my gaze when I would've closed my eyes. Possessed by his stare, I moaned and came harder than I ever had, my body jerking with every pulse of pleasure.

"Fuck, fuck, fuck," he growled, pounding his hips up at me, yanking my hips down to meet his punishing lunges. He hit the end of me with every deep thrust, battering into me. I could feel him growing harder and thicker.

I watched him avidly, needing to see it when he went over the edge for me. His eyes were wild with his need, losing their focus as his control frayed, his gorgeous face ravaged by the brutal race to climax.

"Eva!" He came with an animal sound of feral ecstasy, a snarling release that riveted me with its ferocity. He shook as the orgasm tore into him, his features softening for an instant with an unexpected vulnerability.

Cupping his face, I brushed my lips across his, comforting him as the forceful bursts of his gasping breaths struck my cheeks.

"Eva." He wrapped his arms around me and crushed me to him, pressing his damp face into the curve of my neck.

I knew just how he felt. Stripped. Laid bare.

We stayed like that for a long time, holding each other, absorbing the aftershocks. He turned his head and kissed me softly, the strokes of his tongue into my mouth soothing my ragged emotions.

"Wow," I breathed, shaken.

His mouth twitched. "Yeah."

I smiled, feeling dazed and high.

Gideon brushed the damp tendrils of hair off my temples, his fingertips gliding almost reverently across my face. The way he studied me made my chest hurt. He looked stunned and . . . grateful, his eyes warm and tender. "I don't want to break this moment."

Because I could hear it hanging in the air, I filled it in. "But . . . ?"

"But I can't blow off this dinner. I have a speech to give."

"Oh." The moment was effectively broken.

I lifted gingerly off him, biting my lip at the feel of him slipping wetly out of me. The friction was enough to make me want more. He'd barely softened.

"Damn it," he said roughly. "I want you again."

He caught me before I moved away, pulling a handkerchief out from somewhere and running it gently between my legs. It was a deeply intimate act, on par with the sex we'd just had.

When I was dry, I settled on the seat beside him and dug my lip gloss out of my clutch. I watched Gideon over the edge of my mirrored compact as he removed the condom and tied it off. He wrapped it in a cocktail napkin, then tossed it in a cleverly hidden trash receptacle. After restoring his appearance, he told the driver to head to our destination. Then he settled into the seat and stared out the window.

With every second that passed, I felt him withdrawing, the connection between us slipping further and further away. I found myself shrinking into the corner of the seat, away from him, mimicking the distance I felt building between us. All the warmth I'd felt receded into a marked chill, cooling me enough that I pulled my shawl around me again. He didn't move a muscle as I shifted beside him and put my compact away, as if he weren't even aware I was there.

Abruptly, Gideon opened the bar and pulled out a bottle. Without looking at me, he asked, "Brandy?"

"No, thank you." My voice was small, but he didn't seem to notice. Or maybe he didn't care. He poured a drink and tossed it back.

Confused and stung, I pulled on my gloves and tried to figure out what had gone wrong.

7

I don't remember much of what happened after we arrived. Camera flashes burst around us like fireworks as we walked the length of the press gauntlet, but I scarcely paid them any mind, smiling by rote. I was drawn into myself and desperate to get away from the tension radiating in waves from Gideon.

The moment we crossed over into the building, someone called his name and he turned. I slipped away, darting around the rest of the guests clogging the carpeted entrance.

When I reached the reception hall, I snatched two glasses of champagne from a passing server and searched for Cary as I tossed one back. I spotted him on the far side of the room with my mom and Stanton, and I crossed to them, discarding my empty glass on a table as I passed it.

"Eva!" My mother's face lit up when she

saw me. "That dress is stunning on you!"

She air-kissed each of my cheeks. She was gorgeous in a shimmering, fitted column of icy blue. Sapphires dripped from her ears, throat, and wrist, highlighting her eyes and her pale skin.

"Thank you." I took a gulp of champagne from my second glass, remembering that I'd planned on expressing gratitude for the dress. While I still appreciated the gift, I was no longer so happy about the convenient thigh slit.

Cary stepped forward, catching my elbow. One look at my face and he knew I was upset. I shook my head, not wanting to get into it now.

"More champagne, then?" he asked softly.

"Please."

I felt Gideon approaching before I saw my mother's face light up like the New Year's ball in Times Square. Stanton, too, seemed to straighten and gather himself.

"Eva." Gideon set his hand on the bare skin of my lower back and a shock of awareness moved through me. When his fingers flexed against me, I wondered if he felt it, too. "You ran off."

I stiffened against the reproof I heard in his tone. I shot him a look that said everything I couldn't while we were in public.

"Richard, have you met Gideon Cross?"

"Yes, of course." The two men shook hands.

Gideon pulled me closer to his side. "We share the good fortune of escorting the two most beautiful women in New York."

Stanton agreed, smiling indulgently down at my mother.

I tossed back the rest of my champagne and gratefully exchanged the empty glass for the fresh one Cary handed me. There was a slight warmth growing in my belly from the alcohol, and it loosened the knot that had formed there.

Gideon leaned over and whispered harshly, "Don't forget you're here with me."

He was *mad*? What the hell? My gaze narrowed. "You're one to talk."

"Not here, Eva." He nodded at everyone and led me away. "Not now."

"Not ever," I muttered, going along with him just to spare my mother a scene.

Sipping my champagne, I slid into an autopilot mode of self-preservation I hadn't had to use in many years. Gideon introduced me to people, and I supposed I performed well enough — spoke at the appropriate moments and smiled when necessary — but I wasn't really paying attention. I was too conscious of the icy wall between us and my own hurt anger. If I'd needed any proof that Gideon was rigid about not socializing with women he slept with, I had it.

When dinner was announced, I went with him into the dining room and poked at my food. I drank a few glasses of the red wine they served with the meal and heard Gideon talking to our tablemates, although I didn't pay attention to the words, only to the cadence and the seductively deep, even tone. He made no attempt to draw me into the conversation, and I was glad. I didn't think I could say anything nice.

I didn't become engaged until he stood to a round of applause and took the stage. Then I turned in my seat and watched him cross to the lectern, unable to help admiring his animal grace and stunning good looks. Every step he took commanded attention and respect, which was a feat, considering his easy and unhurried stride.

He looked none the worse for wear after our abandoned fucking in his limo. In fact, he seemed like a totally different person. He was once again the man I'd met in the Crossfire lobby, supremely contained and quietly powerful.

"In North America," he began, "childhood sexual abuse is experienced by one in every four women and one in every six men. Take a good look around you. Someone at your table either is a survivor or knows someone who is. That's the unacceptable truth."

I was riveted. Gideon was a consummate orator, his vibrant baritone mesmerizing. But it was the topic, which hit so close to home, and his passionate and sometimes shocking way of discussing it, that moved me. I began to thaw, my bewildered fury and damaged self-confidence subverted by wonder. My view of him shifted, altering as I became simply another individual in a rapt audience. He wasn't the man who'd so recently hurt my feelings; he was just a skilled speaker discussing a subject that was deeply important to me.

When he finished, I stood and applauded, catching both him and myself by surprise. But others quickly joined me in the standing ovation and I heard the buzz of conversations around me, the quietly voiced compliments that were well deserved.

"You're a fortunate young lady."

I turned to look at the woman who spoke, a lovely redhead who appeared to be in her early forties. "We're just . . . friends."

Her serene smile somehow managed to argue with me.

People began stepping away from their

tables. I was about to grab my clutch so I could leave for home when a young man came up to me. His wayward auburn hair inspired instant envy, and his eyes of grayish-green were soft and friendly. Handsome and sporting a boyish grin, he lured the first genuine smile out of me since the ride over in the limousine.

"Hello there," he said.

He seemed to know who I was, which put me in the awkward position of pretending I wasn't clueless as to who he was. "Hello."

He laughed, and the sound was light and charming. "I'm Christopher Vidal, Gideon's brother."

"Oh, of course." My face heated. I couldn't believe I'd been so lost in my own pity party that I hadn't made the connection at once.

"You're blushing."

"I'm sorry." I offered a sheepish smile. "Not sure how to say I read an article about you without sounding awkward."

He laughed. "I'm flattered you remembered it. Just don't tell me it was in Page Six."

The gossip column was notorious for getting the goods on New York celebrities and socialites. "No," I said quickly. "*Rolling Stone,* maybe?"

"I can live with that." He extended his arm to me. "Would you like to dance?"

I glanced over to where Gideon was standing at the foot of the stairs that led to the stage. He was surrounded by people eager to talk to him, many of whom were women.

"You can see he'll be a while," Christopher said, with a note of amusement.

"Yes." I was about to look away when I recognized the woman standing next to Gideon — Magdalene Perez.

I picked up my clutch and managed a smile for Christopher. "I'd love to dance."

Arm in arm we headed into the ballroom and stepped onto the dance floor. The band began the first strains of a waltz and we moved easily, naturally into the music. He was a skilled dancer, agile and confident in his lead.

"So, how do you know Gideon?"

"I don't." I nodded at Cary when he glided by with a statuesque blonde. "I work in the Crossfire and we've run into each other once or twice."

"You work for him?"

"No. I'm an assistant at Waters Field and Leaman."

"Ah." He grinned. "Ad agency."

"Yes."

"Gideon must really be into you to go

from meeting you once or twice to dragging you out on a date like this."

I cursed inwardly. I'd known assumptions would be made, but I wanted more than ever to avoid further humiliation. "Gideon's acquainted with my mother and she'd already arranged for me to come, so it's just a matter of two people going to the same event in one car rather than two."

"So you're available?"

I took a deep breath, feeling uncomfortable despite how fluidly we moved together. "Well, I'm not taken."

Christopher flashed his charismatic boyish grin. "My night just took a turn for the better."

He filled the rest of the dance with amusing anecdotes about the music industry that made me laugh and took my mind off Gideon.

When the dance ended, Cary was there to take the next one. We danced very well as a couple because we'd taken lessons together. I relaxed into his hold, grateful to have him as moral support.

"Are you enjoying yourself?" I asked him.

"I pinched myself during dinner when I realized I was sitting next to the top coordinator for Fashion Week. And she flirted with me!" He smiled, but his eyes were haunted.

"Whenever I find myself in places like this . . . dressed like this . . . I can't believe it. You saved my life, Eva. Then you changed it completely."

"You save my sanity all the time. Trust me, we're even."

His hand tightened on mine, his gaze hardening. "You look miserable. How'd he fuck up?"

"I think I did that. We'll talk about it later."

"You're afraid I'll kick his ass here in front of everyone."

I sighed. "I'd rather you didn't, for my mom's sake."

Cary pressed his lips briefly to my forehead. "I warned him earlier. He knows it's coming."

"Oh, Cary." Love for him tightened my throat even as reluctant amusement curved my lips. I should've known Cary would give Gideon a big-brother threat of some sort. That was just so like him.

Gideon appeared beside us. "I'm cutting in."

It wasn't a request.

Cary stopped and looked at me. I nodded. He backed away with a bow, his gaze hot and fierce on Gideon's face.

Gideon pulled me close and took over the dance the way he took over everything —

with dominant confidence. It was an entirely different experience dancing with him than with my two previous partners. Gideon had both the expertise of his brother and Cary's familiarity with the way my body moved, but Gideon had a bold, aggressive style that was inherently sexual.

It didn't help that being so close to a man I'd so recently been intimate with seduced my senses despite my unhappiness. He smelled scrumptious, with undertones of sex, and the way he led me through the bold, sweeping steps made me feel the soreness deep inside me, reminding me that he'd been there not long ago.

"You keep taking off," he muttered, scowling down at me.

"Seemed like Magdalene picked up the slack quickly enough."

His brow arched and he drew me closer. "Jealous?"

"Seriously?" I looked away.

He made a frustrated noise. "Stay away from my brother, Eva."

"Why?"

"Because I said so."

My temper ignited, which felt good after all the self-recrimination and doubts I'd been drowning in since we'd screwed like feral bunnies. I decided to see if turnabout was fair play in Gideon Cross's world. "Stay away from Magdalene, Gideon."

His jaw tightened. "She's just a friend."

"Meaning you haven't slept with her . . . ? Yet."

"No, damn it. And I don't want to. Listen—" The music wound down and he slowed. "I have to go. I brought you here, and I would prefer to be the one who takes you home, but I don't want to pull you away if you're enjoying yourself. Would you rather stick around and go home with Stanton and your mother?"

Enjoying myself? Was he kidding or clueless? Or worse. Maybe he'd written me off so completely that he wasn't paying attention to me at all.

I pushed away from him, needing the distance. His scent was messing with my head. "I'll be fine. Forget about me."

"Eva." He reached for me and I stepped back quickly.

An arm came around my back and Cary spoke. "I've got her, Cross."

"Don't get in my way, Taylor," Gideon warned.

Cary snorted. "I get the impression you're doing a smokin' job of that all by yourself."

I swallowed past the lump in my throat. "You gave a wonderful speech, Gideon. It was the highlight of my evening."

He sucked in a sharp breath at the implied insult, then shoved a hand through his hair. Abruptly, he cursed and I realized why when he pulled his vibrating phone out of his pocket and glanced at the screen.

"I have to go." His gaze caught mine and held it. His fingertips drifted over my cheek. "I'll call you."

And then he was gone.

"Do you want to stay?" Cary asked quietly.

"No."

"I'll take you home, then."

"No, don't." I wanted to be alone for a bit. Soak in a hot bath with a bottle of cool wine and pull myself out of my funk. "You should be here. It could be good for your career. We can talk when you get home. Or tomorrow. I'm going the couch potato route all day."

His gaze darted over my face, searching. "You sure?"

I nodded.

"All right." But he looked unconvinced.

"If you could go out and ask a valet to have Stanton's limo brought around, I'll run to the ladies' room real quick."

"Okay." Cary ran his hand down my arm. "I'll get your shawl from the coatroom and see you out front."

It took longer to get to the restroom than it should have. For one, a surprising number of people stopped me for small talk, which had to be because I was Gideon Cross's date. And two, I avoided the nearest ladies' room, which had a steady flow of women pouring in and out of it, and I found one located farther away. I locked myself in a stall and took a few moments longer to finish my business than absolutely required. There was no one else in the room besides the attendant, so there was no one to rush me.

I was so hurt by Gideon it was hard to breathe, and I was so confused by his mood swings. Why had he touched my face like that? Why had he gotten mad when I didn't stay by his side? And why the hell had he threatened Cary? Gideon gave new meaning to the old adage about "running hot and cold."

Closing my eyes, I shored up my composure. *Jesus.* I didn't need this.

I'd bared my emotions in the limo and I still felt horribly vulnerable — a state I'd spent countless therapy hours learning to avoid. I wanted nothing more than to be home and hidden, freed from the pressure of acting like I was completely pulled together when I was anything but.

You set yourself up for this, I reminded myself. *Suck it up.*

Taking a deep breath, I stepped out and was resigned to finding Magdalene Perez leaning against the vanity with her arms crossed. She was clearly there for me, lying in wait at a time when my defenses were already weak. My step faltered; then I recovered and made my way to the sink to wash my hands.

She turned to face the mirror, studying my reflection. I studied her, too. She was even more gorgeous in person than she'd been in her photos. Tall and slender, with big dark eyes and a cascade of straight brown hair. Her lips were lush and red, her cheekbones high and sculpted. Her dress was modestly sexy, a flowing sheath of creamy satin that contrasted beautifully with her olive skin. She looked like a fucking supermodel and exuded an exotic sex appeal.

I accepted the hand towel the bathroom attendant handed me, and Magdalene spoke to the woman in Spanish, asking her to give us some privacy. I capped the request with, *"Por favor, gracias."* That earned me an arched brow from Magdalene and a closer examination, which I returned with equal coolness.

169

"Oh, dear," she murmured, the moment the attendant stepped out of earshot. She made a *tsk*ing noise that scraped over my nerves like nails on a chalkboard. "You've fucked him already."

"And you haven't."

That seemed to surprise her. "You're right, I haven't. You know why?"

I pulled a five-spot out of my clutch and dropped it in the silver tip tray. "Because he doesn't want to."

"And I don't want to either, because he can't commit. He's young, gorgeous, rich, and he's enjoying it."

"Yes." I nodded. "He certainly did."

Her gaze narrowed, her pleasant expression slipping slightly. "He doesn't respect the women he fucks. The minute he shoved his dick in you, you were done. Just like all the others. But I'm still here, because I'm the one he wants to keep around for the long haul."

I maintained my cool even though the blow had been a perfect hit right where the most damage could be done. "That's pathetic."

I walked out and didn't stop until I reached Stanton's limousine. Squeezing Cary's hand as I got in, I managed to wait until the car pulled away from the curb to start crying.

"Hey, baby girl," Cary called out when I shuffled into the living room the next morning. Dressed in nothing but a loose pair of old sweats, he was stretched out on the couch with his feet crossed and propped on the coffee table. He looked beautifully disheveled and comfortable in his own skin. "How'd you sleep?"

I gave him the thumbs-up and headed into the kitchen for coffee. I paused by the breakfast bar, my brows lifting at the massive arrangement of red roses on the counter. The fragrance was divine and I inhaled it with a deep breath. "What's this?"

"They came for you about an hour ago. A Sunday delivery. Pretty and super pricey."

I plucked the card off the clear plastic stake and opened it.

I'M STILL THINKING ABOUT
YOU.

GIDEON

"From Cross?" Cary asked.

"Yes." My thumb brushed over what I assumed was his handwriting. It was bold and masculine and sexy. A romantic gesture for a guy who didn't have romance in his

171

repertoire. I dropped the card on the counter as if it'd burned me and fetched a mug of coffee, praying caffeine would give me strength and restore my common sense.

"You don't seem impressed." He lowered the volume on the baseball game he was watching.

"He's bad news for me. He's like one giant trigger. I just need to stay away from him." Cary had been through therapy with me, and he knew the drill. He didn't look at me funny when I broke things down into therapeutic jargon, and he didn't have any trouble shooting it back to me the same way.

"The phone's been ringing all morning, too. I didn't want it to disturb you, so I shut the volume off."

Aware of the lingering ache between my legs, I curled up on the couch and fought the compulsion to listen to our voice mail to see if Gideon had called. I wanted to hear his voice, and an explanation that would make sense of what happened last night. "Sounds good to me. Let's leave it off all day."

"What happened?"

I blew steam off the top of my mug and took a tentative sip. "I fucked his brains out in his limo and he turned arctic afterward."

Cary watched me with those worldly

172

emerald eyes, eyes that had seen more than anyone should be subjected to. "Rocked his world, did you?"

"Yeah, I did." And I got riled up just thinking about it. We'd connected. I *knew* it. I'd wanted him more than anything last night, and today I wanted nothing to do with him ever again. "It was intense. The best sexual experience of my life, and he was right there with me. I know he was. First time he'd ever made it in a car, and he was kind of resistant at first, but then I got him so hot for it he couldn't say no."

"Really? Never?" He ran a hand over his morning stubble. "Most guys scratch car banging off their fuck list in high school. In fact, I can't think of anyone who didn't, except for the nerds and fuglies, and he's neither."

I shrugged. "I guess car banging makes me a slut."

Cary grew very still. "Is that what he said?"

"No. He didn't say shit. I got that from his 'friend,' Magdalene. You know, that chick in most of the photos you printed off the Internet? She decided to sharpen her claws with a little catty girl chat in the bathroom."

"The bitch is jealous."

"Sexual frustration. She can't fuck him,

because apparently girls who fuck him go into the discard pile."

"Did he say that?" Again, fury laced his quiet question.

"Not in so many words. He said he doesn't sleep with his female friends. He's got issues with women wanting more than a good time in the sack, so he keeps the women he bangs and the women he hangs out with in two separate camps." I took another sip of my coffee. "I warned him that sort of setup wasn't going to work for me and he said he'd make some adjustments, but I guess he's one of those guys who'll say whatever's necessary to get what he wants."

"Or else you have him running scared."

I glared. "Don't make excuses for him. Whose side are you on, anyway?"

"Yours, baby girl." He reached out and patted my knee. "Always yours."

I wrapped my hand around his muscular forearm and stroked my fingers gently along the underside in silent gratitude. I couldn't feel the multitude of fine white scars from cutting that marred his skin, but I never forgot they were there. I was thankful every day that he was alive, healthy, and a vital part of my life. "How'd your night go?"

"I can't complain." His eyes took on a mischievous glint. "I shagged that busty blonde in a maintenance closet. Her tits were real."

"Well, then." I smiled. "You made her night, I'm sure."

"I try." He picked up the phone receiver and winked at me. "What kind of delivery do you want? Subs? Chinese? Indian?"

"I'm not hungry."

"You're always hungry. If you don't pick something, I'll cook and you'll have to eat that."

I lifted my hand in surrender. "Okay, okay. You pick."

I got to work twenty minutes early on Monday, figuring I'd skip running into Gideon. When I reached my desk without incident, I felt such relief that I knew I was in serious trouble where he was concerned. My moods were shifting all over the place.

Mark arrived in high spirits, still floating from his major successes of the week before, and we dug right into work. I'd done some vodka market comparisons on Sunday and he was kind enough to go over those with me and listen to my impressions. Mark was also assigned the account for a new e-reader manufacturer, so we began the initial work on that.

With such a busy morning, time flew

swiftly and I didn't have time to think about my personal life. I was really grateful for that. Then I answered the phone and heard Gideon on the line. I wasn't prepared.

"How's your Monday been so far?" he asked, his voice sending a shiver of awareness through me.

"Hectic." I glanced at the clock and was startled to see it was twenty minutes to noon.

"Good." There was a pause. "I tried calling you yesterday. I left a couple messages. I wanted to hear your voice."

My eyes closed on a deep breath. It had taken every bit of my willpower to make it through the day without listening to the voice mail. I'd even enlisted Cary in the cause, telling him to restrain me forcibly if it looked like I might succumb to the urge. "I did the hermit thing and worked a little."

"Did you get the flowers I sent?"

"Yes. They're lovely. Thank you."

"They reminded me of your dress."

What the hell was he doing? I was beginning to think he had multiple personality disorder. "Some women might say that's romantic."

"I only care what you say." His chair creaked as if he'd pushed to his feet. "I thought about stopping by. . . . I wanted to."

I sighed, surrendering to my confusion. "I'm glad you didn't."

There was another long pause. "I deserved that."

"I didn't say it to be a bitch. It's just the truth."

"I know. Listen . . . I arranged for lunch up here in my office so we don't waste any of the hour leaving and getting back."

After his parting *I'll call you,* I'd wondered if he would want to get together again after he settled down from whatever trip he'd been on. It was a possibility I'd been dreading since Saturday night, aware that I needed to cut him off, but feeling strung out from the desire to be with him. I wanted to experience again that pure, perfect moment of intimacy we'd shared.

But I couldn't justify that one moment against all the other moments when he made me feel like crap.

"Gideon, we don't have any reason to have lunch together. We hashed things out Friday night, and we . . . took care of business Saturday. Let's just leave it at that."

"Eva." His voice turned gruff. "I know I fucked up. Let me explain."

"You don't have to. It's okay."

"It's not. I need to see you."

"I don't want —"

"We can do this the easy way, Eva. Or you can make it difficult." His tone took on a hard edge that made my pulse quicken. "Either way, you'll hear me out."

I closed my eyes, understanding that I wasn't lucky enough to get away with a quick good-bye phone chat. "Fine. I'll come up."

"Thank you." He exhaled audibly. "I can't wait to see you."

I returned the receiver to its cradle and stared at the photos on my desk, trying to formulate what I needed to say and steeling myself for the impact of seeing Gideon again. The ferocity of my physical response to him was impossible to control. Somehow I'd have to get past it and take care of business. Later, I'd think about having to see him in the building over the days, weeks, and months ahead. For the moment, I just had to focus on making it through lunch.

Yielding to the inevitable, I got back to work comparing the visual impact of some blow-in card samples.

"Eva."

I jumped and spun around in my chair, startled to find Gideon standing beside my cubicle. The sight of him blew me away, as

178

usual, and my heart stuttered in my chest. A quick glance at the clock proved that a quarter hour had passed in no time at all.

"Gid— Mr. Cross. You didn't have to come down here."

His face was calm and impassive, but his eyes were stormy and hot. "Ready?"

I opened my drawer and pulled out my purse, taking the opportunity to suck in a deep, shaky breath. He smelled phenomenal.

"Mr. Cross." Mark's voice. "It's great to see you. Is there something — ?"

"I'm here for Eva. We have a lunch date."

I straightened in time to see Mark's brows shoot up. He recovered quickly, his face smoothing into its usual good-natured handsomeness.

"I'll be back at one," I assured him.

"See you then. Enjoy your lunch."

Gideon put his hand at the small of my back and steered me out to the elevators, garnering raised brows from Megumi when we passed reception. I shifted restlessly as he hit the call button for the elevator, wishing I could've made it through the day without seeing the man whose touch I craved like a drug.

He faced me as we waited for the car, running his fingertips down the sleeve of my satin blouse. "Every time I close my eyes, I see you in that red dress. I hear the sounds you make when you're turned on. I feel you sliding over my cock, squeezing me like a fist, making me come so hard it hurts."

"Don't." I looked away, unable to bear the intimate way he was looking at me.

"I can't help it."

The arrival of the elevator was a relief. He caught my hand and pulled me inside. After he put his key in the panel, he tugged me closer. "I'm going to kiss you, Eva."

"I don't —"

He pulled me into him and sealed his mouth over mine. I resisted as long as I could; then I melted at the feel of his tongue stroking slow and sweet over mine. I'd wanted his kiss since we'd had sex. I wanted the reassurance that he valued what we'd shared, that it meant something to him as it had to me.

I was left bereft once again when he pulled away.

"Come on." He pulled the key out as the door opened.

Gideon's redheaded receptionist said nothing this time, although she eyed me strangely. In contrast, Gideon's secretary, Scott, stood when we approached and greeted me pleasantly by name.

"Good afternoon, Miss Tramell."

"Hi, Scott."

Gideon gave him a curt nod. "Hold my calls."

"Yes, of course."

I entered Gideon's expansive office, my gaze drifting to the sofa where he'd first touched me intimately.

Lunch was arranged on the bar — two plates covered in metal salvers.

"Can I take your purse?" he asked.

I looked at him, saw he'd taken off his jacket and slung it over his arm. He stood there in his tailored slacks and vest, his shirt and tie both a pristine white, his hair dark and thick around his breathtaking face, his eyes a wild and dazzling blue. In a word, he amazed me. I couldn't believe I'd made love to such a gorgeous man.

But then, it hadn't meant the same thing to him.

"Eva?"

"You're beautiful, Gideon." The words fell out of my mouth without conscious thought.

His brows lifted; then a softness came into his eyes. "I'm glad you like what you see."

I handed him my purse and moved away, needing the space. He hung his coat and my purse on the coatrack, then moved to the bar.

I crossed my arms. "Let's just get this over with. I don't want to see you anymore."

8

Gideon shoved a hand through his hair and exhaled harshly. "You don't mean that."

I was suddenly very tired, exhausted from fighting with myself over him. "I really do. You and me . . . it was a mistake."

His jaw tightened. "It wasn't. The way I handled it afterward was the mistake."

I stared at him, startled by the fierceness of his denial. "I wasn't talking about the sex, Gideon. I'm talking about my agreeing to this crazy strangers-with-benefits deal between us. I knew it was all wrong from the beginning. I should've listened to my instincts."

"Do you want to be with me, Eva?"

"No. That's what —"

"Not like we discussed at the bar. More than that."

My heart started to pound. "What are you talking about?"

"Everything." He left the bar and came

closer. "I want to be with you."

"You didn't seem like you did Saturday." My arms tightened around my middle.

"I was . . . reeling."

"So? I was, too."

His hands went to his hips. Then his arms crossed like mine. "Christ, Eva."

I watched him squirm and felt a flare of hope. "If that's all you've got, we're done."

"The hell we are."

"We've already hit a dead end if you're going to take a head trip every time we have sex."

He visibly struggled with what to say. "I'm used to having control. I *need* it. And you blew it all to hell in the limousine. I didn't handle that well."

"Ya think?"

"Eva." He approached. "I've never experienced anything like that. I didn't think it was possible for me to. Now that I have . . . I've got to have it. I've got to have *you.*"

"It's just sex, Gideon. Super awesome sex, but that can seriously screw with your head when the two people doing it aren't good for each other."

"Bullshit. I've admitted I fucked up. I can't change what happened, but I can sure as shit get pissed that you want to cut me off because of it. You laid out your rules and

I adjusted to accommodate them, but you won't make even a tiny adjustment for me. You have to meet me halfway." His face was hard with frustration. "At least give me a damn inch."

I stared at him, trying to figure out what he was doing and where this was going. "What do you want, Gideon?" I asked softly.

He caught me to him and cupped my cheek in one hand. "I want to keep feeling the way I feel when I'm with you. Just tell me what I have to do. And give me some room to screw up. I've never done this before. There's a learning curve."

I placed my palm over his heart and felt its pounding rhythm. He was anxious and passionate, and that had me on edge. How was I supposed to respond? Did I go with my gut or my common sense? "Done what before?"

"Whatever it takes to spend as much time with you as possible. In and out of bed."

The rush of delight that swept through me was ridiculously powerful. "Do you understand how much work and time a relationship between us is going to take, Gideon? I'm wiped out already. Plus I'm still working on some personal stuff, and I have my new job . . . my crazy mother . . ." My fingers covered his mouth before he could open it. "But you're worth it, and I want you bad enough. So I guess I don't have a choice, do I?"

"Eva. Damn you." Gideon lifted me, hitching one arm beneath my rear to urge me to wrap my legs around his waist. He kissed me hard on the mouth and nuzzled his nose against mine. "We'll figure it out."

"You say that as if it'll be easy." I knew I was high-maintenance, and he was obviously going to be the same.

"Easy's boring." He carried me over to the bar and set me down on a bar stool. He pulled the dome off my place setting and revealed a massive cheeseburger and fries. The meal was still warm, thanks to a heated granite slab beneath the plate.

"Yum," I murmured, becoming aware of how hungry I was. Now that we'd talked, my appetite had returned full force.

He snapped open my napkin and laid it over my lap with a squeeze to my knee; then he took the seat beside me. "So, how do we do this?"

"Well, you pick it up with your hands and put it in your mouth."

He shot me a wry look that made me smile. It felt good to smile. It felt good to be with him. It usually did . . . for a little while. I took a bite of my burger, moaning when I got a full hit of its flavor. It was a traditional cheeseburger, but the taste was divine.

"Good, right?" he asked.

"Very good. In fact, a guy who knows about burgers this good might be worth keeping to myself." I wiped my mouth and hands. "How resistant are you to exclusivity?"

As he set his burger down, there was an eerie stillness to him. I couldn't begin to guess what he was thinking. "I assumed that was implied in our arrangement. But to avoid any doubts, I'll be clear and say there won't be any other men for you, Eva."

A shiver moved through me at the blunt finality in his tone and the iciness of his gaze. I knew he had a dark side; I'd learned long ago how to spot and avoid men who had dangerous shadows in their eyes. But the familiar alarm bells didn't ring around Gideon as they maybe should have. "But women are okay?" I asked, to lighten the mood.

His brows rose. "I know your roommate is bisexual. Are you?"

"Would that bother you?"

"Sharing you would bother me. It's not an option. Your body belongs to me, Eva."

"And yours belongs to me? Exclusively?"

His gaze turned hot. "Yes, and I expect you to take frequent and excessive advantage of it."

Well, then . . . "But you've seen me naked," I teased, my voice husky. "You know what you're getting. I don't. I love what I've seen of your body so far, but that hasn't been a whole lot."

"We can rectify that now."

The thought of him stripping for me made me squirm in my seat. He noticed and his mouth curved wickedly.

"You'd better not," I said regretfully. "I was late getting back on Friday."

"Tonight, then."

I swallowed hard. "Absolutely."

"I'll be sure to clear my schedule by five." He resumed eating, completely at ease with the fact that we'd both just penciled *mind-blowing sex* into our mental day calendars.

"You don't have to." I opened the mini ketchup bottle by my plate. "I need to hit the gym after work."

"We'll go together."

"Really?" I turned the bottle upside down and thumped the bottom with my palm.

He took it from me and used his knife to coax the ketchup onto my plate. "It's probably best for me to work off some energy before I get you naked. I'm sure you'd like to be able to walk tomorrow."

I stared at him, astonished by the casualness with which he'd made the statement and the rueful amusement on his face that told me he wasn't entirely kidding. My sex clenched in delicious anticipation. I could easily picture becoming seriously addicted to Gideon Cross.

I ate some fries, thinking of someone else who was addicted to Gideon. "Magdalene could be a problem for me."

He swallowed a bite of his burger and washed it down with a swig from his bottled water. "She told me she'd talked to you, and that it didn't go well."

I gave props to Magdalene's scheming and the clever attempt to cut me off at the pass. I'd have to be very careful with her, and Gideon was going to have to do something about her — like cut her off, period.

"No, it didn't go well," I agreed. "But then I don't appreciate being told that you don't respect the women you fuck and that the moment you shoved your dick into me you were done with me."

Gideon stilled. "She said that?"

"Word for word. She also said you're keeping her on ice until you're ready to settle down."

"Did she now?" His low voice had a chilling bite to it.

My stomach knotted, knowing things could go either really right or really wrong, depending on what Gideon said next. "Don't you believe me?"

"Of course I believe you."

"She could be a problem for me," I repeated, not letting it go.

"She won't be a problem. I'll talk to her."

I hated the thought of him talking to her, because it made me sick with jealousy. I figured that was an issue I should disclose up front. "Gideon . . ."

"Yes?" He'd finished his burger and was working on the fries.

"I'm a very jealous person. I can be irrational with it." I poked at my burger with a fry. "You might want to think about that, and whether you want to deal with someone who has self-esteem issues like I do. It was one of my sticking points when you first propositioned me, knowing it was going to drive me nuts having women salivating all over you and not having the right to say anything about it."

"You have the right now."

"You're not taking me seriously." I shook my head and took another bite of my cheeseburger.

"I've never been as serious about anything

190

in my life." Reaching over, Gideon ran a fingertip over the corner of my mouth, then licked off the dab of sauce he'd collected. "You're not the only one who can get possessive. I'm very proprietary about what's mine."

I didn't doubt that for a minute.

I took another bite and thought of the night ahead. I was eager. Ridiculously so. I was dying to see Gideon naked. Dying to run my hands and lips all over him. Dying to have another go at driving him crazy. And I was damn near desperate to be under him, to feel him straining over me, pounding into me, coming hard and deep inside me . . .

"Keep thinking those thoughts," he said roughly, "and you'll be late again."

I looked at him with raised brows. "How did you know what I'm thinking?"

"You get this look on your face when you're turned on. I intend to put that look on your face as often as possible." Gideon covered his plate again and stood, withdrawing a business card from his pocket and setting it down beside me. I could see that he'd written his home and cell phone numbers on the back. "I feel stupid asking this question considering our present conversation, but I need your cell phone number."

"Oh." I forcibly dragged my thoughts out

of the bedroom. "I have to get one first. It's on my to-do list."

"What happened to the phone you were texting with last week?"

My nose wrinkled. "My mother was using it to track my movements around the city. She's a tad . . . overprotective."

"I see." He brushed the backs of his fingers down my cheek. "That's what you were talking about when you said your mom is stalking you."

"Yes, unfortunately."

"Okay, then. We'll take care of the phone after work before we head to the gym. It's safer for you to have one. And I want to be able to call you whenever I feel like it."

I set down the quarter of my burger that I couldn't eat and wiped my hands and mouth. "That was delicious. Thank you."

"It was my pleasure." He leaned over me and pressed his lips briefly to mine. "Do you need to use the washroom?"

"Yes. I need my toothbrush from my purse, too."

A few minutes later, I found myself standing in a washroom hidden behind a door that blended seamlessly with the mahogany paneling behind the flatscreens. We brushed our teeth side by side at the double-sink vanity, our gazes meeting in our mirrored reflections. It was such a domestic, *normal* thing to do and yet we both seemed to delight in it.

"I'll take you back down," he said, crossing his office to the coatrack.

I followed him but veered off when we reached his desk. I went to it and put my hand on the clear space in front of his chair. "Is this where you are most of the day?"

"Yes." He shrugged into his jacket and I wanted to bite him, he looked so delectable.

Instead, I hopped up to sit directly in front of his chair. According to my watch I had five minutes. Barely enough time to get back to work, but still. I couldn't resist exercising my new rights. I pointed at his chair. "Sit."

His brows rose, but he came over without argument and settled gracefully into the seat.

I spread my legs and crooked my finger. "Closer."

He rolled forward, filling the space between my thighs. He wrapped his arms around my hips and looked up at me. "One day soon, Eva, I'm going to fuck you right here."

"Just a kiss for now," I murmured, bending forward to take his mouth. With my hands on his shoulders for balance, I licked across his parted lips; then I slipped inside and teased him with gentleness.

Groaning, he deepened the kiss, eating at my mouth in a way that made me achy and wet.

"One day soon," I repeated against his lips, "I'm going to kneel beneath this desk and suck you off. Maybe while you're on the phone playing with your millions like Monopoly. You, Mr. Cross, will pass Go and collect your two hundred dollars."

His mouth curved against mine. "I can see how this is going to go. You're going to make me lose my mind coming everywhere I can in your tight, sexy body."

"Are you complaining?"

"Angel, I'm salivating."

I was bemused by the endearment, although I liked its sweetness. "Angel?"

He hummed a soft assent and kissed me.

I couldn't believe what a difference an hour made. I left Gideon's office in a completely different frame of mind than when I'd entered it. The feel of his hand at the small of my back made my body hum with anticipation rather than the misery I'd felt on the way in.

I waved bye to Scott and smiled brightly at the unsmiling receptionist.

"I don't think she likes me," I told Gideon, as we waited for the elevator.

"Who?"

"Your receptionist."

He glanced over that way, and the redhead beamed at him.

"Well," I murmured. "She likes you."

"I guarantee her paychecks."

My mouth curved. "Yes, I'm sure that's what it is. It couldn't possibly have anything to do with you being the sexiest man alive."

"Am I now?" He caged me to the wall and burned me with a searing gaze.

I set my hands against his abdomen, licking my lower lip when I felt the hard ridges of muscle tighten under my touch. "Just an observation."

"*I* like you." With his palms pressed flat to the wall on either side of my head, he lowered his mouth to mine and kissed me softly.

"I like you back. You do realize you're at work, don't you?"

"What good is being the boss if you can't do what you want?"

"Hmm."

When a car arrived, I ducked under Gideon's arm and slid into it. He prowled in after me, then circled me like a predator, sliding up behind me to pull me back against him. His hands pushed into my front pockets and splayed against my hip

195

bones, keeping me tucked close. The warmth of his touch so close to where I ached for him was a special brand of torture. In retaliation, I wriggled my butt against him and smiled when he hissed out a breath and hardened.

"Behave," he admonished gruffly. "I have a meeting in fifteen minutes."

"Will you think of me while you're sitting at your desk?"

"Undoubtedly. You'll definitely think about me while you're sitting at yours. That's an order, Miss Tramell."

My head fell back against his chest, loving the bite of command in his voice. "I don't see how I couldn't, Mr. Cross, considering how I think of you everywhere else I go."

He stepped out with me when we reached the twentieth floor. "Thank you for lunch."

"I think that's my line." I backed away. "See you later, Dark and Dangerous."

His brows rose at my nickname for him. "Five o'clock. Don't make me wait."

One of the cars in the left bank of elevators arrived. Megumi stepped out and Gideon stepped in, his gaze locked with mine until the doors closed.

"Whew," she said. "You scored. I'm pea green with envy."

I couldn't think of anything to say to that.

It was all still too new and I was afraid to jinx it. In the back of my mind, I knew these feelings of happiness couldn't last. Everything was going *too* well.

I rushed to my desk and got to work.

"Eva." I looked up to see Mark standing in the threshold of his office. "Could I talk to you a minute?"

"Of course." I grabbed my tablet, even though his grim face and tone warned me it might not be needed. When Mark shut the door behind me, my apprehension increased. "Is everything all right?"

"Yes." He waited until I was seated, then took the chair beside me rather than the one behind his desk. "I don't know how to say this . . ."

"Just say it. I'll figure it out."

He looked at me with compassionate eyes and a cringe of embarrassment. "It's not my place to interfere. I'm just your boss and there's a line that comes with that, but I'm going to cross it because I like you, Eva, and I want you to work here for a long time."

My stomach tightened. "That's great. I really love my job."

"Good. Good, I'm glad." He shot me a quick smile. "Just . . . be careful with Cross, okay?"

I blinked, startled by the direction of the conversation. "Okay."

"He's brilliant, rich, and sexy, so I understand the appeal. As much as I love Steven, I get a little flustered around Cross myself. He's just got that kind of pull." Mark talked fast and shifted with obvious embarrassment. "And I can totally see why he's interested in you. You're beautiful, smart, honest, considerate . . . I could go on, because you're great."

"Thanks," I said quietly, hoping I didn't look as ill as I felt. This sort of warning from a friend, and knowing that others would think of me as just another babe-of-the-week, was exactly the type of thing that preyed on my insecurities.

"I just don't want to see you get hurt," he muttered, looking as miserable as I felt. "Part of that's selfish, I'll admit. I don't want to lose a great assistant because she doesn't want to work in a building owned by an ex."

"Mark, it means a lot to me that you care and that I'm valuable to you around here. But you don't have to worry about me. I'm a big girl. Besides, nothing is going to get me to quit this job."

He blew out his breath, clearly relieved.

"All right. Let's put it away and get to work."

So we did, but I set myself up for future torture by subscribing to a daily Google alert for Gideon's name. And when five o'clock rolled around, my awareness of my many inadequacies was still spreading through my happiness like a stain.

Gideon was as prompt as he'd threatened to be, and he didn't seem to notice my introspective mood as we rode down in a crowded elevator. More than one woman in the car cast furtive glances in his direction, but that sort of thing I didn't mind. He was hot. I would've been surprised if they hadn't looked.

He caught my hand when we cleared the turnstiles, linking his fingers with mine. The simple, intimate gesture meant so much to me in that moment that my grip tightened on his. And I'd really have to watch out for that. The moment I became grateful he was spending time with me would be the beginning of the end. Neither of us would respect me if that happened.

The Bentley SUV sat at the curb and Gideon's driver stood at the ready by the rear door. Gideon looked at me. "I had some workout clothes packed and brought over, in case you were set on visiting your gym.

Equinox, right? Or we can go to mine."

"Where's yours?"

"I prefer to go to the CrossTrainer on Thirty-fifth."

My curiosity over how he knew which gym I frequented vanished when I heard the "Cross" in the name of his gym. "You wouldn't happen to *own* the gym, would you?"

His grin flashed. "The chain. Usually, I practice mixed martial arts with a personal trainer, but I use the gym occasionally."

"The chain," I repeated. "Of course."

"Your choice," he said considerately. "I'll go wherever you want."

"By all means, let's go to your gym."

He opened the back door, and I slid in and over. I set my purse and my gym bag on my lap, and looked out the window as the car pulled away from the curb. The sedan driving next to us was so close I wouldn't have to lean far to touch it. Rush hour in Manhattan was something I was still getting used to. SoCal had bumper-to-bumper traffic, too, but it moved at a snail's pace. Here in New York, speed mixed with the crush in a way that often made me close my eyes and pray to survive the trip.

It was a whole new world. A new city, new apartment, new job, and new man. It was a lot to take on at once. I supposed it was understandable that I felt off-balance.

I glanced at Gideon and found him staring at me with an unreadable expression. Everything inside me twisted into a mess of wild lust and vibrating anxiety. I had no idea what I was doing with him, only that I couldn't stop even if I wanted to.

9

We hit the cellular store first. The associate who helped us seemed highly susceptible to Gideon's magnetic pull. She practically fell all over herself the minute he showed the slightest interest in anything, quickly launching into detailed explanations and leaning into his personal space to demonstrate.

I tried separating from them and finding someone who'd actually help *me,* but Gideon's grip on my hand wouldn't let me move more than touching distance away. Then we argued over who was going to pay, which he seemed to think should be him even though the phone and account were mine.

"You got your way with picking the service provider," I pointed out, pushing his credit card aside and shoving mine at the girl.

"Because it's practical. We'll be on the same network, so calls to me are free." He swapped the cards deftly.

"I won't be calling you at all, if you don't put your damn credit card away!"

That did the trick, although I could tell he was unhappy about it. He'd just have to get over it.

Once we got back in the Bentley, his mood seemed restored.

"You can head to the gym now, Angus," he told his driver, settling back in the seat. Then he pulled his smartphone out of his pocket. He saved my new number into his contact list; then he took my new phone out of my hand and programmed my list with his home, office, and cell numbers.

He'd barely finished when we arrived at CrossTrainer. Not surprisingly, the three-story fitness center was a health enthusiast's dream. I was impressed with every sleek, modern, top-of-the-line inch of it. Even the women's locker room was like something out of a science fiction movie.

But my awe was totally eclipsed by Gideon himself when I finished changing into my workout clothes and found him waiting for me out in the hallway. He'd changed into long shorts and a tank, which gave me my first look at his bare arms and legs.

I came to an abrupt halt and someone coming out behind me bumped into me. I could barely manage an apology; I was too busy visually devouring Gideon's body. His legs were toned and powerful, flawlessly proportional to his trim hips and waist. His arms made my mouth water. His biceps were precisely cut and his forearms were coursing with thick veins that were both brutal looking and sexy as hell. He'd tied his hair back, which showed off the definition of his neck and traps and the sculpted angles of his face.

Christ. I knew this man intimately. My brain couldn't wrap itself around that fact, not while faced with the irrefutable evidence of how uniquely beautiful he was.

And he was scowling at me.

Straightening away from the wall where he'd been leaning, he came toward me, then circled me. His fingertips ran along my bare midriff and back as he made the revolution, sending goose bumps racing over my skin. When he stopped in front of me, I threw my arms around his neck and pulled his mouth down for a quick, playfully smacking kiss.

"What the hell are you wearing?" he asked, looking marginally appeased by my enthusiastic greeting.

"Clothes."

"You look naked in that top."

"I thought you liked me naked." I was secretly pleased with my choice, which I'd made that morning before I'd known he'd be with me. The top was a triangle with long straps at the shoulders and ribs that secured with Velcro and could be worn in a variety of ways to allow the wearer to determine where her breasts needed the most support. It was specially designed for curvy women and was the first top I'd ever had that kept me from bouncing all over the place. What Gideon objected to was the nude color, which coordinated with the racing stripes on the matching black yoga pants.

"I like you naked *in private,*" he muttered. "I'll need to be with you whenever you go to the gym."

"I won't complain, since I'm very much enjoying the view at the moment." Plus, I was perversely excited by his possessiveness after the hurt he'd inflicted with his withdrawal Saturday night. Two very different extremes — the first of many, I was sure.

"Let's get this over with." He grabbed my hand and led me away from the locker rooms, snatching two logo'd towels off a stack as we passed them. "I need to fuck you."

"I need to be fucked."

"Jesus, Eva." His grip on my hand tightened to the point that it hurt. "Where to? Free weights? Machines? Treadmills?"

"Treadmills. I want to run a bit."

He led me in that direction. I watched the way women followed him with their gazes, then their feet. They wanted to be in whatever section of the gym he was, and I couldn't blame them. I was dying to see him in action, too.

When we reached the seemingly endless rows of treadmills and bikes, we found that there weren't two treadmills free adjacent to each other.

Gideon walked up to a man who had one open on either side of him. "I'd be in your debt if you'd move over one."

The guy looked at me and grinned. "Yeah, sure."

"Thanks. I appreciate it."

Gideon took over the man's treadmill and motioned me to the one beside it. Before he programmed his workout, I leaned over to him. "Don't burn off too much energy," I whispered. "I want you missionary style the first time. I've been having this fantasy of you on top, banging the hell out of me."

His gaze burned into me. "Eva, you have no idea."

Nearly giddy with anticipation and a lovely surge of feminine power, I got on my treadmill and started at a brisk walk. While I warmed up, I set my iPod shuffle to random, and when "SexyBack" by Justin Timberlake came on, I hit my stride and went full-out. Running was both a mental and physical exercise for me. Sometimes I wished just running fast could get me away from whatever was troubling me.

After twenty minutes I slowed, then stopped, finally risking a glance at Gideon, who was running with the fluidity of a well-oiled machine. He was watching CNN on the overhead screens, but he flashed a grin at me as I wiped the sweat off my face. I swigged from my water bottle as I moved to the machines, picking one that give me a clear view of him.

He went a full thirty on the treadmill; then he moved to free weights, always keeping me in his line of sight. As he worked out, quickly and efficiently, I couldn't help thinking how virile he was. It helped that I knew exactly what was in his shorts, but regardless, he was a man who worked behind a desk, yet kept his body in combat shape.

When I grabbed a fitness ball to do some crunches, one of the trainers came up to me. As one would expect in a top-of-the-line gym, he was handsome and very nicely built.

"Hi," he greeted me, with a movie star smile that showcased perfect white teeth. He had dark brown hair and eyes of nearly the same color. "First-timer, right? I haven't seen you in here before."

"Yes, first time."

"I'm Daniel." He extended his hand, and I gave him my name. "Are you finding everything you need, Eva?"

"So far so good, thanks."

"What flavor smoothie did you go for?"

I frowned. "Excuse me?"

"Your free orientation smoothie." He crossed his arms and his thick biceps strained the narrow cuffs of his uniform polo shirt. "You didn't get one from the bar downstairs when you signed up? You're supposed to."

"Ah, well." I shrugged sheepishly, thinking it was a nice touch all the same. "I didn't have the usual orientation."

"Did you get the tour? If not, let me take you around." He touched my elbow lightly and gestured toward the stairs. "You also get a free hour of personal training. We could do that tonight or make an appointment for later in the week. And I'd be happy to take you down to the health bar and scratch that off the list, too."

"Oh, I can't really." My nose wrinkled. "I'm not a member."

"Ah." He winked. "You're here on a temp pass? That's fine. You can't be expected to make up your mind if you don't get the full experience. I can assure you, though, that CrossTrainer is the best gym in Manhattan."

Gideon appeared at Daniel's shoulder. "The full experience is included," he said, coming around and behind me to slide his arms around my waist, "when you're the owner's girlfriend."

The word *girlfriend* reverberated through me, sending a crazy rush of adrenaline through my system. It was still sinking in that we had that level of commitment, but that didn't stop me from thinking the designation had a nice ring to it.

"Mr. Cross." Daniel straightened and took a step back, then extended his hand. "It's an honor to meet you."

"Daniel has me sold on the place," I said to Gideon, as they shook hands.

"I thought *I'd* done that." His hair was wet with sweat and he smelled divine. I'd never known a sweaty man could smell so damn good.

His hands stroked down my arms and I

felt his lips on the crown of my head. "Let's go. See you later, Daniel."

I waved good-bye as we walked away. "Thanks, Daniel."

"Anytime."

"I bet," Gideon muttered. "He couldn't keep his eyes off your tits."

"They're very nice tits."

He made a low growling noise. I hid my amusement.

He smacked my butt hard enough to send me forward a step and leave behind a hot sting even through my pants. "That damned Band-Aid you call a shirt doesn't leave much to the imagination. Don't take long in the shower. You're just going to get sweaty again."

"Wait." I caught his arm before he passed the women's locker room on the way toward the men's. "Would it gross you out if I told you I didn't want you to shower? If I said I want to find someplace really close by where I could jump you while you're still dripping sweat?"

Gideon's jaw tightened and his gaze darkened dangerously. "I'm beginning to fear for your safety, Eva. Grab your stuff. There's a hotel around the corner."

Neither of us changed and we were outside in five minutes. Gideon walked briskly and

I hurried to keep up. When he stopped abruptly, turned, and dipped me back in a lavish heated kiss on the crowded sidewalk, I was too stunned to do more than hold on. It was a soul-wrenching melding of our mouths, full of passion and sweet spontaneity that made my heart ache. Applause broke out around us.

When he straightened me again, I was breathless and dizzy. "What was that?" I gasped.

"A prelude." He resumed our dash to the nearest hotel, one I didn't catch the name of as he pulled me past the doorman and crossed straight to the elevator. It was clear to me that the property was one of Gideon's even before a manager greeted him by name just before the elevator doors closed.

Gideon dropped his duffel on the car floor and busied himself with figuring out how to extricate me from my sports top. I was slapping his hands away when the doors opened and he scooped up his bag. There was no one waiting on our floor and no one in the hallway. He pulled a master key out of somewhere, and a moment later we were in a room.

I pounced, pushing my hands up beneath his shirt to feel his damp skin and the hardness of the muscles beneath it. "Get naked.

Like *now*."

He laughed as he toed off his sneakers and yanked his tank over his head.

Oh my God . . . seeing him in the flesh — all of him, as his shorts hit the floor — was synapse frying. There wasn't an ounce of excess flesh on him anywhere, just hard slabs of honed muscle. He had washboard abs and that super sexy V of muscle on his pelvis that Cary called the Loin of Apollo. Gideon didn't wax his chest like Cary did, but he groomed with the same care he showed to the rest of his body. He was pure primal male, the embodiment of everything I coveted, fantasized about, and wished for.

"I've died and gone to heaven," I said, staring unabashedly.

"You're still dressed." He attacked my clothes, whipping my loosened top off before I took a full breath. My pants were wrestled down and I kicked my shoes off in such a hurry that I lost my balance and fell on the bed. I barely caught my breath before he was on me.

We rolled across the mattress in a tangle. Everywhere he touched me left trails of fire behind. The clean, hardworking scent of his skin was an aphrodisiac and intoxicant at once, spurring my desire for him until I felt like I was about to lose my mind.

"You're so beautiful, Eva." He plumped one breast in his hand before taking my nipple into his mouth.

I cried out at the scorching heat and the lash of his tongue, my core tightening with every soft suck. My hands were greedy as they slid over his sweat-damp skin, stroking and kneading, searching for the spots that made him growl and moan. I scissored my legs with his and tried to roll him, but he was too heavy and too strong.

He lifted his head and smiled down at me. "It's my turn this time."

What I felt for him in that moment, seeing that smile and the heat in his eyes, was so intense it was painful. Too fast, I thought. I was falling too fast. "Gideon —"

He kissed me deeply, licking into my mouth in that way of his. I thought he could really make me come with just a kiss, if we stayed at it long enough. Everything about him turned me on, from the way he looked and felt beneath my hands to the way he watched me and touched me. His greed and the silent demands he made on my body, the forcefulness with which he pleasured me and took his pleasure in return, drove me wild.

I ran my hands through the wet silk of his hair. The crisp hairs on his chest teased my tightened nipples, and the feel of his rock-hard body against mine was enough to make me wet and needy.

"I love your body," he whispered, his lips moving across my cheek to my throat. His hand caressed the length of my torso from breast to hip. "I can't get enough of it."

"You haven't had very much of it yet," I teased.

"I don't think I'll ever have enough." Nibbling and licking across my shoulder, he slid down and caught my other nipple between his teeth. He tugged and the tiny dart of pain had my back arching on a soft cry. He soothed the sting with a soft suck, then kissed his way downward. "I've never wanted anything this badly."

"Then do me!"

"Not yet," he murmured, moving lower, rimming my navel with the tip of his tongue. "You're not ready yet."

"What? Ah, God . . . I can't get any readier." I tugged on his hair, trying to pull him up.

Gideon caught my wrists and pinned them to the mattress. "You have a tight little cunt, Eva. I'll bruise you if I don't get you soft and relaxed."

A violent shiver of arousal moved through me. It turned me on when he talked so bluntly about sex. Then he slid lower and I tensed. "No, Gideon. I need to shower for that."

He buried his face in my cleft and I struggled against his hold, flushed with sudden shame. He nipped at my inner thigh with his teeth. "Stop it."

"Don't. Please. You don't have to do that."

His glare stilled my frantic movements. "Do you think I feel differently about your body than you do mine?" he asked harshly. "I want you, Eva."

I licked my dry lips, so crazily turned on by his animal need that I couldn't form a single word. He growled softly and dove for the slick flesh between my legs. His tongue pushed into me, licking and parting the sensitive tissues. My hips churned restlessly, my body silently begging for more. It felt so good I could've wept.

"God, Eva. I've wanted my mouth on your cunt every day since I met you."

As the velvet softness of his tongue flickered over my swollen clit, my head pressed hard into the pillow. "Yes. Like that. Make me come."

He did, with the gentlest of suction and a hard lick. I writhed as the orgasm jolted through me, my core tensing violently, my limbs shaking. His tongue thrust into my

215

sex as it convulsed, rippling along the shallow penetration, trying to pull him deeper. His groans vibrated against my swollen flesh, goading the climax to roll on and on. Tears stung my eyes and coursed down my temples, the physical pleasure destroying the wall that kept my emotions at bay.

And Gideon didn't stop. He circled the trembling entrance to my body with the tip of his tongue and lapped at my throbbing clit until I quickened again. Two fingers pushed inside me, curving and stroking. I was so sensitive I thrashed against the onslaught. When he drew on my clit with steady, rhythmic suction, I came again, crying out hoarsely. Then he had three fingers in me, twisting and opening me.

"No." My head tossed from side to side, every inch of my skin tingling and burning. "No more."

"Once more," he coaxed hoarsely. "Once more, then I'll fuck you."

"I can't . . ."

"You will." He blew a slow stream of air over my wet flesh, the coolness over fevered skin reawakening raw nerve endings. "I love watching you come, Eva. Love hearing the sounds you make, the way your body quivers . . ."

He massaged a tender spot inside me and

an orgasm pulsed through me in a slow, heated roll of delight, no less devastating for being gentler than the two before it.

His weight and heat left me. In a distant corner of my dazed mind, I heard a drawer opening, followed swiftly by the sound of foil tearing. The mattress dipped as he returned, his hands rough now as he yanked me down to the center of the bed. He stretched himself on top of me, pinning me, tucking his forearms on the outside of my biceps and pressing them to my sides, capturing me.

My gaze was riveted to his austerely beautiful face. His features were harsh with lust, his skin stretched tight over his cheekbones and jaw. His eyes were so dark and dilated they were black, and I knew I was staring into the face of a man who'd passed the limits of his control. It was important to me that he'd made it that far for my benefit and that he'd done so to pleasure and prepare me for what I knew would be a hard ride.

My hands fisted in the bedspread, anticipation building. He'd made sure I got mine, over and over again. This would be for him.

"Fuck me," I ordered, daring him with my eyes.

"Eva." He snapped out my name as he

rammed into me, sinking balls-deep in one fierce drive.

I gasped. He was big, hard as stone, and so damn deep. The connection was startlingly intense. Emotionally. Mentally. I'd never felt so completely . . . taken. Possessed.

I wouldn't have thought I could bear to be restrained during sex, not with my past being what it was, but Gideon's total domination of my body ratcheted my desire to an outrageous level. I'd never been so hot for it in my life, which seemed insane after what I'd experienced with him so far.

I clenched around him, relishing the feel of him inside me, filling me.

His hips ground against mine, prodding as if to say, *Feel me? I'm in you. I own you.*

His entire body hardened, the muscles of his chest and arms straining as he pulled out to the tip. The rigid tightening of his abs was the only warning I got before he slammed forward. Hard.

I cried out and his chest rumbled with a low, primitive sound. "Christ . . . You feel so good."

Tightening his hold, he starting fucking me, nailing my hips to the mattress with wildly fierce drives. Pleasure rippled through me again, pushing through me with every hot shove of his body into mine. *Like this,* I thought. *I want you just like this.*

He buried his face in my neck and held me tightly in place, plunging hard and fast, gasping raw, heated sex words that made me crazed with desire. "I've never been so hard and thick. I'm so deep in you . . . I can feel it against my stomach . . . feel my dick pounding into you."

I'd thought of this round as his, and yet he was still with me, still focused on me, swiveling his hips to stroke pleasure through my melting core. I made a small, helpless sound of need and his mouth slanted over mine. I was desperate for him, my nails digging into his pumping hips, struggling with the grinding urge to rock into the ferocious thrusts of his big cock.

We were dripping in sweat, our skin hot and slicked together, our chests heaving for air. As an orgasm brewed like a storm inside me, everything tightened and clenched, squeezing. He cursed and shoved one hand beneath my hip, cupping my rear and lifting me into his thrusts so that his cock head stroked over and over the spot that ached for him.

"Come, Eva," he ordered harshly. "Come now."

I climaxed in a rush that had me sobbing

219

his name, the sensation enhanced and magnified by the way he'd confined my body. He threw his head back, shuddering.

"Ah, Eva!" He clasped me so tightly I couldn't breathe, his hips pumping as he came long and hard.

I've no idea how long we lay like that, leveled, mouths sliding over shoulders and throats to soothe and calm. My entire body tingled and pulsed.

"Wow," I managed finally.

"You'll kill me," he muttered with his lips at my jaw. "We're going to end up fucking each other to death."

"Me? I didn't do anything." He'd controlled me completely, and how freakin' sexy was *that*?

"You're breathing. That's enough."

I laughed, hugging him.

Lifting his head, he nuzzled my nose. "We're going to eat, and then we'll do that again."

My brows lifted. "You can do that again?"

"All night." He rolled his hips and I could feel that he was still semihard.

"You're a machine," I told him. "Or a god."

"It's you." With a soft, sweet kiss, he left me. He removed the condom, wrapped it in a tissue from the nightstand, and tossed the whole thing in the wastebasket by the bed. "We'll shower, then order from the restaurant downstairs. Unless you want to go down?"

"I don't think I can walk."

The flash of his grin stopped my heart for a minute. "Glad I'm not the only one."

"You look fine."

"I feel phenomenal." He sat back on the side of the bed and brushed my hair back from my forehead. His face was soft, his smile warmly affectionate.

I thought I saw something else in his eyes and the possibility closed my throat. It scared me.

"Shower with me," he said, running his hand down my arm.

"Gimme a minute to find my brain, then I'll join you."

"Okay." He went into the bathroom, giving me a prime view of his sculpted back and perfect ass. I sighed with pure female appreciation of a prime male specimen.

The water came on in the shower. I managed to sit up and slide my legs over the side of the bed, feeling exquisitely shaky. My gaze caught on the slightly open bedside drawer and I saw condoms through the gap.

My stomach twisted. The hotel was too upscale to be the kind that provided condoms along with the requisite Bible.

With a slightly trembling hand, I pulled the drawer out further and found a sizable quantity of prophylactics, including a bottle of feminine lubrication and spermicidal gel. My heart started pounding all over again. In my mind, I backtracked through our lust-fueled trip to the hotel. Gideon hadn't asked which rooms were available. Whether he had a master key or not, he'd need to know which rooms were occupied before he took one . . . unless he'd known beforehand that this particular suite would be empty.

Clearly it was *his* suite — a fuck pad outfitted with everything he'd need to have a good time with the women who served that purpose in his life.

As I pushed to my feet and walked over to the closet, I heard the glass shower door open in the bathroom, then close. I caught the two knobs of the louvered walnut closet doors and pushed them apart. There was a small selection of men's clothes hanging on the metal rod, some business shirts and slacks, as well as khakis and jeans. My temperature dropped and a sick misery spread through my orgasmic high.

The right-side dresser drawers held neatly folded T-shirts, boxer briefs, and socks. The top one on the left side held sex toys still in their packages. I didn't look at the drawers below that one. I'd seen enough.

I pulled on my pants and stole one of Gideon's shirts. As I dressed, my mind went through the steps I'd learned in therapy: *Talk it out. Explain what triggered the negative feelings to your partner. Face the trigger and work through it.*

Maybe if I'd been less shaken by the depth of my feelings for Gideon, I could have done all that. Maybe if we hadn't just had mind-blowing sex, I would have felt less raw and vulnerable. I'd never know. What I felt was slightly dirty, a little bit used, and a whole lot hurt. This particular revelation had hit me with excruciating force, and like a child, I wanted to hurt him back.

I scooped up the condoms, lube, and toys, and tossed them on the bed. Then, just as he called out my name in an amused and teasing voice, I picked up my bag and left him.

10

I kept my head down as I made the walk of shame past the registration desk and exited the hotel through a side door. I was red-faced with embarrassment remembering the manager who'd greeted Gideon as we got on the elevator. I could only imagine what he'd thought of me. He had to know what Gideon reserved that suite for. I couldn't stand the thought of being the next in a line of many, and yet that was exactly what I'd been from the moment we entered the hotel.

How hard would it have been to stop by the front desk and secure a room that was ours alone?

I started walking with no direction or destination in mind. It was dark out now, the city taking on a whole new life and energy from what it had during the business day. Steaming food carts dotted the sidewalks, along with a vendor selling framed artwork, another hawking novelty T-shirts, and yet another who had two folding tables covered in movie and television episode scripts.

With every step I took, the adrenaline from my flight burned away. The maliciously gleeful thoughts of Gideon coming out of the bathroom to find an empty room and a paraphernalia-strewn bed ran their course. I began to calm down . . . and seriously think about what had just happened.

Was it a coincidence that Gideon invited me to a gym that just so happened to be conveniently close to his fuck pad?

I remembered the conversation we'd had in his office over lunch and the way he'd struggled to express himself to keep me. He was as confused and torn about what was happening between us as I was, and I knew how easy it was to fall into established patterns. After all, hadn't I just fallen into one of my own by bailing? I'd spent enough years in therapy to know better than to wound and run when I was hurting.

Heartsick, I stepped into an Italian bistro and took a table. I ordered a glass of shiraz and a pizza margherita, hoping wine and food would calm the vibrating anxiety inside me so that I could think properly.

When the waiter returned with my wine, I gulped down half the glass without really tasting it. I missed Gideon already, missed the playful, happy mood he'd been in when I left. His scent was all over me — the smell of his skin and hot, grinding sex. My eyes stung and I let a few tears slide down my face, despite being in a very public, very busy restaurant. My food came and I picked at it. It tasted like cardboard, although I doubted that had anything to do with the chef or the venue.

Pulling over the chair where I'd set my bag, I dug out my new smartphone with the intention of leaving a message with Dr. Travis's answering service. He'd suggested we have video chat appointments until I found a new therapist in New York and I decided to take him up on that offer. That's when I noticed the twenty-one missed calls from Gideon and a text: I fucked up again. Don't break up with me. Talk to me. Pls.

The tears welled again. I held the phone to my heart, at a loss for what to do. I couldn't get the images of Gideon and other women out of my mind. I couldn't stop picturing him fucking the hell out of another woman on that same bed, using toys on her, driving her crazy, taking his pleasure from her body . . .

It was irrational and pointless to think of such things, and it made me feel petty and small and physically sick.

I startled when the phone vibrated against me, nearly dropping it. Nursing my misery, I debating letting it go to voice mail because I could see on the screen that it was Gideon — plus he was the only one who had the number — but I couldn't ignore it, because he was clearly frantic. As much as I'd wanted to wound him earlier, I couldn't stand to do it now.

"Hello." My voice didn't sound like mine, clogged as it was with tears and emotion.

"Eva! Thank God." Gideon sounded so anxious. "Where are you?"

Looking around, I didn't see anything that would tell me the name of the restaurant. "I don't know. I . . . I'm sorry, Gideon."

"No, Eva. Don't. It's my fault. I need to find you. Can you describe where you're at? Did you walk?"

"Yes. I walked."

"I know which exit you took. Which way did you head?" He was breathing quickly and I could hear the sounds of traffic and car horns in the background.

"To the left."

"Did you turn any corners after that?"

"I don't think so. I don't know." I looked around for a server I could ask. "I'm in a restaurant. Italian. There's seating on the sidewalk . . . and a wrought-iron fence. French doors . . . Jesus, Gideon, I —"

He appeared, silhouetted in the entrance with the phone held to his ear. I knew him immediately, watched as he froze when he saw me seated against the wall toward the back. Shoving the phone into the pocket of jeans he'd had stored at the hotel, he strode past the hostess who'd started speaking to him and headed straight for me. I barely managed to get to my feet before he hauled me against him and embraced me tightly.

"God." He shook slightly and buried his face in my neck. "Eva."

I hugged him back. He was fresh from a shower, making me achingly aware of my need for one.

"I can't be here," he said hoarsely, pulling back to cup my face in his hands. "I can't be in public right now. Will you come home with me?"

Something on my face must have betrayed my lingering wariness, because he pressed his lips to my forehead and murmured, "It won't be like the hotel, I promise. My mother's the only woman who's ever been to my place, aside from the housekeeper and staff."

"This is stupid," I muttered. "I'm being stupid."

"No." He brushed the hair back from my face and bent closer to whisper in my ear. "If you'd taken me to a place you reserved for fucking other men, I would've lost it."

The waiter returned and we pulled apart. "Should I get you a menu, sir?"

"That won't be necessary." Gideon dug his wallet out of his back pocket and handed over his credit card. "We're leaving."

We took a cab to Gideon's place and he held on to my hand the entire time. I shouldn't have been so nervous riding a private elevator up to a penthouse apartment on Fifth Avenue. The sight of high ceilings and prewar architecture wasn't new to me, and really, it was all to be expected when dating a man who seemed to own damn near everything. And the coveted view of Central Park . . . well, of course he'd have one.

But Gideon's tension was palpable, and it made me realize that this was a big deal to *him.* When the elevator opened directly into his apartment's marbled entry foyer, his grip on my hand tightened before he released me. He unlocked the double-door entrance to usher me inside, and I could feel his anxiety as he watched for my reaction.

Gideon's home was as beautiful as the

man himself. It was so very different from his office, which was sleek, modern, and cool. His private space was warm and sumptuous, filled with antiques and art anchored by gorgeous Aubusson rugs laid over gleaming hardwood floors.

"It's . . . amazing," I said softly, feeling privileged to see it. It was a glimpse into the private Gideon I was desperate to know, and it was stunning.

"Come in." He tugged me deeper into the apartment. "I want you to sleep here tonight."

"I don't have clothes and stuff . . ."

"All you need is the toothbrush in your purse. We can run by your place in the morning for the rest. I promise to get you to work on time." He pulled me into him and set his chin on the crown of my head. "I'd really like you to stay, Eva. I don't blame you for wanting to get out of the hotel, but finding you gone scared the hell out of me. I need to hang on to you for a while."

"I need to be held." I pushed my hands under the back of his T-shirt to caress the silken hardness of his bare back. "I could also use a shower."

With his nose in my hair, he inhaled deeply. "I like you smelling like me."

But he led me through the living room and down a hall to his bedroom.

"Wow," I breathed when he flicked on the light. A massive sleigh bed dominated the space, the wood dark — which he seemed to prefer — and the linens a soft cream. The rest of the furnishings matched the bed and the accents were brushed gold. It was a warm, masculine space with no art on the walls to detract from the serene night view of Central Park and the magnificent residential buildings on the other side. My side of Manhattan.

"The bathroom's in here."

As I took in the vanity, which appeared to have been made out of an antique claw-footed walnut cabinet, he pulled towels out of a companion armoire and set them out for me, moving with that confident, sensual grace I admired so much. Seeing him in his home, dressed so casually, touched me. Knowing I was the only woman to have this experience with him affected me even more. I felt like I was seeing him more naked now than I ever had. "Thank you."

He glanced at me and seemed to understand that I was talking about more than the towels. His stare burned through me. "It feels good to have you here."

"I have no idea how I ended up like this,

with you." But I really, really liked it.

"Does it matter?" Gideon came to me, tilting my chin up to press a kiss to the tip of my nose. "I'll lay out a T-shirt for you on the bed. Caviar and vodka sound good to you?"

"Well . . . that's quite a step up from pizza."

He smiled. "Petrossian's Ossetra."

"I stand corrected." I smiled back. "Several hundred steps up."

I showered and dressed in the oversized Cross Industries shirt he laid out for me; then I called Cary to tell him I'd be out all night and give him a brief rundown about the hotel incident.

He whistled. "I'm not even sure what to say about that."

A speechless Cary Taylor spoke volumes.

I joined Gideon in the living room, and we sat on the floor at the coffee table to eat the prized caviar with mini toast and crème fraîche. We watched a rerun of a New York–set police procedural that just happened to include a scene filmed on the street in front of the Crossfire.

"I think it'd be cool to see a building I owned on TV like that," I said.

"It's not bad, if they don't close off the street for hours to film."

I bumped shoulders with him. "Pessimist."

We crawled into Gideon's bed at ten thirty and watched the last half of a show while curled up together. Sexual tension crackled in the air between us, but he didn't make any overtures so I didn't either. I suspected he was still trying to make amends for the hotel, trying to prove that he wanted to spend time with me not "actively fucking."

It worked. As much as I desired him, it felt good just hanging out together.

He slept in the nude, which was fabulous for me to cuddle up against. I tossed one leg over his, wrapped an arm around his waist, and rested my cheek over his heart. I don't remember the ending of the show, so I suppose I fell asleep before it was over.

When I woke it was still dark in the room and I'd rolled to the far side of my half of the bed. I sat up to see the digital clock face on Gideon's nightstand and found it was barely three in the morning. I usually slept straight through the night and thought maybe the strange surroundings were keeping me from sleeping deeply; then Gideon moaned and shifted restlessly, and I realized what had disturbed me. The sound he made was pained, his subsequent hiss of breath tormented.

"Don't touch me," he whispered harshly.

"Get your fucking hands off me!"

I froze, my heart racing. His words sliced through the dark, filled with fury.

"You sick bastard." He writhed, his legs kicking at the covers. His back arched on a groan that sounded perversely erotic. "Don't. Ah, Christ . . . It *hurts.*"

He strained, his body twisting. I couldn't bear it.

"Gideon." Because Cary had nightmares sometimes, I knew better than to touch a man in the throes of one. Instead, I knelt on my side of the bed and called his name. "Gideon, wake up."

Stilling abruptly, he fell to his back, tense and expectant. His chest heaved with panting breaths. His cock was hard and lay heavily along his belly.

I spoke firmly, although my heart was breaking. "Gideon. You're dreaming. Come back to me."

He deflated into the mattress. "Eva . . . ?"

"I'm here." Shifting, I moved out of the way of the moonlight but saw no luminous glitter that would tell me his eyes were open. "Are you awake?"

His breathing began to slow, but he didn't speak. His hands were fisted in the bottom sheet. I pulled the shirt I was wearing over my head and dropped it on the bed. I sidled closer, reaching out with a tentative hand to touch his arm. When he didn't move, I caressed him, my fingertips sliding gently over the hard muscle of his biceps.

"Gideon?"

He jerked awake. "What? What is it?"

I sat back on my heels with my hands on my thighs. I saw him blink at me, then shove both hands through his hair. I could feel the nightmare clinging to him, could sense it in the rigidness of his body.

"What's wrong?" he asked gruffly, pushing up onto one elbow. "You okay?"

"I want you." I stretched out against him, aligning my bare body to his. Pressing my face into his damp throat, I sucked gently on his salty skin. I knew from my own nightmares that being held and loved could push the specters back into the closet for a little while.

His arms came around me, his hands running up and down the curve of my spine. I felt him let go of the dream with a long, deep sigh.

Pushing him to his back, I climbed over him and sealed my mouth over his. His erection was notched between the lips of my sex and I rocked against him. The feel of his hands in my hair, holding me to take control of the kiss, quickly made me wet and ready. Fire licked just beneath my skin. I stroked my clit up and down his thick length, using him to masturbate until he made a rough sound of desire and rolled to put me beneath him.

"I don't have any condoms in the house," he murmured before wrapping his lips around my nipple and sucking gently.

I loved that he wasn't prepared. This wasn't his fuck pad; this was his home and I was the only lover he'd brought into it. "I know you mentioned swapping bills of health when we talked about birth control, and that's the responsible way to go, but —"

"I trust you." He lifted his head, looking at me in the faint light of the moon. Kneeing my legs open, he pushed the first bare inch inside me. He was scorching hot and silky soft.

"Eva," he breathed, clutching me tightly to him. "I've never . . . Christ, you feel so good. I'm so glad you're here."

I tugged his lips down to mine and kissed him. "Me, too."

I woke the way I'd fallen asleep, with Gideon on top of me and inside me. His gaze was heavy-lidded with desire as I rose from unconsciousness into heated pleasure. His hair hung around his shoulders and face, looking even sexier for being sleep-tousled. But best of all, there were no shadows in his gorgeous eyes, nothing lingering from the pain that haunted his dreams.

"I hope you don't mind," he murmured with a wicked grin, sliding in and out. "You're warm and soft. I can't help but want you."

I stretched my arms over my head and arched my back, pressing my breasts into his chest. Through the slender arch-topped windows, I saw the soft light of dawn filling the sky. "Umm . . . I could get used to waking up like this."

"That was my thought at three this morning." He rolled his hips and sank deep into me. "I thought I'd return the favor."

My body revved to life, my pulse quickening. "Yes, please."

Cary was gone when we got to my apartment; he'd left a note behind to tell me he was on a job but would be back in plenty of time for pizza with Trey. Since I'd been too upset to enjoy my pie the night before, I was ready to try again when I was having a good time.

"I have a business dinner tonight," Gideon said, leaning over my shoulder to read.

"I was hoping you'd come with me and make it bearable."

"I can't bail out on Cary," I said apologetically, turning to face him. "Chicks before dicks and all that."

His mouth twitched and he caged me to the breakfast bar. He was dressed for work in a suit I'd picked out, a graphite gray Prada with a soft sheen. His tie was the blue one that matched his eyes, and as I'd lain on his bed and watched him dress, I'd had to fight the urge to take it all off him. "Cary isn't a chick. But I get the point. I want to see you tonight. Can I come over after the dinner and stay the night?"

Heated anticipation rushed through me. I smoothed my hands over his vest, feeling like I had a special secret because I knew exactly what he looked like without his clothes on. "I'd love it if you did."

"Good." He gave a satisfied nod. "I'll make us coffee, while you get dressed."

"The beans are in the freezer. The grinder's next to the coffeepot." I pointed. "And I like lots of milk and a little sweetener."

When I came out twenty minutes later, Gideon grabbed two travel mugs of coffee off the breakfast bar and we headed down to the lobby. Paul hustled us out the front door and into the backseat of Gideon's waiting Bentley SUV.

As Gideon's driver pulled into traffic, Gideon checked me out and said, "You're definitely trying to kill me. Are you wearing the garters again?"

Pulling the hem of my skirt up, I showed him where the top of my black silk stockings hooked to my black lace garter belt.

His muttered curse made me smile. I'd chosen a black short-sleeved silk turtleneck sweater paired with a decently short pleated skirt in lipstick red and heeled Mary Janes. Because Cary hadn't been around to manage something fancy with my hair, I'd pulled it back in a ponytail. "You like?"

"I'm hard." His voice was husky, and he adjusted himself in his trousers. "How the hell am I going to get through the day thinking about you dressed like that?"

"There's always lunch," I suggested, fantasizing about a nooner on Gideon's office couch.

"I have a business lunch today. I'd reschedule, if I hadn't moved it already yesterday."

"You rescheduled an appointment for me? I'm flattered."

He reached over and brushed his fingertips over my cheek, a now-habitual gesture of affection that was tender and fiercely intimate. I was coming to depend on receiving those touches.

I leaned my cheek into his palm. "Can you carve fifteen minutes out of your day for me?"

"I'll manage it."

"Call me when you know the time."

Taking a deep breath, I dug into my bag and wrapped my hand around a gift I wasn't sure he'd want, but I couldn't get the memory of his nightmare out of my head. I hoped that what I had for him would remind him of me and three A.M. sex, and help him cope. "I have something. I thought . . ."

It suddenly seemed conceited to give him what I'd brought.

He frowned. "What's wrong?"

"Nothing. It's just . . ." I exhaled in a rush. "Listen, I have something for you, but I just realized it's one of those gifts — well, it's not really a gift. I'm already thinking it's not appropriate and —"

He thrust out his hand. "Give it to me."

"You can totally decide not to take it —"

"Shut up, Eva." He crooked his fingers. "Give it to me."

I pulled it out of my bag and handed it over.

Gideon stared down at the framed photograph in complete silence. It was a novelty frame depicting die-cut images of things relating to graduation, including a digital clock face that read 3:00 A.M. The picture was of me posing on Coronado Beach in a coral bikini with a big floppy straw hat — I was tanned, happy, and blowing a kiss to Cary, who'd playacted the role of a high-fashion photographer by calling out ridiculous encouragements. *Beautiful, dahling. Show me sassy. Show me sexy. Brilliant. Show me catty . . . rawr . . .*

Embarrassed, I squirmed a little on the seat. "Like I said, you don't have to keep —"

"I —" He cleared his throat. "Thank you, Eva."

"Ah, well . . ." I was grateful to see the Crossfire outside my window. I jumped out quickly when the driver pulled over and ran my hands over my skirt, feeling self-conscious. "If you want, I can hang on to it until later."

Gideon shut the door of the Bentley and shook his head. "It's mine. You're not taking it back."

He linked our fingers together and gestured toward the revolving door with the hand holding the frame. I warmed when I realized he intended to take my picture into work with him.

241

■ ■ ■ ■

One of the fun things about the ad business was that no day was ever the same as the one before it. I was hopping all morning and was just beginning to contemplate what to do about lunch when my phone rang. "Mark Garrity's office, Eva Tramell speaking."

"I've got news," Cary said by way of greeting.

"What?" I could tell by his voice that it was good news, whatever it was.

"I landed a Grey Isles campaign."

"Oh my God! Cary, that's awesome! I love their jeans."

"What are you doing for lunch?"

I grinned. "Celebrating with you. Can you be here at noon?"

"I'm already on my way."

I hung up and rocked back in my chair, so thrilled for Cary I felt like dancing. Needing something to do to kill the fifteen minutes remaining before my lunch break, I checked my inbox again and found a Google alert digest for Gideon's name. More than thirty mentions, in just one day.

I opened the e-mail and freaked out a little at the numerous "mystery woman" headlines. I clicked on the first link and found myself landing on a gossip blog.

There, in living color, was a photo of Gideon kissing me senseless on the sidewalk outside his gym. The accompanying article was short and to the point:

Gideon Cross, New York's most eligible bachelor since John F. Kennedy Jr., was spotted yesterday in a passionate public embrace. A source at Cross Industries identified the lucky mystery woman as socialite Eva Tramell, daughter of multimillionaire Richard Stanton and his wife, Monica. When queried about the nature of the relationship between Cross and Tramell, the source confirmed that Miss Tramell is "the significant woman" in the mogul's life at present. We imagine hearts are breaking across the country this morning.

"Oh, crap," I breathed.

11

I quickly clicked through other links in the digest to find the same picture with similar captions and articles. Alarmed, I sat back and thought about what this meant. If one kiss was headline news, what chance would Gideon and I have to make a relationship work?

My hands weren't quite steady as I closed the browser tabs. I hadn't considered the press coverage, but I should have. "Damn it."

Anonymity was my friend. It protected me from my past. It protected my family from embarrassment, and Gideon, too. I didn't even have any social networking accounts, so people who weren't actively in my life couldn't find me.

A thin, invisible wall between me and exposure was gone.

"Hell," I breathed, finding myself in a painful situation I could have avoided if I'd dedicated any of my brain cells to something other than Gideon.

There was also *his* reaction to this mess to consider. . . . I cringed inwardly just thinking about it. And my mother. It wouldn't be long before she was calling and blowing everything out of —

"Shit." Remembering that she didn't have my new cell number, I picked up my desk phone and called my other voice mail to see if she'd already tried to reach me. I winced when I heard that my mailbox was full.

I hung up and grabbed my purse, then headed off to lunch, knowing Cary would help me put it all in perspective. I was so flustered when I reached the lobby level that I rushed out of the elevator with my only thought being to find my roommate. When I spotted him, I didn't take note of anyone else until Gideon sidestepped smoothly in front of me and blocked my path.

"Eva." He frowned down at me. Cupping my elbow, he turned me slightly around. That was when I saw the two women and a man who'd hidden him from my view.

I managed to find a smile for them. "Hello."

Gideon introduced me to his lunch dates. Then he excused us and tugged me off to the side. "What's wrong? You're upset."

"It's all over the place," I whispered. "A picture of us together."

He nodded. "I've seen it."

I blinked up at him, confused at his nonchalance. "You're okay with it?"

"Why wouldn't I be? For once, they're reporting the truth."

A sneaking suspicion niggled at me. "You planned it. You planted the story."

"Not entirely true," he said smoothly. "The photographer happened to be there. I just gave him a picture worth printing, and told PR to make it clear who you are and what you are to me."

"Why? Why would you do that?"

"You have your way of dealing with jealousy and I have mine. We're both off the market and now everyone knows it. Why is that a problem for you?"

"I was worried about your reaction, but there's more . . . There are things you don't know and I —" I took a deep, shaky breath. "It can't be that way between us, Gideon. We can't be public. I don't want — Damn it. I'll embarrass you."

"You couldn't. It's not possible." He brushed a loose lock of hair off my face. "Can we talk about this later? If you need me —"

"No, it's okay. Go."

Cary came over. Dressed in baggy black cargo pants and a V-neck white undershirt, he still managed to look expensive. "Everything all right?"

"Hi, Cary. Everything's fine." Gideon squeezed my hand. "Enjoy your lunch and don't worry."

He could say that because he didn't know better.

And I didn't know whether he'd still want me once he did.

Cary faced me as Gideon walked away. "Worry about what? What's wrong?"

"Everything." I sighed. "Let's get out of here, and I'll tell you over lunch."

"Well," Cary murmured, looking at the link I'd forwarded from my smartphone to his. "That's some kiss. The dip was a great touch. He couldn't look more into you if he tried."

"That's the thing." I took another big gulp of water. "He did try."

He shoved his phone into his pocket. "Last week you kept shooting him down for only wanting your vagina. This week he's publicizing that he's in a committed, passionate relationship with you, and you're still unhappy. I'm starting to feel bad for the guy. He can't win for trying."

That stung. "Reporters are going to dig, Cary, and they're going to find dirt. And since it's juicy dirt, they're going to splash it all over hell and back, and it's going to embarrass Gideon."

"Baby girl." He set his hand over mine. "Stanton buried all that."

Stanton. I straightened. I hadn't thought of my stepfather. He'd see the disaster coming and keep a lid on it because he knew what the revelation would do to my mother. Still . . . "I'll have to talk to Gideon about it. He has a right to be warned."

Just the thought of that conversation made me miserable.

Cary knew how my brain worked. "If you think he's going to cut and run, I think you're wrong. He looks at you like you're the only person in the room."

I poked at my tuna Caesar salad. "He's got a few demons of his own. Nightmares. He's closed himself off, I think, because of whatever's eating at him."

"But he's let you in."

And he'd already shown hints of how possessive he could be about that connection. I accepted that because it was a flaw I shared, but still . . .

"You're analyzing this to death, Eva," Cary said. "You're thinking the way he feels about you has to be a fluke or a mistake. Someone like him couldn't really be into you for your big heart and sharp mind, right?"

"My self-esteem isn't *that* bad," I protested.

He took a sip of his champagne. "Isn't it? So tell me something *you* think he likes about you that doesn't have to do with sex or codependency."

I thought about it and came up empty, which made me scowl.

"Right," he went on with a nod. "And if Cross is anywhere near as messed up as we are, he's thinking the same thing in reverse, wondering what a hot babe like you sees in a guy like him. You've got money, so what has he got going for him besides being a stud who keeps screwing up?"

Sitting back in my chair, I absorbed everything he'd said. "Cary, I love you madly."

He grinned. "Back atcha, sweets. My advice, for what it's worth? Couples therapy. It's always been my plan to get into it when I find the one I want to settle down with. And try to have fun with him. You've got to have as many good times as bad, or it all becomes too painful and too much work."

I reached over and squeezed his hand.

"Thank you."

"For what?" He shrugged off my gratitude with an elegant wave of his hand. "It's easy to pick apart someone else's life. You know I couldn't get through my rough spots without you."

"Which you don't have any of now," I pointed out, shifting the focus to him. "You're about to be splashed across a Times Square billboard. You won't be my secret any longer. Should we upgrade dinner from pizza to something more worthy of the occasion? How about we haul out that case of Cristal Stanton gave us?"

"Now you're talking."

"Movies? Anything in particular you want to watch?"

"Whatever you want. I wouldn't want to screw with your big-dumb-blow-'em-up movie genius."

I grinned, feeling better as I'd known I would after an hour with Cary. "You'll let me know if I'm too dense to figure out when you and Trey want to be alone."

"Ha! Don't worry about that. Your tempestuous love life is making me feel dull and boring. I could use a hot, sweaty bang with my own stud."

"You just had a maintenance closet romp a couple days ago!"

He sighed. "I'd nearly forgotten. How sad is that?"

"It isn't when your eyes are laughing."

I'd just gotten back to my desk when I checked my smartphone and found a text from Gideon letting me know he had fifteen minutes to spare at quarter to three. I nursed a secret rush of anticipation for the next hour and a half, having decided to take Cary's advice and have a little fun. Gideon and I would have to wade through the ugliness of my past soon enough, but for now, I could give us both something to smile about.

I texted him just before I left, letting him know I was on my way. Considering the time constraints, we couldn't waste a minute. Gideon must have felt the same way, because I found Scott waiting for me at reception when I reached the Cross Industries waiting area. He walked me back after the receptionist buzzed me in.

"How's your day been?" I asked him.

He smiled. "Great so far. Yours?"

I smiled back. "I've had worse."

Gideon was on the phone when I entered his office. His tone was clipped and impatient as he told the person on the other end of the line that they should be able to manage the job without him having to oversee it personally.

He held up one finger to me to tell me he'd be another minute. I responded by blowing a big bubble with the gum I was chewing and popping it loudly.

His brows shot up, and he hit the buttons to close the doors and frost the glass wall.

Grinning, I sauntered over to his desk and hopped onto it, curling my fingers around the lip and swinging my legs. He popped the next bubble I blew with a quick jab of his finger. I pouted prettily.

"Deal with it," he said with quiet authority to whoever was on the phone. "It'll be next week before I can get out there, and waiting will set us back further. Stop talking. I have something time-sensitive on my desk and you're keeping me away from it. I guarantee that's not improving my disposition. Fix what needs fixing and report back to me tomorrow."

He returned the phone to its cradle with suppressed violence. "Eva —"

I held up one hand to cut him off and wrapped my gum in a Postit I took from a dispenser on his desk. "Before you reprimand me, Mr. Cross, I want to say that when we reached an impasse in our merger discussions at the hotel yesterday, I shouldn't have walked out. It didn't help to resolve the situation. And I know I didn't react very well to the PR issue with the photo. But still . . . Even though I've been a naughty secretary, I think I should be given another chance to excel."

His gaze narrowed as he studied me, assessing and reevaluating the situation on the fly. "Did I ask for your opinion on the appropriate action to take, Miss Tramell?"

I shook my head and looked up at him from beneath my lashes. I could see the lingering frustration from his phone call falling away from him, replaced by his growing interest and arousal.

Hopping down from the desk, I sidled closer and smoothed his immaculate tie with both hands. "Can't we work something out? I do possess a wide variety of useful skills."

He caught me by the hips. "Which is one of the many reasons you're the only woman I've ever considered for the position."

Warmth flowed through me at his words. Boldly cupping his cock in my hand, I fondled him through his slacks. "Maybe I should reapply myself to my duties? I could demonstrate some of the ways I'm uniquely qualified to assist you."

Gideon hardened with delectable swiftness. "Such initiative, Miss Tramell. But my next meeting is less than ten minutes away. Also, I'm not accustomed to exploring job enrichment opportunities in my office."

I freed the button of his fly and lowered his zipper. With my lips to his jaw, I whispered, "If you think there's anywhere I won't make you come, you'll have to revisit and revise."

"Eva," he breathed, his eyes hot and tender. He cupped my throat, his thumbs brushing over my jaw. "You're unraveling me. Do you know that? Are you doing it on purpose?"

I reached inside his boxer briefs and wrapped my hands around him, offering up my lips for a kiss. He obliged me, taking my mouth with a fierceness that left me breathless.

"I want you," he growled.

I sank to my knees on the carpeted floor, pulling his pants down enough to give me the access I needed.

He exhaled harshly. "Eva, what are you —"

My lips flowed over the wide crown. He reached back for the edge of his desk, his hands curling around the lip with white-knuckled force. I held him with both hands and mouthed the plush head, sucking gently.

The softness of his skin and his uniquely appealing scent made me moan. I felt the vibration ripple through his entire body and heard a rough sound rumble in his chest.

Gideon touched my cheek. "Lick it."

Aroused by the command, I fluttered my tongue across the underside and shivered with delight when he rewarded me with a hot burst of pre-cum. Fisting the root of him with one hand, I hollowed my cheeks and drew rhythmically, hoping for more.

I wished I had the time to make it last. Drive him crazy . . .

He made a sound filled with the sweetest agony. "God, Eva . . . your mouth. Keep sucking. Like that . . . hard and deep."

I was so turned on by his pleasure I squirmed. His hands pushed into my bound hair, pulling and tugging at the roots. I loved how he started out with tenderness, then grew rougher as the lust he felt for me overwhelmed his control.

The soft bite of pain made me hungrier, greedier. My head bobbed as I pleasured him, jacking him with one hand while I sucked and stroked the crest with my mouth. Heavy veins coursed the length of his cock, and I slid the flat of my tongue along them, tilting my head to find and caress each one.

He swelled, growing thicker and longer. My knees were uncomfortable, but I didn't care; my gaze was riveted to Gideon as his head fell back and he fought for breath.

"Eva, you suck me so good." He held my head still and took over. Thrusting his hips. Fucking my mouth. Stripped to a level of base need where only the race to orgasm mattered.

The thought made me crazed, the image in my mind of how we must look: Gideon in all his urbane sophistication, standing at the desk where he ruled an empire, stroking his big cock in and out of my greedy mouth. I gripped his straining thighs in both hands, frantically working my lips and tongue, desperate for his climax. His balls were heavy and big, an audacious display of his powerful virility. I cupped them, rolling them gently, feeling them tighten and draw up.

"Ah, *Eva.*" His voice was a guttural rasp. His grip tightened in my hair. "You're making me come."

The first spurt of semen was so thick, I struggled to swallow. Mindless in his pleasure, Gideon was thrusting against the back of my throat, his cock throbbing with every wrenching pulse into my mouth. My eyes watered and my lungs burned, but still I pumped my fists, milking him. His entire body shuddered as I took everything he had. The sounds he made and the muttered, breathless praise were the most gratifying I'd ever heard.

I licked him clean, marveling at how he didn't fully soften even after an explosive orgasm. He was still capable of fucking me senseless and more than willing to, I knew. But there was no time and I was happy about that. I wanted to do this for him. For us. For me, really, because I needed to know I could indulge in a selfless sexual act without feeling taken advantage of.

"I have to go," I murmured, standing and pressing my lips to his. "I hope the rest of your day is awesome, and your business dinner tonight, too."

I started to move away, but he caught my wrist, his gaze on the clock readout on his desk phone. I noticed my picture then, sitting in a place of prominence where he'd see it all day.

"Eva . . . Damn it. Wait."

I frowned at his tone, which sounded anxious. Frustrated.

He quickly restored his appearance, tucking himself back into his boxer briefs and straightening the tail of his shirt so he could fasten his pants. There was something sweet in watching him pull himself back together, restoring the façade he wore for the world while I knew at least a little of the man beneath it.

Tugging me close, Gideon pressed his lips to my brow. His hands moved through my hair to unclip my tortoise barrette. "I didn't get you off."

"No need." I loved the feel of his hands on my scalp. "That rocked just the way it was."

He was overly focused on fixing my hair, his cheeks flushed from his orgasm. "I know you need an even exchange," he argued gruffly. "I can't let you leave feeling like I used you."

A bittersweet tenderness pierced me. He'd listened. He cared.

I cupped his face in my hands. "You did use me, with my permission, and it was seriously hot. I wanted to give you this, Gideon. Remember? I warned you. I wanted you to have this memory of me."

His eyes widened with alarm. "Why the fuck do I need memories when I have you? Eva, if this is about the photo —"

"Shut up and enjoy the high." We didn't have the time to get into the photo issue now, and I didn't want to. It was going to ruin everything. "If we'd had an hour, I still wouldn't let you get me off. I'm not keeping score with you, ace. And honestly, you're the first guy I can say that to. Now, I have to go. You have to go."

I started away again, but he caught me back.

Scott's voice came through the speaker. "Excuse me, Mr. Cross. But your three o'clock is here."

"It's *okay,* Gideon," I assured him. "You're coming over tonight, right?"

"Nothing could keep me away."

I shoved up onto my tiptoes and kissed his cheek. "We'll talk then."

After work, I took the stairs down to the ground floor to feel less guilty about skipping the gym and seriously regretted it by the time I reached the lobby. Lack of sleep from the night before had left me wiped out. I was contemplating taking the subway rather than walking when I saw Gideon's Bentley at the curb. When the driver got out and greeted me by name, I halted abruptly, surprised.

"Mr. Cross asked that I take you home," he said, looking smart in his black suit and chauffeur hat. He was an older gentleman with graying red hair, pale blue eyes, and the softest of cultured accents.

Considering how much my legs ached, I was grateful for the offer. "Thank you — I'm sorry, what was your name?"

"Angus, Miss Tramell."

How had I not remembered that? The name was so cool, it made me smile. "Thank you, Angus."

He tipped his hat. "My pleasure."

I slid through the back door he opened for me, and as I settled into the seat, I caught a glimpse of the handgun he wore in a shoulder holster beneath his jacket. It appeared that Angus, like Clancy, was both bodyguard and driver.

We pulled away from the curb and I asked, "How long have you been working for Mr. Cross, Angus?"

"Eight years now."

"Quite a while."

"I've known him longer than that," he volunteered, catching my gaze in the rearview mirror. "I drove him to school when he was a boy. He hired me away from Mr. Vidal when the time came."

Once again, I tried to picture Gideon as a child. No doubt he'd been beautiful and charismatic even then.

Had he enjoyed "normal" sexual relationships when he was a teenager? I couldn't imagine that women weren't throwing themselves at him even then. And as innately sexual as he was, I imagined he'd been a horny teen.

Digging in my purse, I pulled out my keys and leaned forward to set them on the front passenger seat. "Can you see that Gideon gets those? He's supposed to come over after whatever it is he's doing tonight, and depending on how late that is, I might not hear him knock."

"Of course."

Paul opened the door for me when we arrived at my apartment and he greeted Angus by name, reminding me that Gideon owned the building. I waved to both men, told the front desk Gideon would be coming over later, and then took myself upstairs. Cary's raised brows when he opened the door to me made me laugh.

"Gideon's coming over later," I explained, "but I'm feeling so hammered right now I may not stay up long. So I gave him my keys to let himself in. Did you order already?"

"I did. And I tossed a few bottles of Cristal in the wine fridge."

"You're the best." I shoved my bag at him.

I showered and called my mom from the phone in my room, wincing at her strident, "I have been trying to reach you *for days*!"

"Mom, if it's about Gideon Cross —"

"Well, of course, it's partly about him! For goodness' sake, Eva. You're being called the significant woman in his life. How could I not want to talk about that?"

"Mom —"

"But there's also the appointment you asked me to make with Dr. Petersen." The note of smug amusement in her voice made me smile. "We're scheduled to meet with him Thursday at six o'clock in the evening. I hope that works for you. He doesn't do many evening appointments."

I plopped backward onto my bed with a sigh. I'd been so distracted by work and Gideon that the appointment had slipped my mind. "Thursday at six will be fine. Thank you."

"Now, then. Tell me about Cross . . ."

When I emerged from my bedroom dressed in jersey pants and a San Diego State University sweatshirt, I found Trey seated with Cary in the living room. Both men stood when I came in, and Trey gifted me with an open, friendly smile.

"I'm sorry I look so ragged," I said sheepishly, running my fingers through my damp ponytail. "Taking the stairs at work almost killed me today."

"Elevator take the day off?" he asked.

"Nope. My brain did. What the hell was I

thinking?" Spending the night with Gideon was enough of a workout.

The doorbell rang and Cary went to get it while I headed into the kitchen for the Cristal. I joined him at the breakfast bar as he signed the credit card receipt, and the look in his eyes when he glanced at Trey had me hiding a smile.

There were a lot of those looks going back and forth between the two men as the evening progressed. And I had to agree with Cary that Trey was a hottie. Dressed in distressed jeans, matching vest, and a long-sleeved shirt, the aspiring veterinarian looked casual but well put together. He was very different personality-wise from the type of guy Cary usually dated. Trey seemed more grounded; not quite somber, but definitely not flighty. I thought he'd be a good influence on Cary, if they stayed together long enough.

The three of us made it through two bottles of Cristal and two pizzas between us, plus all of *Demolition Man* before I called it a night. I urged Trey to stay for *Driven* to round out the Stallone mini-marathon; then I went to my room and changed into a sexy black baby doll I'd been given as part of a bridesmaid gift bag — sans the matching panties.

Leaving a candle burning for Gideon, I crashed.

I woke to darkness and the scent of Gideon's skin, the lights and sounds of the city shut out by soundproofed windows and blackout drapes.

Gideon slid over me, a moving shadow, his bare skin cool to the touch. His mouth slanted over mine, kissing me slowly and deeply, tasting of mint and his own unique flavor. My hands slid down his sleekly muscular back, my legs parting so he could settle comfortably between them. The weight of him against me made my heart sigh and my blood warm with desire.

"Well, hello to you, too," I said breathlessly when he let me up for air.

"You'll come with me next time," he murmured in that sexy and decadent voice, nibbling at my throat.

"Will I?" I teased.

He reached down and cupped my butt in his hand, squeezing and lifting me into a deft roll of his hips. "Yes. I missed you, Eva."

I ran my fingers through his hair, wishing I could see him. "You haven't known me long enough to miss me."

"Shows how much you know," Gideon scoffed, sliding downward and nuzzling between my breasts.

I gasped as his mouth covered my nipple and sucked through the satin, deep pulls that echoed in the clenching of my core. He moved to my other breast, his hand pushing up the hem of my baby doll. I arched into him, lost to the magic of his mouth as it moved over my body, his tongue dipping into my navel, then sliding lower.

"And you missed me, too," he purred with masculine satisfaction, the tip of his middle finger rimming my cleft. "You're swollen and wet for me."

He pulled my legs over his shoulders and licked between my folds, soft and provocative laps of hot velvet against my sensitive flesh. My hands fisted in the sheet, my chest heaving as he circled my clit with the tip of his tongue, then nudged the hypersensitive knot of nerves. I keened, my hips moving restlessly into the devious torment, my muscles tightening with the clawing need to come.

The light, teasing flutters were driving me insane, giving me just enough to make me writhe but not enough to get me off. "Gideon, please."

"Not yet."

He tortured me, coaxing my body to the brink of orgasm, and then letting me slide back down. Over and over. Until sweat misted my skin and my heart felt like it would burst. His tongue was tireless and diabolical, cleverly focusing on my clit until a single stroke would set me off, then moving lower to thrust into me. The soft, shallow plunges were maddening, the flickering against the nerve-laden tissues making me desperate enough to beg shamelessly.

"Please, Gideon . . . let me come . . . I need to come, please."

"Shh, angel . . . I'll take care of you."

He finished me with a tenderness that made the orgasm roll through me like a crashing wave, building and swelling and spreading through me in a warm rush of pleasure.

He threaded his fingers with mine when he came over me again, restraining my arms. The head of his cock aligned with the slick entrance of my body and he pushed inexorably into me. I moaned, shifting to accommodate the heavy surge of his penis.

Gideon's breath gusted hard and humid against my throat, his big frame trembling as he slid carefully inside me. "You're so soft and warm. Mine, Eva. You're mine."

I wrapped my legs around his hips, welcoming him deeper, feeling his buttocks flex and release against my calves as he demonstrated to my body that it would indeed take his thick length all the way to the root.

With our hands linked, he took my mouth and began to move, gliding in and out with languid skill, the tempo precise and relentless yet smooth and easy. I felt every rock-hard inch of him, felt the unmistakable reiteration that every inch of me was his to possess. He drove the message home repeatedly until I was gasping against his mouth, thrashing restlessly beneath him, my hands bloodless from the strength of my grip on his.

He spoke heated praise and encouragement, telling me how beautiful I was . . . how perfect I felt to him . . . how he'd never stop . . . couldn't stop. I came with a sharp cry of relief, vibrating with the ecstasy of it, and he was right there with me. His pace quickened for several slamming thrusts; then he climaxed with a hiss of my name, spilling into me.

I sank lax into the mattress, sweaty and boneless and replete.

"I'm not done," he whispered darkly, adjusting his knees to increase the force of his thrusts. The pace remained expertly measured, each plunge staking a claim — *your body exists to serve me.*

Biting my lip, I fought back the sounds of

helpless pleasure that might've broken the tranquillity of the night . . . and betrayed the frightening depths of emotion I was beginning to feel for Gideon Cross.

12

Gideon found me in the shower the next morning. He strode into the master bath gloriously nude, walking with that sleek, confident grace I'd admired from the beginning. Watching the flexing of his muscles as he moved, I didn't even pretend not to stare at the magnificent package between his legs.

Despite the heat of the water, my nipples beaded tight and goose bumps raced across my skin.

His knowing smile as he joined me told me he knew exactly what kind of effect he had on me. I retaliated by running soapy hands all over his godlike body, then sitting on the bench and sucking him off with such enthusiasm he had to support himself with both palms pressed flat against the tile.

His raw, raspy instructions echoed in my mind the entire time I dressed for work, which I did quickly — before he had a chance to finish his shower and fuck the hell out of me as he'd threatened to just before spurting fiercely down my throat.

He'd had no nightmares during the night. Sex as a sedative seemed to be working, and I was extremely grateful for that.

"I hope you don't think you've gotten away," he said when he prowled after me into the kitchen. Immaculately dressed in a black pinstriped suit, he accepted the cup of coffee I handed him and gave me a look that promised all sorts of wicked things. I saw him in his supremely civilized attire and thought of the insatiable male who'd slipped into my bed during the night. My blood quickened. I was sore, my muscles thrumming with remembered pleasure, and I was still thinking about more.

"Keep looking at me like that," he warned, leaning casually into the counter and sipping his coffee. "See what happens."

"I'm going to lose my job over you."

"I'd give you another one."

I snorted. "As what? Your sex slave?"

"What a provocative suggestion. Let's discuss."

"Fiend," I muttered, rinsing out my mug in the sink and putting it in the dishwasher. "Ready? For *work*?"

He finished his coffee and I held out my hand for his mug, but he bypassed me and rinsed it out himself. Another mortal task that made him seem accessible, less of a fantasy I'd never have a chance of holding on to.

He faced me. "I want to take you out to dinner tonight, and then take you home to my bed."

"I don't want you to burn out on me, Gideon." He was a man used to being alone, a man who hadn't had a meaningful physical relationship in a long time, if ever. How long before his flight instincts kicked in? Besides, we really needed to stay out of the public eye as a couple. . . .

"Don't make excuses." His features hardened. "You don't get to decide I can't do this."

I kicked myself for offending him. He was trying and I needed to make sure he got credit for that, not discouragement. "That's not what I meant. I just don't want to crowd you. Plus we still need to —"

"Eva." He sighed, the hard tension leaving him with that frustrated exhalation. "You have to trust me. I'm trusting you. I've had to or we wouldn't be here now."

Okay. I nodded, swallowing hard. "Dinner and your place it is, then. I honestly can't wait."

Gideon's words about trust lingered in my mind all morning, which was a good thing when the Google alert digest hit my inbox.

There was more than one photo this time around. Each article and blog post had several shots of me and Cary hugging good-bye outside the restaurant where we'd had lunch the day before. The captions speculated on the nature of our relationship, and some noted that we lived together. Others suggested I was reeling in "billionaire playboy Cross" while keeping my up-and-coming model boyfriend on the side.

The reason for the publicity became apparent when I saw the picture of Gideon mingled with the ones of me and Cary. It had been taken last night, while I was watching movies with Cary and Trey — and while Gideon was supposedly at a business dinner. In the photo, Gideon and Magdalene Perez smiled intimately at each other, her hand on his forearm as they stood outside a restaurant. The captions ranged between kudos for Gideon's "bevy of beautiful socialites" to speculation that he was hiding a broken heart over my infidelity by dating other women.

You have to trust me.

I closed my inbox, my breathing too quick and my heartbeat too fast. Jealous confusion twisted my gut. I knew he couldn't possibly have been physically intimate with another woman, and I knew he cared for me. But I hated Magdalene with a passion — certainly she'd given me good reason to during our bathroom chat — and I couldn't stand seeing her with Gideon. Couldn't stand seeing him smiling so fondly at her, especially after the way she'd treated me.

But I put it away. I shoved it into a box in my mind and I focused on my job. Mark was meeting with Gideon tomorrow to go over the RFP for the Kingsman campaign, and I was organizing the information flowing between Mark and the contributing departments.

"Hey, Eva." Mark poked his head out of his office. "Steve and I are meeting at Bryant Park Grill for lunch. He asked if you'd come. He'd like to see you again."

"I'd love to." My whole afternoon brightened at the thought of enjoying lunch at one of my favorite restaurants with two really charming guys. They'd distract me from thinking about the conversation I was hours away from having with Gideon about my past.

My privacy was clearly gone. I would have to grow a set of balls and talk to Gideon before we went out to dinner. Before he was seen in public with me any further. He needed to know the risk he was taking by being associated with me.

When I received an interoffice envelope a short while later, I assumed it was a small mock-up of one of the Kingsman ads, but found a note card from Gideon instead.

NOON. MY OFFICE.

"Really?" I muttered, irritated by the lack of salutation and closing. Not to mention the lack of a request. And who could forget the fact that Gideon hadn't even mentioned running into Magdalene at dinner?

Had he invited her as his date in my stead? That was what she was there for, after all. To be one of the women he socialized with outside his hotel room.

I flipped Gideon's card over and wrote the same number of words with no signature:

Sorry. Have plans.

A bratty reply, but he deserved it. When a quarter to noon rolled around, Mark and I headed down to the ground floor. When I was stopped by security and the guard called up to Gideon to tell him I was in the lobby, my irritation kicked into a temper.

"Let's go," I said to Mark, striding toward the revolving door and ignoring the pleas of the security guard to wait a moment. I felt bad putting him in the middle.

I saw Angus and the Bentley at the curb at the same moment I heard Gideon snap out my name like a whip crack behind me. I faced him as he joined us on the sidewalk with his face impassive and his gaze icy.

"I'm going to lunch with my boss," I told him, my chin lifting.

"Where are you headed, Garrity?" Gideon asked without taking his eyes off me.

"Bryant Park Grill."

"I'll see that she gets there." With that, he took my arm and steered me firmly toward the Bentley and the rear door that Angus held open for me. Gideon crowded in behind me, forcing me to scramble across the seat. The door shut and we were off.

I yanked the skirt of my sheath dress back into place. "What are you doing? Besides embarrassing me in front of my boss."

He draped one arm over the back of the seat and leaned toward me. "Is Cary in love with you?"

"What? No!"

"Have you fucked him?"

"Have you lost your mind?" Mortified, I shot a glance at Angus and found him acting like he was deaf. "Screw you, billionaire playboy with your bevy of beautiful socialites."

"So you did see the photos."

I was so mad I was panting. The nerve. I turned my head away, dismissing him and his idiotic accusations. "Cary's like a brother to me. You know that."

"Ah, but what are you to him? The photos were amazingly clear, Eva. I know love when I see it."

Angus slowed for a herd of pedestrians crossing the street. I shoved the door open and looked at Gideon over my shoulder, letting him take a good look at my face. "Obviously, you don't."

I slammed the door shut and set off briskly, righteous in my anger. I'd fought back my own questions and jealousy with herculean effort, and what did I get for it? An irrationally pissed-off Gideon.

"Eva. Stop right there."

I flipped him the bird over my shoulder and raced up the short steps into Bryant Park, a lushly green and tranquil oasis in the midst of the city. Just crossing up and

276

over from the sidewalk was like being transported to a completely different realm. Dwarfed by the towering skyscrapers surrounding it, Bryant Park was a garden land behind a beautiful old library. A place where time slowed, children laughed over the innocent joy of a carousel ride, and books were treasured companions.

Unfortunately for me, the gorgeous ogre from one world chased me into the other. Gideon caught me by the waist.

"Don't run," he hissed in my ear.

"You're acting like a nut job."

"Maybe because you drive me fucking crazy." His arms tightened into steel bands. "You're mine. Tell me Cary knows that."

"Right. Like Magdalene knows you're mine." I wished he had something near my mouth that I could bite. "You're causing a scene."

"We could've done this in my office, if you weren't so damned stubborn."

"I had plans, asshat. And you're fucking them up for me." My voice broke, tears welling as I felt the number of eyes on us. I was going to get fired for being an embarrassing spectacle. "You're fucking up everything."

Gideon instantly released me, turning me to face him. His grip on my shoulders ensured I still couldn't get away.

"Christ." He crushed me against him, his lips in my hair. "Don't cry. I'm sorry."

I beat my fist against his chest, which was as effectual as hitting a rock wall. "What's *wrong* with you? You can go out with a catty bitch who calls me a whore and thinks she's going to marry you, but I can't have lunch with a dear friend who's been pulling for you from the beginning?"

"Eva." He cupped the back of my head with one hand and pressed his cheek to my temple. "Maggie just happened to be at the same restaurant where I had dinner with my business associates."

"I don't care. You want to talk about a look on someone's face. The look on yours . . . How could you look at her like that after what she said to me?"

"Angel . . ." His lips moved ardently over my face. "That look was for you. Maggie caught me outside and I told her I was heading home to you. I can't help how I look when I'm thinking about us being alone together."

"And you expect me to believe she smiled about that?"

"She told me to tell you hello, but I figured that wouldn't go over well, and there was no way I was ruining our night over her."

My arms slid around his waist beneath his jacket. "We need to talk. Tonight, Gideon. There are things I have to tell you. If a reporter looks in the right place and gets lucky . . . We have to keep our relationship private or end it. Either would be better for you."

Gideon cupped my face and pressed his forehead to mine. "Neither is an option. Whatever it is, we'll figure it out."

I pushed up onto my toes and pressed my mouth to his. Our tongues stroked and dipped, the kiss wildly passionate. I was vaguely aware of the multitude of people milling around us, the buzz of numerous conversations, and the steady rumble of the ceaseless midtown traffic, but none of it mattered while I was sheltered by Gideon. Cherished by him. He was both tormentor and pleasurer, a man whose mood swings and volatile passions rivaled my own.

"There," he whispered, running his fingertips down my cheek. "Let *that* go viral."

"You're not listening to me, you crazy stubborn man. I have to go."

"We'll ride home together after work." He backed away, holding my hand until distance pulled our fingers apart.

When I turned toward the ivy-draped restaurant, I saw Mark and Steven waiting for me by the entrance. They made such a pair with Mark in his suit and tie and Steven in his worn jeans and boots.

Steven stood with his hands in his pockets and a big grin on his attractive face. "I feel like I should applaud. That was better than watching a chick flick."

My face heated and I shifted on my feet.

Mark opened the door and waved me inside. "I think you can ignore my previous words of wisdom about Cross's womanizing."

"Thanks for not firing me," I replied wryly as we waited for the hostess to check our reservation. "Or at least for feeding me first."

Steven patted my shoulder. "Mark can't afford to lose you."

Pulling out a chair for me, Mark smiled. "How else will I give Steven regular updates on your love life? He's a soap opera addict, you know. He loves romantic dramas."

I snorted. "You're kidding."

Steven ran a hand over his chin and smiled. "I'll never admit it one way or the other. A man's got to have his secrets."

My mouth curved, but I was painfully aware of my own hidden truths. And how quickly time was passing before I'd have to reveal them.

Five o'clock found me steeling myself to divulge my secrets. I was tense and somber when Gideon and I slid into the Bentley, and my disquiet only worsened when I felt him studying the side of my averted face. When he took my hand and lifted it to his lips, I felt like crying. I was still trying to adjust after our argument in the park, and that was the least of what we had to deal with.

We didn't speak until we arrived at his apartment.

When we entered his home, he led me straight through his beautiful, expansive living room and down the hall to his bedroom. There, laid out on the bed, was a fabulous cocktail dress the color of Gideon's eyes and a floor-length black silk robe.

"I had a little time to shop before dinner yesterday," he explained.

My apprehension lifted slightly, softened by pleasure at his thoughtfulness. "Thank you."

He set my bag on a chair by the dresser. "I'd like you to get comfortable. You can wear the robe or something of mine. I'll open a bottle of wine and we'll just settle in. When you're ready, we'll talk."

"I'd like to take a quick shower." I wished we could separate what happened in the park from what I had to tell him so that each issue was dealt with on its own merits, but I didn't have a choice. Every day was another opportunity for someone else to tell Gideon what he needed to hear from me.

"Whatever you want, angel. Make yourself at home."

As I kicked off my heels and moved into the bathroom, I felt the weight of his concern, but my revelations would have to hold until I could compose myself better. In an effort to gain that control, I took my time in the shower. Unfortunately, it made me remember the one we'd taken together just that morning. Had that been both our first and last as a couple?

When I was ready, I found Gideon standing by the couch in the living room. He'd changed into black silk pajama bottoms that hung low around his hips. Nothing else. A small blaze flickered in the fireplace and a bottle of wine sat in an ice-filled bucket on the coffee table. A grouping of ivory candles had been clustered as a centerpiece, their golden glow the only illumination besides the fire.

"Excuse me," I said from the threshold of

the room. "I'm looking for Gideon Cross, the man who doesn't have romance in his repertoire."

He grinned sheepishly, a boyish smile so at odds with the mature sexuality of his bared body. "I don't think about it that way. I just try to guess what might please you, and then I give it a shot and hope for the best."

"*You* please me." I crossed to him, the black robe swaying around my legs. I loved that he'd put on something that matched what he had given me.

"I want to," he said soberly. "I'm working on it."

Stopping in front of him, I drank in the beauty of his face and the sexy way the ends of his hair caressed the top of his shoulders. I ran my palms down his biceps, squeezing the hard muscle gently before stepping into him and pressing my face into his chest.

"Hey," he murmured, wrapping his arms around me. "Is this about me being an ass at lunch? Or whatever it is you need to say to me? Talk to me, Eva, so I can tell you it'll be okay."

I nuzzled my nose between his pecs, feeling the tickle of crisp chest hair against my cheek and breathing in the reassuring, familiar scent of his skin. "You should sit down. I have to tell you things about me. Ugly things."

Gideon reluctantly let me go when I pulled away from him. I curled up on his couch with my legs tucked underneath me, and he poured us both glasses of golden wine before taking a seat. Leaning toward me, he draped one arm over the back of the sofa and held his glass with the other hand, giving me every bit of his attention.

"Okay. Here goes." I took a deep breath before starting, feeling dizzy from the elevated rate of my pulse. I couldn't remember the last time I'd been so nervous or sick to my stomach.

"My mother and father never married. I really don't know too much about how they met, because neither of them talks about it. I know my mom came from money. Not as much as she married into, but more than most people have. She was a debutante. Had the whole white dress and presentation thing. Getting pregnant with me was a mistake that got her disowned, but she kept me."

I looked down into my glass. "I really admire her for that. There was a lot of pressure for her to make the baby — make *me* — go away, but she went through with the pregnancy anyway. Obviously."

His fingers sifted through my shower-damp hair. "Lucky me."

I caught his fingers and kissed his knuckles, then held his hand in my lap. "Even with a kid in tow, she was able to land herself a millionaire. He was a widower with a son just two years older than me, so I think they both thought they'd found the perfect arrangement. He traveled a lot and was rarely home, and my mom spent his money and took over raising his son."

"I understand the need for money, Eva," he murmured. "I have to have it, too. I need the power of it. The security."

Our eyes met. Something passed between us with that small admission. It made it easier for me to say what came next.

"I was ten the first time my stepbrother raped me —"

The stem of his glass snapped in his hand. He moved so swiftly he was a blur, catching the bowl of his goblet against his thigh before it spilled its contents.

I scrambled to my feet when he rose to his. "Did you cut yourself? Are you okay?"

"I'm fine," he bit out. He went into the kitchen and threw the broken glass away, shattering it further. I set my own glass down carefully, my hands shaking. I heard cupboards opening and closing. A few minutes later Gideon returned with a tumbler of something darker in his hand.

"Sit down, Eva."

I stared at him. His frame was rigid, his eyes icy cold. He scrubbed a hand over his face and said more gently, "Sit down . . . please."

My weakened knees gave out and I sat on the edge of the sofa, pulling the robe tighter around me.

Gideon remained standing, taking a large swallow of whatever was in his hand. "You said the first time. How many times were there?"

I took conscious breaths, trying to calm myself. "I don't know. I lost count."

"Did you tell anyone? Did you tell your mother?"

"No. My God, if she'd known, she would've gotten me out of there. But Nathan made sure I was too afraid to tell her." I tried to swallow past a tight, dry throat and winced at the painful sandpapery burn. When my voice came again, it was barely a whisper. "There was a time when it got so bad I almost told her anyway, but he knew. Nathan could tell I was close. So he broke my cat's neck and left her on my bed."

"Jesus Christ." His chest was heaving. "He wasn't just fucked up, he was insane. And he was touching you . . . *Eva.*"

"The servants had to know," I went on numbly, staring at my twisted hands. I just wanted to get it over with, to get it all out so I could put it back into the box in my mind where I forgot about it in my day-to-day life. "The fact that they didn't say anything either told me they were scared, too. They were grown-ups and they didn't say a word. I was a child. What could I do if they wouldn't do anything?"

"How did you get out?" he asked hoarsely. "When did it end?"

"When I was fourteen. I thought I was having my period, but there was too much blood. My mother panicked and took me to the emergency room. I'd had a miscarriage. In the course of the exam they found evidence of . . . other trauma. Vaginal and anal scarring —"

Gideon set his glass down on the end table with a harsh thud.

"I'm sorry," I whispered, feeling like I might be sick. "I'd spare you the details, but you need to know what someone might dig up. The hospital reported the abuse to child services. It's all a matter of public record, which has been sealed, but there are people who know the story. When my mom married Stanton, he went back and tightened those seals, paid out in return for nondisclosure agreements . . . stuff like that. But you have a right to know that this could come out and embarrass you."

"*Embarrass* me?" he snapped, vibrating with rage. "Embarrassment isn't on the list of what I'd feel."

"Gideon —"

"I would destroy the career of any reporter who wrote about this, and then I'd dismantle the publication that ran the piece." He was so cold with fury, he was icy. "I'm going to find the monster who hurt you, Eva, wherever he is, and I'm going to make him wish he were dead."

A shiver moved through me, because I believed him. It was in his face. His voice. In the energy he exuded and his sharply honed focus. He wasn't just dark and dangerous in his looks. Gideon was a man who got what he wanted, whatever it took.

I pushed to my feet. "He's not worth the effort. Not worth your time."

"*You* are. You're worth it. Damn it. Goddamn it to hell."

I moved closer to the fireplace, needing the warmth. "There's also a money trail. Cops and reporters always follow the money. Someone may wonder why my mother left her first marriage with two million dollars, but her daughter from a previous relationship left with five."

Without looking, I felt his sudden stillness. "Of course," I went on, "that blood money's probably grown to considerably more than that now. I won't touch it, but Stanton manages the brokerage account I dumped it in and everyone knows he has the Midas touch. If you ever had any concern that I wanted your money —"

"Stop talking."

I turned to face him. I saw his face, his eyes. Saw the pity and horror. But it was what I *didn't* see that hurt the most.

It was my greatest nightmare realized. I'd feared that my past might negatively impact his attraction to me. I'd told Cary that Gideon might stay with me for all the wrong reasons. That he might stay by my side, but that I'd still — for all intents and purposes — lose him anyway.

And it seemed I had.

13

I tightened the belt on my robe. "I'm going to get dressed and go."

"What?" Gideon glared. "Go where?"

"Home," I said, weary to the bone. "I think you need to digest all of this."

His arms crossed. "We can do that together."

"I don't think we can." My chin lifted, grief overwhelming my shame and heartrending disappointment. "Not while you're looking at me like you feel sorry for me."

"I'm not made of fucking stone, Eva. I wouldn't be human if I didn't care."

The emotions I'd run through since lunch coalesced into a searing pain in my chest and a cleansing burst of anger. "I don't want your goddamn pity."

He shoved both hands through his hair. "What the hell do you want, then?"

"You! I want you."

"You have me. How many times do I have to tell you that?"

"Your words don't mean shit when you can't back them up. From the moment we met, you've been hot for me. You haven't been able to look at me without making it damn clear you want to fuck my brains out. And that's gone, Gideon." My eyes burned. "That look . . . it's gone."

"You can't be serious." He stared at me as if I'd grown two heads.

"I don't think you know how your desire makes me feel." My arms wrapped around me, covering my breasts. I suddenly felt naked in the worst way. "It makes me feel beautiful. It makes me feel strong and alive. I — I can't bear to be with you if you don't feel that way about me anymore."

"Eva, I . . ." His voice faded into silence. He was hard-faced and distant, his fists clenched at his sides.

I loosened the sash of my robe and shrugged the whole garment off me. "Look at me, Gideon. Look at my body. It's the same one you couldn't get enough of last night. The same one you were so desperate to get into that you took me to that damn hotel room. If you don't want this any-more . . . if you don't get hard looking at it —"

"Is this hard enough for you?" He broke the drawstring of his pants, pushing them down to expose the heavy, thickly veined length of his erection.

We both lunged at the same time, colliding. Our mouths slid over each other as he lifted me to wrap my legs around his hips. He stumbled to the couch and fell, catching our combined weight with one outstretched hand.

I sprawled beneath him, breathless and sobbing, while he slid to his knees on the floor and tongued my cleft. He was rough and impatient, lacking the finesse I'd become used to, and I loved that he was. Loved it more when he levered over me and shoved his cock into me. I wasn't yet fully wet and the burn made me gasp, and then his thumb was on my clit, rubbing in circles that had my hips churning.

"Yes," I moaned, raking my nails down his back. He wasn't icy anymore. He was on fire. "Fuck me, Gideon. Fuck me hard."

"Eva." His mouth covered mine. He fisted my hair, holding me still as he lunged again and again, pounding hard and deep. He kicked off the armrest with one foot, powering into me, driving toward his orgasm with single-minded ferocity. "Mine . . . mine . . . mine . . ."

The rhythmic slap of his heavy balls against the curve of my buttocks and the harshness of his possessive litany drove me insane with lust. I felt myself quickening with every twinge of pain, felt my sex tightening with my growing arousal.

With a long, guttural groan he started coming, his flexing body quaking as he emptied himself inside me.

I held him as he climaxed, stroking his back, pressing kisses along his shoulder.

"Hold on," he said roughly, pushing his hands beneath me and flattening my breasts against him.

Gideon pulled me up, then sat down with me straddling his hips. I was slick from his orgasm, making it easy for him to push back inside me.

His hands brushed the hair away from my face, then wiped my tears of relief. "I'm always hard for you, always hot for you. I'm always half-crazy with wanting you. If anything could change that, I would've done it before we got this far. Understand?"

My hands wrapped around his wrists. "Yes."

"Now, show me that you still want *me* after that." His face was flushed and damp, his eyes dark and turbulent. "I need to know that losing control doesn't mean I've lost you."

I pulled his palms from my face and urged them down to my breasts. When he cupped them, I splayed my hands on his shoulders and rocked my hips. He was semihard, yet quickly thickened as I began to undulate. His fingers on my nipples, rolling and tugging, sent waves of pleasure through me, the gentle stimulation arrowing to my core. When he urged me closer and took a hardened tip in his mouth I cried out, my body igniting with need for more.

Clenching my thighs, I lifted. I closed my eyes to focus on the way he felt as he slid out; then I bit my lip at the way he stretched me sliding back in.

"That's it," he murmured, licking across my chest to my other nipple, fluttering his tongue over the tight, aching tip. "Come for me. I need you to come riding my cock."

Rolling my hips, I relished the exquisite feel of him filling me so perfectly. I had no shame, no regrets as I worked myself into a frenzy on his stiff penis, adjusting the angle so that the thick crown rubbed right where I needed it.

"Gideon," I breathed. "Oh, yes . . . oh, please . . ."

"You're so beautiful." He gripped the back

of my neck in one hand and my waist in the other, arching his hips to push a little deeper. "So sexy. I'm going to come for you again. That's what you do to me, Eva. It's never enough."

I whimpered as everything tightened, as the sweet tension built from the deep rhythmic strokes. I was panting and frantic, pumping my hips. Reaching between my legs, I rubbed my clit with the pads of my fingers, hastening my climax.

He gasped, his head thrown back into the sofa cushion, his neck corded with strain. "I feel you getting ready to come. Your cunt gets so hot and tight, so greedy."

His words and his voice pushed me over. I cried out when the first hard tremor hit me, then again as the orgasm rippled through my body, my sex spasming around Gideon's steely erection.

Teeth grinding audibly, he held on until the clenches began to fade; then he clutched my hips aloft and pumped upward into me. Once, twice. On the third deep thrust, he growled my name and spurted hotly, laying the last of my fears and doubts to rest.

I don't know how long we sprawled on the couch like that, connected and close, my head on his shoulder and his hands caressing the curve of my spine.

Gideon pressed his lips to my temple and murmured, "Stay."

"Yes."

He hugged me. "You're so brave, Eva. So strong and honest. You're a miracle. My miracle."

"A miracle of modern therapy, maybe," I scoffed, my fingers playing in his luxuriant hair. "And even with that, I was really fucked up for a while and there are still some triggers I don't think I'll ever get past."

"God. The way I came on to you in the beginning . . . I could've ruined us before we even got started. And the advocacy dinner —" He shuddered and buried his face in my neck. "Eva, don't let me blow this. Don't let me chase you away."

Lifting my head, I searched his face. He was impossibly gorgeous. I had trouble taking it in at times. "You can't second-guess everything you do or say to me because of Nathan and what he did. It'll break us apart. It'll end us."

"Don't say that. Don't even think about it."

I smoothed his knit brow with strokes of my thumb. "I wish I could've never told you. I wish you didn't have to know."

He caught my hand and pressed my fingertips to his lips. "I have to know everything, every part of you, inside and out, every detail."

"A woman has to have some secrets," I teased.

"You won't have any with me." He captured me by my hair and an arm banded around my hips, urging me against him, reminding me — as if I could forget — that he was still inside me. "I'm going to possess you, Eva. It's only fair since you've possessed me."

"And what about your secrets, Gideon?"

His face smoothed into an emotionless mask, an act so easily accomplished I knew it had become second nature to him. "I started from scratch when I met you. Everything I thought I was, everything I thought I needed . . ." He shook his head. "We're figuring out who I am together. You're the only one who knows me."

But I didn't. Not really. I was figuring him out, learning him bit by bit, but he was still a mystery to me in so many ways.

"Eva . . . If you just tell me what you want —" His throat worked on a swallow. "I can get better at this, if you give me the chance. Just don't . . . don't give up on me."

Jesus. He could shred me so easily. A few

words, a desperate look, and I was cut wide open.

I touched his face, his hair, his shoulders. He was as broken as I was, in a way I didn't yet know about. "I need something from you, Gideon."

"Anything. Just tell me what it is."

"Every day, I need you to tell me something I don't know about you. Something insightful, no matter how small. I need you to promise me that you will."

Gideon eyed me warily. "Whatever I want?"

I nodded, unsure of myself and what I hoped to get out of him.

He exhaled harshly. "Okay."

I kissed him softly, a silent show of thanks.

Nuzzling his nose against mine, he asked, "Let's go out to dinner. Or do you want to order in?"

"Are you sure we should go out?"

"I want to go on a date with you."

There was no way I could say no to that, not when I knew what a big step it was for him. A big step for both of us, really, since the last time we'd gone on a date it'd ended in disaster. "Sounds romantic. And irresistible."

His joyful smile was my reward, as was the shower we took to clean up. I loved the intimacy of washing his body as much as I loved the feel of his palms gliding over me. When I took his hand and put it between my legs, urging two of his fingers inside me, I saw the familiar and very welcome heat in his eyes as he felt the slick essence he'd left behind.

He kissed me and murmured, "Mine."

Which prompted me to slide both hands over his cock and whisper the same claim back to him.

In the bedroom, I lifted my new blue dress off the bed and hugged it to me. "You picked this out, Gideon?"

"I did, yes. Do you like it?"

"It's beautiful." I smiled. "My mother said you had excellent taste . . . except for your preference for brunettes."

He glanced at me just before his very fine, very firm naked ass disappeared into his massive walk-in closet. "What brunettes?"

"Ooh, nicely done."

"Look in the top drawer on the right," he called out.

Was he trying to distract me from thinking about all the brunettes he'd been photographed with — including Magdalene?

I left the dress on the bed and opened the drawer. Inside were a dozen Carine Gilson lingerie sets, all in my size, in a wide range of colors. There were also garters and silk stockings still in their packages.

I looked up at Gideon as he reappeared with his clothes in hand. "I have a drawer?"

"You have three in the dresser and two in the bathroom."

"Gideon." I smiled. "Working up to a drawer usually takes a few months."

"How would you know?" He laid his clothes on the bed. "You've lived with a man other than Cary?"

I shot him a look. "Having a drawer isn't living with someone."

"That's not an answer." He walked over and brushed me gently aside to grab a pair of boxer briefs.

Sensing his withdrawal and darkening mood, I replied before he moved away. "I haven't lived with any other men, no."

Leaning over, Gideon pressed a brusque kiss to my forehead before returning to the bed. He paused at the footboard with his back to me. "I want this relationship to mean more to you than any others you've had."

"It does. By far." I tightened the knot of the towel between my breasts. "I'm struggling with that a little. It's become important so quickly. Maybe too quickly. I keep thinking it's too good to be true."

Turning, he faced me. "Maybe it is. If so, we deserve it."

I went to him and let him pull me into his arms. It was where I wanted to be more than anywhere else.

He pressed a kiss to the crown of my head. "I can't stand the thought that you're waiting for this to end. That's what you're doing, isn't it? That's what you sound like."

"I'm sorry."

"We just have to make you feel secure." He ran his fingers through my hair. "How do we do that?"

I hesitated a moment, then went for it. "Would you go to couples therapy with me?"

The stroking of his fingers paused. He stood silently for a moment, breathing deeply.

"Just think about it," I suggested. "Maybe look into it, see what it's about."

"Am I doing this wrong? You and me? Am I fucking it up that much?"

I pulled back to look at him. "No, Gideon. You're perfect. Perfect for me, anyway. I'm crazy about you. I think you're —"

He kissed me. "I'll do it. I'll go."

I loved him in that moment. Wildly. And the moment after that. And all through the ride to what turned out to be a dazzling, intimate dinner at Masa. We were one of only three parties in the restaurant and Gideon was greeted by name on sight. The food we were served was otherworldly good and the wine too expensive to think about or I wouldn't have been able to swallow it. Gideon was darkly charismatic; his charm was relaxed and seductive.

I felt beautiful in the dress he'd chosen and my mood was light. He knew the worst of what there was to know about me, but he was still with me.

His fingertips caressed my shoulder . . . drew circles on my nape . . . slid down my back. He kissed my temple and nuzzled beneath my ear, his tongue lightly touching the sensitive skin. Beneath the table, his hand squeezed my thigh and cupped the back of my knee. My entire body vibrated with awareness of him. I wanted him so badly I ached.

"How did you meet Cary?" he asked, eyeing me over the lip of his wineglass.

"Group therapy." I set my hand over his to still its upward slide on my leg, smiling at the mischievous glimmer in his eyes. "My dad's a cop and he'd heard of this therapist who supposedly had mad skills with wild kids, which I was. Cary was seeing Dr. Travis, too."

"Mad skills, huh?" Gideon smiled.

"Dr. Travis isn't like any other therapist I've ever met. His office is an old gymnasium he converted. He had an open-door policy with 'his kids,' and hanging out there was more real to me than lying on a couch. Plus he had a no-bullshit rule. It was straight-up honesty both ways or he'd get pissed. I've always liked that about him, that he cared enough to get emotional."

"Did you choose SDSU because your dad's in Southern California?"

My mouth twisted wryly as he revealed another bit of knowledge about me that I hadn't given him. "How much have you dug up on me?"

"Whatever I could find."

"Do I want to know how extensive that is?"

He lifted my hand to his lips and kissed the back. "Probably not."

I shook my head, exasperated. "Yes, that's why I attended SDSU. I didn't get to spend a lot of time with my dad while I was growing up. Plus my mother was smothering me to death."

"And you never told your dad about what happened to you?"

"No." I rolled the stem of my wineglass between my fingers. "He knows I was an angry troublemaker with self-esteem issues, but he doesn't know about Nathan."

"Why not?"

"Because he can't change what happened. Nathan was lawfully punished. His father paid a large sum for damages. Justice was served."

Gideon spoke coolly. "I disagree."

"What more can you expect?"

He drank deeply before replying. "It's not fit to describe over dinner."

"Oh." Because that sounded ominous, especially when paired with the ice of his gaze, I returned my attention to the food in front of me. There was no menu at Masa, only *omakase,* so every bite was a surprise delight, and the dearth of patrons made it seem almost as if we had the whole place to ourselves.

After a moment, he said, "I love watching you eat."

I shot him a look. "What's that supposed to mean?"

"You eat with gusto. And your little moans of pleasure make me hard."

I bumped my shoulder into his. "By your own admission, you're always hard."

"Your fault," he said, grinning, which made me grin, too.

Gideon ate with more deliberation than I

did and didn't bat an eye at the astronomical check.

Before we stepped outside, he slid his jacket over my shoulders and said, "Let's go to your gym tomorrow."

I glanced at him. "Yours is nicer."

"Of course it is. But I'll go wherever you like."

"Someplace without helpful trainers named Daniel?" I asked sweetly.

He looked at me with an arched brow and a wry curving of his lips. "Watch yourself, angel. Before I think of a suitable consequence for mocking my possessiveness where you're concerned."

I noted he didn't threaten me with a spanking again. Did he understand that administered pain with sex was a major trigger for me? It took me back to a mental place I never wanted to return to.

On the ride back to Gideon's place, I curled into him in the back of the Bentley, my legs slung over one of his thighs and my head on his shoulder. I thought about the ways Nathan's abuse still affected my life — my sex life in particular.

How many of those ghosts could Gideon and I exorcise together? After that brief glimpse of toys I'd seen in the hotel room drawer, it was clear he was more experienced and sexually adventurous than I was. And the pleasure I'd derived from the ferocity of his lovemaking on the couch earlier proved to me that he could do things to me no one else could.

"I trust you," I whispered.

His arms tightened around me. With his lips in my hair, he murmured, "We're going to be good for each other, Eva."

When I fell asleep in his arms later that night, it was with those words in my head.

"Don't . . . No. No, don't. . . . Please."

Gideon's cries had me jackknifing up in the bed, my heart thudding violently. I fought for breath, glancing wild-eyed at the man thrashing next to me.

He snarled like a feral beast, his hands fisted and his legs kicking restlessly. I moved back, afraid he'd strike out at me unknowingly in his dreams.

"Get off me," he panted.

"Gideon! Wake up."

"Get . . . off . . ." His hips arched upward with a hiss of pain. He hovered there, teeth gritted, his back bowed as if the bed were on fire beneath him. Then he collapsed, the mattress jolting as he bounced off it.

"Gideon." I reached for the bedside lamp, my throat burning. I couldn't reach it, had to throw the tangled blankets off to get closer. Gideon was writing in agony, thrashing so violently he shook the bed.

The room lit up in a sudden flare of illumination. I turned toward him . . .

And found him masturbating with shocking viciousness.

His right hand gripped his cock with white knuckled force, pumping brutally fast. His left hand clenched the fitted sheet. Torment and pain twisted his beautiful face.

Fearing for his safety, I shoved his shoulder with both hands. "Gideon, goddamn it. *Wake up!*"

My scream broke through the nightmare. His eyes flew open and he jerked upright, his eyes darting frantically.

"What?" he gasped, his chest heaving. His face was flushed, his lips and cheeks red with arousal. "What is it?"

"Jesus." I shoved my hands through my hair and slid out of bed, snatching up the black robe I'd hung over the footboard.

What was in his mind? What could make someone have such violently sexual dreams?

My voice shook. "You were having a nightmare. You scared the hell out of me."

"Eva." He looked down at his erection, and his color darkened with shame.

I stared at him from my safe place by the

307

window, tying the sash of my robe with a yank. "What were you dreaming about?"

He shook his head, his gaze lowered with humiliation, a vulnerable posture I didn't know or recognize in him. It was as if someone else had taken over Gideon's body. "I don't know."

"Bullshit. Something's in you, something's eating at you. What is it?"

He rallied visibly as his brain struggled free of sleep. "It was just a dream, Eva. People have them."

I stared at him, hurt blooming that he would take that tone with me, as if I were being irrational. "Screw you."

His shoulders squared, and he tugged the sheet over his lap. "Why are you mad?"

"Because you're lying."

His chest expanded on a deep breath; then he released it in a rush. "I'm sorry I woke you."

I pinched the bridge of my nose, feeling a headache gathering strength. My eyes stung with the need to cry for him, to cry for whatever torment he'd once lived through. And to cry for us, because if he didn't let me in, our relationship had nowhere to go.

"One more time, Gideon: What were you dreaming about?"

"I don't remember." He ran a hand

through his hair and slid his legs off the edge of the bed. "I have some business on my mind and it's probably keeping me up. I'm going to work in my home office for a while. Come back to bed, and try to get some sleep."

"There were a few right answers to that question, Gideon. 'Let's talk about it tomorrow' would've been one. 'Let's talk about it over the weekend' would've been another. And even 'I'm not ready to talk about it' would be okay. But you have some nerve acting like you don't know what I'm talking about while speaking to me like I'm unreasonable."

"Angel —"

"Don't." My arms wrapped around my waist. "Do you think it was easy telling you about my past? Do you think it was painless cutting myself open and letting the ugliness spill out? It would've been simpler to cut *you* off and date someone less prominent. I took the risk because I want to be with you. Maybe someday you'll feel the same way about me."

I left the room.

"Eva! Eva, damn it, come back here. What's wrong with you?"

I walked faster. I knew how he felt: the sickness in the gut that spread like cancer, the helpless anger, and the need to curl up in private and find the strength to shove the memories back into the deep, dark hole they still lived in.

It wasn't an excuse for lying or deflecting the blame onto me.

I snatched my purse off the chair where I'd dropped it on the way in from dinner and rushed out the front door into the foyer to the elevator. The car doors were closing with me inside when I saw him step into the living room through the open front door. His nakedness ensured he couldn't come after me, while the look in his eyes ensured I wouldn't stay. He'd donned his mask again, that striking implacable face that kept the world a safe distance away.

Shaking, I leaned heavily against the brass handrail for support. I was torn between my concern for him, which urged me to stay, and my hard-won knowledge, which assured me that his coping strategy wasn't one I could live with. The road to recovery for me was paved with hard truths, not denials and lies.

Swiping at my wet cheeks when I passed the third floor, I took deep breaths and collected myself before the doors opened on the lobby level.

The doorman whistled down a passing

cab for me and was such a consummate professional that he acted like I was dressed for work rather than sporting bare feet and a black dressing gown. I thanked him sincerely.

And I was so grateful to the cabbie for getting me home quickly that I tipped him well and didn't care about the furtive looks I got from my own doorman and the front desk staffer. I didn't even care about the look I got from the stunning, statuesque blonde who stepped out of the elevator I was waiting for, until I smelled Cary's cologne on her and realized the T-shirt she was wearing was one of his.

She took in my half-dressed state with an amused glance. "Nice robe."

"Nice shirt."

The blonde took off with a smirk.

When I reached my floor, I found Cary lounging in the open doorway in a robe of his own.

He straightened and opened his arms to me. "Come here, baby girl."

I walked straight into him and hugged him tight, smelling a woman's perfume and hard sex all over him. "Who's the chick that just left?"

"Another model. Don't worry about her." He drew me into the apartment and shut and locked the door. "Cross called. He said you were heading back and he has your keys. He wanted to be sure I was here and awake to let you in. For what it's worth, he sounded torn up and anxious. You wanna talk about it?"

Setting my purse down on the breakfast bar, I went into the kitchen. "He had another nightmare. A really bad one. When I asked him about it he denied, he lied, then he acted like I was nuts."

"Ah, the classics."

The phone started ringing. I flicked the switch on the base that turned the ringer off and Cary did the same to the handset he'd left on the counter. Then I pulled out my smartphone, closed the alert that said I'd missed numerous calls from Gideon, and sent him a text message: *Home safe. Hope you sleep well the rest of the night.*

I powered the phone off and tossed it back in my purse; then I grabbed a bottle of water from the fridge. "The kicker is that I told him all my junk earlier tonight."

Cary's brows shot up. "So you did it. How'd he take it?"

"Better than I had any right to expect. Nathan ought to hope they never run into each other." I finished the bottle. "And Gideon agreed to the couples counseling you suggested. I thought we'd turned a corner. Maybe we did, but we hit a brick wall anyway."

"You seem okay, though." He leaned into the breakfast bar. "No tears. Really calm. Should I be worried?"

I rubbed my belly to ease the fear that had rooted there. "No, I'll be all right. I just . . . I want it to work out between us. I want to be with him, but lying about serious issues is a deal breaker for me."

God. I couldn't let myself even consider that we might not get past this. I was already feeling antsy. The need to be with Gideon was a frantic beat in my blood.

"You're a tough cookie, baby girl. I'm proud of you." He came to me, linked our arms, and turned off the kitchen lights. "Let's crash and start a new day when we wake up."

"I thought things were going well with you and Trey."

His grin was glorious. "Honey, I think I'm in love."

"With who?" I leaned my cheek against his shoulder. "Trey or the blonde?"

"Trey, silly. The blonde just provided a workout."

I had a lot to say about that, but it wasn't the time to get into Cary's history of sabotaging his own happiness. And maybe focusing on how good things were with Trey was the best way to handle this instance of it. "So you've finally fallen for a good guy. We should celebrate."

"Hey, that's my line."

14

The next morning dawned with an odd surreality. I made it to work, and then through most of my prelunch day in a kind of chilly fog. I couldn't get warm enough, despite wearing a cardigan over my blouse and a scarf that didn't match either one. It took me a few minutes longer to process requests than it should have, and I couldn't shake a feeling of dread.

Gideon made no contact with me whatsoever.

Nothing on my smartphone or e-mail after my text last night. Nothing in my e-mail inbox. No interoffice note.

The silence was excruciating. Especially when the day's Google alert hit my inbox and I saw the photos and phone videos of me and Gideon in Bryant Park. Seeing how we looked together — the passion and need, the painful longing on our faces, and the gratefulness of reconciliation — was bitter-sweet.

Pain twisted in my chest. *Gideon.*

If we couldn't work this out, would I ever stop thinking about him and wishing we had?

I struggled to pull myself together. Mark was meeting with Gideon today. Maybe that was why Gideon hadn't felt pressed to contact me. Or maybe he was just really busy. I knew he had to be, considering his business calendar. And as far as I knew, we still had plans to go to the gym after work. I exhaled in a rush and told myself that things would straighten out somehow. They just had to.

It was quarter to noon when my desk phone rang. Seeing from the readout that the call was coming from reception, I sighed with disappointment and answered.

"Hey, Eva," Megumi said cheerily. "You have a Magdalene Perez here to see you."

"Do I?" I stared at my monitor, confused and irritated. Had the Bryant Park photos lured Magdalene out from under whatever troll bridge she called home?

Regardless of the reason, I had no interest in talking to her. "Keep her up there for me, will you? I have to take care of some-thing first."

"Sure. I'll tell her to have a seat."

I hung up, then pulled out my smartphone and scrolled through the contact list until I found the number to Gideon's office. I dialed and was relieved when Scott answered.

"Hey, Scott. It's Eva Tramell."

"Hi, Eva. Would you like to speak to Mr. Cross? He's in a meeting at the moment, but I can buzz him."

"No. No, don't bother him."

"It's a standing order. He won't mind."

It soothed me immensely to hear that. "I hate to throw this in your lap, but I have a request for you."

"Anything you need. That's also a standing order." The amusement in his voice relaxed me further.

"Magdalene Perez is down here on the twentieth floor. Frankly, the only thing she and I have in common is Gideon, and that's not a good thing. If she has something to say, it's your boss she should be talking to. Could you please have someone escort her up?"

"Absolutely. I'll take care of it now."

"Thanks, Scott. I appreciate you."

"It's my pleasure, Eva."

I hung up the phone and sagged back in my seat, feeling better already and proud of

317

myself for not letting jealousy get the better of me. While I still really hated the idea of her having any of Gideon's time, I hadn't lied when I'd said I trusted him. I believed he had strong, deep feelings for me. I just didn't know if they were enough to override his survival instinct.

Megumi called me again.

"Oh my God," she said, laughing. "You should've seen her face when whoever that was came to get her."

"Good." I grinned. "I figured she was up to no good. Is she gone, then?"

"Yep."

"Thanks." I crossed the narrow strip of hallway to Mark's door and poked my head in to see if he wanted me to pick him up some lunch.

He frowned, thinking about it. "No, thanks. I'll be too nervous to eat until after the presentation with Cross. By then whatever you pick up will be hours old."

"How about a protein smoothie, then? It'll give you some easy fuel until you can eat."

"That'd be great." His smile lit up his dark eyes. "Something that goes good with vodka, just to get me in the mood."

"Anything you don't like? Any allergies?"

"Nada."

"Okay. See you in an hour." I knew just

318

the place to go. The deli I had in mind was a couple blocks up and offered smoothies, salads, and a variety of made-to-order paninis with quick service.

I headed downstairs and tried not to think about Gideon's radio silence. I'd kind of expected to hear *something* after the Magdalene incident. Getting no reaction had me worrying all over again. I pushed out to the street through the revolving door and scarcely paid any attention to the man who climbed out of the back of a town car at the curb until he called my name.

Turning, I found myself facing Christopher Vidal.

"Oh . . . Hi," I greeted him. "How are you?"

"Better, now that I've seen you. You look fantastic."

"Thanks. I can say the same to you."

As different as he was from Gideon, he was gorgeous in his own way with his mahogany waves, grayish-green eyes, and charming smile. He was dressed in loose-fitting jeans and a cream V-neck sweater, a very sexy look for him.

"Are you here to see your brother?" I asked.

"Yes, and you."

"Me?"

"Heading to lunch? I'll join you and explain."

I was briefly reminded of Gideon's warning to stay away from Christopher, but by now I figured he trusted me. Especially with his brother.

"I'm going to a deli up the street," I said. "If you're game."

"Absolutely."

We started walking.

"What did you want to see me about?" I asked, too curious to wait.

He reached into one of two large cargo pockets of his jeans and pulled out a formal invitation in a vellum envelope. "I came to invite you to a garden party we're having at my parents' estate on Sunday. A mix of business and pleasure. Many of the artists signed to Vidal Records will be there. I was thinking it'd be great networking for your roommate — he's got the right look for music video."

I brightened. "That would be wonderful!"

Christopher grinned and passed the invite over. "And you'll both have fun. No one throws a party like my mother."

I glanced briefly at the envelope in my hand. Why hadn't Gideon said anything about the event?

"If you're wondering why Gideon didn't

tell you about it," he said, seemingly reading my mind, "it's because he won't come. He never does. Even though he's the majority shareholder in the company, I think he finds the music industry and musicians too unpredictable for his tastes. By now, you know how he is."

Dark and intense. Powerfully magnetic and hotly sexual. Yes, I knew how he was. And he preferred to know what he was getting into at all costs.

I gestured at the deli when we reached it, and we stepped inside and got in line.

"This place smells awesome," Christopher said, his gaze on his phone as he typed out a quick text.

"The aroma delivers on its promise, trust me."

He smiled a delightful boyish smile that I was sure knocked most women on their asses. "My parents are really looking forward to meeting you, Eva."

"Oh?"

"Seeing the photos of you and Gideon over the last week has been a real surprise. A good surprise," he qualified quickly when I winced. "It's the first time we've seen him really into someone he's dating."

I sighed, thinking he wasn't so into me right now. Had I made a terrible mistake by leaving him alone last night?

When we reached the counter, I ordered a grilled vegetable-and-cheese panini with two pomegranate smoothies, asking them to hold the one with a protein shot for thirty minutes so I could eat in. Christopher ordered the same, and we managed to find a table in the crowded deli.

We talked about work, laughing over both a recent baby food commercial faux-blooper that had gone viral and some backstage anecdotes about acts Christopher had worked with. The time passed swiftly, and when we parted ways at the entrance of the Crossfire, I said good-bye with genuine affection.

I headed up to the twentieth floor and found Mark still at his desk. He offered me a quick smile despite his air of concentration.

"If you don't really need me," I said, "I think it'd be good for me to sit this presentation out."

Although he tried to hide it, I saw the lightning-quick flash of relief. It didn't offend me. Stress was stress, and my volatile relationship with Gideon was something Mark didn't need to think about while he was working on an important account.

"You're golden, Eva. You know that?"

I smiled and set the drink carrier down in front of him. "Drink your smoothie. It's really good, and the protein will keep you from feeling too hungry for a little bit longer. I'll be at my desk if you need me."

Before I put my purse in the drawer, I texted Cary to ask if he had plans on Sunday and if he'd like to go to a Vidal Records party. Then I got back to work. I'd started organizing Mark's files on the server, tagging them and placing them in directories to make it easier for us to assemble portfolios on the fly.

When Mark left for the meeting with Gideon, my heartbeat quickened and a clutch of anticipation tightened my stomach. I couldn't believe my excitement just from knowing what Gideon was doing at that particular moment, and that he'd have to think of me when he saw Mark. I hoped I'd hear from him after that. My mood picked up at the thought.

For the next hour, I was restless waiting to hear how things had gone. When Mark reappeared with a big grin and a spring in his step, I stood up in my cubicle and applauded him.

He took a gallant, exaggerated bow. "Thank you, Miss Tramell."

"I'm so stoked for you!"

"Cross asked me to give you this." He handed me a sealed manila envelope. "Come to my office and I'll give you all the deets."

The envelope had weight and rattled. I knew from touch what I'd find inside before I opened it, but still the sight of my keys sliding out and into my palm hit me hard. Gasping with a pain more intense than any I could remember, I read the accompanying note card.

THANK YOU, EVA. FOR
EVERYTHING.
YOURS, G

A Dear Jane brush-off. It had to be. Otherwise, he would've given me the keys after work on the way to the gym.

There was a dull roaring in my ears. I felt dizzy. Disoriented. I was frightened and agonized. Furious.

I was also at work.

Closing my eyes and clenching my fists, I pulled myself together and fought off the driving urge to go upstairs and call Gideon a coward. He probably saw me as a threat, someone who'd come in, unwanted and uninvited, and shaken up his orderly world. Someone who'd demanded more from him than just his hot body and hefty bank account.

I shut my emotions behind a glass wall, where I was aware of them waiting in the background, but I was able to get through the rest of my workday. By the time I clocked out and headed downstairs, I still hadn't heard from Gideon. I was such an emotional disaster at that point I felt only a single, sharp twinge of despair as I exited the Crossfire.

I made it to the gym. I shut my brain off and ran full-bore on the treadmill, fleeing the anguish that would hit me soon enough. I ran until sweat coursed in rivulets down my face and body, and rubber legs forced me to stop.

Feeling battered and exhausted, I hit the showers. Then I called my mother and asked her to send Clancy to the gym to pick me up for our appointment with Dr. Petersen. As I put my work clothes back on, I mustered the energy to get through that last task before I could go home and collapse on my bed.

I waited for the town car at the curb, feeling separate and apart from the city teeming around me. When Clancy pulled up and hopped out to open the back door for me, I was startled to see my mom already inside.

It was early yet. I'd expected to be driven solo to the apartment she shared with Stanton and wait on her for twenty minutes or so. That was our usual routine.

"Hey, Mom," I said wearily, settling on the seat beside her.

"How could you, Eva?" She was crying into a monogrammed handkerchief, her face beautiful even while reddened and wet with tears. *"Why?"*

Jolted out of my torment by her misery, I frowned and asked, "What did I do now?"

The new cell phone, if she'd somehow found out about it, wouldn't trigger this much drama. And it was too soon after the fact for her to know about my breakup with Gideon.

"You told Gideon Cross about . . . what happened to you." Her lower lip trembled with distress.

My head jerked back in shock. How could she know that? My God . . . Had she bugged my new place? My purse . . . ? *"What?"*

"Don't act clueless!"

"How do you know I told him?" My voice was a pained whisper. "We just talked last night."

"He went to see Richard about it today."

I tried to picture Stanton's face during

326

that conversation. I couldn't imagine my stepfather taking it well. "Why would he do that?"

"He wanted to know what's been done to prevent information leaks. And he wanted to know where Nathan is —" She sobbed. "He wanted to know everything."

My breath hissed out between my teeth. I wasn't sure what Gideon's motivation was, but the possibility that he'd dumped me over Nathan and was now making sure that he was safe from scandal hurt worse than anything. I twisted in pain, my spine arching away from the seat back. I'd thought it was *his* past that drove a wedge between us, but it made more sense that it was *mine.*

For once I was grateful for my mother's self-absorption, which kept her from seeing how devastated I was.

"He had a right to know," I managed in a voice so raw it sounded nothing like my own. "And he has a right to try to protect himself from any blowback."

"You've never told any of your other boy-friends."

"I've never dated anyone who makes national headlines by sneezing either." I stared out the car window at the traffic that boxed us in. "Gideon Cross and Cross Industries are global news, Mother. He's light-years away from the guys I dated in college."

She spoke more, but I didn't hear her. I shut down for self-protection, cutting off the reality that was suddenly too painful to be endured.

Dr. Petersen's office was exactly as I remembered. Decorated in soothing neutrals, it was both professional and comfortable. Dr. Petersen was the same — a handsome man with gray hair and gentle, intelligent blue eyes.

He welcomed us into his office with a wide smile, commenting on how lovely my mother looked and how like her I was. He said he was happy to see me again and that I looked well, but I could tell he spoke for my mother's benefit. He was too trained an observer to miss the raging emotions I suppressed.

"So," he began, settling into his chair across from the sofa my mother and I sat on. "What brings you both in today?"

I told him about the way my mom had been tracking my movements via my cell phone signal and how violated I felt. Mom told him about my interest in Krav Maga and how she took it as a sign that I wasn't feeling safe. I told him about how my mom and Stanton had pretty much taken over Parker's studio, which made me feel suffocated and claustrophobic. She told him I'd betrayed her trust by divulging deeply personal matters to strangers, which made her feel naked and painfully exposed.

Through it all, Dr. Petersen listened attentively, took notes, and spoke rarely, until we'd purged everything.

Once we'd quieted, he asked, "Monica, why didn't you tell me about tracking Eva's cell phone?"

The angle of her chin altered, a familiar defensive posture. "I didn't see anything wrong with it. Many parents track their children through their cell phones."

"Underage children," I shot back. "I'm an adult. My personal time is exactly that."

"If you were to envision yourself in her place, Monica," Dr. Petersen interjected, "would it be possible that you might feel as she does? What if you discovered someone was monitoring your movements without your knowledge or permission?"

"Not if the someone was my mother and I knew it gave her peace of mind," she argued.

"And have you considered how your actions affect Eva's peace of mind?" he queried gently. "Your need to protect her is understandable, but you should discuss the steps you wish to take openly with her. It's important to gain her input — and expect cooperation only when she chooses to give it. You have to honor her prerogative to set limits that may not be as broad as you'd like them to be."

My mother sputtered indignantly.

"Eva needs her boundaries, Monica," he continued, "and a sense of control over her own life. Those things were taken from her for a long time, and we have to respect her right to establish them now in the manner that best suits her."

"Oh." My mother twisted her handkerchief around her fingers. "I hadn't thought of it that way."

I reached out for my mother's hand when her lower lip trembled violently. "Nothing could've stopped me from talking to Gideon about my past. But I could have forewarned you. I'm sorry I didn't think of it."

"You're much stronger than I ever was," my mother said, "but I can't help worrying."

"My suggestion," Dr. Petersen said, "would be for you to take some time, Monica, and really think about what sorts of events and situations cause you anxiety. Then write them down."

My mother nodded.

"When you have what will surely not be an exhaustive list but a strong start," he went on, "you can sit down with Eva and discuss strategies for addressing those concerns — strategies you can both live with comfortably. For example, if not hearing from Eva for a few days troubles you, perhaps a text message or an e-mail will alleviate that."

"Okay."

"If you like, we can go over the list together."

The back-and-forth between the two made me want to scream. It was insult to injury. I hadn't expected Dr. Petersen to smack some sense into my mom, but I'd hoped he would at least take a harder line — God knew someone needed to, someone whose authority she respected.

When the hour ended and we were on our way out, I asked my mom to wait a moment so I could ask Dr. Petersen one last personal and private question.

"Yes, Eva?" He stood in front of me, looking infinitely patient and wise.

"I just wondered . . ." I paused, needing to swallow past a lump in my throat. "Is it possible for two abuse survivors to have a functional romantic relationship?"

"Absolutely." His immediate, unequivocal

answer forced the trapped air from my lungs.

I shook his hand. "Thank you."

When I got home, I unlocked my door with the keys Gideon had returned to me and went straight to my room, offering a lame wave to Cary, who was practicing yoga in the living room to a DVD.

I stripped off my clothes as I crossed the distance from my closed bedroom door to the bed, finally crawling between the cool sheets in just my underwear. I hugged a pillow and closed my eyes, so tired and drained I had nothing left.

The door opened at my back, and a moment later Cary sat beside me.

He brushed my hair away from my tear-streaked face. "What's the matter, baby girl?"

"I got kicked to the curb today. Courtesy of a fucking note card."

He sighed. "You know the drill, Eva. He's going to keep pushing you away, because he's expecting you to fail him like everyone else has."

"And I keep proving him right." I recognized myself in the description Cary had just given. I ran when the going got tough, because I was so sure it was all going to end badly. The only control I had was to be the one who left, instead of the one who was left behind.

"Because you're fighting to protect your own recovery." He lay down and spooned against my back, wrapping one leanly muscular arm around me and tucking me tight against him.

I snuggled into the physical affection I hadn't realized I needed. "He might've dumped me because of *my* past, not his."

"If that's true, it's good it's over. But I think you two will find each other eventually. At least I'm hoping you will." His sigh was soft on my neck. "I want there to be happily-ever-afters for the fucked-up crowd. Show me the way, Eva honey. Make me believe."

15

Friday found Trey sharing breakfast with Cary and me after an overnighter. As I drank the day's first cup of coffee, I watched him interact with Cary and was genuinely thrilled to see the intimate smiles and covert touches they gave each other.

I'd had easy relationships like that and hadn't appreciated them at the time. They had been comfortable and uncomplicated, but they'd been superficial in a fundamental way, too.

How deep could a love affair get if you didn't know the darkest recesses of your lover's soul? That was the dilemma I'd faced with Gideon.

Day Two After Gideon had begun. I found myself wanting to go to him and apologize for leaving him. I wanted to tell him I was there for him, ready to listen or simply offer silent comfort. But I was too emotionally invested. I got wounded too easily. I was too afraid of rejection. And knowing he wouldn't let me get too close only intensified that fear. Even if we did figure things out, I'd only tear myself apart trying to live with just the bits and pieces he decided to share with me.

At least my job was going well. The celebratory lunch the executives gave in honor of the agency landing the Kingsman account made me genuinely happy. I felt blessed to work in such a positive environment. But when I heard that Gideon had been invited — although no one expected him to show up — I returned quietly to my desk and focused on work the rest of the afternoon.

I hit the gym on the way home, then picked up some items to make fettuccini alfredo for dinner with crème brûlée for dessert — comfort food guaranteed to put me in a carbohydrate coma. I expected sleep to offer me a break from the endless what-ifs my brain was recycling, hopefully long into Saturday morning.

Cary and I ate in the living room with chopsticks, his idea to cheer me up. He said dinner was great, but I couldn't tell. I snapped out of it when he fell silent, too, and I realized I was being a less than stellar friend.

"When are the Grey Isles campaign ads going up?" I asked.

"I'm not sure, but get this . . ." He grinned. "You know how it is with male models — we're tossed around like condoms at an orgy. It's tough to stand out from the crowd, unless you're dating someone famous. Which I'm suddenly reported to be doing since those photos of you and me were plastered everywhere. I'm the side piece of action in your relationship with Gideon Cross. You've done wonders for making me a hot commodity."

I laughed. "You didn't need my help for that."

"Well, it certainly didn't hurt. Anyway, they called me back for a couple more shoots. I think they might just use me for more than five minutes."

"We'll have to celebrate," I teased.

"Absolutely. When you're up for it."

We ended up hanging out and watching the original *Tron*. His smartphone rang twenty minutes into the movie and I heard him speaking to his agency. "Sure. I'll be there in fifteen, tops. I'll call you when I get there."

"Got a job?" I asked after he'd hung up.

"Yeah. A model showed up for a night shoot so trashed he's worthless." He studied me. "You wanna come?"

I stretched my legs out on the couch. "Nope. I'm good right here."

"You sure you're okay?"

"All I need is mindless entertainment. Just the thought of getting dressed again exhausts me." I'd be happy wearing my flannel pajama bottoms and holey old tank top all weekend. As much as I hurt inside, total comfort outside seemed like a necessity. "Don't worry about me. I know I've been a mess lately, but I'll get it together. Go on and enjoy yourself."

After Cary rushed out, I paused the movie and went to the kitchen for some wine. I stopped by the breakfast bar, my fingertips gliding over the roses Gideon had sent me the previous weekend. Petals fell to the countertop like tears. I thought about cutting the stems and using the flower food packet that came with the bouquet, but it was pointless hanging on to them. I'd throw the arrangement away tomorrow, the last reminder of my equally doomed relationship.

I'd gotten further with Gideon in one week than I had with other relationships that lasted two years. I would always love him for that. Maybe I'd always love him, period.

And one day, that might not hurt so badly.

"Rise and shine, sleepyhead," Cary sing-songed as he yanked the comforter off me.

"Ugh. Go away."

"You've got five minutes to get your ass up and in the shower, or the shower's coming to you."

Opening one eye, I peeked at him. He was shirtless and wearing baggy pants that barely clung to his hips. As far as wake-up calls went, he was prime. "Why do I have to get up?"

"Because when you're flat on your back you're not on your feet."

"Wow. That was deep, Cary Taylor."

He crossed his arms and shot me an arch look. "We need to go shopping."

I buried my face in the pillow. "No."

"Yes. I seem to remember you saying this was a 'Sunday garden party' and 'rock star gathering' in the same sentence. What the hell do I wear to something like that?"

"Ah, well. Good point."

"What are you wearing?"

"I . . . I don't know. I was leaning toward the 'English tea with hat' look, but now I'm not so sure."

He gave a brisk nod. "Right. Let's hit the

shops and find something sexy, classy, and cool."

Growling a token protest, I rolled out of bed and padded over to the bathroom. It was impossible to shower without thinking of Gideon, without picturing his perfect body and remembering the desperate sounds he made when he came in my mouth. Everywhere I looked, Gideon was there. I'd even started hallucinating black Bentley SUVs all around town. I thought I spotted one damn near everywhere I went.

Cary and I had lunch; then we bounced all over the city, hitting the best of the Upper East Side thrift stores and Madison Avenue boutiques before taking a taxi downtown to SoHo. Along the way, Cary had two teenage girls ask for his autograph, which tickled me more than him, I think.

"Told you," he crowed.

"Told me what?"

"They recognized me from an entertainment news blog. One of the posts about you and Cross."

I snorted. "Glad my love life is working out for someone."

He was due at another job around three and I went with him, spending a few hours in the studio of a loud and brash photographer. Remembering it was Saturday, I slipped into a far corner and made my weekly call to my dad.

"You still happy in New York?" he asked me above the background noise of dispatch talking over the radio in his cruiser.

"So far so good." A lie, but the truth helped no one.

His partner said something I didn't catch. My dad snorted and said, "Hey, Chris insists he saw you on television the other day. Some cable channel, celebrity gossip thing. The guys won't leave me alone about it."

I sighed. "Tell them watching those shows is bad for their brain cells."

"So you're not dating one of the richest men in America?"

"No. What about your love life?" I asked, quickly diverting. "Are you seeing anyone?"

"Nothing serious. Hang on." He responded to a call on the radio, then said, "Sorry, sweetheart. I have to run. I love you. Miss you like crazy."

"I miss you, too, Daddy. Be careful."

"Always. Bye."

I killed the call and went back to my former spot to wait for Cary to wrap things up. In the lull, my mind tormented me. Where was Gideon now? What was he doing?

Would Monday bring me an inbox full of photos of him with another woman?

Sunday afternoon I borrowed Clancy and one of Stanton's town cars for the drive out to the Vidal estate in Dutchess County. Leaning back in the seat, I looked out the window, absently admiring the serene vista of rolling meadows and green woodlands that stretched to the distant horizon. I realized I was working on Day Four After Gideon. The pain I'd felt the first few days had turned into a dull throbbing that felt almost like the flu. Every part of my body ached, as if I were going through some sort of physical withdrawal, and my throat burned with unshed tears.

"Are you nervous?" Cary asked me.

I glanced at him. "Not really. Gideon won't be there."

"You're sure about that?"

"I wouldn't be going if I thought otherwise. I do have some pride, you know." I watched him drum his fingers on the armrest between our two seats. For all the shopping we'd done yesterday, he'd made only one purchase: a black leather tie. I'd teased him mercilessly about it, he of the perfect fashion sense going with something like that.

He caught me looking at it. "What? You still don't like my tie? I think it works well with the emo jeans and my lounge lizard jacket."

"Cary" — my lips quirked — "you can wear anything."

It was true. Cary could pull off any look, a benefit of having a sculpted, rangy body and a face that could make angels weep.

I set my hand over his restless fingers. "Are *you* nervous?"

"Trey didn't call last night," he muttered. "He said he would."

I gave his hand a reassuring squeeze. "It's just one missed call, Cary. I'm sure it doesn't mean anything serious."

"He could've called this morning," he argued. "Trey's not flaky like the others I've dated. He wouldn't have forgotten to call, which means he just doesn't want to."

"The rat bastard. I'll be sure to take lots of pictures of you having a great time looking sexy, classy, and cool to torment him with on Monday."

His mouth twitched. "Ah, the deviousness of the female mind. It's a shame Cross won't see you today. I think I got a semi when you came out of your room in that dress."

"Eww!" I smacked his shoulder and mock-glared when he laughed.

The dress had seemed perfect to both of us when we'd found it. It was cut in a classic garden party style — fitted bodice with a knee-length skirt that flared out from the waist. It was even white with flowers. But that was where the tea-and-crumpets style ended.

The edginess came from the strapless form, the alternating layers of black and crimson satin underskirts that gave it volume, and the black leather flowers that looked like wicked pinwheels. Cary had picked the red Jimmy Choo peep-toe pumps out of my closet and the ruby drop earrings to give it all the finishing touch. We'd decided to leave my hair loose around my shoulders, in case we arrived and learned that hats were required. All in all, I felt pretty and confident.

Clancy drove us through an imposing set of monogrammed gates and turned into a circular driveway, following the direction of a valet. Cary and I got out by the entrance, and he took my arm as my heels sank into blue-gray gravel on the walk to the house.

Upon entering the Vidals' sprawling Tudor-style mansion, we were warmly greeted by Gideon's family in a receiving line — his mother, his stepfather, Christopher, and their sister.

I took in the sight, thinking the Vidal family could only look more perfect if Gideon were lined up with them. His mother and sister had his coloring, both women boasting the same glossy obsidian hair and thickly lashed blue eyes. They were both beautiful in a finely wrought way.

"Eva!" Gideon's mother drew me toward her, then air-kissed both of my cheeks. "I'm so pleased to finally meet you. What a gorgeous girl you are! And your dress. I love it."

"Thank you."

Her hands brushed over my hair, cupped my face, and then slid down my arms. It was hard for me to bear it, because touching was sometimes an anxiety trigger for me when the person was a stranger. "Your hair, is it naturally blond?"

"Yes," I replied, startled and confused by the question. Who asked a question like that of a stranger?

"How fascinating. Well, welcome. I hope you have a wonderful time. We're so glad you could make it."

Feeling strangely unsettled, I was grateful when her attention moved to Cary and zeroed in.

"And you must be Cary," she crooned.

"Here I'd been certain my two boys were the most attractive in the world. I see I was wrong about that. You are simply divine, young man."

Cary flashed his megawatt smile. "Ah, I think I'm in love, Mrs. Vidal."

She laughed with throaty delight. "Please. Call me Elizabeth. Or Lizzie, if you're brave enough."

Looking away, I found my hand clasped by Christopher Vidal Sr. In many ways, he reminded me of his son, with his slate green eyes and boyish smile. In others, he was a pleasant surprise. Dressed in khakis, loafers, and a cashmere cardigan, he looked more like a college professor than a music company executive.

"Eva. May I call you Eva?"

"Please do."

"Call me Chris. It makes it a little easier to distinguish between me and Christopher." His head tilted to the side as he contemplated me through quirky brass spectacles. "I can see why Gideon is so taken with you. Your eyes are a stormy gray, yet they're so clear and direct. Quite the most beautiful eyes I think I've ever seen, aside from my wife's."

I flushed. "Thank you."

"Is Gideon coming?"

"Not that I'm aware of." Why didn't his parents know the answer to that question?

"We always hope." He gestured at a waiting servant. "Please head back to the gardens and make yourself at home."

Christopher greeted me with a hug and a kiss on the cheek, while Gideon's sister, Ireland, sized me up in a sulky way that only a teenager could pull off. "You're a blonde," she said.

Jeez. Was Gideon's preference for dark-haired women a damn law or something? "And you're a very lovely brunette."

Cary offered me his arm and I accepted it gratefully.

As we walked away, he asked me quietly, "Were they what you expected?"

"His mom, maybe. His stepdad, no." I looked back over my shoulder, taking in the elegant floor-length cream sheath dress that clung to Elizabeth Vidal's svelte figure. I thought of what little I knew about Gideon's family. "How does a boy grow up to be a businessman who takes over his stepfather's family business?"

"Cross owns shares in Vidal Records?"

"Controlling interest."

"Hmm. Maybe it was a bailout?" he offered. "A helping hand during a trying time for the music industry?"

"Why not just give him the money?" I wondered.

"Because he's a shrewd businessman?"

With a sharp exhalation, I waved the question away and cleared my mind. I was attending the party for Cary, not Gideon, and I was going to keep that first and foremost in my thoughts.

Once we'd moved outside, we found a large, elaborately decorated marquee erected in the rear garden. Although the day was beautiful enough to stay out in the sun, I found a seat at a circular table covered in white damask instead.

Cary patted my shoulder. "You relax. I'll network."

"Go get 'em."

He moved away, intent on his agenda.

I sipped champagne and chatted with everyone who stopped by to strike up a conversation. There were a lot of recording artists at the party whose work I listened to, and I watched them covertly, a bit starstruck. For all the elegance of the surroundings and the endless number of servants, the overall vibe was casual and relaxed.

I was starting to enjoy myself when someone I'd hoped never to see again stepped out of the house onto the terrace: Magdalene Perez, looking phenomenal in a rose-hued chiffon gown that floated around her knees.

A hand settled on my shoulder and squeezed, setting my heart racing because it reminded me of the night Cary and I had gone to Gideon's club. But the figure that rounded me this time was Christopher.

"Hey, Eva." He took the chair next to mine and set his elbows on his knees, leaning toward me. "Are you having fun? You're not mingling much."

"I'm having a great time." At least I had been. "Thank you for inviting me."

"Thank you for coming. My parents are stoked you're here. Me, too, of course." His grin made me smile, as did his tie, which had cartoon vinyl records all over it. "Are you hungry? The crab cakes are great. Grab one when the tray comes by."

"I'll do that."

"Let me know if you need anything. And save a dance for me." He winked, then hopped up and away.

Ireland took his seat, arranging herself with the practiced grace of a finishing-school graduate. Her hair fell in a single length to her waist, and her beautiful eyes were direct in a way I could appreciate. She looked worldlier than the seventeen years I'd calculated her to be, based on the newspaper clippings Cary had collected. "Hi."

"Hello."

"Where's Gideon?"

I shrugged at the blunt question. "I'm not sure."

She nodded sagely. "He's good at being a loner."

"Has he always been that way?"

"I guess. He moved out when I was little. Do you love him?"

My breath caught for a second. I released it in a rush and said simply, "Yes."

"I thought so when I saw that video of you two in Bryant Park." She bit her lush lower lip. "Is he fun? You know . . . to hang around with?"

"Oh. Well . . ." God. Did *anyone* know Gideon? "I wouldn't say he's fun, but he's never boring."

The live band began playing "Come Fly with Me," and Cary appeared beside me as if by magic. "Time to make me look good, Ginger."

"I'll try my best, Fred." I smiled at Ireland. "Excuse me a minute."

"Three minutes, nineteen seconds," she corrected, displaying some of her family's expertise in music.

Cary led me onto the empty dance floor and pulled me into a swift foxtrot. It took me a minute to get into it, because I'd been stiff and tight with misery for days. Then the synergy of longtime partners kicked in and we glided across the floor with sweeping steps.

When the singer's voice faded with the music, we stopped, breathless. We were pleasantly surprised by applause. Cary gave an elegant bow and I held on to his hand for stability as I dipped into a curtsy.

When I lifted my head and straightened, I found Gideon standing in front of me. Startled, I stumbled back a step. He was seriously underdressed in jeans and an untucked white dress shirt that was open at the collar and rolled up at the sleeves, but he was so damn fine he still put every other man in attendance to shame.

The tremendous yearning I felt at the sight of him overwhelmed me. Distantly I was aware of the band's singer pulling Cary away, but I couldn't tear my gaze away from Gideon, whose wildly blue eyes burned into mine.

"What are you doing here?" he snapped, scowling.

I recoiled from his harshness. "Excuse me?"

"You shouldn't be here." He grabbed me by the elbow and started hauling me toward the house. "I don't want you here."

If he'd spit in my face, it couldn't have devastated me more. I yanked my arm free of him and walked briskly toward the house with my head held high, praying I could make it to the privacy of the town car and Clancy's protective watch before the tears started falling.

Behind me, I heard a come-hither female voice call out Gideon's name, and I sent up a prayer that the woman would stall him long enough for me to get out without further confrontation.

I thought I just might make it when I passed into the cool interior of the house.

"Eva, wait."

My shoulders hunched at the sound of Gideon's voice and I refused to look at him. "Get lost. I can show myself out."

"I'm not done —"

"I am!" I pivoted to face him. "You don't get to talk to me that way. Who do you think you are? You think I came here for *you*? That I was hoping I'd see you and you'd throw me a goddamn scrap or bone . . . some pathetic acknowledgment of my existence? Maybe I'd be able to harass you into a quick, dirty fuck in a corner somewhere in a pitiful effort to win you back?"

"Shut up, Eva." His gaze was scorching

hot, his jaw tight and hard. "Listen to me
—"

"I'm only here because I was told you
wouldn't be. I'm here for Cary and his
career. So you can go back to the party and
forget about me all over again. I assure you,
when I walk out the door, I'll be doing the
same to you."

"Shut your damned mouth." He caught
me by the elbows and shook me so hard my
teeth snapped together. "Just shut up and
let me talk."

I slapped him hard enough to turn his
head. "Don't touch me."

With a growl, Gideon hauled me into him
and kissed me hard, bruising my lips. His
hand was in my hair, fisting it roughly, holding me in place so I couldn't turn away. I
bit the tongue he thrust aggressively into
my mouth, then his lower lip, tasting blood,
but he didn't stop. I shoved at his shoulders
with everything I had, but I couldn't budge
him.

Goddamn Stanton! If not for him and my
crazy-assed mother, I'd have had a few Krav
Maga classes under my belt by now. . . .

Gideon kissed me as if he were starved for
the taste of me, and my resistance began to
melt. He smelled so good, so familiar. His
body felt so perfectly *right* against mine. My

352

nipples betrayed me, hardening into tight points, and a slow, hot trickle of arousal gathered in my core. My heart thundered in my chest.

God, I wanted him. The craving hadn't gone away, not even for a minute.

He picked me up. Imprisoned by his tight grip, I had trouble breathing and my head began to spin. When he carried me through a door and kicked it shut behind him, I couldn't do more than make a feeble sound of protest.

I found myself pressed against a heavy glass door on the other side of a library, Gideon's hard and powerful body subduing my own. His arm at my waist slid lower, his hand delving beneath my skirts and finding the curves of my butt exposed by my lacy boy shorts underwear. He wrenched my hips hard to his, making me feel how hard he was, how aroused. My sex trembled with want, achingly empty.

All the fight left me. My arms fell to my sides, my palms pressing flat to the glass. I felt the brittle tension drain from his body as I softened in surrender, the pressure of his mouth easing and his kiss turning into a passionate coaxing.

"Eva," he breathed gruffly. "Don't fight me. I can't take it."

My eyes closed. "Let me go, Gideon."

He nuzzled his cheek against mine, his breath gusting hard and fast over my ear. "I can't. I know you're disgusted by what you saw the other night . . . what I was doing to myself —"

"Gideon, no!" *God.* Did he think I left him because of that? "That's not why —"

"I'm losing my mind without you." His lips were gliding down my neck, his tongue stroking over my racing pulse. He sucked on my skin, and pleasure radiated through me. "I can't think. I can't work or sleep. My body aches for you. I can make you want me again. Let me try."

Tears slipped free and ran down my face. They splashed on the upper swell of my breasts and he licked at them, lapping them away.

How would I ever recover if he made love to me again? How would I survive if he didn't?

"I never stopped wanting you," I whispered. "I can't stop. But you hurt me, Gideon. You have the power to hurt me like no one else can."

His gaze was stark and confused on my face. "I hurt you? How?"

"You lied to me. You shut me out." I cupped his face, needing him to understand this one thing without question. "Your past doesn't have the power to push me away. Only you can do that, and you did."

"I didn't know what to do," he rasped. "I never wanted you to see me like that . . ."

"That's the problem, Gideon. I want to know who you are, the good *and* the bad, and you want to keep parts of yourself hidden from me. If you don't open up, we're going to lose each other down the road and I won't be able to take it. I'm barely surviving it now. I've crawled through the last four days of my life. Another week, a month . . . It'll break me to give you up."

"I can let you in, Eva. I'm trying. But your first response when I screw up is to run away. You do it every time and I can't stand feeling like any moment I'm going to do or say something wrong and you're going to bolt."

His mouth was tender again as he brushed his lips back and forth over mine. I didn't argue with him. How could I, when he was right?

"I had hoped you'd come back on your own," he murmured, "but I can't stay away anymore. I'll carry you out of here if I have to. Whatever it takes to get you back in the same room with me, talking this out."

My heart stuttered. "You were hoping I'd

come back? I thought . . . You gave me back my keys. I thought we were over."

He pulled back, his face set in fierce lines. "We'll *never* be over, Eva."

I looked at him, my heart aching like an open wound at how beautiful he was, how broken and in pain he was — pain I'd caused to some degree.

On tiptoes, I kissed the reddened handprint I'd left on his cheek, clutching his thick silky hair in my hands.

Gideon bent his knees to align our bodies, his breathing harsh and erratic. "I'll do whatever you want, whatever you need. Anything. Just take me back."

Maybe I should have been scared by the depth of his need, but I felt the same passionate insanity for him.

Running my hands down his chest in an effort to soothe his trembling, I gave him the hard truth. "We can't seem to stop making each other miserable. I can't keep doing this to you and I can't keep going through these crazy highs and lows. We need help, Gideon. We're seriously dysfunctional."

"I saw Dr. Petersen on Friday. He's going to take me on as a patient, and — if you agree — he'll take us both on as a couple. I figured if you can trust him, I can try."

"Dr. Petersen?" I remembered the brief

jolt I'd felt at seeing a black Bentley SUV when Clancy pulled away from the doctor's office. At the time, I'd told myself it was wishful thinking. After all, there were countless black SUVs in New York. "You had me followed."

His chest expanded on a deep breath. He didn't deny it.

I bit back my anger. I could only imagine how terrible it must be for him to be so dependent on something — *someone* — he couldn't control. What mattered most at that moment were his willingness to try and the fact that it wasn't just talk. He'd actually taken steps. "It's going to be a lot of work, Gideon," I warned him.

"I'm not afraid of work." He was touching me restlessly, his hands sliding over my thighs and buttocks as if caressing my bare skin were as necessary to him as breathing. "I'm only afraid of losing you."

I pressed my cheek to his. We completed each other. Even now, as his hands roamed possessively over me, I felt a thawing in my soul, the desperate relief of being held — finally — by the man who understood and satisfied my deepest, most intimate desires.

"I need you." His mouth was sliding over my cheek and down my throat. "I need to be inside you . . ."

"*No.* My God. Not here." But my protest sounded weak even to my own ears. I wanted him anywhere, anytime, any way. . . .

"It has to be here," he muttered, dropping to his knees. "It has to be now."

He chafed my skin ripping the lace of my panties away; then he shoved my skirts to my waist and licked my cleft, his tongue parting my folds to stroke over my throbbing clit.

I gasped and tried to recoil, but there was nowhere to go. Not with the door at my back and a grimly determined Gideon in front, one hand keeping me pinned while the other lifted my left leg over his shoulder, opening me to his ardent mouth.

My head thudded against the glass, heat pulsing through my blood from the point where his tongue was driving me mad. My leg flexed against his back, urging him closer, my hands cupping his head to hold him still as I rocked into him. Feeling the rough satin strands of his hair against my sensitive inner thighs was its own provocation, heightening my awareness of everything around me. . . .

We were in Gideon's parents' house, in the midst of a party attended by dozens of famous people, and he was on his knees, growling his hunger as he licked and sucked my slick, aching cleft. He knew just how to get to me, knew what I liked and needed. He had an understanding of my nature that went above and beyond his incredible oral skills. The combination was devastating and addicting.

My body shook, my eyelids heavy from the illicit pleasure. "Gideon . . . You make me come so hard."

His tongue rubbed over and over the clenching entrance to my body, teasing me, making me grind shamelessly into his working mouth. His hands cupped my bare butt, kneading, urging me onto his tongue as he thrust it inside me. There was reverence in the greedy way he enjoyed me, the unmistakable sense that he worshipped my body, that pleasuring it and taking pleasure from it was as vital to him as the blood in his veins.

"Yes," I hissed, feeling the orgasm building. I was buzzed by champagne and the heated scent of Gideon's skin mixed with my own arousal. My breasts strained within the increasingly too-tight confines of my strapless bra, my body trembling on the edge of a desperately needed orgasm. "I'm so close."

A movement on the far side of the room caught my eye and I froze, my gaze locking with Magdalene's. She stood just inside the door, halted midstride, staring wide-eyed and openmouthed at the back of Gideon's moving head.

But he was either oblivious or too impassioned to care. His lips circled my clit and his cheeks hollowed. Sucking rhythmically, he massaged the hypersensitive knot with the tip of his tongue.

Everything tightened viciously, then released in a fiery burst of pleasure.

The orgasm poured through me in a scorching wave. I cried out, pumping my hips mindlessly into his mouth, lost to the primal connection between us. Gideon held me up as my knees weakened, tonguing my quivering flesh until the last tremor faded.

When I opened my eyes again, our audience of one had fled.

Standing in a rush, Gideon picked me up and carried me to the couch. He dropped me lengthwise on the cushion, then hauled my hips up to rest on the armrest, arching my spine.

I eyed him up the length of my torso. Why not just fold me over and fuck me from behind?

Then he ripped open his button fly and pulled his big, beautiful penis out, and I didn't care how he took me just so long as he did. I whimpered as he shoved into me, my body struggling to accommodate the wonderful fullness I craved. Yanking my hips to meet his powerful thrusts, Gideon battered my tender sex with that brutally thick column of rigid flesh, his gaze dark and possessive, his breath leaving him in primitive grunts every time he hit the end of me.

A trembling moan left me, the friction of his drives stirring my never-sated need to be fucked senseless by him. Only him.

A handful of strokes and his head fell back as he gasped my name, his hips rolling to stir me into a frenzy. "Squeeze me, Eva. Squeeze my dick."

When I complied, the ragged sound he made was so erotic my sex trembled in appreciation. "Yeah, angel . . . just like that."

I tightened around him and he cursed. His gaze found mine, the stunning blue hazed with sexual euphoria. A convulsive shudder racked his powerful frame, followed by an agonized sound of ecstasy. His cock jerked inside me, once, twice, and then he was coming long and hard, spurting hotly into the clutching depths of my body.

I didn't have time to climax again, but it didn't matter. I watched him with awe and pure female triumph. *I* could do this to *him.*

In the moments of orgasm, I owned him as completely as he owned me.

16

Gideon folded over me, his hair falling forward to tickle my chest, his lungs heaving. "God. I can't go days without this. Even the hours at work are too long."

I ran my fingers through the sweat-damp roots of his hair. "I missed you, too."

He nuzzled my breasts. "When you're not with me, I feel — Don't run anymore, Eva. I can't take it."

He pulled me up to stand in front of him, keeping his cock in me until the soles of my heels touched the hardwood floor. "Come home with me now."

"I can't leave Cary."

"Then we'll drag him out of here with us. Shh . . . Before you complain, whatever he hopes to get out of this party, I can make happen. Being here accomplishes nothing."

"Maybe he's having fun."

"I don't want you here." He suddenly seemed distant, his tone far too controlled.

"Do you know how badly it hurts me when you say that?" I cried softly, my chest tight with the pain of it. "What's wrong with me that you don't want me around your family?"

"Angel, no." He hugged me, his hands roaming my back in soothing caresses. "There's nothing wrong with you. It's this place. I don't — I *can't* be here. You want to know what's in my dreams? It's this house."

"Oh." My stomach knotted with worry and confusion. "I'm sorry. I didn't know."

Something in my voice lured him to press a kiss between my eyebrows. "I've been rough with you today. I'm sorry. I'm edgy and agitated being here, but that's no excuse."

I cupped his face and stared into his eyes, seeing the tumultuous emotions he was so used to hiding. "Don't ever apologize for being yourself with me. It's what I want. I want to be your safe place, Gideon."

"You are. You don't know how much, but I'll find a way to tell you." He rested his forehead against mine. "Let's go home. I bought some things for you."

"Oh? I love gifts." Especially when they came from my self-professed unromantic boyfriend.

Cautiously, he began to pull out of me. I was shocked to feel how wet I was, how copiously he'd come. The final few inches of his cock slid out in a rush and semen slicked my inner thighs. A moment later, two audacious droplets fell to the hardwood floor between my spread legs.

"Oh, shit." He groaned. "That's so damn hot. I'm getting hard again."

I stared at the brazen display of his virility and felt warm. "You can't go again after *that.*"

"Hell if I can't." Cupping my sex in his hand, he rubbed the slickness all over me, coating the outer lips and massaging it into the folds. Euphoria spread through me like the warmth of fine liquor, a sense of contentment that came solely from the knowledge that Gideon found gratification in me and my body.

"I'm an animal with you," he murmured. "I want to mark you. I want to possess you so completely there's no separation between us."

My hips began to move in tiny circles as his words and touch reignited the desire he'd goaded with the thrusts of his cock. I wanted to come again, knew I'd be miserable if I had to wait until we reached his bed. I was a sexual creature with him, too, so physically attuned to him and so positive that he would never physically hurt me, that I was . . . free.

I encircled his wrist with my fingers and gently directed his hand around my hip to reach for me from behind. Nipping his jaw with my teeth, I gathered the courage he inspired in me and whispered, "Touch me here with your fingers. Mark me there."

He froze, his chest lifting and falling rapidly. "I don't" — his voice strengthened — "I don't do anal play, Eva."

Looking into his eyes, I saw something dark and volatile. Something very painful.

Of all the things for us to have in common. . . .

The raw passion of our lust gentled into the warm familiarity of love. With my heart breaking, I confessed, "I don't either. At least not voluntarily."

"Then . . . why?" The confusion in his voice moved me deeply.

I hugged him, pressing my cheek to his shoulder and listening to the slightly panicked beat of his heart. "Because I believe your touch can erase Nathan's."

"Oh, Eva." His cheek pressed to the crown of my head.

I snuggled closer. "You make me feel safe."

We held each other for long moments. I

listened as his heartbeat slowed and his breathing smoothed out. I inhaled deeply, relishing the mix of his personal scent mixed with the scent of hard lust and harder sex.

When the tip of his middle finger slid gossamer-soft over the pucker of my anus, I stilled and pulled back to look at him. "Gideon?"

"Why me?" he asked softly, his beautiful eyes dark and stormy. "You know I'm fucked up, Eva. You saw what I . . . that night you woke me . . . You *saw*, damn it. How can you trust me with your body this way?"

"I trust my heart and what it tells me." I smoothed the frown line between his brows. "You can give my body back to me, Gideon. I believe you're the only one who can."

His eyes closed and his damp forehead touched mine. "Do you have a safeword, Eva?"

Startled, I pulled back again to study his face. A few members of my therapy group had talked about Dom/sub relationships. Some required total control to feel safe during sex. Others fell on the opposite side of the line, finding that bondage and humiliation satisfied their deep-seated need to feel pain to experience pleasure. For those who practiced that lifestyle, a safeword was an unambiguous way to say *Stop*. But I couldn't see how that had any relevance to me and Gideon. "Do you?"

"I don't need one." Between my legs, the gentle stroke of his finger became less tentative. He repeated his question, "Do you have a safeword?"

"No. I've never needed one. Missionary, doggy style, B.O.B. . . . that's about the extent of my mad skills in the sack."

That brought a touch of amusement to his otherwise severe face. "Thank God. I wouldn't survive you otherwise."

And still that fingertip massaged me, spurring a dark yearning. Gideon could do that to me, make me forget everything that happened before. I had no negative sexual triggers with him, no hesitation or fears. He'd given that to me. In return, I wanted to give him the body he'd freed from my past.

The long case clock near the door began to chime the hour.

"Gideon, we've been gone a long time. Someone will come looking for us."

He put the slightest pressure against my sensitive rosette, barely pressing. "Do you really care if they do?"

My hips arched into the touch. Anticipation was making me hot all over again. "I don't care about anything but you when you're touching me."

His free hand lifted to my hair and held it at the roots, keeping my head still. "Did you ever enjoy anal play? Accidentally or by deliberation?"

"No."

"And yet you trust me enough to ask me for this." He kissed my forehead as he drew the slickness of his semen back to my rear.

I gripped his waistband. "You don't have to —"

"Yes, I do." His voice had that wickedly assertive bite to it. "If you crave something, I'll be the one to give it to you. All of your needs, Eva, are mine to fulfill. Whatever it costs me."

"Thank you, Gideon." My hips shifted restlessly as he continued to lubricate me gently. "I want to be what you need, too."

"I've told you what I need, Eva — control." He brushed his parted lips back and forth over mine. "You're asking me to lead you back into painful places, and I will, if that's what you need. But we have to be extremely careful."

"I know."

"Trust is hard for both of us. If we break it, we could lose everything. Think of a word you associate with power. *Your* safeword, angel. Choose it."

The pressure of that single fingertip became more insistent. I moaned, "Crossfire."

"Umm . . . I like it. Very fitting." His tongue dipped into my mouth, barely touching mine before retreating. His finger rimmed my anus over and over, pushing his semen into the puckered hole, a soft growl escaping him as it flexed in a silent plea for more.

The next time he pressed against the ring, I pushed out and he slipped his fingertip inside me. The feeling of penetration was shockingly intense.

Just as before, surrender weighted my body, leaving me languid.

"Are you okay?" Gideon asked harshly as I sagged against him. "Should I stop?"

"No . . . Don't stop."

He pushed fractionally deeper and I clenched around him, a helpless reaction to the feel of something gliding across tender tissues. "You're snug and scorching hot," he murmured. "And so soft. Does it hurt?"

"No. Please. More."

Gideon withdrew to his fingertip; then he slid in to the knuckle, slow and easy. I quivered in delight, astonished by how good it felt, that teasing bit of fullness in my rear.

"How's that?" he asked hoarsely.

"Good. Everything you do to me feels good."

He withdrew again, glided deep again. Leaning forward, I thrust my hips back to give him easier access and pressed my breasts against his chest. His fist in my hair tightened, pulling my head back so he could take my mouth in a lush, wet kiss. Our open mouths slid across each other, growing more frantic as my arousal built. The feel of Gideon's finger in that darkly sexual place, thrusting in that gentle rhythm, had me rocking backward to meet his inward drives.

"You're so beautiful," he murmured, his voice infinitely gentle. "I love making you feel good. Love watching an orgasm move through your body."

"Gideon." I was lost, drowning in the powerful joy of being held by him, loved by him. Four days alone had taught me how miserable I'd be if we couldn't work things out, how dull and colorless my world would be without him in it. "I need you."

"I know." He licked across my lips, making my head spin. "I'm here. Your cunt's trembling and tightening. You're going to come for me again."

With shaking hands, I reached between us for his cock, finding it hard. I lifted the layers of my underskirts so I could insert him into my drenched sex. He slid in a few inches, our standing positions preventing deeper penetration, but the connection alone was enough. I wrapped my arms around his shoulders, burying my face in his neck as my knees weakened. His hand left my hair, his arm clasping my back and holding me close.

"Eva." The tempo of his finger thrusts quickened. "Do you know what you do to me?"

His hips nudged against mine, the wide crest of his penis massaging a sweetly tender spot. "You're milking the head of my dick with those hungry little squeezes. You're going to make me come for you. When you go off, I'm going with you."

I was distantly aware of the helpless noises spilling from my throat. My senses were overloaded by Gideon's scent and the heat of his hard body, the feel of his cock rubbing inside me and his finger pumping into my rear. I was surrounded by him, filled with him, blissfully possessed in every way. A climax was building in force, pounding through me, pooling in my core. Not just from the physical pleasure but from the knowledge that he'd been willing to take a risk. Once again. For me.

His finger stilled and I made a sound of protest.

"Hush," he whispered. "Someone's coming."

"Oh God! Magdalene came in earlier and saw us. What if she told —"

"Don't move." Gideon didn't let me go. He stood just as he was, filling me front and back, his hand caressing the length of my spine and smoothing my dress down. "Your skirts hide everything."

With my back to the room's entrance, I pressed my flaming face into his shirt.

The door opened. There was a pause, then, "Is everything all right?"

Christopher. I felt awkward being unable to turn around.

"Of course," Gideon said smoothly, coolly in control. "What do you want?"

To my horror, he resumed the push and withdrawal of his finger. Not with the deep strokes of before, but slow, shallow thrusts that didn't disturb my skirts. Already aroused to a fever pitch and hovering on the verge of orgasm, I dug my nails into his neck. The tension in my body from having Christopher in the room only ramped up the erotic sensations.

"Eva?" Christopher asked.

I swallowed hard. "Yes?"

"Are you okay?"

Gideon adjusted his stance, which moved his cock inside me and bumped his pelvis against my pulsing clit.

"Y-yes. We're just . . . talking. About. Dinner." My eyes closed as Gideon's fingertip grazed the thin wall separating his penis from his touch. If he nudged my clit again, I'd come. I was too wound up to stop it.

Gideon's chest vibrated against my cheek as he spoke. "We'd be done sooner if you'd go, so tell me what you need."

"Mom's looking for you."

"Why?" Gideon shifted again, rocking into my clit at the same moment he gave a quick, deep thrust of his finger into my rear.

I climaxed. Afraid of the wail of pleasure that wanted out of me, I sank my teeth into Gideon's hard pectoral. He grunted softly and started coming, his cock jerking as it pumped thick spurts of scorching semen into me.

The rest of the conversation was lost beneath the roar of my blood. Christopher said something, Gideon replied, and then the door shut again. I was lifted to sit on the armrest and Gideon started thrusting between my spread thighs, using my body to rub out the rest of his orgasm, growling in my mouth as we finished off the rawest, most exhibitionistic sexual encounter of my life.

Afterward, Gideon led me by the hand to a bathroom, where he lightly soaped a washcloth and cleansed between my legs before he paid the same attention to his cock. The way he took care of me was sweetly intimate, demonstrating yet again that as primal as his desire for me was, I was precious to him.

"I don't want us to fight anymore," I said quietly from my perch on the counter.

He tossed the washcloth down a concealed laundry chute and refastened his fly. Then he came to me, brushing his cool fingertips down my cheek. "We don't fight, angel. We just have to learn not to scare the hell out of each other."

"You make it sound so easy," I grumbled. To call either of us virgins would be ridiculous, yet emotionally that was just what we were. Fumbling in the dark and too eager, completely out of our depths and self-conscious, trying to impress and missing all the subtle nuances.

"Easy or hard, doesn't matter. We'll get through this because we have to." He pushed his fingers through my hair, restoring order to the disheveled strands. "We'll discuss when we get home. I think I've discovered the crux of our problem."

His conviction and determination soothed the restlessness I'd been feeling the last few days. Closing my eyes, I relaxed and enjoyed the tactile delight of having my hair played with. "Your mother seemed startled that I'm a blonde."

"Did she?"

"My mother was, too. Not about me being a blonde," I qualified. "That you'd be interested in one."

"Was she?"

"Gideon!"

"Hmm?" He kissed the end of my nose and ran his hands down my arms.

"I'm not the type you usually go for, am I?"

His brow arched. "I have one type: Eva Lauren Tramell. That's it."

I rolled my eyes. "Okay. Whatever."

"What does it matter? You're the woman I'm with."

"It doesn't matter. I'm just curious. People don't usually stray from their preferred type."

Stepping between my legs, he put his arms around my hips. "Lucky for me that I fit your type."

"Gideon, you don't fit any type," I drawled. "You're in a class by yourself."

His eyes sparkled. "Like what you see, do you?"

"You know I do, which is why we really should get out of here before we start screwing like minks again."

Pressing his cheek to mine, he murmured, "Only you could blow my mind in a place that's always made my skin crawl. Thank you for being exactly what I want and need."

"Oh, Gideon." I wrapped my arms and legs around him, holding him as close to me as possible. "You came here for me, didn't you? To take me away from this place you hate."

"I'd walk into hell for you, Eva, and this is pretty damn close." He exhaled harshly. "I was about to go to your apartment and drag you away with me when I learned you'd come here. You have to stay away from Christopher."

"Why do you keep saying that? He seems very nice."

Gideon pulled back, sifting my hair through his fingers. His eyes stayed fiercely locked to mine. "He takes sibling rivalry to the extreme, and he's unstable enough to make him dangerous. He's reaching out to you because he knows he can hurt me through you. You have to trust me on this."

Why was Gideon so suspicious of his half

brother's motives? He had to have a good reason. It was yet another thing he didn't fully share with me. "I do trust you. Of course I do. I'll keep my distance."

"Thank you." Catching me by the waist, he lifted me off the counter and set me on my feet. "Let's grab Cary and get the hell out of here."

We made our way back outside with my hand in his. I was uncomfortably aware that we'd been gone a very long time. The sun was going down. And I was pantyless. My ruined boy shorts were presently stuffed into the front pocket of Gideon's jeans.

He glanced at me as we entered the marquee. "I should've told you before. You look gorgeous, Eva. That dress is amazing on you and so are those fuck-me red heels."

"Well, clearly they work." I bumped my shoulder into him. "Thank you."

"For the compliment? Or the fucking?"

"Hush," I admonished, flushing.

His dark velvet laugh turned every female head in hearing distance and some of the men's, too. Placing our linked hands at the small of my back, he pulled me close and smacked a kiss on my mouth.

"Gideon!" His mother glided toward us with sparkling eyes and a wide smile on her lovely face. "I'm so happy you're here."

She looked like she might hug him, but his posture altered subtly, charging the air around him with an invisible field of power that encompassed me as well.

Elizabeth drew to an abrupt halt.

"Mother," he greeted her with all the warmth of an arctic storm. "You can thank Eva for my being here. I've come to take her away."

"But she's having a good time, aren't you, Eva? You should stay for her sake." Elizabeth looked at me with a plea in her eyes.

My fingers flexed around Gideon's hand. He came first, that was never in question, but I couldn't help but wish I knew the story behind his coldness toward a mother who seemed to love him. Her adoring gaze slid over the face that had shades of her own, drinking in every feature hungrily. How long had it been since the last time she'd seen him in person?

Then I wondered if maybe she'd loved him *too much.* . . .

Revulsion made my spine stiffen.

"Don't put Eva on the spot," Gideon said, rubbing his knuckles against my tense back. "You've gotten what you wanted — you've met her."

"Perhaps you'll both come to dinner later this week?"

His only answer was an arched brow. Then his gaze lifted, luring my attention to follow it. I found Cary emerging from what appeared to be a hedgerow maze with a very recognizable pop princess on his arm. Gideon gestured him over.

"Oh, not Cary, too!" Elizabeth protested. "He's the life of the party."

"I thought you might like him." Gideon bared his teeth in something that was too sharp to be a smile. "Just remember that he's Eva's friend, Mother. That makes him mine as well."

I was hugely relieved when Cary joined us, breaking the tension in his easygoing way.

"I was looking for you," he said to me. "I was hoping you'd be ready to go. I got that call I was expecting."

Looking into his sparkling eyes, I knew Trey had reached him. "Yes, we're ready."

Cary and I walked around to say our good-byes and offer our thanks. Gideon remained at my side like a possessive shadow, his demeanor calm but markedly aloof.

We were all walking toward the house when I spotted Ireland off to the side staring at Gideon. I stopped and looked up at him. "Go get your sister so we can say good-bye."

"What?"

"She's standing to your left." I looked to our right to hide my prodding from the young girl whom I suspected might hero-worship her eldest brother.

He gestured Ireland over with a brusque wave of his hand. She took her time ambling over, her pretty face schooled into an expression of militant boredom. I looked at Cary with a shake of my head, remembering those days all too well.

"Listen." I squeezed Gideon's wrist. "Tell her you're sorry you two didn't get to catch up while you were here and she should call you sometime, if she wants."

Gideon shot me an arch look. "Catch up on what?"

Rubbing his biceps, I said, "She'll do all the talking if given a chance."

He scowled. "She's a teenage girl. Why would I give her a chance to talk my ear off?"

I pushed onto my tiptoes and whispered in his ear, "Because I'll owe you one."

"You're up to something." He eyed me warily for a moment; then he pressed a hard kiss to my lips with a growl. "So we'll leave it open and say you owe me more than one.

Quantity to be determined."

I nodded. Cary rocked back on his heels and twirled one index finger around another in a sign meaning *wrapped around your finger.*

Only fair, I thought, since he was wrapped around my heart.

I was surprised when Gideon accepted the keys to the Bentley SUV from one of the valets. "*You* drove? Where's Angus?"

"Day off." He nuzzled against my temple. "I missed you, Eva."

I settled into the front passenger seat, and he shut the door behind me. As I secured my seat belt, I saw him pause by the hood, making eye contact with two men dressed in black who waited beside a sleek black Mercedes sedan at the end of the drive. They nodded and got in the Benz. When Gideon pulled out of the Vidal driveway, they followed directly behind us.

"Security detail?" I asked.

"Yes. I took off fast when I was told you were here, and they lost the tail for a while."

Cary went home with Clancy, so Gideon and I headed straight to the penthouse. I found myself getting turned on from watching Gideon drive. He handled the luxury vehicle the way he handled everything —

confidently, aggressively, and with skillful control. He drove fast but not recklessly, weaving easily over the curves and straight-aways of the scenic route back to the city. There was almost no traffic until we hit the gridlock of Manhattan.

When we arrived at his apartment, we both went straight into the master bathroom and undressed for a shower. As if he couldn't stop touching me, Gideon washed me from head to toe; then he dried me with a towel and wrapped me in a new robe of embroidered teal silk with kimono sleeves. He finished by pulling a pair of similarly hued drawstring silk pants out of a drawer for himself.

"Don't I get panties?" I asked, thinking about my drawer of sexy underwear.

"No. There's a phone hanging on the wall in the kitchen. Hit speed dial one and tell the man who answers that I want him to pick up double my usual dinner order from Peter Luger."

"All right." I headed out to the living room and made the call; then I had to search for Gideon. I found him in his home office, a room I hadn't been in before.

I didn't get a good look at the space at first because the only lighting came from an angled picture light on the wall and a barrister's lamp on his polished wood desk. Plus my eyes were more interested in focusing on him. He looked utterly sensual and compelling sprawled in his big black leather chair. He held a tulip glass of some liquor that he warmed between his hands, and the beauty of his flexing biceps sent tingles racing through me, as did the tight lacing of muscles on his abdomen.

His gaze was on the wall illuminated by the picture light, which snagged my attention, too. I was startled when I saw the art — a huge collage of blown-up photos of him and me: the picture of our kiss on the street outside the gym . . . a shot of us from the press gauntlet at the advocacy dinner . . . a candid of the tender aftermath of our fight in Bryant Park . . .

The focal point was the image in the center that had been taken while I slept in my own bed, lit only by the candle I'd left burning for him. It was an intimate voyeuristic shot, one that said more about the photographer than it did the subject.

I was deeply touched by the proof that he'd been falling along with me.

Gideon gestured at the drink he'd poured for me in advance and set on the edge of his desk. "Have a seat."

I complied, curious. There was an edge to

him that was new, a sense of purpose and calm determination paired with laser-precise focus.

What had brought on his mood? And what did it mean for the rest of our evening?

Then I saw the small photo collage frame lying on the desktop next to my drink, and my worry faded. The frame was very similar to the one already on my desk, but this one held three photos of Gideon and me together.

"I want you to take that to work," he said quietly.

"Thank you." For the first time in days, I was happy. I hugged the frame to my chest with one hand and picked up my glass with the other.

His eyes glittered as he watched me take a seat. "You blow kisses at me all day from your picture on my desk. I think it's only fair that you be equally reminded of me. Of us."

I exhaled in a rush, my heartbeat not quite steady. "I never forget about you or us."

"I wouldn't let you if you tried." Gideon took a deep drink, his throat working on a swallow. "I think I've figured out where we made our first misstep, the one that's led to all the stumbles we've had since."

"Oh?"

"Take a drink of your Armagnac, angel. I think you'll need it."

I took a cautious sip of the liquor, feeling the instantaneous burn, followed by recognition that I liked the flavor. I took a bigger drink.

Rolling his glass between his palms, Gideon took another drink and eyed me thoughtfully. "Tell me which was hotter, Eva: sex in the limo when you were in charge or sex in the hotel when I was?"

I shifted restlessly, unsure of where the conversation was leading. "I thought you enjoyed what happened in the limo. While it was happening, I mean. Obviously not later."

"I loved it," he said with quiet conviction. "The image of you in that red dress, moaning and telling me how good my cock feels inside you, will haunt me as long as I live. If you'd like to top me again in the future, I'm definitely game."

My stomach tensed. The muscles in my shoulders began to knot. "Gideon, I'm starting to freak out a little. All this talk of safewords and topping . . . it feels like this conversation is leading somewhere I can't go."

"You're thinking of bondage and pain. I'm talking about a consensual power exchange." Gideon studied me intently. "Would you like more brandy? You're very pale."

"You think?" I set the drained glass down. "It sounds like you're telling me you're a Dominant."

"Angel, you knew that already." His mouth curved in a soft, sexy smile. "What I'm telling you is that you're submissive."

17

I pushed to my feet in a rush.

"Don't," he warned in a dark purr. "You're not running yet. We're not done."

"You don't know what you're talking about." Being under someone else's thumb — *losing my right to say no!* — was never going to happen again. "You know what I went through. I need control as much as you do."

"Sit down, Eva."

I stayed on my feet, just to prove my point.

His smile widened and my insides melted. "Do you have any idea how crazy I am about you?" he murmured.

"You're crazy all right, if you think I'm going to put up with being ordered around, especially sexually."

"Come on, Eva. You know I don't want to beat you, punish you, hurt you, demean you, or order you around like a pet. Those aren't needs either of us has." Straightening, Gideon leaned forward and placed his elbows on the desktop. "You're the most important thing in my life. I treasure you. I want to protect you and make you feel safe. That's why we're talking about this."

God. How could he be so wonderful and so insane at the same time? "I don't need to be dominated!"

"What you need is someone to trust — No. Close your mouth, Eva. You'll wait until I'm finished."

My protest spluttered into silence.

"You've asked me to reacquaint your body with acts previously used to hurt and terrorize you. I can't tell you what your trust means to me or what it would do to me if I broke that trust. I can't risk it, Eva. We have to do this right."

I crossed my arms. "I guess I'm dumber than bricks. I thought our sex life was rockin'."

Setting his glass down, Gideon kept going as if I hadn't spoken. "You asked me to meet a need of yours today and I agreed. Now we need to —"

"If I'm not what you want, just spit it out!" I set the picture frame and my glass down before I did something with them I'd regret. "Don't try to pretty it up with —"

He was around the desk and on me before

I could stumble back more than a couple steps. His mouth sealed over mine; his arms caged me. As he'd done earlier, he carried me to a wall and restrained me against it, his hands banding my wrists and lifting them high above my head.

Trapped, I could do nothing as he bent his knees and stroked my cleft with the rigid length of his erection. Once, twice. Silk rasped against my swollen clit. The bite of his teeth on my covered nipple sent a shiver through me, while the clean scent of his warm skin intoxicated me. With a gasp, I sagged into his embrace.

"See how easily you submit when I take over?" His lips followed the arch of my brow. "And it feels good, doesn't it? It feels right."

"That's not fair." I stared up at him. How could he expect me to respond any differently? As disturbed and confounded as I was, I was helplessly drawn to him.

"Of course it is. It's also true."

My gaze roamed over that glorious mane of inky hair and the chiseled lines of his incomparable face. The longing I felt was so acute it was painful. The hidden damage inside him only made me love him more. There were times when I felt like I'd found the other half of myself in him.

"I can't help it that you turn me on," I muttered. "My body is physiologically supposed to soften and relax, so you can shove that big cock inside me."

"Eva. Let's be honest. You *want* me to have total control. It's important to you that you can trust me to take care of you. There's nothing wrong with that. The reverse is true for me — I need you to trust me enough to give up that control."

I couldn't think when he was pressed up against me, my body achingly aware of every hard inch of him. "I am *not* submissive."

"You are with me. If you look back, you'll see you've been yielding to me all along."

"You're good in bed! And have more experience. Of course I let you do what you want to me." I bit my lower lip to stop it from quivering. "I'm sorry I haven't been as exciting for you."

"Bullshit, Eva. You know how much I enjoy making love to you. If I could get away with it, I'd do nothing else. We're not talking about games that get me off."

"Then we're talking about what gets *me* off? Is that what this is?"

"Yes. I thought so." He frowned. "You're upset. I didn't mean — Damn it. I thought discussing this would help us."

"Gideon." My eyes stung, then flooded

with tears. He looked as wounded and confused as I felt. "You're breaking my heart."

Releasing my wrists, he stepped back and swept me up in his arms, carrying me out of his office and down the hallway to a closed door. "Turn the knob," he said quietly.

We entered a candlelit room that still smelled faintly of new paint. For a few seconds I was disoriented, unable to comprehend how we'd stepped out of Gideon's apartment and into my bedroom.

"I don't understand." A serious understatement, but my brain was still trying to get past the feeling of being teleported from one residence to another. "You . . . moved me in with you?"

"Not quite." He set me down, but kept an arm around me. "I recreated your room based on the photo I took of you sleeping."

"Why?"

What the hell? Who did something like that? Was this all to keep me from witnessing his nightmares?

The thought shattered my heart further. I felt like Gideon and I were drifting further away from each other by the moment.

His hands sifted through my damp hair, which only increased my agitation. I felt like batting his touch away and putting at least the length of the room between us. Maybe two rooms.

"If you feel the need to run," he said softly, "you can come in here and shut the door. I promise not to bother you until you're ready. This way, you have your safe place and I know that you haven't left me."

A million questions and speculations roared through my mind, but the one thing that stuck out was, "Are we still going to share a bed when we're sleeping?"

"Every night." Gideon's lips touched my forehead. "How could you think otherwise? Talk to me, Eva. What's going through that beautiful head of yours?"

"What's going through *my* head?" I snapped. "What the fuck is going on in yours? What happened to you in the four days we were broken up?"

His jaw tightened. "We never broke up, Eva."

The phone rang in the other room. I cursed under my breath. I wanted us to talk and I wanted him to go away, both at the same time.

He squeezed my shoulders, and then let me go. "That's our dinner."

I didn't follow him when he left, feeling too unsettled to eat. Instead, I crawled onto the bed that was exactly like my own and curled around a pillow, closing my eyes. I didn't hear Gideon come back, but I felt him as he drew to a stop at the edge of the bed.

"Please don't make me eat alone," he said to my rigid back.

"Why don't you just order me to eat with you?"

He sighed, and then slid onto the bed to spoon behind me. His warmth was welcome, chasing away the chill that had brought goose bumps to my skin. He didn't say anything for a long while, just gave me the comfort of having him close. Or maybe he was taking comfort in me.

"Eva." His fingers caressed the length of my silk-clad arm. "I can't stand you being unhappy. Talk to me."

"I don't know what to say. I thought we were finally coming to a point where things would smooth out between us." I hugged the pillow tighter.

"Don't tense up, Eva. It hurts when you pull away from me."

I felt like he was *pushing* me away.

Rolling, I shoved him to his back; then I mounted him, my robe parting as I straddled his hips. I ran the palms of my hands over his powerful chest and raked the tanned flesh with my nails. My hips undulated over him, stroking my bare cleft over his cock. Through the thin silk of his pants, I could feel every ridge and thick vein. From the way his eyes darkened and his sculpted mouth parted on quickened breaths, I knew he could feel the outline and damp heat of me as well.

"Is this so awful for you?" I asked, rocking my hips. "Are you lying there thinking you're not giving me what I want because I'm in charge?"

Gideon set his hands on my thighs. Even that innocuous touch seemed dominating.

The edginess and sharpened focus I'd detected not long ago abruptly made sense to me — he wasn't restraining his force of will anymore.

The tremendous power coiled inside him was now directed at me like a blast of heat.

"I've told you before," he said huskily. "I'll take you however I can get you."

"Whatever. Don't think I don't know you're topping from the bottom."

His mouth curved with unapologetic amusement.

Sliding down, I teased the flat disk of his nipple with the tip of my tongue. I blanketed him as he'd done to me in the past, stretching my body over his hips and legs, my hands shoving beneath his gorgeous ass to squeeze the firm flesh and hold him tight against me. His cock was a thick column against my belly, renewing my fierce appetite for him.

"Are you going to punish me with pleasure?" he asked quietly. "Because you can. You can bring me to my knees, Eva."

My forehead dropped to his chest and the air left my lungs in an audible rush. "I wish."

"Please don't be so worried. We'll get through this along with everything else."

"You're so positive you're right." My gaze narrowed. "You're trying to prove a point."

"And you might prove yours." Gideon licked his lower lip and my sex clenched in silent demand.

There was a brilliant depth of emotion in his eyes. Whatever else was going on in our relationship, there was no doubt we were seriously twisted up over each other.

And I was about to demonstrate that in the flesh.

Gideon's neck arched as my mouth moved over his torso. "Oh, Eva."

"Your world's about to be rocked, Mr. Cross."

It was. I made sure of it.

Feeling goofy with feminine triumph, I sat

at Gideon's dining table and remembered him as he'd been just a short time ago — damp with sweat and panting, cursing as I took my time savoring his luscious body.

He swallowed a bite of his steak, which had been kept hot courtesy of a warming drawer, and said calmly, "You're insatiable."

"Well, duh. You're gorgeous, sexy, and very well hung."

"I'm glad you approve. I'm also extremely wealthy."

I waved one hand carelessly, encompassing the whole of what had to be a fifty-million-dollar apartment. "Who cares about that?"

"Well, I do, actually." His mouth curved.

I stabbed my fork into a German fried potato, thinking that Peter Luger food was almost as good as sex. Almost. "I'm interested in your money only if it means you can afford to stop working in favor of lounging around naked as my sex slave."

"I could afford to financially, yes. But you'd get bored and dump me, and then where would I be?" His look was warmly amused. "Think you proved your point, do you?"

I chewed, then said, "Should I prove it again?"

"The fact that you're still horny enough

to want to proves *my* point."

"Hmm." I drank my wine. "Are you projecting?"

He shot me a look and casually chewed another bite of the tenderest steak I'd ever had.

Restless and worried, I took a deep breath and asked, "Would you tell me if our sex life didn't satisfy you?"

"Don't be ridiculous, Eva."

What else could have prompted him to bring this up after our four-day breakup? "I'm sure it doesn't help that I'm not the type you usually go for. And we haven't used any of those toys you had in the hotel —"

"Stop talking."

"Excuse me?"

Gideon set his utensils down. "I'm not going to listen to you shred your self-esteem."

"What? You're the only one who gets to do all the talking?"

"You can pick a fight with me, Eva, but it's still not going to get you fucked."

"Who said —" I shut up when he glared. He was right. I still wanted him. I wanted him on top of me, explosively lustful, completely in control of both my pleasure and his.

Pushing away from the table, he said curtly, "Wait here."

When he returned a moment later, he set a black leather ring box beside my plate and resumed his seat. The sight of it hit me like a physical blow. Fear struck me first, icy cold. Followed swiftly by a longing that was white-hot.

My hands shook in my lap. I clasped my fingers together and realized my whole body was shaking. Lost, I lifted my gaze to Gideon's face.

The feel of his fingertips brushing down my cheek soothed much of the vibrating anxiety inside me, leaving behind the terrible yearning.

"It's not *that* ring," he murmured gently. "Not yet. You're not ready."

Something inside me wilted. Then relief flooded me. It *was* too soon. Neither of us was ready. But if I'd ever wondered how deeply I had fallen in love with Gideon, now I knew.

I nodded.

"Open it," he said.

With cautious fingers, I pulled the box closer and thumbed open the lid. "Oh."

Nestled inside the black leather and velvet was a ring like no other. Gold ropelike bands were intertwined and decorated with

Xs covered in diamonds.

"Bonds," I murmured, "secured by crosses." Gideon *Cross*.

"Not quite. I see the ropes as representative of the many threads of you, not bondage. But yes, the Xs are me holding on to you. By my fingernails, it feels like." He finished his glass of wine and refilled both our glasses.

I sat unmoving, stunned, trying to take it all in. Everything he'd done in the time we'd been apart — the photos, the ring, Dr. Petersen, the replicated bedroom, and whoever had been following me around — told me I'd never been far from his mind, if I'd even left it at all.

"You gave me my keys back," I whispered, still remembering the pain.

His hand reached out and covered mine. "There are a lot of reasons why I did that. You left me wearing nothing but a robe, Eva, and without your keys. I can't stand thinking about what could've happened if Cary hadn't been home to let you in right away."

Lifting his hand to my mouth, I kissed the back, then released him and closed the lid of the ring box. "It's beautiful, Gideon. Thank you. It means a lot to me."

"But you won't wear it." It wasn't a question.

"After the conversation we've had tonight, it feels like a collar."

After a moment, he nodded. "You're not altogether wrong."

My brain hurt and my heart ached. Four nights of restless sleeping didn't help. I couldn't understand why he felt I was so necessary, even though I felt that way about him. There were thousands of women in New York alone who could replace me in his life, but there was only one Gideon Cross.

"I feel like I'm disappointing you, Gideon. After everything we've talked about tonight . . . I feel like this is the beginning of the end."

Pushing his chair back, he angled toward me and touched my cheek. "It's not."

"When do we see Dr. Petersen?"

"I'll go alone on Tuesdays. After you talk to him and agree to couples counseling, we can go together on Thursdays."

"Two hours of your week, every week. Not including the travel back and forth. That's a big commitment." I reached up and brushed the hair back from his cheek. "Thank you."

Gideon caught my hand and kissed the palm. "It's no sacrifice, Eva."

He went into his office to work a bit before bed, and I carried the ring box into the master bathroom with me. I studied it further while I brushed my teeth and hair.

There was a soft hum of need beneath my skin, a persistent level of arousal that shouldn't have been possible considering the number of orgasms I'd already had over the course of the day. It was an emotionally driven need to connect to Gideon, to reassure myself that we were okay.

Clutching the ring box in my hand, I went to my side of Gideon's bed and set it on the nightstand. I wanted it where I'd see it first thing in the morning, after a good night's sleep.

With a sigh, I draped my beautiful new robe over the footboard and crawled into bed. After tossing and turning for a long while, I finally crashed.

I woke sometime in the middle of the night to a racing pulse and quick, shallow breathing. Disoriented, I lay still for a moment, gathering my bearings and remembering where I was. I tensed when it sank in, my ears straining to hear if Gideon was having another nightmare. When I discovered him lying quietly beside me, his breathing deep and even, I relaxed with a sigh.

What time had he finally come to bed? After the days we'd spent apart, it worried me that he might have felt a need to be alone.

Then it hit me. I was *aroused.* Painfully so.

My breasts were full and heavy, my nipples furled and tight. My core was aching and my cleft wet. As I lay there in the moonlit darkness, I realized that my own body had woken me with its demands. Had I dreamed something erotic? Or was it enough that Gideon was lying beside me?

Pushing up onto my elbows, I looked at him. The sheet and comforter clung to his waist, leaving his sculpted chest and biceps bared. His right arm was tossed over his head, framing the fall of dark hair around his face. His left arm lay between us on the blankets, the hand fisted and bringing to relief the network of thick veins that coursed up his forearms. Even in repose he looked fierce and powerful.

I became more aware of the tension inside me, the sense that I was drawn to him by the silent exertion of his formidable will. It wasn't possible that he could demand my surrender while he was sleeping, yet it felt that way, felt like that invisible rope between us was pulling me to him.

The throbbing between my legs grew unbearable and I pressed one hand against the violent pulsing, hoping to dull the ache. The pressure worsened it instead.

I couldn't stay still. Throwing the covers off, I slid my legs off the side of the mattress and thought about trying a glass of warm milk with the brandy Gideon had given me earlier. Abruptly, I paused, riveted by the moonlight gleaming off the leather of the ring box on the nightstand. I thought of the jewelry inside it and my desire surged. At that moment, the thought of being collared by Gideon filled me with heated yearning.

You're just horny, I scolded myself.

One of the girls in group had talked about how her "master" could use her body any time and in any way he wanted, for his pleasure alone. There was nothing about that I'd found sexy . . . until I put Gideon in the picture. I loved getting him off. I loved making him come. Just because.

My fingers brushed over the lid of the tiny box. Exhaling a shaky breath, I picked it up and opened it. A moment later I was sliding the cool band onto the ring finger of my right hand.

"Do you like it, Eva?"

A shiver moved through me at the sound

of Gideon's voice, deeper and rougher than I'd ever heard it. He'd been awake, watching me.

How long had he been conscious? Was he as attuned to me while sleeping as I seemed to be to him?

"I love it." *I love you.*

Setting the box aside, I turned my head to find him sitting up. His eyes glittered in a way that made me impossibly aroused but also sent a bite of fear through me. It was an unguarded look, like the one that had literally knocked me on my ass when we met — scorching and possessive, filled with dark threats of ecstasy. His gorgeous face was harsh in the shadows, his jaw taut as he lifted my right hand to his mouth and kissed the ring he'd given me.

I moved to kneel on the bed and draped my arms around his neck. "Take me. Carte blanche."

He cupped my butt and squeezed. "How does it feel to say that?"

"Almost as good as the orgasms you're going to give me."

"Ah, a challenge." The tip of his tongue teased the seam of my lips, tempting me with the promise of a kiss he deliberately withheld.

"Gideon!"

"Lie back, angel, and grip your pillow with both hands." His mouth curved in a wicked smile. "Don't let go for any reason. Understand?"

Swallowing hard, I did as I was told, so turned on I thought I might come from just the relentless spasming of my needy sex.

He kicked the covers down to the footboard. "Spread your legs and pull up your knees."

My breath caught audibly as my nipples hardened further, causing a deep ache in my breasts. God, Gideon was hot as hell like this. I was panting with excitement, my mind spinning with the possibilities. The flesh between my legs trembled with want.

"Oh, Eva," he crooned, running his index finger through my slick cleft. "Look how greedy you are for me. It's a full-time job keeping this sweet little cunt satisfied."

That single rigid finger pushed into me, parting the swollen tissues. I tightened around him, so close to coming I could taste it. He withdrew and lifted his hand to his mouth, licking my flavor from his skin. My hips arched without volition, my body straining toward his.

"Your fault I'm so hot for you," I gasped. "You slacked on the job for days."

"Then I better make up for lost time."

Sliding down into a prone position, he settled his shoulders beneath my thighs and rimmed the quivering entrance to my body with the tip of his tongue. Around and around. Ignoring my clit and refraining from fucking me even when I begged.

"Gideon, please."

"Shh. I have to get you ready first."

"I'm ready. I was ready before you woke up."

"Then you should've woken me earlier. I'll always take care of you, Eva. I live for it."

Whimpering in distress, I rocked my hips into that teasing tongue. Only when I was soaked with my own arousal, creaming desperately for the feel of any part of him I could get inside me, did he crawl over me and settle between my spread thighs, placing his forearms flat on the bed.

He held my gaze. His cock, feverishly hot and hard as stone, lay against the lips of my sex. I wanted it inside me more than I wanted to breathe. "Now," I gasped. "Now."

With a practiced shift of his hips, he rammed deep into me, shoving me up the bed.

"Ah, God," I gasped, convulsing ecstatically around the thick column of flesh that possessed me. This was what I'd needed since we'd talked in his home office, what I'd craved as I rode up and down his steely erection before dinner, what I'd needed even as I climaxed around his thick length.

"Don't come," he murmured in my ear, cupping my breasts in his hands and rolling my nipples between his thumb and forefingers.

"What?" I was pretty sure if he'd just take a deep breath I'd go off.

"And don't let go of the pillow."

Gideon began to move in a slow, lazy rhythm. "You're going to want to," he murmured, nuzzling the sensitive spot beneath my ear. "You love to grab my hair and rake your nails down my back. And when you're close to coming, you like to squeeze my ass and yank me deeper. Makes me so damn hard when you go wild like that, when you show me how much you love how I feel inside you."

"No fair," I moaned, knowing he was deliberately provoking me. The cadence of his raspy voice was perfectly timed with the relentless surging of his hips. "You're torturing me."

"Good things come to those who wait." His tongue traced the shell of my ear, and then dipped inside at the same moment he tugged on my nipples.

I bucked into his next thrust and nearly came. Gideon knew my body so well, knew all its secrets and erogenous zones. He was expertly stroking his cock inside me, rubbing over and over the tender bundle of nerves that quivered in delight.

Rolling his hips, he screwed into me, exploiting other spots. I made a plaintive sound, on fire for him, desperately infatuated. My fingers cramped with the grip I had on my pillow, my head thrashing against the driving need to orgasm. He could get me there just by rubbing inside me, the only man who'd ever been skilled enough to give me an intense vaginal orgasm.

"Don't come," he repeated, his voice hoarse. "Make it last."

"I c-can't. It feels too good. God, Gideon . . ." Tears leaked out of the corners of my eyes. "I . . . I'm lost in you."

I cried softly, afraid to say the other L-word too soon and risk upsetting the delicate balance between us.

"Oh, Eva." He rubbed his cheek against my damp face. "I must've wished for you so hard and so often you had no choice but to come true."

"Please," I begged softly. "Slow down."

Gideon lifted his head to look at me, choosing that moment to pinch my nipples with just enough force to inflict a hint of pain. The tender muscles inside me clenched down so hard that his next thrust caused him to groan.

"Please," I pleaded again, trembling with the effort to stave off my building climax. "I'm going to come if you don't slow down."

His gaze was hot on my face, his hips still lunging in a measured tempo that was slowly stealing my sanity. "Don't you want to come, Eva?" he purred in that voice that could lure me into hell with a dreamy smile. "Isn't that what you've been working toward all night?"

My neck arched as his lips drifted across my throat. "Only when you say I can," I gasped. "Only . . . when you say."

"Angel." One hand moved to my face, brushing back the strands of hair that clung to the perspiration on my skin. He kissed me deeply, reverently, licking deep into my mouth.

Yes . . .

"Come for me," he coaxed, quickening his pace. "Come, Eva."

On command, the orgasm struck me like a blow, shocking my system with an overload of sensation. Wave after wave of pulsing heat rolled through me, contracting my sex and tightening my core. I cried out, first with an

410

inarticulate sound of agonized pleasure, then with his name. Chanting it over and over as he drove his beautiful cock into me, prolonging my climax, before pushing me into another one.

"Touch me," he rasped, as I fell apart beneath him. "Hold me."

Freed from his command to hold the pillow, I bound him to my sweat-slick body with arms and legs. He pounded deep and hard, driving strenuously toward his climax.

He came with a growl, his head thrown back as he spurted into me for long minutes. I held him until our bodies cooled and our breathing evened.

When Gideon finally rolled off me, he didn't go far. He wrapped himself around my back and whispered, "Sleep now."

I don't remember if I stayed awake long enough to reply.

18

Monday mornings could be awesome, when they began with Gideon Cross. We rode to work with my back propped against his side and his arm slung over my shoulder so that his fingers could link with mine.

As he toyed with the ring he'd given me, I kicked out my legs and eyed the classic nude heels he'd bought me along with some outfits to wear on the occasions I slept over. To start out the new week, I'd decided on a black pinstriped sheath dress with a thin blue belt that reminded me of his eyes. He had excellent taste; I had to give him that.

Unless he was sending one of his brunette "acquaintances" out on buying sprees . . . ?

I pushed the unpleasant thought aside.

When I'd checked out the drawers he had set aside for me in his bathroom, I found all of my usual cosmetics and toiletries in all my usual shades. I didn't bother to ask how he knew, which might've led to me freaking out. Instead, I chose to look at it as more proof of his attentiveness. He thought of everything.

The highlight of my morning had been helping Gideon dress in one of his seriously sexy suits. I'd buttoned his shirt; he'd tucked it into his pants. I'd fastened his fly; he had knotted his tie. He'd shrugged into his vest; I'd smoothed the finely tailored material over his equally fine shirt, amazed to find that it could be just as sexy putting clothes *on* him as it was to take them *off*. It was like wrapping my own gift.

The world would see the beauty of the packaging, but only I knew the man inside it and how precious he was. His intimate smiles and his deep husky laugh, the gentleness of his touch and the ferocity of his passion were all reserved for me.

The Bentley bounced lightly over a pothole in the road and Gideon tightened his hold. "What's the plan after work?"

"I get to start my Krav Maga classes today." I couldn't keep the excitement out of my voice.

"Ah, that's right." His lips brushed over my temple. "You know I'm going to have to watch you go through drills. Just thinking about it makes me hard."

"Didn't we already establish that *every-*

thing makes you hard?" I teased, nudging him with my elbow.

"Everything about *you.* Which is lucky for us, since you're insatiable. Text me when you're done and I'll meet you at your place."

Digging in my purse, I pulled out my smartphone to see if it still had a charge and saw a message from Cary. I opened it and found a video plus a text: Does X know his bro is a douche? Stay away from CV, baby girl *smooches*

I started the playback but it took me a minute to figure out what I was seeing. When comprehension set in, I froze.

"What is it?" Gideon asked with his lips in my hair. Then he stiffened behind me, which told me he was looking over my shoulder.

Cary had filmed the video at the Vidals' garden party. From the eight-foot-high hedges in the background, he was in the maze, and from the leaves framing the screen, he was in hiding. The star of the show was a couple locked in a passionate embrace. The woman was beautifully teary, while the man kissed over her frantic words and soothed her with gentle strokes of his hands.

They were talking about me and Gideon, talking about how I was using my body to

414

get my hands on his millions.

"Don't worry," Christopher crooned to a distraught Magdalene. "You know Gideon gets bored fast."

"He's different with her. I — I think he loves her."

He kissed her forehead. "She's not his type."

The fingers I had linked with Gideon's tightened.

As we watched, Magdalene's demeanor slowly changed. She began to nuzzle into Christopher's touch, her voice softening, her mouth seeking. To an observer, it was clear he knew her body well — where to pet and where to rub. When she responded to his skilled seduction, he lifted her dress and fucked her. That he was taking advantage of her was obvious. It was there in the contemptuously triumphant look on his face as he screwed her until she was limp.

I didn't recognize the Christopher on the screen. His face, his posture, his voice . . . it was like he was a different man.

I was grateful when my smartphone battery died and the screen abruptly winked off. Gideon wrapped his arms around me.

"Yuck," I whispered, snuggling carefully into him so I didn't get makeup on his lapel. "Majorly creepy. I feel bad for her."

He exhaled harshly. "That's Christopher."

"Asshole. That smug look on his face — ugh." I shuddered.

Pressing his lips to my hair, he murmured, "I thought Maggie would be safe from him. Our mothers have known each other for years. I forget how much he hates me."

"Why?"

I wondered briefly if the nightmares Gideon had were related to Christopher, then put the thought aside. No way. Gideon was older by several years and tougher all the way around. He'd kick Christopher's ass.

"He thinks I got all the attention when we were younger," Gideon said wearily, "because everyone was worried about how I was handling my father's suicide. So he wants what's mine. Everything he can get his hands on."

I turned into him, pushing my arms underneath his jacket to get closer. There was something in his voice that made me hurt for him. His family home was a place he said haunted his nightmares and he was terribly distant from his family.

He'd never been loved. It was as simple — and as complicated — as that.

"Gideon?"

"Hmm?"

I pulled back to look at him. Reaching up,

416

I traced the bold arch of his brow. "I love you."

A violent shudder moved through him, one hard enough to shake me, too.

"I don't mean to freak you out," I reassured him quickly, averting my face to give him some privacy. "You don't have to do anything about it. I just didn't want another minute to go by without you knowing how I feel. You can tuck it away now."

One of his hands gripped my nape; the other dug almost painfully into my waist. Gideon held me there, immobile, locked against him as if I might blow away. His breathing was ragged, his heartbeat pounding. He didn't say another word the rest of the ride to work, but he didn't let me go either.

I planned on telling him again one day in the future, but as far as first times went, I thought we'd both done okay.

At ten o'clock sharp, I had two dozen long-stemmed red roses delivered to Gideon's office with the note:

In celebration of red dresses and limo rides.

Ten minutes later, I received an interoffice

envelope with a note card that read:

LET'S DO THAT AGAIN. SOON.

At eleven o'clock, I had a black-and-white calla lily arrangement delivered to his office with the note:

In honor of black & white garden party dresses and being dragged into libraries . . .

Ten minutes later, I received his reply:

I'LL BE DRAGGING YOU TO THE FLOOR IN A MINUTE . . .

At noon, I went shopping. Ring shopping. I hit six different shops before I found a piece that struck me as being absolutely perfect. Made of platinum and studded with black diamonds, it was an industrial-looking ring that made me think of power and bondage. It was a dominant ring, very bold and masculine. I had to open a new charge account with the store to cover the hefty cost, but I considered the months of payments ahead of me worth it.

I called Gideon's office and talked with Scott, who helped me arrange a fifteen-minute window in Gideon's packed day for me to stop by.

"Thank you so much for your help, Scott."

"You're very welcome. I've enjoyed watching him receive your flowers today. I don't think I've ever seen him smile like that."

A warm rush of love flowed through me. I wanted to make Gideon happy. As he'd said, I lived for it.

I went back to work with a smile of my own. At two o'clock, I had a tiger lily arrangement delivered to Gideon's office followed by a private note sent via interoffice envelope:

In gratitude for all the jungle sex.

His reply:

SKIP THE KRAV MAGA. I'LL GIVE YOU A WORKOUT.

When three forty rolled around — five minutes before my appointment with Gideon — I got nervous. I stood up from my chair on shaky legs and paced in the elevator on the way up to his floor. Now that the time had come to give him my gift, I worried that maybe he didn't like rings . . . after all, he didn't wear any.

Was it too presumptuous and possessive of me to want him to wear one just because I did?

The redheaded receptionist didn't give me any trouble getting in and when Scott spotted me emerging from the hallway, he stood from his desk and greeted me with a wide grin. When I stepped into Gideon's office, Scott closed the door behind me.

I was immediately struck by the lovely fragrance of the flowers and the way they warmed the starkly modern office.

Gideon looked up from his monitor, his brows lifting when he saw me. He pushed fluidly to his feet. "Eva. Is something wrong?"

I watched him shift gears from professional to personal, his gaze softening as he looked at me.

"No. It's just . . ." I took a deep breath and went to him. "I have something for you."

"More? Did I forget a special occasion?"

I set the ring box down in the center of his desk. Then I turned away, feeling queasy. I seriously doubted the wisdom of my impetuous gift. It seemed like a stupid idea now.

What could I say to absolve him of guilt for not wanting it? As if it weren't bad enough I'd dropped the L-bomb on him today; then I had to follow it up with a damned ring. He was probably feeling the ball and chain already, dragging after him as he ran. And the noose tightening —

I heard the ring box snap open and Gideon's sharply drawn breath. *"Eva."*

His voice was dark and dangerous. I turned carefully, wincing at the austerity of his features and the starkness of his gaze. His hands were white-knuckled on the box.

"Too much?" I asked hoarsely.

"Yes." He set the box down and rounded the desk. "Too damn much. I can't sit still, I can't concentrate. I can't get you out of my head. I'm fucking restless, and I never am when I'm at work. I'm too busy. But you have me under siege."

I knew damn well how demanding his work had to be, yet I hadn't taken that into consideration when the mood to surprise him — again and again — hit me. "I'm sorry, Gideon. I wasn't thinking."

He approached with the sexy stride that hinted at how great he was in the sack. "Don't be sorry. Today has been the best day of my life."

"Really?" I watched him slide the ring onto his right ring finger. "I wanted to please you. Does it fit? I had to guess . . ."

"It's perfect. You're perfect." Gideon caught up my hands and kissed my ring, then watched as I repeated the gesture with his. "What you make me feel, Eva . . . it hurts."

My pulse leaped. "Is that bad?"

"It's wonderful." He cupped my face, his ring cool against my cheek. He kissed me passionately, his lips demanding against mine, his tongue thrusting with wicked skill into my mouth.

I wanted more, but restrained myself, thinking that I'd already gone overboard enough for one day. Plus, he'd been too distracted by my unexpected appearance to frost the glass wall to give us privacy.

"Tell me again what you said in the car," he whispered.

"Hmm . . . I don't know." I brushed my free hand over his vest. I was afraid to tell him again that I loved him. He'd taken it hard the first time, and I wasn't sure he'd fully taken in what it meant for us. For him. "You're ridiculously handsome, you know. It's a sucker punch every time I see you. Anyway . . . I don't want to risk scaring you away."

Leaning toward me, he touched his forehead to mine. "You regret what you said, don't you? All the flowers, the ring —"

"Do you really like it?" I asked anxiously, pulling back to study his face and see if he was hedging on the truth. "I don't want you to wear it for me if you hate it."

His fingers traced the shell of my ear. "It's perfect. It's how you see me. I'm proud to wear it."

I loved that he got it. Of course, that was because he got me.

"If you're trying to soften the blow of taking back what you said —" he began, his gaze betraying a surprising anxiety.

I couldn't resist the soft plea in his eyes. "I meant every word, Gideon."

"I'll make you say it again," he threatened in a seductive purr. "You'll scream it by the time I'm done with you."

I grinned and backed away. "Get back to work, fiend."

"I'll give you a lift home at five." He watched me move to the door. "I want your cunt naked and wet when you come down to the car. If you touch yourself to get there, don't make yourself come or there will be consequences."

Consequences. A little shiver moved through me, but it carried a level of fear I could deal with. I trusted Gideon to know just how far to push me. "Will you be hard and ready?"

A wry smile twisted his lips. "When am I not, with you? Thank you for today, Eva. Every minute of it."

I blew him a kiss and watched his eyes darken. The look on his face stayed with me the rest of the day.

It was six o'clock before I made it back to my apartment in a state of well-fucked dishevelment. I'd known what I was in for when I found Gideon's limousine at the curb after work instead of the Bentley. He'd damn near tackled me as I climbed into the back, then proceeded to demonstrate his phenomenal oral skills before nailing me into the seat with vigorous enthusiasm.

I was grateful that I kept in shape. Otherwise, Gideon's insatiable sexual appetite combined with his seemingly endless stamina might've exhausted me by now. Not that I was complaining. Just an observation.

Clancy was already waiting for me in the lobby of my apartment building when I came rushing in. If he noted my hideously wrinkled dress, flushed cheeks, and messy hair, he didn't point it out. I changed swiftly upstairs and we took off for Parker's studio. I hoped the orientation would start out easy because my legs were still a bit jellied from two toe-curling orgasms.

By the time we arrived at the converted warehouse in Brooklyn, I was excited and ready to learn. About a dozen students were engaged in various exercises, with Parker overseeing and offering encouragement from the edge of the mats. When he saw me, he came over and directed me to a far corner of the sparring area where we could work one-on-one.

"So . . . how's it going?" I asked, to break my own tension.

He smiled, showing off a very interesting and arresting face. "Nervous?"

"A little."

"We're going to work on your physical strength and stamina, as well as your awareness. I'm also going to start training you not to freeze or hesitate in unexpected confrontations."

Before we began, I thought I had pretty good physical strength and stamina, but I learned both could be better. We started out with a brief introduction to the equipment and layout of the space, and then moved on to an explanation of both fighting and neutral/passive stances. We warmed up with basic bodyweight calisthenics, then progressed to "tagging," where we tried to tag each other's shoulders and knees while standing face-to-face and blocking counter-moves.

Parker was amazing at tagging, of course, but I started to get the hang of it. The majority of the time, however, was spent covering groundwork and I really sank my teeth into that. I knew very well what it was like to be down and at a disadvantage.

If Parker noted my underlying vehemence, he didn't comment on it.

When Gideon showed up at my apartment later that evening, he found me soaking my aching body in my bathtub. Although I could tell he was fresh from a shower after his own workout with his personal trainer, he stripped and slid into the bath behind me, cradling me with his arms and legs. I whimpered as he rocked me.

"That good, huh?" he teased, catching my earlobe in his teeth.

"Who knew rolling around for an hour with a hot guy could be so exhausting?" Cary had been right about Krav Maga causing bruises; I could see a few shadows blooming beneath my skin already and we hadn't even gotten to the hard stuff yet.

"I might be jealous," Gideon murmured, squeezing my breasts, "if I didn't know Smith was married with children."

I snorted at yet another tidbit of knowledge he shouldn't know. "Do you also know his shoe and hat sizes?"

"Not yet." He laughed at my exasperated growl and I couldn't hold back a smile at hearing the rare sound.

One day soon we were going to have to talk about his obsession with information gathering, but today wasn't the day to get into it. We'd been at odds too much lately and Cary's warning about making sure we had as much fun as not was ever-present in my mind.

Playing with the ring on Gideon's finger, I told him about the conversation I'd had with my dad on Saturday and how his fellow cops had been ribbing him over the gossip about me dating *the* Gideon Cross.

He sighed. "I'm sorry."

Turning, I faced him. "It's not your fault you're news. You can't help being insanely attractive."

"One of these days," he said dryly, "I'll figure out whether my face is a curse or not."

"Well, if my opinion counts for anything, I'm rather fond of it."

Gideon's lips twitched and he touched my cheek. "Your opinion is the only one that means anything. And your dad's. I want him to like me, Eva, not think I'm exposing his daughter to invasions of her privacy."

"You'll win him over. He just wants me to be safe and happy."

He visibly relaxed and pulled me closer. "Do I make you happy?"

"Yes." I rested my cheek over his heart. "I love being with you. When we're not together, I wish we were."

"You said you didn't want to fight anymore," he murmured in my hair. "It's been bugging me. Are you getting tired of me fucking up all the time?"

"You do *not* fuck up all the time. And I've screwed up, too. Relationships are hard, Gideon. Most of them don't have kick-ass sex like we do. I put us in the lucky column."

He cupped water in his hand and poured it down my back, over and over, soothing me with its sinuous warmth. "I don't really remember my dad."

"Oh?" I tried to not tense up and reveal my surprise. Or my agitated excitement and desperate hunger to learn more about him. He'd never talked about his family before. It killed me not to prod with questions, but I didn't want to push if he wasn't ready. . . .

His chest lifted and fell on a deep exhale. There was something in the sound of his sigh that brought my head up and ruined my intention to be cautious.

I ran my hand over his hard pectorals. "Want to talk about what you *do* remember?"

"Just . . . impressions. He wasn't around much. He worked a lot. I guess I get my drive from him."

"Maybe workaholism — is that a word? — is something you have in common, but that's it."

"How would you know?" he shot back, defiant.

Reaching up, I brushed the hair back from his face. "I'm sorry, Gideon, but your father was a fraud who took the easy, selfish way out. You don't have it in you to be that way."

"Not that way, no." He paused. "But I don't think he ever learned how to connect to people, how to care about anything but his own immediate needs."

I studied him. "Do you think that describes you?"

"I don't know," he answered quietly.

"Well, I know, and it doesn't." I pressed a kiss to the tip of his nose. "You're a keeper."

"I better be." His arms tightened around me. "I can't think about you with someone else, Eva. Just the idea of another man seeing you the way I do, seeing you like this . . . putting his hands on you . . . It takes me to a dark place."

"It's not going to happen, Gideon." I knew how he felt. I wouldn't be able to bear it if he was intimate with another woman.

"You've changed everything for me. I couldn't stand losing you."

I hugged him. "The feeling's mutual."

Tilting my head back, Gideon took my mouth in a fierce kiss.

In moments it became clear we were soon going to be sloshing water all over the floor. I pulled away. "I need to eat if you want to go at it again, fiend."

"Says the girlfriend rubbing her wet naked body all over me." He sat back with a sinful smile.

"Let's order cheap Chinese and eat it out of the box with chopsticks."

"Let's order good Chinese and do that."

19

Cary joined us in the living room for excellent Chinese, a sweet plum wine, and Monday night television. As we flipped channels and laughed over the hilarious names of some reality television shows, I watched as two of the most important men in my life enjoyed some relaxation time and each other. They got along well, ribbing and playfully insulting each other in that way men had. I'd never seen that side of Gideon before and I loved it.

While I hogged one whole side of our sectional sofa, the two guys sat cross-legged on the floor and used the coffee table as a dining table. Both were wearing loose sweatpants and fitted T-shirts, and I appreciated the view. Was I a lucky girl or what?

Cracking his knuckles, Cary dramatically prepared to open his fortune cookie. "Let's see. Will I be rich? Famous? About to meet Mr. or Ms. Tall, Dark, and Tasty? Traveling to distant lands? What'd you guys get?"

"Mine's lame," I said. "*In the end all things will be known.* Duh. I didn't need a fortune to figure that out."

Gideon opened his and read, *"Prosperity will knock on your door soon."*

I snorted.

Cary shot me a look. "I know, right? You snatched someone else's cookie, Cross."

"He better not be anywhere near someone else's cookie," I said dryly.

Reaching over, Gideon plucked half of mine out of my fingers. "Don't worry, angel. Your cookie is the only one I want." He popped it in his mouth with a wink.

"Gag," Cary muttered. "Get a room." He cracked his fortune with a flourish, and then scowled. "What the fuck?"

I leaned forward. "What's it say?"

"Confucius say," Gideon ad-libbed, "man with hand in pocket feel cocky all day."

Cary threw half his cookie at Gideon, who caught it deftly and grinned.

"Give me that." I snatched the fortune out from between Cary's fingers and read it. Then laughed.

"Fuck you, Eva."

"Well?" Gideon prodded.

"Pick another cookie."

Gideon smiled. "*Pwned* by a fortune."

Cary threw the other half of his cookie.

I was reminded of similar evenings spent with Cary when I was attending SDSU, which made me try to picture what Gideon had been like in college. From the articles I'd read, I knew he'd attended Columbia for his undergraduate studies, then left to focus on his expanding business interests.

Had he associated with the other students? Did he go to frat parties, screw around, and/or drink too much? He was such a controlled man that I had a hard time picturing him that carefree, and yet here he was being exactly that with me and Cary.

He glanced at me then, still smiling, and my heart turned over in my chest. He looked his age for once, young and seriously fine and so very normal. At that moment, we were just a twenty-something couple relaxing at home with a roommate and a remote control. He was just my boyfriend, hanging out. It was all so sweet and uncomplicated, and I found the illusion a poignant one.

The intercom buzzed and Cary leaped to his feet to answer it. He glanced at me with a smile. "Maybe it's Trey."

I held up a hand with my fingers crossed.

But when Cary answered the door a few minutes later, it was the leggy blonde from the other night who came in.

"Hey," she said, taking in the remnants of dinner on the table. She eyed Gideon appraisingly as he politely unfolded and stood in that powerfully graceful way of his. She shot me a smirk, then unleashed a dazzling supermodel smile on Gideon and held out her hand. "Tatiana Cherlin."

He shook her hand. "Eva's boyfriend."

My brows lifted at his introduction. Was he protecting his identity? Or his personal space? Either way, I liked his response.

Cary came back into the room with a bottle of wine and two glasses. "Come on," he said, gesturing down the hallway to his bedroom.

Tatiana gave a little wave and preceded Cary out. I mouthed behind her back to Cary, *What are you doing?*

He winked and whispered, "Picking another cookie."

Gideon and I called it a night shortly after and headed to my room. As we got ready for bed, I asked him something I'd wondered about earlier. "Did you have a fuck pad in college, too?"

His T-shirt cleared his head. "Excuse me?"

"You know, like the hotel room. You're a randy guy. I just wondered if you'd had some kind of setup even then."

He was shaking his head as I ogled his divinely perfect torso and lean hips. "I've had as much sex since I met you as I've had in the last two years combined."

"No way."

"I work hard and I work out harder, both of which keep me pleasantly exhausted most of the time. Occasionally, I might've gotten an offer I didn't refuse, but otherwise I could take or leave sex until I met you."

"Bullshit." I found that impossible to believe.

He shot me a look before he headed toward the bathroom with a black leather toiletry bag. "Keep doubting me, Eva. See what happens."

"What?" I followed him, enjoying the sight of his delectable ass. "You're going to prove that you can take or leave sex by doing me again?"

"It takes two." He opened his bag and pulled out a new toothbrush that he extricated from its packaging and dropped into my toothbrush holder. "You've initiated sex between us as much as I have. You need the connection as much as I do."

"You're right. It's just . . ."

"Just what?" He pulled open a drawer, frowned at finding it full, and moved on to pull open another.

"Other sink," I said, smiling at his presumption that he would get drawers at my place, too, and his scowl when he couldn't find them. "They're all yours."

Gideon moved over to the second sink and began unpacking his bag into the drawers. "Just what?" he repeated, taking shampoo and body wash over to my shower.

Leaning my hip into the sink and crossing my arms, I watched him stake his claim all over my bathroom. There was no doubt that was what he was doing, just as there was no doubt that anyone walking into the room would know right away there was a man in my life.

It struck me then that I had a similar claim on his private space. His household staff had to know their boss was in a committed relationship now. The thought gave me a little thrill.

"I was thinking about you in college earlier," I went on, "when we were eating dinner, imagining what it would be like to see you around on campus. I would've been obsessed with you. I would have gone out of my way to see you around just to enjoy the view. I would've tried to get in the same classes as you, so I could daydream during lectures about getting into your pants."

"Sex maniac." He kissed the tip of my

nose as he passed me and went to brush his teeth. "We both know what would've happened once I saw you."

I brushed my hair and teeth, then washed my face. "So . . . did you have a sex pad for the rare occasions some lucky bitch got you in bed?"

His gaze caught my soapy reflection in the mirror. "I've always used the hotel."

"That's the only place you've had sex? Before me?"

"The only place I've had consensual sex," he said quietly, "before you."

"Oh." My heart broke.

I walked over to him, hugging him from behind. I rubbed my cheek against his back.

We went to bed and wrapped ourselves around each other. I buried my face in his neck and breathed him in, snuggling. His body was hard, yet it was wonderfully comfortable against mine. He was so warm and strong, so powerfully male. I only had to think of him to want him.

I slid my leg over his hips and rose above him, my hands splayed atop the ridges of his abdomen. It was dark. I couldn't see him, but I didn't need to. As much as I loved that face of his — the one he resented at times — it was the way he touched me and murmured to me that really got to me.

437

As if there were no one else in the world for him, nothing he wanted more.

"Gideon." I didn't need to say anything else.

Sitting up, he wrapped his arms around me and kissed me deeply. Then he rolled me beneath him and made love to me with a tender possessiveness that rocked me to my soul.

I woke with a jolt of surprise. A heavy weight crushed me and a harsh voice spit ugly, nasty words into my ear. Panic gripped me, cutting off my air.

Not again. No . . . Please, no . . .

My stepbrother's hand covered my mouth and he yanked my legs apart. I felt the hard thing between his legs poking blindly, trying to push into my body. My scream was muffled by his palm smashed over my lips and I cringed away, my heart pounding so hard I thought it would burst. Nathan was so heavy. So heavy and strong. I couldn't buck him off. I couldn't shove him away.

Stop it! Get off me. Don't touch me. Oh, God . . . please don't do that *to me . . . not again . . .*

Where was Mama? *Mama!*

I screamed, but Nathan's hand covered my mouth. It pressed down on me, squash-

438

ing my head into the pillow. The more I fought, the more excited he became. Panting like a dog, he rammed against me over and over . . . trying to shove himself inside me . . .

"You're going to know what it feels like."

I froze. I knew that voice. I knew it wasn't Nathan's.

Not a dream. Still a nightmare.

God, no. Blinking madly in the darkness, I struggled to see. The blood was roaring through my ears. I couldn't hear.

But I knew the smell of his skin. Knew his touch, even when it was cruel. Knew the feel of his body on mine, even as it tried to invade me.

Gideon's erection battered into the crease of my thigh. Panicked, I heaved upward with all my strength. His hand on my face dislodged.

Sucking air into my lungs, I screamed.

His chest heaved as he growled, "Not so neat and tidy when you're the one getting fucked."

"Crossfire," I gasped.

A flash of light from the hallway blinded me, followed by the blessed removal of Gideon's smothering weight. Rolling to my side, I sobbed, my eyes streaming tears that blurred my view of Cary shoving Gideon across the room and into the wall, denting the drywall.

"Eva! Are you okay?" Cary turned on the bedside light, cursing when he saw me curled in a fetal position, rocking violently.

When Gideon straightened, Cary rounded on him. "Move one fucking muscle before the cops get here and I'll beat you to a bloody pulp!"

Swallowing past my burning throat, I pushed up to a seated position. My gaze locked with Gideon's and I watched the haze of sleep leave his eyes, replaced by a dawning horror.

"Dream," I choked out, catching Cary's arm as he reached for the phone. "He's d-dreaming."

Cary glanced at where Gideon crouched naked on the floor like a wild animal. Cary's arm dropped back to his side. "Jesus Christ," he breathed. "And I thought I was fucked up."

Sliding off the bed, I stood on shaky legs, sick with lingering fear. My knees gave out and Cary caught me, lowering to the floor with me and holding me as I cried.

"I'm gonna crash on the couch." Cary ran a hand through his sleep-mussed hair and leaned into the hallway wall. The door to my bedroom was open behind me and Gideon was inside, looking pale and haunted. "I'll set out some blankets and pillows for him, too. I don't think he should go home alone. He's shredded."

"Thanks, Cary." The arms I had wrapped around my middle tightened. "Is Tatiana still here?"

"Hell, no. It's not like that. We just fuck."

"What about Trey?" I asked quietly, my mind already drifting back to Gideon.

"I love Trey. I think he's the best person I've ever met aside from you." He bent forward and kissed my forehead. "And what he doesn't know won't hurt him. Stop worrying about me and take care of you."

I looked up at him, my eyes swimming in tears. "I don't know what to do."

Cary sighed, his green eyes dark and serious. "I think you need to decide if you're in over your head, baby girl. Some people can't be fixed. Look at me. I've got a great guy and I'm giving it to a girl I can't stand."

"Cary . . ." Reaching out, I touched his shoulder.

He caught my hand and squeezed it. "I'm here if you need me."

Gideon was zipping up his duffel bag when I returned to my room. He looked at me and fear slithered in my gut. Not for me, but for him. I'd never seen anyone look so desolate, so utterly broken. The bleakness in his beautiful eyes frightened me. There was no life in him. He was gray as death with deep shadows in all the angles and planes of his breathtaking face.

"What are you doing?" I whispered.

He backed up, as if he wanted to be as far away from me as he could get. "I can't stay."

It worried me that I felt a surge of relief at the thought of being alone. "We agreed — no running."

"That was before I attacked you!" he snapped, showing the first sign of spirit in more than an hour.

"You were unconscious."

"You're not going to be a victim ever again, Eva. My God . . . what I almost did to you . . ." He turned his back to me, his shoulders hunched in a way that scared me as much as the attack had.

"If you leave, we lose and our pasts win." I saw my words hit him like a blow. Every light in my room was on, as if electricity alone could banish all the shadows on our souls. "If you give up now, I'm afraid it'll be easier for you to stay away and for me to let you. We'll be over, Gideon."

"How can I stay? Why would you want me to?" Turning around, he looked at me with such longing it brought fresh tears to my eyes. "I'd kill myself before I hurt you."

Which was one of my fears. I had a difficult time picturing the Gideon I knew — the dominant, willful force of nature — taking his own life, but the Gideon standing before me was an entirely different person. And he was the child of a suicidal parent.

My fingers plucked at the hem of my T-shirt. "You'd never hurt me."

"You're afraid of me," he said hoarsely. "I can see it on your face. *I'm* afraid of me. Afraid of sleeping with you and doing something that will destroy us both."

He was right. I was afraid. Dread chilled my stomach.

Now I knew the explosive violence in him. The festering fury. And we were so impassioned with each other. I'd slapped his face at the garden party, lashing out physically when I *never* did that.

It was the nature of our relationship to be lusty and emotional, earthy and raw. The trust that held us together also opened us up to each other in ways that made us both vulnerable and dangerous. And it would get worse before it got better.

He shoved a hand through his hair. "Eva, I —"

"I love you, Gideon."

"God." He looked at me with something that resembled disgust. Whether it was directed at me or himself, I didn't know. "How can you say that?"

"Because it's the truth."

"You just see this —" He gestured at himself with a wave of his hand. "You're not seeing the fucked-up, broken mess inside."

I inhaled sharply. "You can say that to me? When you know I'm fucked up and broken, too?"

"Maybe you're wired to go for someone who's terrible for you," he said bitterly.

"Stop it. I know you're hurting, but lashing out at me is only going to make you hurt worse." I glanced at the clock and saw it was four in the morning. I walked toward him, needing to get past my fear of touching him and being touched by him.

He held up a hand as if to hold me off. "I'm going home, Eva."

"Sleep on the couch here. Don't fight me about this, Gideon. Please. I'll worry myself sick if you go."

"You'll be more worried if I stay." He stared at me, looking lost and angry and filled with terrible yearning. His eyes pleaded with me for forgiveness, but he

444

wouldn't accept it when I tried to give it to him.

I went to him and took his hand, fighting back the surge of apprehension that hit me when we touched. My nerves were still raw, my throat and mouth still sore, the memory of his attempts at penetration — so like Nathan's — still too fresh. "We'll g-get through this," I promised him, hating that my voice quavered. "You'll talk to Dr. Petersen and we'll go from there."

His hand lifted as if to touch my face. "If Cary hadn't been here —"

"He was, and I'll be fine. I love you. We'll get past this." I walked into him, hugging him, pushing my hands beneath his shirt to touch his bare skin. "We're not going to let the past get in the way of what we have."

I wasn't sure which of us I was trying to convince.

"Eva." His returning hug squeezed all of the air out of me. "I'm sorry. It's killing me. Please. Forgive me . . . I can't lose you."

"You won't." My eyes closed, focusing on the feel of him. The smell of him. Remembering that I once feared nothing when I was with him.

"I'm so sorry." His shaking hands stroked the curve of my spine. "I'll do anything . . ."

"Shh. I love you. We'll be okay."

Turning his head, he kissed me softly. "Forgive me, Eva. I need you. I'm afraid of what I'll become if I lose you . . ."

"I'm not going anywhere." My skin tingled beneath the restless glide of his hands on my back. "I'm right here. No more running."

He paused, his breath gusting harshly against my lips. Then he tilted his head and sealed his mouth over mine. My body responded to the gentle coaxing of his kiss. I arched into him without volition, pulling him closer.

He cupped my breasts in his hands, kneading them, circling the pads of his thumbs over my nipples until they peaked and ached. I moaned with a mixture of fear and hunger, and he quivered at the sound.

"Eva . . . ?"

"I — I can't." The memory of how I'd woken up was too fresh in my mind. It hurt me to deny him, knowing he needed the same thing from me as I'd needed from him when I told him about Nathan — proof that the desire was still there, that as ugly as the scars of our pasts were, they didn't affect what we were to each other now.

But I couldn't give him that. Not yet. I felt too raw and vulnerable. "Just hold me, Gideon. Please."

He nodded, wrapping his arms around me.

I urged him to sink to the floor with me, hoping I could get him to fall asleep. I curled into his side, my leg thrown over his, my arm draped over his hard stomach. He squeezed me gently, pressing his lips to my forehead, whispering over and over again how sorry he was.

"Don't leave me," I whispered. "Stay."

Gideon didn't answer, didn't make any promises, but he didn't let me go either.

I woke sometime later, hearing Gideon's heart beating steadily beneath my ear. All the lights were still on, and the carpeted floor was hard and uncomfortable.

Gideon lay on his back, his beautiful face youthful in sleep, his shirt lifted just enough to expose his navel and the ripped muscles of his abdomen.

This was the man I loved. This was the man whose body gave me such pleasure, whose thoughtfulness moved me over and over again. He was still here. And from the frown that marred the space between his brows, he was still hurting.

I slid my hand into his sweatpants. For the first time since we'd been together, he wasn't hot steel in my palms, but he quickly swelled and thickened as I tentatively stroked him from root to tip. Fear lingered just beneath my arousal, but I was more afraid of losing him than of living with the demons inside him.

He stirred, his arm tightening around my back. "Eva . . . ?"

This time I answered him the way I couldn't before. "Let's forget," I breathed into his mouth. "Make us forget."

"Eva."

He rolled into me, peeling my shirt off with cautious movements. I was similarly tentative in undressing him. We approached each other as if each of us were breakable. The bond between us was fragile just then, both of us apprehensive about the future and the wounds we could inflict with all of our jagged edges.

His lips wrapped around my nipple, his cheeks hollowing slowly, his seduction subdued. The tender suckling felt so good I gasped and arched into his hand. He caressed my side from breast to hip and back again, over and over, gentling me as my heart raced wildly.

He kissed across my chest to the other breast, murmuring words of apology and need in a voice broken by regret and misery. His tongue lapped at the hardened point, worrying it, before surrounding it with wet heat and suction.

"Gideon." The delicate pulls expertly coaxed desire through my skittish mind. My body was already lost in him, greedily seeking the pleasure and beauty of his.

"Don't be afraid of me," he whispered. "Don't pull away."

He kissed my navel and then moved lower, his hair caressing my stomach as he settled between my legs. He held me open with shaking hands and nuzzled my clit. His light, teasing licks through my cleft and the fluttering dips into my trembling sex took me to the edge of insanity.

My back bowed. Hoarse pleas left my lips. Tension spread through my body, tightening everything until I felt like I might snap under the pressure. And then he pushed me into orgasm with the softest nudge of the tip of his tongue.

I cried out, heated relief pulsing through my writhing body.

"I can't let you go, Eva." Gideon levered over me as I vibrated with pleasure. "I can't."

Brushing away the tear tracks from his face, I stared into his reddened eyes. His torment was painful for me to witness, hurting my heart. "I wouldn't let you if you tried."

He took himself in hand and fed his cock slowly, carefully into me. My head pressed hard into the floor as he sank deeper, possessing my body one thick inch at a time.

When I'd taken all of him, he began to move in measured, deliberate thrusts. I closed my eyes and focused on the connection between us. Then he settled onto me, his stomach pressed to mine, and my pulse leaped with panic. Abruptly frightened, I hesitated.

"Look at me, Eva." His voice was so hoarse it was unrecognizable.

I did, and saw his anguish.

"Make love to me," he begged in a breathless whisper. "Make love *with* me. Touch me, angel. Put your hands on me."

"Yes." My palms pressed flat to his back, then stroked over the quivering muscles to his ass. Squeezing the hard, flexing flesh, I urged him to move faster, plunge deeper.

The rhythmic strokes of his heavy cock through the clenching depths of my sex pushed ecstasy through me in heated waves. He felt so good. My legs wrapped around his plunging hips, my breath quickening as the cold knot inside me began to melt. Our gazes held.

Tears coursed down my temples. "I love you, Gideon."

"Please . . ." His eyes squeezed shut.

"I love you."

He lured me to orgasm with the skilled rolling of his hips, stirring his cock inside me. My sex clenched tightly, trying to hold him, trying to keep him deep in me.

"Come, Eva," he gasped against my throat.

I struggled for it, struggled to get past the lingering apprehension that came from having him on top of me. The anxiety mingled with the desire, keeping me on edge.

He made a hoarse sound filled with pain and regret. "Need you to come, Eva . . . need to feel you . . . Please . . ."

Cupping my buttocks, he angled my hips and stroked over and over that sensitive spot inside me. He was tireless, relentless, fucking me long and hard until my mind lost control of my body and I came violently. I bit his shoulder to stem my cries as I shook beneath him, the tiny muscles inside me trembling with ecstatic ripples. He groaned deep in his chest, a serrated sound of tormented pleasure.

"More," he ordered, deepening his drives to give me that delectable bite of soreness. That he once again trusted us both enough to introduce that little touch of pain chased away the last of my reservations. As much as we trusted each other, we were learning to trust our instincts, too.

I came again, ferociously, my toes curling until they cramped. I felt the familiar tension grip Gideon and tightened my grasp on his hips, spurring him on, desperate to feel him spurting inside me.

"No!" He wrenched away, falling to his back and throwing an arm over his eyes. Punishing himself by denying his body the comfort and pleasure of mine.

His chest heaved and glistened with sweat. His cock lay heavily on his belly, brutal-looking with its broad purpled head and thick roping of veins.

I dove for it with hands and mouth, ignoring his vicious curse. Pinning his torso with my forearm, I pumped him hard with my other fist and sucked voraciously on the sensitive crown. His thighs quivered, his legs kicking restlessly.

"Damn it, Eva. Fuck." He stiffened and gasped, his hands shoving into my hair, his hips bucking. "Oh, fuck. Suck it hard . . . Ah, Christ . . ."

He exploded in a powerful rush that almost choked me, coming hard, flooding my mouth. I took it all, my fist milking pulse after pulse up the throbbing length of his cock, swallowing repeatedly until he shuddered with the surfeit of sensation and begged me to stop.

I straightened and Gideon sat up and wrapped himself around me. He took me back down to the floor, where he buried his face in my throat and cried until dawn.

I wore a black, long-sleeved silk blouse and slacks to work on Tuesday, feeling the need to have a barrier between myself and the world. In the kitchen, Gideon cupped my face in his hands and brushed his mouth across mine with heartrending tenderness. His gaze remained haunted.

"Lunch?" I asked, feeling like we needed to cling to the connection between us.

"I have a business lunch." He ran his fingers through my loose hair. "Would you come? I'll make sure Angus gets you back to work on time."

"I'd love to come along." I thought of the schedule of evening events, meetings, and appointments he'd sent to my smartphone. "And tomorrow night we have a benefit dinner at the Waldorf-Astoria?"

His gaze softened. Dressed for work, he looked somber yet collected. I knew he was anything but.

"You really won't give up on me, will

you?" he asked quietly.

I held up my right hand and showed him my ring. "You're stuck with me, Cross. Get used to it."

On the drive to work, he cuddled me in his lap, and again on the ride to lunch at Jean Georges. I didn't speak more than a dozen words during the meal, which Gideon ordered for me and I enjoyed immensely.

I sat quietly at his side, my left hand resting on his hard thigh beneath the tablecloth, a wordless affirmation of my commitment to him. To us. One of his hands rested over mine, warm and strong, as he discussed a new property in development on St. Croix. We kept that connection throughout the entire meal, each of us choosing to eat one-handed rather than separate.

With each hour that passed, I felt the horror of the night before drain away from both of us. It would be another scar to add to his collection, another bitter memory he'd always have, a memory I would share and fear along with him, but it wouldn't rule us. We wouldn't let it.

Angus was waiting to take me home when my day ended. Gideon was working late and then going directly from the Crossfire to

Dr. Petersen's office. I used the length of the drive to steel myself for the next round of training with Parker. I debated skipping it but ended up deciding it was important to keep to a routine. So much in my life was uncontrollable at the moment. Following a schedule was one of the few things totally within my power.

After an hour and a half of tagging and groundwork with Parker at the studio, I was relieved when Clancy dropped me off at home and proud of myself for working out when it was the last thing I'd wanted to do.

When I stepped into the lobby, I found Trey talking to the front desk.

"Hey," I greeted him. "Going up?"

He turned to face me, his hazel eyes warm and his smile open. Trey had a gentleness to him, a kind of straightforward naïveté that was different from the other relationships Cary'd had before. Or maybe I should just say Trey was "normal," which so few of the people in my and Cary's lives were.

"Cary's not in," he said. "They just tried calling."

"You're welcome to come up with me and wait. I won't be going out again."

"If you really don't mind." He fell into step beside me as I waved at the gal at the front desk and moved toward the elevators.

"I brought something for him."

"I don't mind at all," I assured him, returning his sweet smile.

He eyed my yoga pants and tank top. "You just get back from the gym?"

"Yeah. Despite it being one of those days when I'd rather have done *anything* else."

He laughed as we stepped into the elevator. "I know that feeling."

As we rode up, silence descended. It was weighted.

"Everything all right?" I asked him.

"Well . . ." Trey adjusted the sling of his backpack. "Cary's just seemed a little off the last few days."

"Oh?" I bit my lower lip. "In what way?"

"I don't know. It's hard to explain. I just feel like maybe something's up with him and I'm missing what it is."

I thought of the blonde and winced inwardly. "Maybe he's stressed about the Grey Isles job and he doesn't want to bother you with it. He knows you've got your hands full with your job and school."

The tension in his shoulders softened. "Maybe that's it. It makes sense. Okay. Thank you."

I let us in to the apartment and told him to make himself at home. Trey headed to Cary's room to drop his stuff, while I went to the phone to check the voice mail.

A shout from down the hallway had me reaching for the phone for a different reason, my heart thudding with thoughts of intruders and imminent danger. More yelling followed, with one voice clearly belonging to Cary.

I exhaled in a rush, relieved. With the phone in my hand, I ventured to see what the hell was going on. I was nearly run over by Tatiana rounding the hallway corner, still buttoning her blouse.

"Oops," she said, with an unapologetic grin. "See ya."

I couldn't hear the door shut behind her over Trey's shouting.

"Fuck you, Cary. We talked about this! You promised!"

"You're blowing this out of proportion," Cary barked. "It's not what you think."

Trey came storming out of Cary's bedroom in such a rush that I plastered myself to the hallway wall to get out of his way. Cary followed, with a sheet slung around his waist. As he passed me, I shot him a narrow-eyed glance that earned me a fuck-off middle finger.

I left the two men alone and escaped into my shower, angry at Cary for once again ruining something good in his life. It was a pattern I kept hoping he'd break, but he couldn't seem to kick it.

When I came out to the kitchen a half hour later, the stillness in the apartment was absolute. I focused on cooking dinner, deciding to go with a pork roast and new potatoes with asparagus, one of Cary's favorite dinners, in case he was home for dinner and needed some cheering up.

The sight of Trey stepping into the hallway while I was putting the roast in the oven surprised me, and then it made me sad. I hated to see him leave looking flushed, disheveled, and crying. My pity turned to fierce disappointment when Cary joined me in the kitchen with the scent of male sweat and sex clinging to him. He shot me a scowl as he passed me on his way to the wine fridge.

I faced him with my arms crossed. "Screwing a heartbroken lover on the same sheets he's just caught you cheating on isn't going to make things better."

"Shut up, Eva."

"He's probably hating himself right now for giving in."

"I said shut the fuck up."

"Fine." I turned away from him and focused on seasoning the potatoes to put in the oven with the roast.

Cary grabbed wineglasses out of the cupboard. "I can feel you judging me. Stop it. He wouldn't be half as pissed if it'd been a man he caught me fucking."

"It's all his fault, huh?"

"Newsflash: Your love life isn't perfect either."

"Low blow, Cary. I'm not going to be your punching bag over this. You messed up, and then you made it worse. It's all on you."

"Don't get on your damn high horse. You're sleeping with a man who's going to rape you any day now."

"It's not like that!"

He snorted and leaned his hip against the counter, his green eyes filled with pain and anger. "If you're going to make excuses for him because he's sleeping when he attacks you, you'll have to make those same excuses for drunks and druggies. They don't know what they're doing either."

The truth of his words struck me hard, as did the fact that he was deliberately trying to wound me. "You can put down a bottle. You can't quit sleeping."

Straightening, Cary opened the bottle he'd selected and poured two glasses, sliding one across the counter toward me. "If anyone knows what it's like to be involved with people who hurt you, it's me. You love him. You want to save him. But who's going to save you, Eva? I'm not always going to be around when you're with him, and he's a ticking time bomb."

"You wanna talk about being in relationships that hurt, Cary?" I shot back, deflecting him away from my painful truths. "Did you screw Trey over to protect yourself? Did you figure you'd push him away before he had the chance to disappoint you?"

Cary's mouth curved bitterly. He tapped his glass to mine, which still sat on the counter. "Cheers to us, the seriously fucked up. At least we have each other."

He stalked out of the room and I deflated. I'd known this was coming — the unraveling of circumstances too good to be true. Contentment and happiness didn't exist in my life for more than a few moments at a time, and they were really only illusionary.

There was always something hidden. Lying in wait to spring up and ruin everything.

20

Gideon arrived just as dinner was coming out of the oven. He had a garment bag in one hand and a laptop case in the other. I'd worried that he would try to go home alone after his session with Dr. Petersen and was relieved when he'd called to say he was on his way. Still, when I first opened the door and saw him on the threshold, a shiver of unease slid through me.

"Hey," he said quietly, following me back into the kitchen. "Smells delicious in here."

"I hope you're hungry. There's a lot of food and I'll be surprised if Cary joins us to help eat it all."

Gideon dropped his stuff on the breakfast bar and approached me cautiously, his gaze searching my face as he neared. "I brought some things with me to stay the night, but I'll go if you want. At any time. Just tell me."

I blew out my breath in a harsh rush, determined not to let fear dictate my actions. "I want you here."

"I want to be here." He paused beside me. "Can I hold you?"

I turned into him and squeezed him hard. "Please."

He pressed his cheek against mine and hugged me close. The embrace wasn't as natural and easy as we'd grown used to. There was a new wariness between us that was different from anything we'd felt before.

"How are you doing?" he murmured.

"Better now that you're here."

"But still nervous." He pressed his lips to my forehead. "Me, too. I don't know how we're ever going to fall asleep next to each other again."

Pulling back slightly, I looked at him. That was my fear as well, and my earlier conversation with Cary didn't help matters. *He's a ticking time bomb. . . .*

"We'll figure it out," I said.

He was quiet for a long moment. "Has Nathan ever contacted you?"

"No." Although I had a deep-rooted fear that I might see him again one day, whether accidentally or deliberately. He was out there somewhere, breathing the same air . . . "Why?"

"It was on my mind today."

I pulled back to search his face, a knot

forming in my throat at how tormented he looked. "Why?"

"Because we've got a lot of baggage between us."

"Are you thinking it's too much?"

Gideon shook his head. "I can't think that way."

I didn't know what to do or say. What assurances could I give him, when I wasn't sure my love and his need would be enough to make our relationship work?

"What's going through your mind?" he asked.

"Thoughts of food. I'm starving. Why don't you go see if Cary wants to eat? Then we can get started on dinner."

Gideon found Cary sleeping, so he and I ate a candlelit dinner for two at the dining table, a somewhat formal meal while lounging in the worn T-shirts and pajama bottoms we'd put on after our respective showers. I was worried about Cary, but spending quiet downtime alone with Gideon felt like just what we needed.

"I had lunch with Magdalene in my office yesterday," he said after we'd enjoyed a few initial bites.

"Oh?" While I'd been ring shopping, Magdalene had been enjoying private time with my man?

"Don't take that tone," he admonished. "She ate a meal in an office covered in your flowers, with you blowing kisses from my desk. You were as much there as she was."

"Sorry. Knee-jerk reaction."

He lifted my hand to his mouth and pressed a quick, hard kiss to the back. "I'm relieved you can still get jealous over me."

I sighed. My emotions had been all over the map all day; I couldn't decide how I felt about anything. "Did you say anything to her about Christopher?"

"That was the point of the lunch. I showed her the video."

"What?" I frowned, remembering my phone had died in his car. "How'd you do that?"

"I took your phone up to my office and pulled the video off via USB. Didn't you notice I brought it back last night, fully charged?"

"No." I set my silverware down. Dominant or not, Gideon and I were going to have to work on which lines crossed over into my freak-out zone. "You can't just hack into my phone, Gideon."

"I didn't hack into it. You haven't set a password yet."

"That's not the point! It's a serious invasion of my fucking privacy. Jesus . . ." Why in hell did no one in my life understand that I had boundaries? "Would you like me rummaging through your stuff?"

"I've got nothing to hide." He pulled his smartphone out of an inner pocket of his sweats and held it out to me. "And you won't either."

I didn't want to get into a fight now — things were too shaky as it was — but I'd let this go long enough. "It doesn't matter whether I have something I don't want you to see. I have a right to space and privacy, and you need to ask before you help yourself to my information and my belongings. You have to stop taking whatever you want without my permission."

"What was private about it?" he asked with a frown. "You showed it to me yourself."

"Don't be like my mother, Gideon!" I shouted. "There's only so much crazy I can handle."

He jerked back at my vehemence, clearly surprised by how upset I was. "Okay. I'm sorry."

I gulped down my wine, trying to rein in my temper and unease. "Sorry I'm mad? Or sorry you did it?"

After the length of several heartbeats, Gideon said, "I'm sorry you're mad."

He really didn't get it. "Why don't you see how weird this is?"

"Eva." He sighed and shoved a hand through his hair. "I spend a quarter of every day *inside* you. When you set limits outside that I can't help but see them as arbitrary."

"Well, they're not. They're important to me. If there's something you want to know, you need to ask me."

"All right."

"Don't do it anymore," I warned. "I'm not kidding, Gideon."

His jaw tightened. "Okay. I get it."

Then, because I really didn't want to fight, I moved on. "What did she say when she saw it?"

He visibly relaxed. "It was difficult, of course. Even more difficult to know I'd seen it."

"She saw us in the library."

"We didn't talk about that directly, but then, what was there to say? I won't apologize for making love to my girlfriend in a closed room." He leaned back in his chair and exhaled harshly. "Seeing Christopher's face on the video — seeing what he really thought of her — *that* hurt her. It's hard to see yourself being used that way. Especially by someone you think you know, someone who's supposed to care about you."

To hide my reaction, I busied myself with refilling both my glass and his. He spoke as if from experience. What exactly had been done to him?

After a quick gulp of wine, I asked, "How are *you* doing with it?"

"What can I do? Over the years, I've made every attempt to talk to Christopher. I've tried throwing money at him. I've tried threatening him. He's never shown any inclination to change. I realized long ago that I can only do damage control. And keep you as far away from him as possible."

"I'll be helping you with that, now that I know."

"Good." He took a drink, eyeing me over the lip of his glass. "You're not asking me about my appointment with Dr. Petersen."

"It's none of my business. Unless you want to share." I met his gaze, willing him to do just that. "I'm here to listen whenever you need an ear, but I'm not going to pry. When you're ready to let me in, you will. That said, I'd love to know if you like him."

"So far." He smiled. "He talks me around in circles. Not many people can do that."

"Yes. Talks you back around and makes you come at it from a different angle that has you thinking, 'Now why didn't I see it like that?' "

Gideon's fingers stroked up and down the stem of his glass. "He prescribed something for me to take at night before bed. I filled it before I came over."

"How do you feel about taking drugs?"

He looked at me with dark, haunted eyes. "I feel it's necessary. I have to be with you and I have to make that safe for you, whatever it takes. Dr. Petersen says the drug combined with therapy has been successful for other 'atypical sexual parasomniacs.' I have to believe that."

I reached over to squeeze his hand. Taking medication was a big step, especially for someone who'd avoided facing his problems for a long time. "Thank you."

Gideon's grip tightened. "Apparently there are enough people with this problem that there have been sleep studies on it. He told me about a documented case where a man sexually assaulted his wife in his sleep for twelve years before they sought help."

"Twelve years? Jesus."

"Apparently part of the reason they waited so long was because the man was a better lay when he was asleep," he said dryly. "And if that's not a killer blow to the ego, I don't know what is."

I stared at him. "Well, shit."

"I know, right?" His wry smile faded. "But I don't want you to feel pressured to share a bed with me, Eva. There is no magic pill. I can sleep on the couch or I can go home, although of the two choices I'd prefer the couch. My whole day is better after getting ready for work with you."

"For me, too."

Reaching over, Gideon caught my hand and lifted it to his lips. "I never imagined I could have this . . . Someone in my life who knows what you do about me. Someone who could talk about my fuck-ups over dinner because they accept me anyway . . . I'm grateful for you, Eva."

My heart twisted with a sweet pain in my chest. He could say such beautiful things, the perfect things.

"I feel the same way about you, ace." Deeper, maybe, because I loved him. But I didn't say that aloud. He'd get there someday. I wasn't going to give up until he was absolutely, irrevocably mine.

With his bare feet propped on the coffee table and his computer on his lap, Gideon looked so at home and relaxed that he kept distracting me from my television shows.

How did we get here? I asked myself. This extravagantly sexy man and me?

"You're staring," he murmured, his gaze on his laptop screen.

I stuck my tongue out at him.

"Is that a sexual suggestion, Miss Tramell?"

"How do you see me while staring at whatever you're working on?"

He looked up then and caught my gaze. His blue eyes blazed with power and heat. "I've always seen you, angel. From the moment you found me, I've seen nothing but you."

Wednesday started with Gideon's cock pushing into me from behind, my new favorite way to wake up.

"Well, then," I said hoarsely, rubbing the sleep from my eyes as his arm hitched around my waist and hauled me closer to his warm, hard chest. "You're frisky this morning."

"You're gorgeous and sexy every morning," he murmured, nibbling on my shoulder. "I love waking up to you."

We celebrated a night of uninterrupted sleep with a handful of orgasms between us.

Much later in the day, I had lunch with Mark and Steven at a lovely Mexican restaurant tucked beneath the street. We descended a short set of cement stairs into a surprisingly spacious restaurant with black-vested waitstaff and plenty of light.

"You'll need to bring your man back here," Steven said, "and have him buy you one of the pomegranate margaritas."

"Good stuff?" I asked.

"Oh, yeah."

When the waitress came to take our orders, she flirted outrageously with Mark, fluttering enviously long lashes. Mark flirted back. As the meal progressed, the exuberant redhead — whose name tag introduced her as Shawna — became bolder, touching Mark's shoulders and the back of his neck every time she came by. In return, Mark's banter became more suggestive, until I eyed Steven nervously, watching his face redden and his scowl deepen by the moment. Shifting uncomfortably, I was counting down the minutes until the tension-fraught meal was over.

"Let's get together tonight," Shawna said to Mark when she brought the check. "One night with me and I'll cure you."

I gaped. Seriously?

"Seven o'clock work for you?" Mark purred. "I'll ruin you, Shawna. You know what happens once you go black. . . ."

I inhaled my water down the wrong pipe

and choked.

Steven leaped to his feet and rounded the table, pounding me on the back. "Hell, Eva," he said, laughing. "We're just playing with you. Don't die on us."

"What?" I gasped, my eyes watering.

Grinning, he came around my shoulder and tossed his arm around the waitress. "Eva, meet my sister, Shawna. Shawna, Eva here is the one who makes Mark's life easier."

"That's good," Shawna said, "since he's got you to make things harder."

Steven winked at me. "That's why he keeps me around."

Seeing the brother and sister pair so close together, I finally caught the resemblance I'd missed before. I sagged into my seat and narrowed my eyes at Mark. "That was rotten. I thought Steven was going to blow a gasket."

Mark held up his hands in a show of surrender. "It was all his idea. He's the drama queen, remember?"

Rocking back on his heels, Steven grinned and said, "Now, Eva. You know Mark's the idea man in this relationship."

Shawna dug a business card out of her pocket and handed it to me. "My number's on the flipside. Gimme a call. I've got the

472

inside dirt on these two. You can pay 'em back really good."

"Traitor!" Steven accused.

"Hey." Shawna shrugged. "Us girls have to stick together."

After work, Gideon and I went to his gym. Angus dropped us off at the curb and we headed inside. The place was hopping and the locker room crowded. I changed and stowed my stuff, then met Gideon in the hallway.

I waved at Daniel, the trainer who'd talked to me on my first visit to CrossTrainer, and got a smack on the ass for it.

"Hey," I protested, swatting at Gideon's chastising hand. "Cut it out."

He tugged my ponytail and gently urged my head back, tilting my mouth up so he could mark his territory with a deep, lush kiss.

The way he pulled my hair sent electricity sweeping across my skin. "If this is your idea of a deterrent," I whispered against his lips, "I have to say it's much more of an incentive."

"I'm quite willing to take it up a notch." He nipped my lower lip with his teeth. "But I wouldn't suggest testing my limits that way, Eva."

"Don't worry. I have other ways to do it."

Gideon hit the treadmill first, affording me the pleasure of seeing his body glistening with sweat . . . in public. As often as I saw him that way in private, it never ceased to be a major turn-on.

And God, I loved the way he looked with his hair tied back. And the flex of his muscles beneath lightly tanned skin. And the graceful power of his movements. Seeing such an elegantly urbane man shed the suits and show off his animal side hit all my hot buttons.

I couldn't stop staring and was happy I didn't have to. He was mine, after all, a fact that sent warm pleasure sliding through me. Besides, every other woman in the gym was checking him out, too. As he moved from station to station, dozens of admiring eyes followed.

When he caught me ogling, I shot him a suggestive glance and ran my tongue along my lower lip. His arched brow and rueful half-smile made me tingly. I couldn't remember the last time I'd been so motivated while working out. An hour and a half just flew by.

By the time we got back in the Bentley and headed to the penthouse, I was squirming in my seat. My gaze slid repeatedly to

Gideon in silent invitation.

He linked his fingers with mine. "You'll wait for it."

That pronouncement startled me. *"What?"*

"You heard me." He kissed my fingers and had the nerve to give me a wicked smile. "Delayed gratification, angel."

"Why would we do that?"

"Think of how crazed we'll be for each other after dinner."

I leaned closer so Angus didn't overhear me, although I knew he was professional enough to ignore us. "That's a given, waiting or not. I say we go with not."

But he wouldn't budge. Instead, he tortured us both. Having us undress each other for a steamy shower, our hands petting and caressing the curves and hollows of each other's bodies, then dressing for dinner. He went all out in black tie, but skipped the tie. His crisp white shirt was unbuttoned at the collar, revealing a flash of skin. The cocktail dress he selected for me was a champagne silk Vera Wang with a strapless bustier bodice, an open back, and a tiered skirt that ended a few inches above my knees.

I smiled when I saw it, knowing it was going to drive him nuts seeing me in that dress all night. It was gorgeous and I loved it, but it was a style meant for tall, slender models, not short curvy girls. In a pitiful bid for modesty, I left my hair down to hang over my breasts, but it didn't help much if Gideon's expression was any indication.

"My God, Eva." He adjusted himself in his slacks. "I've changed my mind about that dress. You shouldn't wear it in public."

"We don't have time for you to change your mind."

"I thought there was more material than that."

I shrugged with a grin. "What can I say? You bought it."

"I'm having second thoughts. How long could it possibly take to remove it?"

Sliding my tongue along my lower lip, I said, "I don't know. Why don't you find out?"

His eyes turned dark. "We'd never get out of here."

"I wouldn't complain." He looked so damn hot and I wanted him — as always — really damned bad.

"Isn't there a jacket or something you can put over that? A parka, maybe? Or a trench coat?"

Laughing, I grabbed my clutch off the dresser and wrapped my arm around his. "Don't worry. Everyone will be too busy checking you out to even bother noticing me."

He scowled as I tugged him out of the bedroom. "Seriously. Have your tits gotten bigger? They're spilling out over the top of that thing."

"I'm twenty-four years old, Gideon," I said dryly. "I stopped developing years ago. What you see is what you get."

"Yes, but I'm the only one who's supposed to be seeing, since I'm the only one who's allowed to be getting."

We moved into the living room. In the short time it took us to pass through to the foyer, I relished the quiet beauty of Gideon's home. I loved how warm and inviting it was. The Old World charm of the décor was so elegant, yet it was also remarkably comfortable. The stunning view out of the arched windows complemented the interior, but didn't distract from it.

The mixture of dark woods, distressed stone, warm colors, and vivid jeweled accents was clearly expensive, as was the art hung on the walls, but it was a tasteful display of wealth. I couldn't imagine anyone feeling awkward about what to touch or where to sit. It just wasn't that kind of space.

We caught the private elevator and Gideon faced me as the doors closed. He immediately tried tugging my bodice up.

"If you're not careful," I warned, "you'll expose my crotch instead."

"Damn it."

"We could have fun with this. I could play the role of a bubble-headed blond bimbo who's after your cock and your millions, and you can be yourself — the billionaire playboy with his latest toy. Just look bored and indulgent while I rub up against you and coo about how brilliant you are."

"That's not funny." Then he brightened. "What about a scarf?"

Once we checked in for the gala dinner benefitting a new crisis shelter for women and children, we were directed to a press gauntlet, triggering my fear of exposure. I focused on Gideon because nothing distracted me as thoroughly as he did. And because I was paying such close attention, I was able to watch the change from private man to public persona as it happened.

The mask slipped smoothly into place. His irises chilled to an icy blue and his sensual mouth lost any hint of curve. I could almost feel the force of his will enclosing us. There was a shield between us and the rest of the world simply because he wished it to be there. Standing beside him, I knew no one would approach or speak to me until he gave them some sign that they could.

Still, the don't-touch vibe didn't extend to looking. Gideon turned heads as we walked to the ballroom and eyes followed him. I got a nervous twitch from all the attention he garnered, but he seemed oblivious and completely unruffled.

If I'd had my heart set on cooing and rubbing all over Gideon, I would've had to wait in line. He was pretty much mobbed the moment we stopped walking. I stepped away to make room for those vying to catch his attention and wandered off to find some champagne. Waters Field & Leaman had done the pro bono advertising for the gala, and I spotted a few people I knew.

I'd managed to snag a glass off a passing waiter's tray when I heard someone call out my name. Turning, I saw Stanton's nephew approaching with a broad smile. Dark-haired and green-eyed, he was around my age. I knew him from the times I'd visited my mother on holiday breaks and was glad to see him.

"Martin!" I greeted him with open arms and we hugged briefly. "How are you? You look fabulous."

"I was about to say the same." He eyed my dress appreciatively. "I'd heard you'd moved to New York and meant to look you up. How long have you been in town?"

"Not long. A few weeks."

"Drink your champagne," he said. "And let's dance."

The wine was still bubbling nicely through my system when we moved onto the dance floor to the sound of Billie Holiday singing "Summertime."

"So," he began, "are you working?"

As we danced, I told him about my job and I asked what he was up to. I wasn't surprised to hear he was working for Stanton's investment firm and doing well.

"I'd love to come uptown and take you out to lunch sometime," he said.

"That would be great." I stepped back as the music ended and bumped into someone behind me. Hands went to my waist to steady me and I looked over my shoulder to find Gideon at my back.

"Hello," he purred, his icy gaze on Martin. "Introduce us."

"Gideon, this is Martin Stanton. We've known each other for a few years now. He's my stepfather's nephew." I took a deep breath and went for it. "Martin, this is the significant man in my life, Gideon Cross."

"Cross." Martin grinned and held out his hand. "I know who you are, of course. It's a pleasure to meet you. If things work out, maybe I'll be seeing you at some of the family gatherings."

Gideon's arm slid around my shoulders. "Count on it."

Martin was hailed by someone he knew, and he leaned forward to kiss my cheek. "I'll call you about lunch. Next week maybe?"

"Great." I was highly conscious of Gideon vibrating with energy beside me, although when I glanced at him, his face with calm and impassive.

He pulled me into a dance, with Louis Armstrong singing "What a Wonderful World." "Not sure I like him," he muttered.

"Martin's a very nice guy."

"Just so long as he knows you're mine." He pressed his cheek to my temple and placed his hand within the cutout back of my dress, skin to skin. There was no way to doubt that I belonged to him when he was holding me like that.

I relished the opportunity to be so close to his scrumptious body in public. Breathing him in, I relaxed into his expert hold. "I like this."

Nuzzling against me, he murmured, "That's the idea."

Bliss. It lasted as long as the dance did.

We were exiting the dance floor when I caught sight of Magdalene off to the side. It took me a moment to recognize her because she'd cut her hair into a sleek bob. She looked slender and classy in a simple black cocktail dress but was eclipsed by the striking brunette she was speaking to.

Gideon's stride faltered, slowing fractionally before resuming his usual pace. I was looking down, thinking he'd avoided something on the floor, when he said quietly, "I need to introduce you to someone."

My attention shifted to see where we were going. The woman with Magdalene had spotted Gideon and turned to face him. I felt his forearm tense beneath my fingers the moment their gazes met.

I could see why.

The woman, whoever she was, was deeply in love with Gideon. It was there on her face and in her pale, otherworldly blue eyes. Her beauty was stunning, so exquisite as to be surreal. Her hair was black as ink and hung thick and straight almost to her waist. Her dress was the same icy hue as her eyes, her skin golden from the sun, her body long and perfectly curved.

"Corinne," he greeted her, the natural rasp in his voice even more pronounced. He released me and caught her hands. "You didn't tell me you were back. I would've picked you up."

"I left a few messages on your voice mail at home," she said, in a voice that was cultured and smooth.

"Ah, I haven't been there much lately." As if that reminded him I was next to him, he released her and drew me up to his side. "Corinne, this is Eva Tramell. Eva, Corinne Giroux. An old friend."

I extended my hand to her and she shook it.

"Any friend of Gideon's is a friend of mine," she said with a warm smile.

"I hope that applies to girlfriends as well."

When her gaze met mine, it was knowing. "Especially girlfriends. If you could spare him a moment, I've been hoping to introduce him to an associate of mine."

"Of course." My voice was calm; I was anything but.

Gideon gave me a perfunctory kiss on the temple before he stepped closer to Corinne and offered his arm to her, leaving Magdalene standing awkwardly next to me.

I actually felt sorry for her, she looked so dejected. "Your new hairstyle is very flattering, Magdalene."

She glanced at me, her mouth tight, and then it softened with a sigh that sounded filled with resignation. "Thank you. It was time for a change. Time for many changes, I think. Also, there was no reason to imitate the one who got away now that she's back."

I frowned in confusion. "You lost me."

"I'm talking about Corinne." She studied my face. "You don't know. She and Gideon were engaged, for more than a year. She broke it off, married a wealthy Frenchman, and moved to Europe. But the marriage fell apart. They're now getting divorced and she's moved back to New York."

Engaged. I felt the blood drain from my face, my gaze shifting to where the man I loved stood with the woman he must've once loved, his hand moving to the small of her back to steady her as she leaned into him with a laugh.

As my stomach twisted with jealousy and sick fear, it struck me that I'd assumed he had never had a serious romantic relationship before me. Stupid. As hot as he was, I should've known better.

Magdalene touched my shoulder. "You should sit down, Eva. You're very pale."

I knew I was breathing too fast and my speeding pulse rate was dangerously high. "You're right."

Moving to the nearest available chair, I got off my feet. Magdalene sat beside me.

"You love him," she said. "I didn't see it. I'm sorry. And I'm sorry for what I said to you the first time we met."

"You love him, too," I replied woodenly, my gaze unfocused. "And at that time, I didn't. Not yet."

"Doesn't excuse me, does it?"

I gratefully accepted another glass of champagne when it was offered to me and took a second for Magdalene before the waiter straightened to move on. We clinked glasses in a pitiful display of scorned female solidarity. I wanted to leave. I wanted to get up and walk out. I wanted Gideon to realize I'd left, to be forced to leave after me. I wanted him to feel some of the pain I felt. Stupid, immature, hurtful imaginings that made me feel small.

I took comfort from Magdalene sitting silently beside me in commiseration. She knew how it felt to love Gideon and want him too much. That I sensed she was as miserable as I was confirmed what a threat Corinne might be.

Had he been pining for her this whole time? Was she the reason he'd closed himself off from other women?

"There you are."

I looked up as Gideon found me. Of course Corinne was still on his arm and I got the full effect of the two of them as a couple. They were, quite simply, impossibly gorgeous together.

Corinne took a seat beside me and Gideon brushed his fingertips over my cheek. "I have to speak with someone," he said. "Would you like me to bring you back anything?"

"Stoli and cranberry. Make it a double." I needed a buzz. Bad.

"All right." But he frowned at my request before he walked away.

"I'm so glad to meet you, Eva," Corinne said. "Gideon has told me so much about you."

"It can't have been too much. You two weren't gone that long."

"We talk nearly every day." She smiled, and there was nothing fake or malicious in her expression. "We've been friends a long time."

"More than friends," Magdalene said pointedly.

Corinne frowned at Magdalene, and I realized I wasn't supposed to know. Was it she or Gideon or both of them that had decided it was best not to tell me? Why cover up something if there was nothing to hide?

"Yes, that's true," she admitted with obvious reluctance. "Although that was some

486

years ago now."

I twisted in my seat to face her. "You still love him."

"You can't blame me for that. Any woman who spends time with him falls in love with him. He's beautiful and untouchable. That's an irresistible combination." Her smile softened. "He tells me you've inspired him to start opening up. I'm grateful to you for that."

I was about to say, *I didn't do it for you.* Then an insidious doubt drifted through my mind, making a vulnerable spot inside me fold in on itself.

Was I doing it for her without knowing it?

I twisted the base of my empty champagne flute around and around on the table. "He was going to marry you."

"And it was the biggest mistake of my life walking away." Her hand went to her throat, her slender fingers restlessly stroking, as if toying with a necklace she'd normally find there. "I was young and in some ways he frightened me. He was so possessive. It wasn't until after I married that I realized possessiveness is much better than indifference. At least for me."

I looked away, fighting the nausea that rose in my throat.

"You're awfully quiet," she said.

"What is there to say?" Magdalene tossed out.

We all loved him. We were all available to him. In the end, he would make a choice between us.

"You should know, Eva," Corinne began, looking at me with those clear aquamarine eyes, "he's told me how special you are to him. It took me some time to gather the courage to come back here and face you two together. I even canceled a flight I had booked a couple weekends ago. I interrupted him at some charity event he was giving a speech at, poor guy, to tell him I was on my way and to ask for his help getting settled."

I froze, feeling as brittle as cracked glass. She had to be talking about the advocacy center dinner, the night Gideon and I had sex for the first time. The night we'd christened his limo and he'd immediately withdrawn, then left me abruptly.

"When he called me back," she continued, "he told me he'd met someone. That he wanted you and me to meet when I got into town. I ended up chickening out. He's never asked me to meet a woman in his life before."

Oh my God. I glanced at Magdalene. Gideon had left me in a rush that night for *her*. For Corinne.

21

"Excuse me." I pushed back from the table and searched for Gideon. I saw him at the bar and went to him.

He was just turning away from the bartender with two glasses in his hands when I intercepted him. I took my drink and gulped it down, my teeth aching as the cubes of ice knocked against them.

"Eva —" There was a soft note of chastisement in his voice.

"I'm leaving," I said flatly, stepping around him to set my empty glass on the bar top. "I don't consider that running, because I'm telling you in advance and giving you the option of coming with me."

He exhaled harshly and I could see that he understood my mood. He knew I knew. "I can't leave."

I turned away.

He caught my arm. "You know I can't stay if you go. You're upset over nothing, Eva."

"Nothing?" I stared at where his hand gripped me. "I warned you I get upset and jealous. This time, you've given me good reason."

"Warning me is supposed to excuse you when you get ridiculous about it?" His face was relaxed, his voice low and calm. No one looking from a distance would pick up on the tension between us, but it was there in his eyes. Burning lust and icy fury. He was so good at putting those two together.

"Who's ridiculous? What about Daniel, the personal trainer? Or Martin, a member of my stepfamily?" I leaned closer and whispered, "I've never fucked either of them, let alone agreed to a marriage! I sure as hell don't talk to them every damn day!"

Abruptly, he caught me by the waist and hauled me up tight against him. "You need to be fucked now," he hissed in my ear, nipping the lobe with his teeth. "I shouldn't have made us wait."

"Maybe you were planning ahead," I shot back. "Saving it up in case an old flame popped back into your life, one you'd prefer to screw instead."

Gideon tossed back his drink, then secured me to his side with a steely arm around my waist and led me through the crowd to the door. He pulled his smart-

491

phone out of his pocket and ordered the limo brought around. By the time we reached the street, the long, sleek car was there. Gideon pushed me through the door Angus held open and told him, "Drive around the block until I say otherwise."

Then he slid in directly behind me, so closely I could feel his breath against my bare back. I scrambled toward the opposite seat, determined to get away from him. . . .

"Stop," he snapped.

I sank to my knees on the carpeted floor, breathing hard. I could run to the ends of the earth and I still wouldn't be able to escape the fact that Corinne Giroux had to be better for Gideon than I was. She was calm and cool, a soothing presence even to me — the person freaking out over the unwelcome fact of her existence. My worst nightmare.

His hand twisted into my loose hair, restraining me. His spread legs surrounded mine, his grip tightening so that my head was pulled back gently to touch his shoulder. "I'm going to give you what we both need, Eva. We're going to fuck as long as it takes to dull the edge enough to get through dinner. And you're not going to worry about Corinne, because while she's inside the ballroom, I'll be deep inside you."

"Yes," I whispered, licking dry lips.

"You forget who submits, Eva," he said gruffly. "I've given up control for you. I've bent and adjusted for you. I'll do anything to keep you and make you happy. But I won't be tamed or topped. Don't mistake indulgence for weakness."

I swallowed hard, my blood on fire for him. "Gideon . . ."

"Reach up with both hands and hold on to the grab handle above the window. Don't let go until I tell you, understand?"

I did as he ordered, pushing my hands through the leather loop. As my grip secured, my body sparked to life, making me aware of how right he was about what I needed. He knew me so well, this lover of mine.

Shoving his hands into my bodice, Gideon squeezed my full, aching breasts. When he rolled and tugged my nipples, my head lolled against him, the tension leaving my body in a rush.

"God." He nuzzled his mouth against my temple. "It's so perfect when you give yourself over to me like that . . . all at once, as if it's a huge relief."

"Fuck me," I begged, needing the connection. "Please."

Releasing my hair, he reached under my

dress and pulled my panties down my thighs. His jacket flew past me to land on the seat; then his hand pushed between my legs from the front. He growled at finding me wet and swollen. "You were made for me, Eva. You can't go long without me inside you."

Still he primed me, running his skilled fingers through my cleft, spreading the moisture over my clit and the lips of my sex. He pushed two fingers into me, scissoring them, preparing me for the thrust of his long, thick cock.

"Do you want me, Gideon?" I asked hoarsely, needing to ride his thrusting fingers, but hampered by how far I had to reach to grab the strap.

"More than my next breath." His lips moved over my throat and the top of my shoulder, the warm velvet of his tongue sliding seductively across my skin. "I can't go long without you either, Eva. You're an addiction . . . my obsession . . ."

His teeth bit gently into my flesh, conveying his animal need with a rough sound of desire. All the while he fucked me with his fingers, his other hand massaging my clit, making me come again and again from the simultaneous stimulation.

"Gideon!" I gasped, when my damp fingers began to slip from the leather.

His hands left me and I heard the erotic rasp of his zipper lowering. "Let go and lie on your back with your legs spread."

I moved to the seat and stretched along it, offering my body to him in quivering anticipation. His gaze met mine, his face briefly lit by a passing swath of headlights.

"Don't be afraid." He came over me, setting his weight onto me with excruciating care.

"I'm too horny to be scared." I caught him and pulled my body up to press against the hardness of his. "I want you."

His cock head nudged against the lips of my sex. With a flex of his hips, he pushed into me, his breath hissing just as mine did at the searing connection. I went lax against the seat, my fingers barely clinging to his lean waist.

"I love you," I whispered, watching his face as he began to move. Every inch of my skin burned as if from the sun, and my chest was so tight with longing and emotion that it was hard to breathe. "And I need you, Gideon."

"You have me," he whispered, his cock sliding in and out. "I couldn't be more yours."

I quivered and tensed, my hips meeting

his relentlessly measured drives. I climaxed with a breathless cry, shuddering as the ecstasy rippled through my sex, milking him until he grunted and started powering into me.

"Eva."

I rocked into his ferocious lunges, urging him on. He clutched at me, riding me hard and fast. My head thrashed and I moaned shamelessly, loving the feel of him, that decadent sensation of being possessed and ruthlessly pleasured.

We were wild for each other, fucking like feral beasts, and I was so turned on by our primal lust I thought I'd die from the orgasm building inside me.

"You're so good at this, Gideon. So good . . ."

He gripped my buttock and yanked me up to meet his next thrust, hitting the end of me, forcing a gasp of pleasure/pain from my throat. I came again, clenching down hard on him.

"Ah, God. *Eva.*" With a serrated groan, he erupted violently, flooding me with his heat. Pinning my hips, he ground against me, emptying himself as deep in me as he could get.

When he finished, he sucked in a harsh breath and gathered my hair in his hands, kissing the side of my damp throat. "I wish you knew what you do to me. I wish I could tell you."

I held him tightly. "I can't help it that I'm stupid over you. It's just too much, Gideon. It's —"

"— uncontrollable." He started over again, thrusting rhythmically. Leisurely. As if we had all the time in the world. Thickening and lengthening with each push and pull.

"And you need control." I lost my breath on a particularly masterful stroke.

"I need *you,* Eva." His gaze was fierce on my face as he moved inside me. "I need you."

Gideon didn't leave my side, or allow me to leave his, the rest of the evening. He kept his right hand linked with my left all the way through dinner, once again choosing to eat one-handed rather than release his hold on me.

Corinne — who'd taken a seat on the other side of him at our table — gave him a curious look. "I seem to remember you being right-handed."

"I still am," he said, lifting our joined hands from under the table and kissing my fingertips. I felt foolish and insecure when he did that — and conscious of Corinne's scrutiny.

Unfortunately, the romantic gesture didn't keep him from talking to Corinne throughout the meal, not me — which left me feeling fidgety and unhappy. I saw more of the back of Gideon's head than his face.

"At least it's not chicken."

I turned my head toward the man sitting beside me. I'd been so focused on trying to eavesdrop on Gideon's conversation that I hadn't paid any mind to our tablemates.

"I like chicken," I said. And I had liked the tilapia served for dinner — I'd cleaned my plate.

"Not rubberized, certainly." He grinned and suddenly looked much younger than his pure-white hair would suggest. "Ah, there's a smile," he murmured. "And it's a beautiful one."

"Thank you." I introduced myself.

"Dr. Terrence Lucas," he said. "But I prefer Terry."

"Dr. Terry. It's lovely to meet you."

He smiled again. "Just Terry, Eva."

Over the course of the few minutes we'd spoken, I'd come to believe Dr. Lucas wasn't a whole lot older than me, just prematurely gray. Aside from that, his face was handsome and unlined, his green eyes intelligent and kind. I revised my guesstimate of his age to be mid-to-late thirties.

"You look as bored as I feel," he said. "These events raise a considerable amount of money for the shelter, but they can be dull. Would you like to accompany me to the bar? I'll buy you a drink."

Beneath the table, I tested Gideon's grip by flexing my hand. His tightened.

"What are you doing?" he murmured.

Looking over my shoulder, I saw him watching me. Then I watched his gaze lift as Dr. Lucas stood behind me. Gideon's gaze noticeably cooled.

"She's going to alleviate the boredom of being ignored, Cross," Terry said, setting his hands on the back of my chair, "by spending time with someone who's more than happy to pay attention to such a beautiful woman."

I was immediately uncomfortable, aware of the crackling animosity between the two men. I tugged on his hand, but Gideon wouldn't release me.

"Walk away, Terry," Gideon warned.

"You've been so preoccupied with Mrs. Giroux, you didn't even notice when I sat at your table." Terry's smile took on an edge. "Eva. Shall we?"

"Don't move, Eva."

I shivered at the ice in Gideon's voice but felt stung enough to say, "It's not his fault he has a point."

Gideon's grip tightened painfully. "Not now."

Terry's gaze moved to my face. "You don't have to tolerate him talking to you that way. All the money in the world doesn't give anyone the right to order you around."

Infuriated and horribly embarrassed, I looked at Gideon. "Crossfire."

I wasn't sure I could use the safeword outside the bedroom, but he released me as if I'd burned him. I shoved my chair back and threw my napkin onto my plate. "Excuse me. Both of you."

With my clutch in hand, I walked away from the table, my stride easy and smooth. I made a beeline toward the restrooms, intending to freshen my makeup and collect myself, but then I saw the lighted exit sign and went with my urge to bail.

I pulled out my smartphone when I hit the sidewalk and texted Gideon: Not running. Just leaving.

I managed to hail a passing cab and headed home to nurse my anger.

I was jonesing for a hot bath and a bottle of wine when I reached my apartment. Shoving my key into the lock, I turned the knob and stepped into a porn video.

In the few shocked seconds it took for my brain to register what I was seeing, I stood riveted on the threshold, flooding the hallway behind me with blaring technopop. There were so many body parts involved, I had time to hastily slam the door behind me before I pieced them all together. One woman was spread-eagled on the floor. Another woman's face was in her crotch. Cary was banging the hell out of her while another man was drilling him in the ass.

I threw my head back and screamed bloody murder, completely fed up with everyone in my life. And because I was competing with the sound system, I ripped off one of my heels and threw it in that direction. The CD skipped, which jolted the *ménage à quatre* in progress on my living room floor into awareness of my presence. I limped over and shut off the volume, then faced the lot of them.

"Get the fuck out of my house," I snapped. "Right now."

"Who the hell is that?" the redhead at the bottom of the pile asked. "Your wife?"

There was a brief flash of embarrassment and guilt on Cary's face, and then he shot me a cocky smile. "My roommate. There's room for more, baby girl."

"Cary Taylor. Don't push me," I warned. "It's really, *really* not a good night."

The dark-haired male on top disengaged from Cary and stood, sauntering toward me. As he got closer, I saw that his brown eyes were unnaturally dilated and the pulse in his neck was throbbing viciously. "I can make it better," he offered with a leer.

"Back the fuck up." I adjusted my stance, preparing to ward him off physically if necessary.

"Leave her alone, Ian," Cary snapped, pushing to his feet.

"Come on, baby girl," Ian coaxed, making me sick by using Cary's pet name for me. "You need a good time. Let me show you one."

One minute he was inches in front of me, the next he was sailing into the couch with a scream. Gideon moved into place between me and the others, vibrating with fury. "Take it to your room, Cary," he bit out. "Or take it somewhere else."

Ian was squealing on my sofa, his nose spraying blood despite the two hands he tried to stanch it with.

Cary snatched his jeans off the floor. "You're not my fucking mother, Eva."

I sidestepped around Gideon. "Wasn't

screwing up with Trey enough of a fucking lesson for you, you idiot?"

"This isn't about Trey!"

"Who's Trey?" the bottle blonde asked as she got to her feet. When she caught a good look at Gideon, she visibly preened, showing off an admittedly pretty body.

Her efforts earned her a glance so disdainfully dismissive and unimpressed that she finally had the grace to blush and cover herself with a slinky gold lamé dress she picked up off the floor. And because I was in a mood, I said, "Don't take it personally. He prefers brunettes."

The look Gideon shot me was lethal. I'd never seen him look so livid. He was literally vibrating with suppressed violence.

Frightened by that glare, I took an involuntary step back. He cursed viciously and shoved both of his hands through his hair.

Suddenly bone weary and desperately disappointed with the men in my life, I turned away. "Get this mess out of my house, Cary."

I headed down the hallway, kicking off my other heel en route. I was out of my dress before I reached my bathroom and in the shower less than a minute beyond that. I stayed out of the range of the spray until the water warmed, and then I stood directly beneath it. Too tired to stand for long, I sank to the floor and just sat beneath the stream with my eyes closed and my arms wrapped around my knees.

"Eva."

I cringed when I heard Gideon's voice, and tucked into an even tighter ball.

"Goddamn it," he snapped. "You piss me off worse than anyone else I know."

I looked at him through the veil of my wet hair. He was pacing the length of my bathroom, his jacket shed somewhere and his shirt untucked. "Go home, Gideon."

He halted and shot me an incredulous look. "I'm not fucking leaving you here. Cary's lost his damned mind! That amped-up asshole was seconds away from putting his hands on you when I got here."

"Cary wouldn't have let that happen. But either way, I can't deal with him and you at the same time." I didn't want to deal with either of them, actually. I just wanted to be alone.

"Then you'll just deal with me."

I scooped my hair back from my face with an impatient swipe of my hand. "Oh? I'm supposed to make *you* the priority?"

He recoiled as if I'd hit him. "I was under the impression we were both each other's priorities."

"Yeah, I thought that, too. Until tonight."

"Jesus. Will you drop it with Corinne already?" He spread his arms wide. "I'm here with you, aren't I? I barely said good-bye to her because I was chasing after you. *Again.*"

"Fuck you. Don't do me any favors."

Gideon lunged into the shower fully dressed. He yanked me to my feet and kissed me. Hard. His mouth devoured mine, his hands gripping my upper arms to hold me in place.

But I didn't soften this time. I didn't give in. Even when he tried coaxing me with lush, suggestive licks.

"Why?" he muttered, his lips sliding down to my throat. "Why are you driving me insane?"

"I don't know what your problem is with Dr. Lucas, and I honestly don't give a shit. But he was right. Corinne got way too much of your attention tonight. You pretty much ignored me during dinner."

"It's impossible for me to ignore you, Eva." His face was hard and tight. "If you're in the same room with me, I don't see anyone else."

"Funny. Every time I looked at you, you were looking at her."

"This is stupid." He released me and

shoved the wet hair out of his face. "You know how I feel about you."

"Do I? You want me. You need me. But do you love Corinne?"

"Oh, for fuck's sake. *No.*" He shut the water off, caging me to the glass with both arms. "You want me to tell you I love you, Eva? Is that what this is about?"

My stomach cramped as if he'd struck me with the full force of his fist. I'd never felt that kind of pain before, hadn't known it existed. My eyes burned and I ducked under his arm before I embarrassed myself by crying. "Go home, Gideon. Please."

"I *am* home." He caught me from behind and buried his face in my soaked hair. "I'm with you."

I struggled to get free, but I was too wiped out. Physically. Emotionally. The tears came in a torrent and I couldn't stop them. And I hated crying in front of anyone. "Go away. *Please.*"

"I love you, Eva. Of course I do."

"Oh my God." I kicked at him, flailing. Anything to get away from the person who'd become a massive source of pain and misery. "I don't want your fucking pity. I just want you to *go away.*"

"I can't. You know I can't. Eva, stop fighting. Listen to me."

"Everything you're saying *hurts,* Gideon."

"It's not the right word, Eva," he pressed on stubbornly, his lips at my ear. "That's why I haven't said it. It's not the right word for you and what I feel for you."

"Shut up. If you care about me at all, you'll just shut up and go away."

"I've been loved before — by Corinne, by other women . . . But what the hell do they know about me? What the hell are they in love with when they don't know how fucked up I am? If that's love, it's nothing compared to what I feel for you."

I stilled, trembling, my gaze on the mirror's reflection of my mascara-smeared face and bedraggled wet hair next to Gideon's ravaged beauty. His features were overcome by volatile emotion as he wrapped himself tightly around me. We looked all wrong for each other.

And yet I understood the alienation of being around others who couldn't really see you or chose not to. I'd felt the self-loathing that came with being a fraud, portraying an image of what you wished you could be but weren't. I'd lived with the fear that the people you loved might turn away from you if they ever got to know the true person hidden inside.

"Gideon —"

His lips touched my temple. "I think I loved you the moment I saw you. Then we made love that first time in the limo and it became something else. Something more."

"Whatever. You cut me off that night and left me behind to take care of Corinne. How could you, Gideon?"

He released me only long enough to scoop me up and carry me over to where my bathrobe hung from a hook on the back of the door. He bundled me up, then had me sit on the edge of the tub while he went to the sink and pulled my makeup remover wipes out of the drawer. Crouching in front of me, he stroked the cloth over my cheek.

"When Corinne called during the advocacy dinner, it was the perfect time to make me do something stupid." His gaze was soft and warm on my tear-streaked face. "You and I had just made love, and I wasn't thinking clearly. I told her I was busy and that I was with someone, and when I heard the pain in her voice, I knew I had to deal with her so I could move forward with you."

"I don't understand. You left me behind for her. How does that move us forward?"

"I screwed up with Corinne, Eva." He tilted my chin back to rub at my raccoon eyes. "I met her my first year at Columbia. I noticed her, of course. She's beautiful and

508

sweet, and never had an unkind word to say about anyone. When she pursued me, I let myself be caught and she became my first consensual sexual experience."

"I hate her."

That made his mouth curve slightly.

"I'm not kidding, Gideon. I'm sick with jealousy right now."

"It was just sex with her, angel. As raw as you and I fuck, it's still making love. Every time, from the very first time. You're the only one who's ever gotten to me that way."

I heaved out a breath. "Okay. I'm marginally better."

He kissed me. "I guess you could say we dated. We were exclusive sexually and we often ended up going to the same places as a couple. Still, when she told me she loved me, I was surprised. And flattered. I cared about her. I enjoyed spending time with her."

"Still do, apparently," I muttered.

"Keep listening." He chastised me with a tap of his finger to the end of my nose. "I thought maybe I might love her, too, in my own way . . . the only way I knew how. I didn't want her to be with anyone else. So I said yes when she proposed."

I jerked back to look at him. "*She* proposed?"

"Don't look so shocked," he said wryly. "You're bruising my ego."

Relief flooded me in a rush that made me dizzy. I threw myself at him, hugging him as tight as I could.

"Hey." His returning embrace was just as fierce. "You okay?"

"Yes. Yes, I'm getting there." I pulled back and cupped his jaw in my hand. "Keep going."

"I said yes for all the wrong reasons. After two years of hanging out, we'd never spent a full night together. Never talked about any of the things I talk to you about. She didn't know me, not really, and yet I convinced myself that being loved at all was something to hang on to. Who else was going to do it right, if not her?"

He moved his attention to my other eye, cleaning away the black streaks. "I think she was hoping that being engaged would take us to a different level. Maybe I'd open up more. Maybe we'd stay the night at the hotel — which she thought was romantic, by the way — instead of calling it an early night because of classes in the morning. I don't know."

I thought it sounded terribly lonely. My poor Gideon. He'd been alone for so long. Maybe his whole life.

"And maybe when she broke it off after a year," he went on, "she was hoping that would kick-start things, too. That I'd make a bigger effort to keep her. Instead, I was relieved because I'd started to realize it was going to be impossible to share a home with her. What excuse was I going to come up with to sleep in separate rooms and have my own space?"

"You never considered telling her?"

"No." He shrugged. "Until you, I didn't consider my past an issue. Yes, it affected certain ways I did things, but everything had its place and I wasn't unhappy. In fact, I thought I had a comfortable and uncomplicated life."

"Oh, boy." My nose wrinkled. "Hello, Mr. Comfortable. I'm Miss Complicated."

His grin flashed. "Never a dull moment."

22

Gideon tossed the makeup remover wipe in the trash. Then he grabbed a towel to throw over the puddle he'd left on the floor and toed off his shoes. To my utter delight, he began stripping out of his wet clothes.

Watching him raptly, I said, "You feel guilty because she still loves you."

"I do, yes. I knew her husband. He was a good guy and he was crazy about her, until he figured out she didn't feel the same way and things fell apart."

He looked at me as he peeled his shirt off. "I couldn't figure out why he let it get to him. He was married to the girl he wanted, they lived in a different country away from me, so what was his problem? Now, I understand. If *you* loved someone else, Eva, it'd shred me to pieces, every single day. It'd kill me even if you were with me and not him. But unlike Giroux, I wouldn't let you go. Maybe I wouldn't have all of you, but you'd still be mine and I'd take what I could get."

My fingers laced in my lap. "That's what scares me, Gideon. You don't know what you're worth."

"Actually, I do. Twelve bill—"

"Shut up." My head spun and I pressed my fingertips to my eyes. "It shouldn't be such a mystery that women fall in love with you and stay in love. Did you know that Magdalene kept her hair long hoping it'd remind you of Corinne?"

He dropped his slacks and frowned at me. "Why?"

I sighed at his cluelessness. "Because she believes Corinne is who you want."

"Then she's not paying attention."

"Isn't she? Corinne told me she talks to you almost every day."

"Not quite. I'm often not available. You know how busy I am." His gaze took on the heated look I was so familiar with. I knew he was thinking about the times he got busy with me.

"That's nuts, Gideon. Her calling every day. That's stalking." Which reminded me of her assertion that he'd been as possessive over her as he was about me. That niggled at me in a terrible way.

"Where are you going with this?" he

asked, in a voice laced with warm amusement.

"Don't you get it? You drive women off the deep end because you're the ultimate. You're the grand prize. If a woman can't have you, they know they're settling for less than the best. So they can't think about not having you. They just think of crazy ways to try to get you."

"Except for the one I want," he retorted dryly, "who spends a lot of time running in the opposite direction."

I stared unabashedly, drinking him in as he stood naked in front of me. "Answer one question for me, Gideon. Why do you want me, when you can have your pick of perfection instead? And I'm not fishing for compliments or reassurances. I'm asking an honest question."

He caught me up and moved us into the bedroom. "Eva, if you don't stop thinking of us as temporary, I'm going to take you over my knee and make damn sure you like it."

Setting me down in a chair, he went to rifle through my drawers.

I watched him pulling out underwear, yoga pants, and a top. "Have you forgotten I sleep in the nude with you?"

"We're not staying here." He faced me. "I

don't trust Cary not to bring more intoxicated jerks home, and once we turn in for the night I'll be drugged on the medication Dr. Petersen prescribed and possibly unable to protect you. So we're going to my place."

I looked down at my twisted hands, thinking about how I might need protection from Gideon, too. "I've been down this road with Cary before, Gideon. I can't just hole up at your place and hope he comes out of it on his own. He needs me to be around more than I have been."

"Eva." Gideon brought me my clothes and crouched in front of me. "I know you need to support Cary. We'll figure out how tomorrow."

I cupped his face. "Thank you."

"I need you, too, though," he said quietly.

"We need each other."

He pushed to his feet. Moving back to the dresser, he pulled open his drawers and grabbed clothes for himself.

Standing, I began to dress. "Listen . . ."

He pulled on a pair of low-slung jeans. "Yes?"

"I feel tons better now that I know the score, but Corinne is still going to be a problem for me." I paused with my shirt in my hands. "You wanna nip her hopes in the bud real quick. Stow the guilt, Gideon, and start weaning her off."

He sat on the edge of the bed to pull on his socks. "She's a friend, Eva, and she's in a rough spot. It's a cruel time to cut her off."

"Think carefully, Gideon. I have exes in my past, too. You're setting the precedent now for how I'll handle them. I'm taking my cues from you."

He stood with a scowl. "You're threatening me."

"I prefer to see it as coercion. Relationships work both ways. You're not her only friend. She can find someone more appropriate to lean on in her time of crisis."

We grabbed what we needed and walked back into the living room. I saw the mess left behind — an aqua-hued bra beneath an end table and blood spray on my cream sectional — and I wished Cary were still around to smack some sense into.

"I'm digging into it with him tomorrow," I bit out, my jaw tight with anger and worry. "Goddamn it, I should've decked him when I had the chance. I should've knocked him out cold, and then locked him up in his room until he gets his brain working again."

Gideon's hand at the small of my back rubbed soothingly. "It'll be better to do that tomorrow, when he's alone and hungover.

More effective that way."

Angus was waiting for us when we got downstairs. I was about to climb into the back of the limo when Gideon cursed under his breath, stopping me.

"What?" I asked him.

"I forgot something."

"Let me get my keys." I reached for the overnight bag Gideon was holding, which had my purse inside.

"No need. I have a set." He shot me an unapologetic grin when my brows rose. "I had copies made before I gave them back to you."

"Seriously?"

"If you'd paid attention" — he kissed the top of my head — "you might've noticed that you've had the key to my place on your key ring since I returned it."

I gaped after him as he darted past the doorman and back into the building. I remembered the torment of those four days when I'd thought we'd broken up and the excruciating pain I'd felt when those keys slid out of the envelope and into my palm.

I'd had the key to being with him all along.

Shaking my head, I looked around at my adopted city, loving everything about it and feeling grateful for the crazy well of happiness I'd found here.

Gideon and I still had so much work ahead of us. As much as we loved each other, it was no guarantee that we'd survive our personal wounds. But we communicated, we were honest with each other, and God knew we were both too stubborn to quit without a fight.

Gideon reappeared just as two large, beautifully groomed poodles walked by with their equally coiffed owner.

I climbed into the limo. As we pulled away from the curb, Gideon tugged me onto his lap and cuddled me close. "We had a rough night, but we got through it."

"Yeah, we did." Tipping my head back, I offered my mouth for a kiss. He obliged me with one that was slow and sweet — a simple reaffirmation of our precious, complicated, maddening, necessary connection.

Cupping his nape, I ran my fingers through his silky hair. "I can't wait to get you back in bed."

He gave a sexy little growl and attacked my neck with tickling nips and kisses, banishing our ghosts and their shadows.

At least for a little while . . .

■ ■ ■ ■

READERS GUIDE FOR BARED TO YOU

BY SYLVIA DAY

■ ■ ■ ■

DISCUSSION QUESTIONS

1. Eva's move from California to New York brings her closer to her mother. While the move was a good one for both her and Cary's careers, it could have been avoided. Why do you think she chose to start her new life in New York?

2. Cary is dependent on Eva materially and emotionally, even though she turns to him as a sounding board more often than he turns to her. What needs does Eva meet for Cary?

3. Initially, it's the physical attraction that draws Gideon to Eva, but by the time he lures her to his nightclub there's something deeper involved. What is it about Eva that causes Gideon to pursue her so relentlessly?

4. Gideon has a difficult time accepting any

privacy barriers between him and Eva. Do you think Eva is too soft or too tough on the issue? How would you respond?

5. Eva values transparency in her relationships, but she allows Gideon to keep his secrets. Why do you think that is? Do you agree or disagree?

6. Gideon's life revolves around his work and his philanthropic commitments; Eva's social life is more personal. How do these differences affect them as a couple?

7. Gideon and Eva have a very sexual relationship. Considering their pasts, why do you think sex is such an important way for them to communicate?

ABOUT THE AUTHOR

Sylvia Day is the *New York Times* and *USA Today* bestselling author of more than a dozen novels. Her résumé includes a variety of odd jobs ranging from amusement park employee to Russian linguist/interrogator for U.S. Army military intelligence. She's presently a full-time writer. Sylvia's work has been called an "exhilarating adventure" by *Publishers Weekly* and "wickedly entertaining" by *Booklist.* Her stories have been translated into several languages. She's been honored with the RT Book Reviews Reviewers' Choice Best Book Award, the EPPIE Award, the National Readers' Choice Award, the Readers' Crown, and multiple finalist nominations for Romance Writers of America's prestigious RITA Award of Excellence. She's now hard at work on *Reflected in You,* the sequel to *Bared to You,* but would love for you to visit with her on her website, www.SylviaDay.com, on Facebook at www.facebook.com/AuthorSylviaDay, or on Twitter at www.twitter.com/SylDay.